Making Perfect Sense

When Only The Truth Matters

Beth Gelman

Cindy Ziegelman Enterprises LLC

Making Perfect Sense

For information, address Beth Gelman directly at: BethGelman.com or at BethGelmanWrites@gmail.com.

KDP ISBN: 979-8389003729 (Paperback)

KDP ISBN: 979-8989946747 (Hardback)

This book is registered with the Library of Congress: ISBN: 979-8-9899467-4-7 (Paperback)

This book is registered with the Library of Congress: ISBN: 979-8-9905873-2-8 (Hardback)

Summary: The conclusion to *The Perfect Lessons*

When Trudie returns home from the glamorous New York gala, shattered by the lies Dr. Alexander Pierce has told her, she is forced to untangle truth from fiction. As she is forced to work alongside the pompous, gorgeous, and selfish Alex, Trudie must find a way to regain her focus on her students and her own life.

With a past filled with childhood trauma still affecting them as adults, Trudie and Alex must learn to trust each other if they are to heal and pave the way for their future. Alex still has lessons to teach Trudie's wanton body, and Trudie continues teaching him how to get what he wants without being a jerk. They must figure it out before the school year ends, if not for themselves, then for the kids whose lives depend on it.

Making Perfect Sense is the third book in The Perfect Series by Beth Gelman. This is the conclusion to *The Perfect Lessons*.

[1. Romance 2. Contemporary romance 3. Romantic comedy 4. Multiracial romance 5. Teacher love story 6. Healing love story]

Copy Editor: Megan Rubiner-Zinn, Cherry & Parsons Writing and Editing

Formatting Editor: Jennifer Haskin, Frontpage Editing

Cover Design: Christine Cover Designs

First Edition

Contents

"Baby, I can't fight this feeling anymore."

—REO Speedwagon

PROLOGUE

TRUDIE

This week had been a real ballbuster. After the Great Dr. Alexander Pierce played me like a fiddle at his family gala, my mom called to tell me my disaster of a father was in the hospital. Why the hell would I care where he was? He'd never found the time to check in on me in the past fifteen years. My only saving graces were: one, I was able to get onto a midnight flight back to Detroit, and two, because of the broken heel on my sky-high stiletto, I had the help of Gus, who had kindly offered me a ride in his stylish golf cart thingy and whisked me down to my gate. And, three, Ruby could pick me up in the middle of the night and bring me home from the airport. *Have I mentioned recently what a great friend she is?*

Ruby walked me inside and forced me to wash my face. It was dripping and smeared with makeup, thanks to all the crying I did in the cab because Alex neglected to tell me he was still fooling around with his ex, Sheila. Who, by the way, had the resting bitch face of a crocodile. Never trust a crocodile! While I got ready for bed, my bestie set a cup of hot cocoa on my nightstand while I stripped and got into bed. She then did the same so she could cuddle with me. I don't know if she'd ever seen me look and feel so bad—even when we were in college and I drank my weight in beer our freshman year. That was one week I'll never remember!

I propped up my pillows and after sinking back comfortably, I warmed my hands on the mug while I blew little swirls into the liquid.

"My brain hurts," I whimpered.

"I know, sweetie. I know." Ruby ran her knuckles down my cheek. "You've had a rough go of it this weekend. Tell me, was any part of your weekend good?"

She was distracting me, and I loved her for it. "Most of it was amazing. Central Park, the Belvedere Castle, and the best Chinese food I've ever had." I took another sip, trying to stay focused on the best parts, but a tear slipped from my eye and dropped into my cup.

Ruby took both of my cheeks in her hands and looked me in the eyes to search for the absolute truth in my sorrow.

"I know it wasn't bad sex that has you upset. No man that pretty can be that bad in bed. Why didn't you stay and call him out on his assholery? Why didn't you lay into him about lying to you? Trudie, be honest with me. I want to help you."

She's right. So right. Why had I run like the scared rabbit he had accused me of being? Was I so broken that I couldn't stand up for myself? Did I have such low self-esteem that I would let someone take advantage of me that way? I didn't know. I felt so helpless, much like when I was a girl. Wasn't this why I spent so much time and money attending psychology conferences to figure out my shit? Had I learned nothing in five years? Why did I feel so bad?

I hiccupped, sloshing my drink so it dripped down my hand. "I'm broken."

I was numb. I needed sleep. I needed to crawl into my woman cave and let myself heal so I could produce a new plan for working with Alex for the next six months. If it weren't for my commitment to my principal and students, I would have taken a sabbatical and run further away than home.

"Maybe for now, sweetheart. Tomorrow you'll try again. I love you, Trudes." She kissed my forehead and curled up under the covers, leaving me to my thoughts and my spilled milk.

CHAPTER 1
TRUDIE

"Thank you for coming over so soon, *cariño*. I'm sorry this couldn't wait." My mom hugged me and pressed my hair down after I removed my knit cap. It was the beginning of October, and mornings were already dipping into the forties.

"I'm not going to lie, Mom. When you called about Dad, I almost told you to tell him to go to hell. Why does his health need to concern me? He never cared about my health or anyone's health in this family. Besides, where has he been for the past fifteen years? Calculating weather damage that giant conglomerates created with pollution and chemical spills?" My disgust was palpable.

I didn't expect any answers to the questions I fired at my mother. She was as affected as we all were. My daddy issues weren't the typical abuse stuff you hear on podcasts and *Dateline*-type shows. Mine were of the neglected genre of abuses. The "all promises and no follow-through" kind. Hello today, goodbye in ten minutes, kind of abuse. After thousands of dollars of therapy, I'd discovered that leaving wasn't the biggest problem I had to deal with, it was the reentry into our family unit that caused all my issues.

"What am I expected to do now? And where are my brothers? Aren't they part of this 'happy family' equation?"

My shoes were off, and I marched into the kitchen looking for coffee during my tirade. My mom fell in tow, letting me have my rant. She'd learned that the only way to get me to listen was to let me have diarrhea of the mouth first.

I dumped several large dollops of my favorite chemical creamer into a giant mug that I'd bought off Etsy for my mom on Mother's Day when I was fifteen. It said, "Happy Mother's Day, Mom. Keep That Shit Up!" Best mug ever. It was a toss-up between that, and "I'd walk through fire for you, Mom. Well, not fire. That would be dangerous. But a super humid room. Okay, not too humid, because you know ... my hair." Those Etsy sayings get me every time.

"Cariño, sweetheart, listen to me. You have to do some things in life, and this is one of them. Your father needs all of us to help him. He has cancer. From asbestos. From all those buildings he had to go into that were filled with toxic smoke and materials. He has no one else to help him, and I hoped, prayed even, that you'd find it in your heart to ease his suffering by spending what little time he has left with him. Think of it as an opportunity to put your mind at rest and give a stubborn old man some peace. Please, Mija, he needs you. I need my children to find peace with their father. He once had his finer moments and his charms."

I hated it when she turned on the puppy dog eyes and pleading hands. It was my kryptonite. I flopped onto one of the kitchen chairs with my eyes closed in frustration. I hated having to be the one that always had to travel the high road. Why did I have to abide by a higher moral compass than everyone else? It exhausted me. I fell forward over the table, rubbing my eyes with the heels of my hands, grappling with my feelings and the reality of what happened to me as a child vs. what it means to me as an adult. I guess my therapy was working.

"Fine. I'll take the fucking high road—again!" I screamed my anger and helplessness into the universe. I suppose I could have walked away from this situation. But even if I had, it would have haunted me like the rest of the crap inflicted on my life. I was tired of carrying these emotions. Tired of thinking my rightness was the most essential thing to me. It wasn't. I needed to put this down. I was enough. I wouldn't be the one left with regret when he died. No way!

My mom and I didn't say anything else. She fell to her knees in front of me and grabbed my hands as if we were both in prayer. Our foreheads touched, and we drew energy from each other in hopes of finding homeostasis. I was doing this as much for her as for myself. Whatever my father thought would happen from our meeting, he was going to have to be the bigger person to have a breakthrough.

I spent the rest of the afternoon helping my mom organize her new library, a.k.a. my old bedroom. I dropped several books on her counter every month. After several month she needed the Dewey decimal system for her collection. We also moved her knitting materials into the room, along with a comfortable chair that was collecting clothes in her bedroom and a Tiffany-style light extracted from the basement. Now that she had her indoor she-shed set up, I yawned and dragged myself to the front door to leave.

"Hey, Mom! I'm going now," I called across the house and pulled on my coat. She came running over to give me a hug along with a sack full of her Mexican wedding cookies. My favorite. "You're the best." I kissed her and mumbled, a cookie in my mouth, "Text me where to find him."

"Thank you, baby. You're a class act." Her sweet smile got me right where it counted.

I mumbled under my breath again as I walked down the front steps, "All the praise in the world isn't going to make this any better for me." I let out a huge sigh after I started my car. This Sunday Funday hadn't been fun at all. Neither would the rest of my Sundays as long as he was alive.

It was seven o'clock when I realized I still had my phone off. I didn't want to hear from or look at Alex ever again. I didn't care that I sounded like a petulant teenager. That's how I felt. I had all the bad feels: anger, frustration, betrayal, and mostly embarrassment. I burrowed my butt into a nest made of blankets and a scarf. I wrapped my head and barricaded myself before turning on the phone, then waited for all the beeps and pings to stop. Most of them were from Alex.

Where are you?

Why won't you pick up?

What did she say to you?

All good questions—I was still deciding whether I wanted to respond to any of them. Then his tone changed. Dr. Alexander Pierce, king of psychology and my personal sex education teacher, was now threatening me.

You need to speak with me... NOW!

Ooh. Shouty. Not answering that one.

Damn it, Trudie. You're going to feel stupid when you hear the whole story.

Will I?

And my not so favorite, "*You're acting like a child. Grow a pair and call me.*"

Then, there was the frustrated father text. That one made me a little moist.

Ugh! I was too tired to deal with this. It had been almost twenty-four hours since I ran away from that lying sack of shit, Dr. Alexander Pierce. All I wanted to do was rewind time to the trip I took to California this past summer. I had wanted an adventure. One that included a hot sexy guy with great lips, knowing hands, and a dick that knew how to please me. No more vanilla sex. That's all I wanted. And, of course, the real reason I had traveled was my psychology conference. Suddenly, I wondered what Jared, the hot guy I met on the plane, was up to. He checked all the boxes—minus the dick—which I didn't have the opportunity to test drive. *Hmm.*

I needed to get ahead preparing for this week and went to my tiny kitchen to pack lunch for tomorrow and start some laundry.

Girl's gotta have clean panties. Realization hit that I had left my luggage in New York and should probably figure out how to get it back when the banging on my front door startled me. *Crap!* I was pretty sure I knew who it was and I wasn't sure I wanted to answer the door. What if he broke up with me? Were we even together? He was always intimidating me and leaving me confused. Was Alex my peer? Or client? A teacher or mentor? My lover or my boyfriend? I was so confused.

Shucking all the self-doubt from my mind, I walked to the door, opened it, then walked away. I knew he'd barge in and scream at me about how childish it was of me to run away and that I should have trusted him to explain everything. He might be right about that, though it still didn't excuse what he did. He hid a very important piece of his past from me. He knew there was a high probability I'd run into his ex at the foundation gala his family hosted, yet he had said nothing.

There weren't too many places to hide in my tiny apartment, so I returned to the spot that brought me the most comfort: my couch nest. I waited for Alex to begin, but he didn't. I tilted my chin up, looked over my shoulder toward the front door, and found it empty. The only thing in my doorway was my luggage and my purse. My heart stopped. I knew in that instant not only had I hurt him terribly, but I'd also hurt myself irrevocably as well.

CHAPTER 2

ALEXANDER

She wouldn't even look at me. She opened the door, and all I wanted to do was blast her for acting stupid or squeeze the living daylights out of her. In the end, I was just happy she was home safe and sound. I'd spent the last twenty-four hours out of my mind trying to figure out what that hoyden, Sheila, had said to Trudie to make her leave me without so much as a goodbye. *God damn it!* I'd finally found a woman who challenged me intellectually, sexually, and emotionally. I could feel myself becoming a better person when was with her even though she frustrated the fuck out of me.

I'd planned to have it out with her, but she didn't even have it in her heart to look at me. She threw me away like old garbage, and I'd be damned if I'd beg at her feet for another chance. I barely had enough self-respect to drop her things at her apartment, knowing I'd see her tomorrow at school. I felt paralyzed. Defeated. I wished she would have stood up to me. Hoped she would try to put me in my place so we could have hedonistic makeup sex. That wasn't going to happen and now, neither was our relationship. We were over in an instant.

I walked out to my car and glanced up at her window. She stood there with a look I'd never seen before. Sadder than sad. Lost.

Huh. "Honey, I feel you," I said. And I drove away.

That particular Monday morning, I felt like I had on the first day of football practice in high school—achy. My shoulders and neck were racked with tension, and my lower back felt twisted and out of shape from a lousy night's sleep. All I wanted to do was stand in a hot shower all day. After chucking my phone across the room when the alarm went off, I headed to my treadmill, honoring the obligatory routine of running. I protested, though: I wasn't doing five miles, and I wasn't doing any weights. When I finally made it to the kitchen island for breakfast, I found several emails from Eloise bringing me up to speed on the high-risk student program we'd been discussing for Hart Middle School. She reminded me we'd meet at nine in the counseling office to hammer out the details and which roles each person would be responsible for. She also wanted to know if I had secured the funds to back this little endeavor of ours while I also carried out my responsibilities for helping the school reach exemplary status.

I needed to get my head on straight and remember why the school board hired me for this one task alone. Everything else was the frosting on the proverbial cake. Then why did I care so much? Oh, yeah, Trudie. She was the reason I'd become so invested in this extra project. Seeing her light up while helping her students was contagious. Every time she leaned into a conversation with one of them or clapped at their genius, she exuded love, kindness, and professionalism. She was the poster child for Teacher of the Year.

I swallowed my last sip of coffee and clicked on a message with the subject line containing the word "opportunity." Once opened, I scanned the document and was pleasantly surprised to learn that I was offered a job opportunity in Texas. I felt numb, though, thinking about leaving Trudie. This was my career—traveling the world, speaking, and doing research. Our separation was inevitable, but I strongly believed she had no idea how that might affect us.

Packing lunch was foreign to me since most of my work fell into a corporate setting. So when I looked in the fridge and found a jar of jelly and bread, I immediately fell through a wormhole back to third grade. PB&J had been a staple in my life, and I supposed it would be for the foreseeable future.

Twenty minutes later I stepped through the school lobby, getting sideswiped by prepubescent boys and wannabe grown-up girls. You couldn't pay me enough to live through middle school again.

"Hello there, Dr. Pierce. Did you have a nice weekend?" Ricky propped his hand under his chin and gave me his version of a dreamy-eyed fan girl. He was so amusing.

"Well, hello there, Ricky. You're in good spirits this morning. I think the real question is did *you* have a nice weekend?" I waggled my eyebrows just for fun.

He flushed pink and clasped his hands together, looking toward the ceiling.

"As a matter of fact, I did. Some pals and I went to Drag Queen Bingo and I won a very lewd T-shirt that I can't wear to work. You know—the kids. Nonetheless, it was a blast." He was practically bubbling over with his description.

I laughed, finishing the conversation as I knocked on Eloise's door. "It sounds like it. I'll have to try that sometime. Maybe a staff outing?" I made a nasal grunt hidden under a laugh.

"Oh! For sure!" He clapped his hands ecstatically.

Eloise motioned for me to come in and stood to shake my hand. "Let's go down to the counseling office and have our meeting," she said. "I want to make sure that both staff and students are being represented well for our projects."

Eloise had a gleam in her eye that scared me. She looked like she knew something, and for all I knew, Trudie had blabbed to her about the whole weekend, with an emphasis on how I seemingly betrayed her. I'd had forty-eight hours to digest the fun that Trudie and I'd had before my ex-fiancée showed up. Ripping off her panties and fucking her at the top of the Waldorf Astoria was a dream come true. Getting her off before other guests found us—priceless. She positively glowed up until my speech. As soon as all the pomp and circumstance were over, I had planned on fulfilling every desire she articulated, and a few she didn't know she wanted.

When I saw Sheila slide up next to her it was as if I was struck by a nail gun through my heart. That vicious woman had spun a web so thick it would take me weeks to break through. If only Trudie would tell me what she said, I'd know which strand to cut first. In the meantime, it was back to business. As Yoda would say, "The force you are is not strong today," or something like that. My senses were mushy and my focus wasn't much better. I hoped I could get through this meeting without needing any Jedi mind-reading.

I smiled as Eloise ushered me down a short hallway, around another corner, and into a small conference room. I took a seat on the opposite side of the room and opened my laptop, preparing to deliver my updates. Eloise sighed and sat back in a blue upholstered swivel armchair, waiting to begin.

"Is it me, or are these days zipping by? We have barely begun school, and I already need a vacation." Her friendly smile was meant to relax me, though I knew better. She was a sly woman, and nothing but my A-game would suffice here.

"I couldn't agree more. I'm finally feeling like I can remember more of the teachers' names and can locate at least three bathrooms around the school because you never know when nature will call." I chuckled.

She laughed back. "I'm in my fifties, Dr. Pierce, that is no joke. Anyhow, we need to finalize our projects and establish goals and pathways to get there. Now, I have my ideas, but I'd like to hear what you're thinking." She sat back and took a sip of her coffee, crossing her legs in anticipation.

I stood up. "I think better on my feet. Feel free to look at my computer presentation as I go through the points and interrupt me whenever you need to." I shoved my hands in my pockets and proceeded to walk her through the school board's requirements and how they matched with those of the State Board of Education so that we didn't spend time on steps that wouldn't work in our favor. Then, I shared with her a list of teachers who I felt needed some tweaking here and there in either their mannerisms, verbiage, communication skills, or lesson plans.

"You see, I'm not trying to cramp anyone's style. It's that everyone needs to raise their skill set to be equal to the guy or gal next to them. Yes, it's comparing apples and oranges. Yes, they're both fruit. However, they are ripe in different seasons and the school board and everyone else who works with these kids wants every teacher to be 'in season' all school year. That's a big ask. So here are a few ways to help them along."

Eloise nodded her understanding and did a sort of wave thing over her head to keep me moving forward.

"The cool thing about becoming an exemplary school is that it fits exactly into the high-risk program we are creating alongside it. Both the kids and their teachers need to understand their function in the school better so both can excel in and out of it. Follow me?" I placed my hands flat on the table at the opposite end of the room and stared straight into her eyes. I hoped she was picking up what I was putting down because this was my only option.

"Hmm." She ruminated. I was getting worried until I could see a figurative light bulb go on above her head. "So, if I understand you, Dr. Pierce, you'd like the kids to do the same thing the teachers have to do and vice versa?"

My cheeks hurt from the smile I gave her. "Exactly. We roll out the program as a seamless project that the whole school adopts. We will pair up teachers and students with contrasting personalities and help them overcome their misconceptions and improve their communication skills. I'm sure there will be the usual twenty percent who will not want to adopt any program, so we'll have to offer some kind of incentive for both adults and children. Maybe a pizza party, zip lining, or axe throwing to get them excited. Though no axes for the kids. As we mentioned before, the mentors will get an additional stipend for their additional responsibilities. What do you think?"

"Not bad, Dr. P. Not bad," she remarked, reducing my name to a single letter. "We still need to tighten it up, but I think we have the makings of a positive long-term program. The only thing that you haven't mentioned is how we will measure our success. Smiling faces aren't enough. We'll need data."

Eloise stood and walked the opposite way around the table, thinking about it herself. "I still think with the improvement in morale, friendship, and reduced stress, test scores will rise organically, though if you can think of anything specific, please don't hold back." She paused, then added, "There have been several studies that suggest games, writing, and speech exercises can help students retain information and gain a deeper understanding of concepts."

"Oh! How about creating Friday Fun Games? Instead of the regular curriculum being taught after lunch, teachers incorporate those things you suggested into games for the rest of the afternoon. It would create more engagement for the kids, there'd be less stress on keeping their attention at the end of the week, and parents would get happy kids at the end of the day. Eloise! I'm loving this. You know who else is going to love this?" I waggled my eyebrow "Trudie."

Just then, the conference room door opened, and low and behold, there was my little vixen. Shocked but present.

Eloise looked at her, then back at me, then back at her. "You're right on time, Trudie." She smiled conspiratorially.

Trudie's confusion was evident as she looked from me to Eloise. Did she know I had been talking about her?

"Ah, yeah. You said to come down to your office at nine-thirty to go over lunchroom duties for October."

Eloise waved her in and pulled a seat out for her. Thankfully, she brought Trudie up to speed so I could study her nonverbal communication. Her posture was ramrod stiff, and she'd take her skin off if she kept wringing her hands the way she was. I didn't know whether to be angry or sad at that moment, so I pasted on the fake smile I used when attending my parents' functions. Placid and impenetrable.

TRUDIE

I knew Eloise was up to something. In the five years I'd worked at Hartland Middle School, I'd only doled out lunchroom duties once. She was an evil woman with a hidden agenda, and I was going to punch Ricky in his long, smooth throat for not giving me a heads-up.

I watched Alex through my peripheral vision as Eloise detailed their plan. He was plastic. I had seen that look all weekend long as he had weathered his parents' onslaught. Now he was using it on me. Great. Just thinking about having a conversation with him made my stomach turn over. It was the same pain I experienced last night when my mom begged me to see my father. Helpless.

"So, what do you think?" Eloise exclaimed with excitement.

I managed to formulate a response in seconds, even though I was barely listening.

"That ticks off all the S.M.A.R.T. goal requirements: specific, measurable, achievable, realistic, and timely. My only concern is the realistic part. Do you really think we can get all our teachers and all our students on the same page as one big happy family? I'm usually the eternal optimist, but this seems like a stretch." I tried not to look over at Alex. His chiseled jaw was ticking away, and he looked twitchy. Not a look I'd seen on him before.

Eloise scratched her neck and pondered my assessment of what they had presumed was their flawless plan. "Yeah, I knew it was too good to be true. What changes do you suggest?"

"Well," I took my time, then sized up Alex. I wanted this moment to reflect on who actually was the "stupid" person he accused me of being during his text tirade. Perhaps I was twisting things out of context, but I'm also still feeling petulant. "I'm surprised Dr. Pierce didn't point out how ridiculous it would be to assume everyone would get on board. I mean, he is the specialist, right? Nevertheless," I pressed on, "If the incentive is alluring, we could expect eighty to ninety percent compliance. I'm not worried about our high-risk kids. We will make sure they receive the attention they deserve."

Alex seemed ready to attack, then reeled himself in, shrugging his shoulders and pulling his suitcoat back on straight. "Ms. Gonzalez, I don't think accusations are helpful or professional," he retorted. It's the same behavior we are trying to eradicate from this school."

Crap! Caught in my own snare.

"Sustained," I muttered. "What do you propose are enticing bribes to get everyone to play nicely?" I crossed my arms under my chest, giving him my mean-girl look. Actually, I didn't have a mean-girl look, so I'm sure I looked as stupid as charged.

"Kids!" Eloise shouted. "I'm not sure what's flown up your butts but knock it off. Here's what we're going to do. You two are going to sit here and figure out some incentives. Then you're going to write out a brief description of the dozen kids who have been recommended for the high-risk group. I've already secured our mentors, so all you have to do is come up with a rotation for them and a way to track their progress."

I flung my arms out in front of me. "What am I supposed to do with my classes? They are already waiting on me."

Alex fired out, "I have two conference calls starting at eleven and won't finish until one this afternoon. Eloise, I'll do all the hard lifting on this one this afternoon."

I felt my face separate and a tiny alien crepy out of it screeching, "Hell, no! These are my kids and my friends. Not yours. I get a say in all of this, so back off." I could feel a headache working its way up from my shoulders. This was all too much.

Eloise smacked her hands down on the table in disgust. "Enough. You," she pointed at me, "have ten minutes to get your things out of your classroom, go to the bathroom, and return to this room. And you, sir, have ten minutes to cancel whatever you think is more important than your job here. You will eat here and stay here until you have figured all this crap out, and I'd better not hear any raised voices or chairs being tossed about or there will be hell to pay. Capisce?"

"Capase," we said in unison, like two siblings ready to kill each other as soon as their parents left the room. My jaw clenched, and his fists squeezed open and shut. We were both ready for a knockdown, no-holds-barred showdown. *Come on, big boy!*

I moved like lightning out the door to collect my things and returned in eight minutes flat. As soon as I had the conference room door closed the staring contest began. He crossed his arms in front of that ridiculously chiseled chest in an Armani suit that looked like it had been painted on. His eyes turned that deep, deep green that was almost obsidian. I was in big trouble now. I knew it, and he knew it. The only time his eyes looked like that was when he was teaching me the most resplendent of all magnificent sexual pleasures known to womankind. My thighs trapped a rush of moisture that was sure to attract his senses. He walked around the table like I was a gazelle he would eat for lunch. I trembled. I always thought that was the overactive sensation of weak women. Either it's a real thing or I'm a weak woman.

Refusing to believe the latter, I stood up, crossed my arms under my chest, and stared at him as hard as I could. I wouldn't give him anything. No words. No drama. No contact. I was a strong, resilient, and super-fucking-smart woman who would hold her ground. That's right! I'm not a snowflake like his stupid crocodile-looking bitch of a fiancée.

He stopped in front of me, close enough that I couldn't shake off his fucking pheromones and delicious manly scent. Then he took one more step and leaned into my face, holding himself like a statue, waiting for me to cave. One … two … three seconds passed and neither of us moved an inch. Both of us were as stubborn as three-year-olds wanting to stay up past bedtime.

I'm not sure what happened after that because his lips were on mine, devouring me whole. I couldn't breathe and my legs wobbled. He caught me in an embrace as tightly as he ever had and my only choice was to hold onto his lapels for dear life or kick him in the balls. *So tempting.* Sadly, I loved his lips on mine even when I was angry with him, and his balls might hold my future family. It was a hate kiss! I hoped that was a thing because I had missed his pillowy Greek-godlike lips on mine.

He growled and grabbed my ass with both hands, pulling me against his hips. That was when reality broke through.

I shoved at his chest, hissing, "Stop."

When he let go of me, I took several steps back and tried to clear my head. He'd always had the power to dislocate my brain from my skull and make me—okay—talk me into doing unspeakable sexual acts, but not that day. That day, we were … doing something important … God, I couldn't remember why we were in that room together.

Oh, yeah, work. "You can't do that to me. I'm mad at you, and we're at work." I paced back and forth in front of the whiteboard, trying to figure out a way to shove last weekend's debacle into the deepest recesses of my mind. I was hurt and needed more time to take the emotions out of what had happened in New York. Shit, I still didn't even know if he was currently engaged.

He pushed his large hand into those beautiful waves of thick brown hair trying to gain what appeared to be his composure, unfortunately for him, it looked more like frustration.

"Trudie. Listen," he begged.

I put my hand up to stop him. "Don't come any closer. You don't deserve to touch me," I whisper-shouted.

"I had to break the sexual tension so we could focus on these projects," he rationalized.

"Had to? Seriously? You think you're all that—that you can throw yourself all over me and expect me just to let you have your way after the bullshit you pulled in New York? Hell no!"

"I don't understand. Didn't you have a great time in New York before the gala? How about when we hung your panties on the diorama of the Empire State Building? I know you had a great time up there. Everything was amazing until my fucking ex-fiancée—EX-fiancée, Trudie—stuck her forked tongue in your ear. Can't you see why I left her … three years ago? I never lied to you,

Trudie. You were the one who should be apologizing to me for not trusting me. I've never lied to you. Not then, not now, and not ever. What do you want me to say?" He scrubbed his face with his hand and stormed away from me.

I bit my lip, tears already staining my face. He was right. I needed to own my freak-out. "I just wanted you to say you're sorry. Sorry for leaving me with all those people I didn't know, sorry that you didn't check to see if she would be there, and sorry that my feelings were hurt, because they hurt a lot, Alex." I sounded like a child even to my own ears.

"Baby, please accept my apologies for all the shit that happened when I should have had you by my side. I'm sorry your feelings were hurt and that Sheila rattled you about our relationship. I am truly sorry for all those things. I'm most sorry, though, that we didn't have a chance to talk it through that evening so neither of us would have had to suffer these past few days." He walked over and took my hands in his and brought them to his trembling lips. I didn't realize how upset he was about me leaving. I knew he liked me, but I thought perhaps not as much as I liked him.

He brushed away more tears with his thumb and looked deeply into my water-laden eyes. The creases on his forehead were grooved in a way that made him look concerned, not angry. "Trudie, you captured my attention in San Francisco and have consumed my thoughts every day since. Finding you here and working with you at your school has shown me so many of your beautiful facets that I can't deny how deeply connected I am to you. I'm falling for you Trudie, and I'm scared as hell about it."

Wow! That was some confession. I was so selfish and wrapped up in my own pain that I didn't consider what our relationship meant to him. I thought he just wanted to have fun and mind-blowing sex. Sure, he was thoughtful, kind, attentive, and . . . *oh shit. Was he falling for me? Was I falling for him?* I'd already thrown in the towel of fighting our attraction. So what if he was an asshole sometimes? I was no prize either. I think stubborn would be his first word to describe me to others. He apologized so sincerely that I cried all over again. Geez, this man was something else.

Alex knelt before me taking my hands in both of his, remorse written all over his face. "Sheila and I had been on and off again since college. My parents decided that she was from, and I quote, "good stock." They made plans and for whatever stupid reasons at the time we stayed together––until I wanted to see what life without her would be like. We were apart for almost ten years. It was the idea that I was getting older and should probably settle down did the idea of getting back together sounded good. I was all in. I was ready for a family. She was the best of the best of any woman I had been with––but, you know how that ended. Unfortunately, she thought she could cheat and get away with it. That was much different than me breaking things off first before fucking my way across the country. Needless to say, now she regrets it and is making it difficult for both of us."

I pulled my hands from his and cupped his jaw. "You astound me, Alex. There are so many sides to you I couldn't have imagined. You always seem to see all of me, and that's one of the best parts about you. Thank you for your very sincere apologies. I accept every one of them, and we will work through them soon." I brushed my thumbs over his long-lashed eyes and held them shut while I purged myself of my sorrow. "I am truly sorry for running away and not giving you a chance to explain yourself. It was wrong, hurtful and selfish of me to do that to you."

He opened his eyes. I needed to get the words out of my mouth before letting him see how raw and broken I was. He was so in tune with me that he understood me before I even understood myself. It was uncanny how often he found ways to heal my past before I'd even said the words.

I continued. "It's been my go-to thing since I was young—running and hiding. You probably already get this, but I felt lied to and deceived about your promises, just like I had with my dad, except you came back and demanded we talk it through. That never happened when I was a kid. You're forcing me out of my comfort zone, and it's scaring me, too. You aren't just my sex healer"—we both laughed at that— "you are my soul healer. I just need some time to let each piece fall into place. Am I making any sense?" I kissed his salty lips sweetly, hoping my olive branch was accepted.

"Perfect sense." He kissed me back softly.

There was a knock at the door, and we broke apart, each of us walking in the opposite direction: me to the whiteboard, him to the window.

"Hi there. Eloise wanted me to drop off these snacks for you and a thermos full of coffee to keep you juiced up. Okay, I used the word 'juiced'; she said 'coherent.' All right then, I'll be on my way.

Good luck!" Ricky was like a walking sitcom. He placed everything on the barren conference table and all but skipped out of the room.

"I guess we better get busy, huh?" I smirked at his confused face.

"Ah, yeah. Has he always been so cheerful?" Alex shook his head again.

"Incredibly so."

CHAPTER 3

ALEXANDER

It was the only way I knew to shut her down. She loved it when I kissed her. The submissive way she let go was such a turn-on that I almost forgot we were in a school. I pulled away from that smoldering kiss bereft of her warmth and sensuality. I could still taste the salt bagel she'd had for breakfast on my lips, and God, was I hungry for more. She did have a point, though. We were at a school, with children and her boss close by—it wouldn't be prudent to continue groping each other. I supposed it was good timing that Ricky had dropped by.

The way we were able to hash out our differences was incredible. I'd never argued with someone so willing to fix a problem and not overdramatize the situation. Sure, she was pissed off. So was I. She needed to vent, and so did I. Our shared goal though was to identify problems while being mindful of each other's baggage. My family had a history of shoving your weaknesses and slip-ups in your face, over and over again. You could never move on from it. At one time, I thought it was my dad who was the biggest perpetrator, but it was actually my mother. Constant shaming to get my sisters and I to do their bidding. The proverbial music started, and before you knew it you were dancing to the figurative beat.

I sat back down at my computer and found the place where I had begun with Eloise an hour earlier. Twenty minutes later I had brought Trudie up to speed, and I could feel the excitement rolling off her.

"That's a great start, Alex. Once we get our incentives in place, how would you like to roll this out? School assembly? Email? Skywriter?" *She was cute.*

"I'd rather like a skywriter, though the kids would miss it if they were at school. How about an email to the teachers to give them a heads-up, then an email to the parents the following day? Hopefully, the teachers will have a head start on wrapping their brains around the idea. Maybe, though, we should wait a few days before letting the parents know of the assembly. Our teachers may have questions before we roll it out."

I felt like I was rambling. I hadn't executed a program like this before and there were so many variables to consider. We just had to come up with a realistic plan and hope for the best.

Trudie walked around the table twice before replying, her face moved like she was stretching every muscle the whole time.

"I hear what you're saying, but we need to hone this even more. Our statement needs to be precise and tie up as many loopholes as we can identify. Let's make a list of those loopholes and then craft a statement. I like the email rollout. Maybe give teachers forty-eight hours to add their feedback or concerns, and then send the email to the parents with the updated verbiage. How does that sound?"

I leaned back in my chair steepling my fingers in front of my mouth. I loved watching her mind work. "Genius. Good job. Okay, what's next?" I leaned forward to type out our process and then followed her over to the whiteboard.

For the next fifteen minutes, we hashed out all known variables to ensure a smooth rollout. Then we spent an equal amount of time nailing down a process for running the program for the next several months. We needed measurable goals and a plan to achieve those.

At twelve thirty there was another knock on the door. It was Eloise with the look of a stern jailer on her face.

"Well, look what we have here. Two professionals who put their differences aside to meet a common goal. Fantastic. Gold stars for the both of you." She smiled brightly as she dropped two Panera bags on the table. "Eat and go for a walk. You have forty-five minutes, and I want you back here to finish up." She strutted back to the door. "Oh, and don't forget the high-risk program processes. I hope you don't have plans tonight, because you're not leaving until it's all done."

Harsh! Wasn't there a clause in her contract that said she's entitled to her time off? I was sure there was one in mine.

"Uh, thanks?" Trudie muttered and dove into the bags. "All this brain work is exhausting."

"Brain work?" I chuckled. "Isn't everything we do brain work?" I snatched the macaroni from her hands.

"Hey! I wanted that."

"Maybe I'll share if you talk nice to me."

She swiveled her body and stepped behind me, planting her hands on my hips. Next thing I knew she was sliding them up my torso under my suit coat and rubbing my nipples through my shirt.

"Maybe I don't want to talk at all." *Fuck!* She could have all the macaroni if she would just keep doing that.

"You're not playing fair," I moaned.

"I didn't realize that was part of our negotiation," she crooned.

I spun around and placed my hands on her breasts and massaged them the way she liked. "Great. Let's continue our negotiations."

"Fuck, Alex. That feels too good to dispute. How about a truce?" She dropped her head to my chest purring like a kitten and I felt like I'd do anything for her.

"Yeah. How about I feed you your portion and I can eat mine off your tummy?"

The look on her face was priceless. "You're hilarious! Give me the fork."

TRUDIE

By the time I walked through my apartment door that evening, my head was throbbing and I shook from not having eaten since the Panera eight hours earlier. In order to keep Alex off me I all but had to tranquilize him. As much as I'd have liked to fuck him in the school conference room or play handsies under a restaurant table, I was spent. My phone rang and my mom's face appeared. She usually waited for me to call, which meant something important was on her mind.

"Hi, Mom. How was your day?" I dropped all my bags and walked the five steps to my kitchen and opened the fridge, collecting items to make grilled cheese.

"Mija. The hospital called and said your father refuses to eat. I need you to go now and encourage him to fight for his life." Her emphatic tone fell on deaf ears.

"What?! I can't just drop what I'm doing, Mom. I am required to be at school during the day, and I just walked through the door this evening. Besides, I have a ginormous project that I'm getting paid to do. I can't leave anytime I feel like it." I slammed the orange juice container on the counter and tore open the bag of bread.

"Honey, your dad is dying. I have no idea how long he has. He needs you."

I almost threw up—he needs me? That's a laugh. "Well, he better hang on until Friday night, because I don't have a moment until then to even think about this."

"Trudie! You've pushed me to my limits. Go and see your father tomorrow. Make it happen. You don't have to speak to him. Sit by his bed and let him do all the talking. Do the right thing and see the man. He loved you even if he couldn't be the father you needed him to be. Show him a little respect."

Whoa! My mother had never taken that tone with me. His time must truly be running out for her to be so stern.

"Okay, okay. I'll see him after work tomorrow, but I can't stay long." I let out a long breath trying to settle my nerves.

"Thank you, darling. I'm sorry I raised my voice at you. Your father isn't doing well and I know deep in my heart neither of you will rest peacefully until you've worked out your problems." She made kissing sounds and I clicked off the call.

Fuck! Fuck! Fuck!

Now my hunger was nonexistent, though I knew I had to eat. I finished going through the motions of making my dinner and taking a shower before collapsing into a slumber coma.

The next day was hectic with a new module to start in English. A rash of sickness that permeated the school forced me to slow down my lesson plans so the absent kids didn't get too far behind. And, of course, there was Dr. Pierce.

I didn't have time for him that day. I put off all the reports and emails that needed to be written and organized for Eloise's approval and instead did damage control with Ella, who had proceeded to have a panic attack in the middle of my classroom in front of her peers.

"Ella, sweetheart, please, take a breath and follow me. Everyone! Please pair up and review your vocabulary words for the next ten minutes, and then we'll have our quiz." Gasps of anxiety filled the room.

I motioned for Ella to sit on the shag carpet that made my classroom's Rest and Return area cozy, and I joined her, sitting on a meditation cushion.

"Let's breathe together—in for a count of four, and then slowly out for a count of four. Let's do those four times, okay?" I smiled, nodding my head, and when she reciprocated, we started the breathing exercise together.

"Good girl. That's better, right?

"Miss Trudie?"

"Yes, sweetheart."

"My parents told me they are getting a divorce and that I'd have to pick where I want to live." Her eyes welled up full of tears and her shoulders curled into her chest. *Poor dear.*

"Oh, no." I patted her shoulder. "I'm so sorry to hear that. What are your feelings about it?" I knew I wasn't to give her any professional advice since I wasn't a psychologist, but she needed a shoulder to cry on and a friend who could guide her in the right direction.

"Mostly scared. They've been fighting for so long that I hardly notice it anymore. Who will be home for me and take me to my activities and help me with my homework and. . .?" She cried harder.

The rest of the class got very quiet and tried to understand why Ella was so upset.

"Hey, guys. Can I trust you to control yourselves while I walk Ella down to the office? She isn't feeling well."

Delano, smart-ass that he was, said, "We've got you, Ms. G," and winked at me.

"Thank you, Delano. You're in charge. Anything that goes wrong is your responsibility." I gave him a wink, then. That shut him down from anything he was planning.

When Ella and I reached the office, I walked her back to the conference room. Alex was working there, and I sat Ella across from him.

"Dr. Pierce, we could use your help. Would you mind?" I nodded my head at Ella.

He pushed his papers and computer aside and folded his hands in front of him on the table. "How can I help?"

"I'm going to grab Ella's counselor so she can join you. You should know that Ella's parents told her this morning that they were getting a divorce right before she left for school, and she's having a panic attack." I stood behind her chair rolling my eyes at how selfish her parents were to notify her as she left for school. What the hell was she supposed to do with that information?

"That's awful, Ella. I'm so sorry to hear that. I'll wait for your counselor and maybe we can figure out a few ways to make your situation better before you leave today. One thing I can tell you is that parents don't always do things the best way." *Ha! Wasn't that the truth?*

I shook my purse out onto my desk, looking for some Tylenol. My head was pounding from thinking about Ella and what assholes her parents were. Of course, I knew this additional traumatic episode would haunt her not only for the rest of this school year but for the rest of her life. I think the real reason I was so upset about her was that she represented another statistic of people who become damaged through no fault of their own. You could say, spiritually, her soul chose this family so that she could work out her issues in hopes of elevating herself to a higher plane. Yeah, maybe, but at that moment, she felt totaled, crushed, and broken. No amount of higher thinking could fix that now. How do you teach a kid she has to "walk through the fire" to learn she wasn't the problem?

If that weren't enough, there was my visit to my father I had to contend with. I'd been playing our last conversation in my head for almost fifteen years.

"You don't understand what it was like to have to pick up and leave your family time after time, not knowing when you were coming back or if you were coming back. I might as well have been in the military for all the notice these insurance companies gave me." His monologue was followed by his drinking a full can of beer in two gulps. *Typical.*

My response was closer to my heart and I'm positive he wasn't catching on.

"Dad. I know your job was hard. We missed you so much every time you'd leave. It's only that you were so mean to us when you came home. What did we do to make you so angry? It's not fair." My twelve-year-old self remembered saying one particular afternoon when I was feeling brave.

In response, he stared me down, grabbed his tan Carhartt jacket, got into his rusty pickup, and drove away. I prayed so hard that he wouldn't hit anyone while driving under the influence. I had a father who I now realize was as traumatized as we were about his coming and going. The difference was he was a grown-ass man and we were children. That was fifteen years ago. I couldn't imagine what else needed to be said now.

I found my pills and took a long swig of water out of the Tervis mug Robin and Jody had given me for my twenty-fifth birthday. The flower design usually lifted my spirits, but not at this moment. I'd have needed a séance to get my spirits to rise. I had finished my day with my "happy teacher" façade, and now I was packed up and ready to take the drive downtown to Grace Hospital to fight the devil.

I was two steps out of my classroom when I got a call from my best friend, Ruby. I'm sure whatever she had to tell me would at least make me laugh.

"Hello, Princess! I've missed you since you returned from the ball and left me sleeping in your bed." She was so dramatic—though I did leave her a note when I left to visit my mom on Sunday.

"Yes, it is I, your queen … what's up?" I waved at a few teachers as I exited the building, one hand holding my phone to my ear. The sky looked gloomy and matched my attitude perfectly. Robin waved at me and put her hand up to her head, extending her thumb and pinky, indicating she wanted me to call. I nodded, then dug out my keys to open my car door. I couldn't wait for the new car I'd buy when I got the bonus from working as a liaison with Alex. How sad was I that a keyless entry system made me swoon? Pathetic, I know.

"Are you in your car yet? I can hear you huffing and puffing."

"Yeah, yeah, I just got in. Hang on a second while the call switches over."

I threw my stuff on the front seat and buckled myself in. After a big breath and sigh, I encouraged her to continue.

"You are never going to believe where I'm going Saturday night?" Ruby's excitement was over the top. Her new voice-over career was going great and last I heard her boss made her drool-worthy.

"I can't even imagine. The Whitney Restaurant so you can hang out at the Ghostbar? Or maybe the Townsend Hotel for their amazing brick chicken?" I knew I was being a smart-ass. I wasn't in the mood to get excited, except she *was* and I didn't want to let her down.

"Oh my God, those both sound amazing. It's been years since I've been to either, but, no! Even better..." She was dragging this out.

"What, Ruby? Where are you going already?" I signaled to get on the expressway and checked my dashboard clock. Four o'clock. With any luck I could get to the hospital in time for his dinner so I could excuse myself and remove myself quickly.

"Daniel, Patrick, and his wife and I are going to a hockey game! I'm freaking out, Trudes. Friday night, Daniel and I have a very important meeting with Stella from Stella Lingerie about her campaign with Miles & Stone, the advertising agency I'm working with, and then the next night I'm out with him again. Again, Trudie. Do you know what that means?"

"Uh, hot boss problems two nights in a row?" I asked sarcastically.

"Yes, Trudie, that's exactly what that means," she deadpanned.

"Honey, listen, it's obvious you have feelings for this guy, and from what you said, the feelings are mutual. The bigger issue is human resources. How do they feel about you dating your boss?"

"Ugh!" she moaned in despair. "You see, this is why I called you. I don't know how to bring it up. Shouldn't he be the one to toe the company line here?" Her whininess was escalating.

"Come on, sweetheart. Put on your big girl panties and ask the hard questions. Do you report to him or this Patrick guy?"

The phone went silent and I waited a full minute before I got concerned.

"Ruby, are you still there?"

"Yeah, I'm here. In reality, I report to Patrick, so that would make Daniel..."

"Not your direct supervisor, henceforth which-not, you could date him."

There was a hissing sound coming through the receiver that made my ears ache. "Yeesssss! Trudie, you're a genius. I'm so happy I called you. I've got to get back into the studio but thank you so much. BFFs forever!" she cheered and then hung up.

You're welcome. Anytime.

CHAPTER 4

TRUDIE

I hated hospitals. The sterile white walls and checkered linoleum floors screamed insane asylum. The acrid smell of disinfectant or the occasional leaking bodily fluids infiltrated my nose and nauseated me. The third floor of Grace Hospital was no exception. If not for the bright flowers that punctuated the view and the whooshing of nurses and aides brushing by me, I'd have thought I was in purgatory. I smiled at the cute doctor whose badge read "Resident," noticing as he brushed by me. He reciprocated by pulling his hand through his blond locks and smiling back, treating me to the sight of a beautiful set of teeth and a delicious dimple in his left cheek. Too bad I was here on a death mission or I would have followed him to wherever he was going, just to see that dimple again. Yeah, even in my nauseated, brain-dead state, I was still checking out hot doctors. Something was seriously wrong with me.

"Excuse me," I said to the nurse at the floor desk, "can you direct me to Room 312?" Without lifting her head from the chart she was engrossed in, she pointed down the hall, and then used her thumb to indicate I should hang a right—at least, I think she meant right.

I followed her remedial instructions and found my dad's room. The blinds were closed and no evidence of well-wishers was to be found. The fluorescent light above his head was the only light in the room and, well, it felt bleak and sad. I walked slowly forward, not wanting to wake him if he was asleep, when I heard my name whispered from his bluish lips.

Time had not been kind to my father. It appeared to me that he had gotten his comeuppance for all the years he stole from our family. I wasn't sure if I was happy or sad about that, except that it was a fair trade. I didn't come up here to be his friend or offer love. That well inside me was bone-dry. I had promised my mom I would let him speak his truth, whatever that was, so I wouldn't have any regrets when he passed. *When exactly did the doctors think that might happen?*

It was weird and heartbreaking to see such a strong man withered down to this. Dry skin, sallow eyes, matted hair, and a week's worth of scruff. The beeps in the background and whining sound of oxygen being pushed through tubes were my only sign that he was physically still alive, until I heard that same whisper again.

"Cariño."

In every movie I had ever watched, the daughter would spring from her seat and grab her father's hand when he woke from his coma. Cries and gasps of joy would echo throughout the room and happy music would usher out the end of the scene. Not this movie. Not this daughter. This daughter was more like a deer in headlights. Frozen and unable to speak.

"You came." His gravely words caught in his throat as he turned his eyes to capture mine. "You came," he repeated.

I walked toward the pleather chair situated next to his bed. My mother must have been visiting earlier and set it there. She proved herself to be a caregiver-for-life even after their divorce. I hung my purse over the back of the seat and hung my coat there too, then settled myself down to look at him more carefully. It had been fifteen hard years of battling my depression over his behavior. Fifteen years of feeling abandoned and unworthy. Didn't he know how much damage he'd inflicted on every relationship I'd ever had? Who would abandon me next? Don't get too emotionally attached to anyone … they'll leave you. God forbid, don't try to love anyone. For sure you'll never get over it. The fact that I had maintained a six-year relationship with Sam was a miracle. Perhaps it lasted as long as it did was that I was never fully invested in him or his plans, or especially his boring bedroom skills.

It baffled me that even though my father chose this lifestyle, he didn't try to stay in touch. A simple card, call, or even a text on my birthday would have made a huge difference in my self-worth. I was invisible to him and therefore he became invisible to me—except that you can't "un-father" your father. It was an infestation in my mind that even five years of therapy couldn't completely remove. Everyone said, "Just get over it. Forget about it. Let it go." God, if only I could. This had become part of my tapestry and unfortunately, no matter how much "getting over" or "forgetting about it" I did, it still hid in the shadows of my mind.

I cleared the voice in my head and decided to take myself out of the equation and just focus on letting him have his peace.

"Dad." *Okay, that was a start.* My lips pressed into a line and I took in a breath to steady myself. "What have you gotten yourself into now?"

His laugh was choked and pained. I reached for his water on the tray table and handed it to him.

"Thank you." You could hear the clock ticking on the wall and the monitors going off down the hall. What was I doing here?

"Sweetie, I can't remember a time I wasn't in trouble, but this time may be my last." He closed his eyes, presumably feeling the weight of his statement.

"What exactly is the problem? Mom said it was cancer, I think." I returned the glass to the table and sat back down for the full story.

"Asbestos poisoning. All those buildings I had to comb through finally caught up with me." He coughed a few times for emphasis.

"That is quite ironic since you now have an insurance claim with the people who hired you to do those jobs."

"Exactly. I filed one six months ago. I only hope I live to collect on it. You and your brothers deserve something good from my poor choices."

The guilt!

"Listen, I don't need anything from you now or in the future. I needed you years ago, but I'm over that now. Mom said you had some things to say to me, so why don't you say them and we both can go back to our own lives." I hated sounding like a bitch, especially given his circumstances. But opening my heart now would incapacitate me for days or weeks, and I just didn't have the energy for that.

His eyes squeezed shut and when they opened again, they were moist. His voice shook as he prepared his speech.

"Your mom and I were so in love, and each time one of our children was born we committed ourselves to each other and to giving you a life better than the ones we had. When the catastrophic adjuster position became available, it presented an opportunity to move from a regular claims agent to something more meaningful and definitely more lucrative. We discussed the pros and cons of this move and what it might mean to our relationship and our kids, but ultimately, we decided that for three years we would accept the downside so that we would have a lifetime of upside." He motioned to his water glass and I complied with his request for assistance.

"The first couple of assignments weren't bad, and we were happy that our decision was paying off. We were able to update our home and provide dance classes for you and martial arts classes for your brothers. Things were good. Until Hurricane Katrina. I remember the call came shortly after dinner and I looked at your mom and the despair on her face. She knew this was the downside of this job—months away from home. I packed and hugged each one of you so hard. You remember, *cariño*, you said, 'Daddy, you're squishing me,' and we laughed. Do you remember?"

I nodded. It was weird remembering a good moment in all the bad.

"I kissed your mother goodbye and then my life became mayhem. I didn't sleep for days on end. The ravages of that storm still keep me up at night. Did you know that most of those poor people who lived near the 17th Street Canal levee that broke only got $1200 in compensation? $50 billion in damages. I still can't get my head around it. I was in and out of the reconstruction of the area for five years and still, it looked like a war scene. If you haven't already done the math, this assignment took me two years past the agreement I made with your mom. We agreed, though, that it was my patriotic duty to stay and help those people get as much money as they could to rebuild their lives."

My brain worked hard fitting his timeline to my memories, but it all started to make sense. I held my thoughts and let him finish. I watched his rough hands twist in his lap and his legs twitch periodically, showing the pain as he purged the memories from his mind. My heart was nicked by his words and I gulped back my tears.

"Obviously, you know the rest of the story. Home for a few days and then gone again for weeks, only to come back again angrier and more intolerable," he said.

That's when my resolve broke.

"Exactly! You were a real asshole. Do you have any idea how stressed out we were knowing that you'd come home like some Jekyll and Hyde character? We ran around the house doing our best to make it all comfortable, and we were so excited when you arrived, but then you were the biggest jerk in the history of jerks!"

I had to breathe. I had to disengage. I knew this would happen, and now I was screaming at a dying man. The knock on the door confirmed I had lost my shit and was too loud.

"Hey, hi, uh, everything okay in here? It's time for Mr. Gonzalez's medication." The nurse scrunched up her face, embarrassed to be interrupting our *tête-à-tête*.

"Sure. Just let me step out of the room. I'll be back shortly." I grabbed my purse and bolted. I made it to the bathroom and started sobbing uncontrollably in a stall. This was why I didn't want to see him again. I knew my healing wouldn't be complete without this last confrontation. Even though I was glad to let go of the pain, I still felt like I was going to barf. I took several long yoga-style breaths—might as well since I paid to learn them—and calmed myself to the point where I could open the door. I laughed as I looked into the mirror—I was a picture of sheer madness: tear-streaked lines that dripped down my cheeks to my chin, ruddy complexion, quivering lips, and smudged mascara that looked like tire tracks across my eyes. A real beauty queen. My face resembled how I felt inside—disfigured and distraught.

I needed to finish this Greek tragedy, so I splashed water on my face, wiped my hands, and dabbed at the errant black marks. I just had to make myself more presentable. I reapplied my lip gloss and pressed my hands down my shirt, pulling myself together before walking back to the final act of today's rendition of Dante's *Inferno*.

I settled back into my seat as the nurse finished taking his vital signs.

"Mr. Gonzalez, your blood pressure is up. I'd like you to finish your visit quickly and get some rest. I'll come back in twenty minutes to check it again."

"Sure. Thank you, nurse." He wiggled his fingers goodbye and turned back to me.

"I'm so sorry this is upsetting to you. I didn't want to leave this world without clearing the air." His voice rattled as he spoke.

Humph." Are you even dying? They have so many treatments now, can't one of them help you?" My callousness was grating even on me. These thoughts kept slipping out, and even though it appeased my anger to say them, I knew they were cruel.

"From your mouth to God's ears, I wish there were. I've been through three types of treatments already and two clinical trials. Nothing seems to help." He adjusted his canula, which hung from his nose and then went up around his ears. "This oxygen is the only thing keeping me from gasping for air."

"I'm sorry for saying that. It was rude and callous. When were you diagnosed?" I handed him his water again.

"Five years ago. I didn't reach out to your mom until last year. I didn't want to be a burden to her again. There isn't anyone in my family anymore, and I needed an executor of my estate to handle my funeral. Everything is paid for, it's only, I was afraid no one would know that I was gone. I have been alone for a long time. After your mom and I broke up all I had was regret and shame."

What do you even say to that? "Yeah, you dick, your fault, not ours"? I thought. I breathed in and out again for strength and calm.

"Trudie. My rage was never at you, or your brothers, and especially not at your mother. I was angry with myself for not leaving that job before I felt so disconnected from my family. I felt humiliated that I wasn't caring for everyone the way a man should. Every time I walked away from our home to go back to the field, I chastised myself horribly for being a son of a bitch. It hurt so much that I talked myself into thinking that you'd be better off without me, and that maybe I shouldn't come back at all. I'm pathetic, cariño. I don't deserve your love or attention. Please, sweetheart, you have to know that even through all of this I loved you so very much." His tears fell from his weathered face and he became racked with a coughing fit.

Without thinking I stood and pulled him forward and patted his back, encouraging him to calm himself down and breathe deeply. Minutes went by before I heard him take a settling breath, and then I fluffed his pillows so he could sink back into the bed. I was surprised when I sat again. *Was I helping a man in pain or was I helping my father unburden his soul?* Compassion was a strange feeling. It seemed to have a mind of its own, acting and reacting without thought. That must have been why I offered my help. Maybe we both could find some peace in taking a step forward in our assumptions. Maybe my absolving him, just a little, would soften the pain and heal my heart and mind.

I took his hand and his eyes went wide. My lips twisted into what only could be called a grimace, since a smile was giving him too much. "We all make mistakes, Dad. I'm not sure what to make of all you said, but I'll think about it. Try to get some rest and I'll be by again soon." I patted his hand and gave him a gentle squeeze before I took my leave.

I was almost to the door when he wheezed out, "Thank you for coming." I stopped short and looked over my shoulder, remembering that he was only human, even if he was an asshole, and gave him a small smile.

CHAPTER 5
ALEXANDER

I chose to work from home in hopes of getting some quality work done. When I was at the school my thoughts wandered to Trudie too often, and between Ricky begging for my attention and the kids realizing I was fun to hang around with, nothing was getting done.

I hadn't had any meaningful conversation with Trudie in two days. She was acting weird and, of course, I made it about myself. Our last meeting had been intense and filled with contradicting emotions. It felt like whiplash. One moment I was deliriously happy to see her and the next I wanted to wring her neck for running out on me at the gala. When would this woman understand that she could trust me and talk to me about her feelings instead of always bolting out the door? When she pulled that trick in San Francisco this past summer, it was nearly two months before our paths impossibly crossed again.

The Exemplary School Project was well underway, and from what I could tell, this school was already above average for most of the national requirements. Sure, there were a few minor things that the school board wanted tweaked, like a more uniform approach to teaching, except that would never happen. Not at this school, nor any other in the world. Teachers needed to have freedom to execute their visions. The school board should have understood this, and I was concerned that pushing these teachers too far would alienate them to the point that they would quit.

The principal had wrangled me into a school board meeting the previous night, leading me around like her prized pony in a way that was reminiscent of my parents' practice of showing off their family. Being so well versed in these machinations, I played my role perfectly, right up to the point when the board president demanded that I require the teachers to record all conversation made directly to students in case their parents took issue with how their child was spoken to.

"With all due respect, Dr. Williams, much like your office, what happens in the classroom stays in the classroom. How can a teacher build trust if everything they say is recorded? It's absurd to think an educator has to stop and detail every conversation to protect their ass and the school's ass."

I can't remember all the deliberation that followed, but I can tell you that it was a good thing there wasn't a stapler in front of me because I would have chucked it at this guy's head. Of all the stupid things to ask of a teacher. Don't they have enough to deal with? All incidents that are relevant are reported to the kid's counselor or the principal anyway—why create a hostile environment?

Once again, I was torn between my moral compass and the demands of my clients. I wondered if I should consider private practice again. At least then I had control of the beginning and end of the conversation.

I got up to stretch and noticed it was almost ten o'clock and I needed another jolt of coffee. My phone rang as I dropped a pod into the single-cup coffee maker my sister had sent me. The coffee tasted like shit, but it worked in a pinch. I clicked the button on the machine while I clicked the green icon on my phone.

"Jacob, my long-lost friend. To what do I owe the honor?" My brother from another mother and I met back in college. We'd go months between conversations, but we had no trouble picking up where we'd left off.

"Douchebag! I missed you and your hard pecs rubbing against mine." He was always the funniest of our pair. "I'm in town this Friday and you're coming out with me. The wife and kids are going to South Carolina to visit her parents, so you and I are going to stretch our badass bachelor muscles together."

"You? Badass? Ha! The last time you did anything badass was ten years ago when you asked your wife to marry you. Since then, she's owned your dick, and let's be frank, you hurt my feelings when you said her tits felt better than my pecs against yours. So, fuck you!" Bantering with this guy felt so good. I missed it, a lot.

"Spoilsport. I'll give you that last remark, but I still want to feel your ass rub against mine at the bar while I pretend to be picking up chicks." I knew I should want to pick up chicks with my best buddy, but like him, I had already found my chick. Every day since I had met Trudie, I'd felt less and less driven to look for anyone else.

Her smile, that curvy ass, those voluptuous tits, and the way she looked at me got me hard every time.

"I'll tell you what—how about you and I have dinner somewhere, and then move on to drinks at a downtown establishment? I'll invite my friend Trudie to hang with us." *Yeah, this could be fun.*

"A friend, huh? I'm your only friend, Doofus. That name sounds familiar. Have you mentioned her before?'

"Uhh, maybe?" I dragged out my response as my brain flipped through the past four months of conversations.

"I got it! The kids and I were in an escape room. You said, and I quote, 'The most infuriating woman in my workshop is scheduled with me for the whole week and I am going to lose my mind.' That woman?"

"Shit!" Maybe I had mentioned something like that. I was lost in thought, still trying to figure out exactly what I had said when he chimed in again.

"Aww, boy-eee! You found the girl! Now I have to meet her. Dude, this trip will be the best ever."

I could imagine him punching the air like he always did when he put everything together.

"Oh, and I'm staying with you while I'm on this recruiting weekend." Jacob was a professional athletic recruiter for what I called "the not-so-important sports." Sports like soccer, tennis, and golf. I was impressed with how keenly in touch he was with his needs. He knew how much pressure he wanted to live with and still make millions. The Big Four sports were brutal on a marriage and that lifestyle would be detrimental to both his physical and mental health.

"Yay, me!" I waved imaginary tiny flags in my head. "I'll be sure to load up on carbs for you. Are those still your favorite treats?" The stories I could tell about how many bagels that guy could shove into his face would make anyone vomit.

"Nope. Ellen has brainwashed me into eating old-man food like oatmeal and bananas. Soft foods that I don't need my teeth to eat. It's humiliating." I roared a big belly laugh at my emasculated friend and assured him I'd have a bagel with lox and cream cheese on hand, and it would be our secret.

"You're the best friend ever. Just so you know, this weekend is about soccer. The tournament is at Oakland University and I expect you to show up. Bring Trudie so she can see what a badass friend you have." I'm sure he was winking through the phone. He was such a dork.

"Again, you're not a badass, and your breakfast proves it. I love you, man. I'll text you Thursday night."

I capped my coffee cup and returned to my desk, ruminating over our conversation. Did Jacob illuminate what my subconscious desperately wanted? Was Trudie the one? More importantly, was I ready to try committing to a relationship again? Both of us had so many hang-ups in our past and I couldn't see how we could make it work if we didn't trust each other. We had to have more than just a physical relationship. She had to trust me emotionally too, and unfortunately, I had some collateral damage to fix first—like Sheila.

My lips pursed as I pulled up Sheila's phone number. I'd been pondering the best way to get that viper out of my life for a long time, and I truly thought I finally had it figured out. Not thinking about her or hearing from her until her stunt at the gala felt good, normal, and easy. It was time to put my plan into action, so I dialed her number.

Sheila loved drama and worked very hard at creating it even when there wasn't any. That was my in.

"Alex!" she shrieked.

"Sheila," I deadpanned.

"I was just thinking about you and all the wonderful times we had at your parents' lake house when we were kids, and…"

I was not going down memory lane with her. Not now. Not ever again. "You acted like a shrew at the gala. Your ability to stoop lower and lower to get what you want is stupefying. You are to stay away from me, my girlfriend, my friends, and if you're smart, my family. You're acting manic and sociopathic, and that's my professional opinion. I'll use it if or when I need to get a restraining order."

I heard her gasping and stomping. "Well … you … why are you doing this to me, Alex? I made a mistake. I apologized and prostrated myself to you. How much lower do you want me to feel? I'm sorry I cheated on you."

"I'm glad you found therapy helpful in exonerating yourself from your past. That's what you should do. Now, put our relationship there too. There never will be a future for us, so let it go."

"Please, Alex. Can't we even be friends? Our parents socialize together all the time. We are bound to end up at a table sometime. Can't we be civil for their sake?"

She had a point. Which made me think harder about how that situation needed to change as well. My parents' manipulation of me and my sisters was coming to an end. But, first things first.

"No. I can't. If I can't trust my parents to have me at their table without you or your parents present, then I won't be joining them again."

"You can't be serious! You have a place in the community and a foundation that needs you to be present. What about duty, Alex? Don't you care how this will affect your family?"

"My relationship with my family is mine to deal with. Not yours. I'm blocking your number in case you can't control yourself, so goodbye, good luck, and remember, you have been warned."

I hung up the phone to the sounds of her histrionics. Then I blocked her number as promised and changed into my workout clothes for the second time that day. This conversation had been a long time coming, and both the pain and promise it gave needed to be burned off with five more miles of running.

I was back on my phone, showered, and fed, in less than two hours. It always amazed me how slowly time passed when you kept getting distracted. The project at Hart Middle School would, for the most part, be over for me in February and I wouldn't be required to come back until the end of the school year in June. Eloise, Trudie, and I had put in place a plan to help high-risk kids, and now we needed traction to make it successful. I sent our mentors a list of preselected students and requested a meeting the next day after school. Hopefully, this would become a weekly meeting time for our program, and I needed their buy-in immediately. Each one of our mentors held a different skill set and would need a specific weekly plan to move all the kids in the same direction, much like a herd of sheep. We also needed plans B and C for the stragglers and outliers who would need more one-on-one mentoring. Eloise, Trudie, and I had the nuts and bolts worked out, but we needed to cultivate a complete program as soon as possible.

The following day, water pitchers and a bowl of fruit sat on the conference room table, and we were ready for our teachers to assume their new roles. Each seat had a folder that included a notepad and a detailed description of the program, the funding, and our mission guidelines.

Eloise stood with hands clasped in front of her, shouting at us to take a seat and get started.

"Ladies and gentlemen and all shades of gray, thank you for being here and accepting this opportunity because it really is an opportunity. Not just to help some great kids who are struggling, but to help you dig deep individually and figure out how to rise above your own childhood traumas to guide and protect these kids as they work through theirs." She waited for the cumulative sigh to settle.

"First off, each mentor will have a 'lane' to stay in. If you need to pass into another lane, please contact either myself or Dr. Pierce for guidance. We absolutely must work in tandem and without ego. You all have essential skills that make you an asset to this team.

We don't want anyone treading on the others to prove how much more fabulous they are. Check your attitude at the door. Our team motto will be, "For the Greater Good."

"Next, Dr. Pierce will introduce each mentor and explain why they were selected. I know you all know each other, though you don't really know everything you should about everyone else."

I looked at this group of people and chuckled. They were as goofy as the kids we were trying to help, and it made me smile.

"I'm not a medium, nor do I have any channeling skills, but I know you all represent the kids we are trying to help, only in adult form. Your life baggage is exactly what you'll need to help these kids," I explained. Ask yourself what and why you made the choices you did to stay out of trouble. Who made a difference in your life? What lessons did you learn, or what phrases did you connect with that kept you moving forward into a positive and productive life? That is your mission in this program. Guide these kids—don't tell them what to do. Ask them to do the reflecting and the hard work to find their inner beauty. Give them your shoulder to cry on when they can't do it alone. It's a huge undertaking. You have been identified as the best of the best this school has to offer, and I truly believe you will make a difference in these kids' lives."

I stepped back from the table to let that sink in while I took a swig of water. I winked at Trudie and signaled her to step up for her part.

"Whew! Was that intense for all of you, too?" She had a way of diffusing the tension that had built. "Let's get to what everyone will be focused on, okay?"

She stepped over to her computer, which was set up to project onto the screen at the end of the room. She spun around, and her ponytail swished near my face. I shuddered a little at the possibilities of what I could do with that hairdo.

"As most of you know, I'm a yogi. I will implement meditation and yoga strategies to settle the kids' minds and to use them as tools to identify when their breathing changes. This will be the clue that they are in distress. As our art teacher, Jody will use color and texture to help the kids express themselves in healthy ways. Robin will do the same, using various genres of music. She'll also use the dramatic arts to allow kids to take on other personas and expel their feelings without exposing their inner hurt.

"I'd also like to welcome Bobby to our group. He isn't a regular teacher here at Hart Middle School but he is the middle school wrestling coach for the district and has a background in physical education and psychology. His focus will be on healthy outward-aggression therapies. And our fearless leader, Dr. Alexander Pierce, will handle the nuances of each of the kid's issues. He will coach us on best practices when working with each child's situation or condition. Any questions?"

No one had any at that moment, so Eloise finished selecting a weekly mentor meeting time and assigning names and rooms for each rotation of kids.

Our long game needed to be that we give these kids the emotional tools and resources to stave off their fight or flight impulse—to become more empowered by their own internal mantras instead of letting external forces crush their spirit and limit their abilities. The goal was to build confidence, trust, and self-worth to last a lifetime and, in my most humble opinion, securing these qualities in their teenage years would prevent a downward spiral during adulthood.

It exhausted me to think about how much work it would take to accomplish what we'd set out to do. And if that goal wasn't hard enough, clearing the air with Trudie looked insurmountable. I broke all the accepted meeting rules and snuck a look at my phone under the table. I wanted to see if Trudie had posted anything on her social media in the last couple of days, but there was only one entry with four sad emoji regarding the visit with her father. No specifics or drama, just, "It's finally time to see my dad." It sounded more like a cry for help, and the four people who responded must have known her well enough to comment. I wondered what had happened during that visit.

She was taking notes on some of the questions the group had, and she must have sensed me, because she looked over her right shoulder to where I was sitting. I gave her a quick smile, remembering her earlier comments about her daddy issues. He sounded like a real piece of work. I needed to spend some time alone with her and finish processing what had happened the previous weekend in New York. Plus, my attachment to her was addictive and I needed to get another fix. Maybe our next lesson would involve a ponytail, a blindfold, and some cold water. *Hmm.*

TRUDIE

"I need a drink," I whined at Ruby. I hadn't had a minute to process my visit with my dad, and this Sheila business with

Alex was still looming. All I wanted to do was drink, get laid, or meditate. I'd been pondering which to do first. Of course, one of them involved Alex, so probably not that one. Although using sex to medicate would be a new one for me, it would also involve difficult conversations that I wasn't sure I had the strength for at that moment.

It was time to enlist Ruby.

"I wish I could meet you tonight," she said apologetically. "But Daniel needs me to record some new tag lines and go over some upcoming scripts that he and Patrick have been working on."

Ruby was running ragged with her new voice-over job and I was pretty sure that the only thing that would be upcoming that night would be Daniel's dick. Those two were so into each other—it was clear she was falling fast for him. We'd been each other's emotional support person for ten years, and now it was weird watching her fall for someone. Her normally erratic self was mellowing and I supposed Daniel had something to do with it. She was happy and that was all that mattered to me.

"That's all right, babe. Another time." I sighed into the phone. "I probably should spend some time on my yoga mat reflecting on all my issues. There are so many to choose from." I gave a self-deprecating laugh and said goodbye, promising I would make time this weekend for coffee.

I shoved through my front door with all my school bags, two sacks of groceries, my purse, and Chinese takeout. One day, I was going to leave with just my purse and come home with just my purse. I felt like a bag lady most of the time. Dumping my stuff on the counter, I unzipped my coat and hung it on the hook next to the front door. I turned on two mood lamps with the hope that the calm lighting would settle my head and my heart.

Too hungry to wait until dinnertime, I collected my food, napkins, fork, knife, and plate, plopped down on the meditation cushion that sat under my coffee table, and began scooping out chicken ho fun. I loved this stuff, as was clear from the humming sounds I made while I ate. I clicked on the television and turned on a movie I had previously been watching—finishing by the time I was done eating. Then it was time to get serious about meditating.

I cleaned up my mess and changed into a not-so-supportive sports bra in a terribly unfashionable gray color and black yoga pants that bunched at my ankles. The previous month, I had found a great hack in Cosmo that suggested applying a twenty-minute mask just before meditating would do double duty for a clear mind and clear face. Why didn't I ever put these things together for myself?

Finally seated and ready to free my mind for some helpful guidance, I asked the universe the hardest question first: Did I truly want to heal my relationship with my dad? Using my mantra breathing, I inhaled the word "truth" and exhaled the word "love." Almost instantly, my outside chatter dissipated, and my jaw relaxed. My shoulders dropped, and moments later, so did my breathing. The swirls of energy behind my eyes became small waves measured with my breath, and the lightness I'd been craving hummed through me. And there, creeping up from my spine through my neck and over my head to my third eye, came a vision of me and my father snuggled on the couch, his arms tightly wrapped around my shoulders while he read to me. I looked to be about six years old, with my soft, silky brown locks draped over my shoulders, messy and innocent. I noticed him rubbing my hair between his calloused fingers, and his smile said it all: He loved me then. I loved him then. And, I knew now that his circumstances robbed us of our time together. How could he not be upset about that?

My phone sang a tune, alerting me that my time was up, so I repeated my mantra, thanking the universe for showing me what I needed at that moment, and stretched into a restorative pose for another minute. Afterward, I felt truly restored—refreshed and pointed in the right direction. A hot bath sounded like the perfect way to end the night, except I was too tired. I settled instead for rinsing the dried mask and crawling into bed to read.

A loud knocking on my door startled me. Ruby was busy, and I wasn't expecting anyone, so I wasn't sure who it could be. Looking through the peephole, I gasped. *Alex. Crap!* I looked like shit, and I just got all relaxed—now I would be ramped up again. This guy's timing was horrible, but since he'd come all the way here, I felt obligated to open the door. The universe was funny that way: ask for guidance, and you got it. I guess I should have told the universe to stop for the night.

CHAPTER 6

TRUDIE

He looked edible. Tight dark blue denim jeans that outlined his sculpted thighs and tight ass and a white formfitting button-down with a woven design that ebbed and flowed depending on how his body moved. I envisioned myself grabbing hold of the material at his chest and ripping it off, complete with buttons flying across the room. I may have drooled a little.

My fixation was interrupted by a smirk and a devilish smile.

"Hungry, sweetheart?" His fingers lifted my chin so he could bore his sparkling green eyes into mine. The look was consuming, and that melty feeling I got when he went all alpha on me heated my blood to scorching.

"Starving," I muttered.

Alex pulled me toward him with his perfectly formed hand and began to suck on my lower lip. His tongue penetrated my mouth, going deeper and circling my tongue, making me moan. Wetness pooled between my legs, soaking my thong. My hands on his neck pulled him closer, wanting more. I was so aroused that I forgot to stand and my knees buckled. His strong arms caught me and carried me to the counter, where he sat me down and pressed my knees open wide with his body, stepping into the open space like it was something he did every day.

I could feel him smile as he slowly drew his hands down to the tops of my thighs, leaving me all tingly.

"Wow! That was the best reception I have ever received. Does that mean we're back on solid ground?" I knew he was treading carefully, and rightfully so. Our physical relationship wasn't our problem, and I also knew that sex shouldn't be my drug of choice. *But look at him!* He was spectacular, and his kisses—mind-blowing.

I had to answer him honestly. I needed to face this like an adult. He needed to hear my truth—we couldn't dance around it like we did earlier.

"No, we are not."

I pressed against his chest, pushing him out from between my legs and slid off the counter. I put as much distance between us as I could. It was the prudent thing to do. We needed to talk without the draw of pheromones wafting up our noses, so I dragged one of the barstools around to the other side of the counter and took a seat. Rethinking, I got up, opened the refrigerator, grabbed the pitcher of filtered water, and then got two glasses from the cupboard alongside it.

"Water?" I offered.

"I think something stronger is called for tonight. Bourbon?" he countered.

Now that he mentioned it, drinking did sound like a good plan. I grabbed a light beer for myself and put some ice in a short glass, pushing it across the counter. I cracked the lid off my beer and spun around to reach on top of the fridge to get the bourbon when his hips bumped into my ass as he reached over my head for the bottle.

"Oh no you don't. You—back to your side of the counter. I can't think straight when I'm all hot and bothered." I ducked under his arm and pushed my stool another foot farther away. He rolled his eyes and took the bottle to his side of the counter.

"Look! I'm safely away from you. Please, unload that beautiful mind of yours, but be gentle. I'm a fragile flower." We both laughed at that.

I went back to my yoga breathing and quickly asked for help from above to speak clearly, unemotionally, and compassionately. He sipped his drink and waited patiently like a good psychologist should, giving me space to formulate my thoughts.

I lifted my head to look at the man who was changing my world. He deserved honesty, plain and simple. I owed him that, at least.

"If I didn't care so much about you, this whole situation would be moot, but I do."

He smiled and leaned forward in his seat; my lips quivered at his appreciation.

"I believed you when you said your relationship was over with Sheila. Her comments were toxic and threatening and meant to get a rise out of me—and she did. Though not from what she said, but from what you didn't. You did a great job preparing me for your family's shenanigans. I knew exactly what to expect from them, and when they went above and beyond, I found the right place to put it in my head for further review at a later time. I didn't have that option with her. If you had been upfront about her behavior toward you and her viper-like tongue, I would have known what to do. I was blindsided, Alex. In all your efforts to protect me, you left me—and us—the most vulnerable to her."

He sat back deflated. I almost couldn't believe how articulately I had presented my thoughts. Usually, they were disjointed and unorganized. The words seemed channeled directly to my mouth from above, and it was as perfect a presentation as I could have hoped for. My eyes dropped and my nose tickled, as tears of relief threatened to fall. I stood up to him without causing a confrontation. This was a new sensation and it filled me with joy.

I was startled when his chair screeched on the wood floor, and my heartbeat sped up as he rounded the counter and threw his arms around me tightly. He stroked my hair and whispers of an apology spilled from his beautiful mouth. Minutes of this solace went by, and my heart swelled, knowing he was truly remorseful.

I tried to push back from his embrace, but he wouldn't let me. His hands slid up my body to cup my face, and looking into his eyes, I saw the hurt my words had created. He was right. I should have stayed and had this conversation back then, but I didn't have the clarity I did now. I needed time to move away from the pain and understand why I had been so upset. I couldn't do that in the moment.

"You said that perfectly, baby. And you are right. I let you down, and I'm so sorry I did. It appears that my cowardice bit me in the ass. I was afraid that if you knew that I had called off the wedding it would put you off. Or worse, make me look like a complete asshole. It has been instilled in me to always consider the optics of a situation. To avoid suffering any consequences. That's the price I paid for growing up in my family."

"It sounds like both our parents damaged us for the worse." I laughed.

"Yes and no. Yes, because that's what they did back then for their own purposes, but no, because we don't have to accept that any longer. We worked to change who we are, and in the process, we became better people.

"You're always the teacher. Why does everything have to be a lesson? It's exhausting."

He rolled his eyes and then hugged me again. "I have no idea, it just comes out that way, I guess."

He walked back around the counter and took his seat. I wondered if he had more to say. I was all talked out. This must have been "bleeding heart" week because I felt completely drained.

"Trudie, I hope we're in a better place so I can share two more things with you." He was so serious in his tone that I became concerned.

"Ah, yeah, as long as you don't commit more sins of omission, I think I'm good." I clasped my hands together on the counter and leaned toward him, anticipating his next words.

"The first is that I'd like you to meet my best friend this Friday night. He will be in town for the weekend recruiting potential pro athletes. I'm meeting him for dinner and thought you could meet us afterward. There is a tournament he invited us to attend this Saturday, as well. He wants to impress you for some weird reason.

Would you do me the honor of attending both?" He poured on his charm and even winked at me. Did he think he was offering me the chance of a lifetime?

"Yeah," I said, nodding slowly, and added, just to taunt Alex, "He can impress me."

"What about me impressing you?" he said, feigning dejection.

"Sorry, you already impressed me. I'm on to the next guy."

That got him riled up. "Let's talk about my second point then. There will be no next guy. I want you to myself, like a real girl-friend."

I swooned a little and sat back, letting his request settle deep into my fluttering chest. *Girlfriend. I liked the sound of that.*

"That's a big step, Alex. Are you sure? I mean, I've heard you introduce me to your family as your girlfriend, but we never discussed it. What does that really mean to you anyhow?"

He was quiet for a bit, until the ice in his bourbon shifted, breaking the silence. He looked as though his answer would determine his life or death.

"It means that I have more than *like* for you. Honestly, saying how I truly feel may freak you out, but I'll say it anyway. I'm falling in love with you, Trudie. When you ran away from me, I didn't want to live anymore. I didn't have our life planned out, but I knew if you weren't in mine, the sun would never shine again."

It was my turn now to come around the counter. Alex pulled me between his legs as I cupped his face.

"Baby, I feel the same way, and I am falling in love with you too." That was all it took for him to kiss me breathless.

I wanted all of him all the time, and our professional life would have to be figured out quickly for this to work. We had so much to work through and I still needed to learn to trust him. Words were cheap, and only time would tell how this relationship would go.

ALEXANDER

She smelled so good, and the outfit she had on had been driving me wild since her eyes had devoured me at the door. We had covered a lot of emotional ground today, and hearing those three little words solidified everything I'd felt since the moment I met her. She challenged me, and that was no easy achievement. I may be a specialist in human thought and behavior, nonetheless, I wasn't exempt from being human myself. I was as flawed as the next person. The only difference was that I was quicker and more equipped to catch myself speaking or making decisions that adversely affected myself and others. But now, Trudie was on her A game and so was I. I've said it before and I'll say it again, we made an incredible team once we got past our bullshit.

I pressed her shoulder straps down her arms and appraised her gorgeous tits, rubbing my thumbs over her peaked nipples.

"Now that you're my girlfriend, you're required to let me touch every inch of you wherever and whenever I want. Are you okay with that?" I could see her chest rising in short breaths at my request. She liked it when I made sexual demands of her. She could let go and let me take her body away from her mind.

"Yes ... except at school." Her moans increased as I rolled her nubs between my thumbs and forefingers.

"Yes, at school. Through your clothes when no one is around," I countered.

"Alex." Her head fell back. "You're too much of a distraction already. How am I supposed to face my students when you touch me?" She had a point.

"Final negotiation: lunchtime only or after school." I pinched harder to get her attention when she didn't answer.

"Ouch!" she cried. Her look of surprise made me growl.

"Answer me."

"Fine! Yes, but you better be sure no one sees us."

I nuzzled into her neck, giving her wet kisses up and down her collarbone.

Trudie licked her pink lips and I gave her my thumb to wrap them around. *Fuck, that felt good.*

"Sweet girl, I need you naked. Go to your room and get those clothes off. I'm locking up for the night." She reminded me of a little girl as she ran toward her bedroom, knowing there was a big surprise for her when I arrived.

I secured the front door, pulled the shades, and turned off the two lamps that dimly lit the room, then skirted the ottoman and rounded the love seat. Her place was so tiny. I wondered if she would consider moving in with me. Another question for another day.

The only light in Trudie's bedroom was a candle with an aroma that reminded me of her—vanilla and cinnamon. Her creamy tan legs were crossed as she sat at the end of the bed, her tits full and heaving.

"Spread your legs, baby." She made a small noise and unwrapped her limbs.

"You didn't follow my instructions, Trudie. I asked you to get naked, and your panties are still on." I tsked and walked a few steps, stopping directly in front of her. My cock strained against the denim fabric and was becoming very uncomfortable. She had a front row seat of my predicament. I wanted her mouth on me—however, we had the little matter of her panties to address.

"Do you still want a teacher, baby?" Her eyes widened, and she nodded like the naughty little girl she was.

"When I ask you nicely to do something, I expect you to do it the way I prescribe. Understood?" She pouted her lips and nodded again.

"Then why didn't you take your panties off like a good girl?"

She blinked several times and swallowed. "I wanted you to do that for me."

Sweet Jesus. "Oh, baby, aren't you sweet. Of course, I'll help you this time—only listen better next time." She nodded her understanding.

I knelt between her legs, bending forward to smell her through the lavender lace material. Licking her seam through the fabric, I could taste her sopping wet pussy throbbing under my tongue. I played with her clit through the fabric as she moaned out my name, begging for more.

Sitting back on my heels, I hooked my fingers around the strings and pulled her panties down, exposing a nearly bare pussy glistening with her juices. *Fuck.* I was a starved man, and this pussy would be my appetizer, dinner and dessert. Trudie was meant to be mine, and I would dine on her nonstop until we were both sated.

"You are exquisite, Trudie." I flicked at the raised rose of her clit and she whipped her head back, loving the sensations.

"Move up the bed and get on your hands and knees." It took her a minute to understand my words, and then she flipped herself and crawled up the comforter.

I nudged her knees apart and massaged her curvy ass cheeks, parting them to see her sweet pucker. One day, that would be mine too. For now, I kissed it and moved from hole to hole, placing kisses along the way.

"Damn it, Alex. You're killing me. Fuck me, please!"

I gave her a throaty laugh and reminded her of our first lesson. "You will address me as Dr. Pierce when I'm teaching you. And, my dear little girl, you are surely being taught a lesson tonight."

Her gasp ignited my desire to teach her everything I knew and discover what I didn't. She loved my filthy mouth, and I loved it when she complied. My kink wasn't over the top—I just needed to have complete control in the bedroom. If past history was anything to go by, that's what my vixen wanted too, and she would be rewarded for her compliance.

I continued my onslaught of her pussy from behind. Her moans of desire grew louder and faster, encouraging me to increase her pleasure. Unfortunately for her, I had a lesson to deliver. Along with patience, she would learn to trust me. Implicitly. Without question.

When she begged for more, I pulled away, placing my hands on her hips to flip her over. She crashed back to the mattress shocked and disoriented.

"What's going on? Why did you stop?" She was near tears. I pulled a pillow from the pile at the head of her bed and stripped it of the pillowcase.

"What's that for, Al—Dr. Pierce."

Good save.

"Do you remember the first time we played?" Her jaw dropped. "You were blindfolded." Her gulp was answer enough. "Do you trust me, baby? Really trust me?"

Her eyes warmed and her eyebrows scrunched together as her lips pursed. "Absolutely. I do."

I wanted to believe her. I think she wanted to believe her words too. But I couldn't forget all the times she ran away when things got too stressful. That needed to be fixed. Once and for all.

"I know you want to believe that, and so do I. I have a little test to see just how committed we both are. Are you ready to find out?"

My eyes were locked on hers, challenging her resolve. Tiny lines around her eyes quirked and her mouth quivered as she considered what I might ask her to do. What she didn't realize was that I, too, needed to trust myself with her. To be able to push her without breaking her. I also had to know that I was capable of loving her even when it wasn't comfortable for me.

"I love you, Alex," she whispered, and my heart zinged. "I want Dr. Pierce to test me, to prove to both of us now and forever that we can trust one another."

I crashed my lips onto hers, savoring her sweet taste and sealing my unending commitment and love. I removed her ponytail and wrapped the folded pillowcase around her eyes.

"Don't move," I instructed. I went to her dresser to find something I could use to secure her arms and legs. Grabbing two pairs of tights, I shoved the drawer closed and walked back to the bed. Gently taking her left hand, I tied a knot around her wrist and stretched the material to the end of her headboard, and then did the same on the other side, all the while telling her what a beautiful girl she was and how proud I was of her bravery. Being a dirty girl didn't make her a bad person. She needed to see that her sexual desires enhanced who she was as a woman while not defining her completely. Every facet of her was spectacular.

With her feet and hands bound, I now had the opportunity to sit between her legs and fully take her in. A man doesn't often get a chance to see his woman spread out so completely for him to enjoy, and I didn't take for granted what she gave to me . . . her everything.

"I could look at you all night, sweetheart. You take my breath away." I leaned forward again, flattening my tongue to lap at her sweet pussy and squeeze her tits until she screamed my name.

It didn't take long for my girl to peak. When her voice croaked with hysterical pleas, "Doctor, please, please fuck me," I knew she was moments away from climax.

"It's nice to know that you've retained your new skill of using your words to describe what you want," I growled between licks. "Do you also remember that you're not allowed to come until I give you permission?" My menacing taunt was received just as I had hoped.

"Fuck you, Alex. You ca—"

I didn't need to hear her diatribe. To make sure she knew I was serious, I stopped licking her pussy and then got off the bed.

"Wait! Where are you going? Get back here and make me come. Please. I'm sorry I didn't call you Dr. Pierce. I won't forget it again. I promise."

I loved her fake repentance, but I knew all too well how she flipped her approach if she wasn't getting what she wanted. She needed to learn that when we were role-playing, she was the submissive. Not the other way around. I didn't respond to her cries, though I did unbutton my shirt and take off my socks before unbuttoning my pants to give myself some relief.

I perused her room and found a delightful torture device stuck behind her mirror and walked slowly back toward the bed. She couldn't see what I had, but I knew Trudie would enjoy how it felt.

I knelt on the side of the bed to alert her of my return.

"There you are. I thought you were going to leave me tied up all night." Her relief was palpable, and it was clear she needed reassurance.

"I've been with you the whole time. As I said before, I would never leave you exposed like that again. Your body is aching for me, isn't it?"

"So much, Dr. Pierce. Please touch me." She said it so sweetly I couldn't resist another long deep kiss that left both of us panting. "Thank you. Thank you," she whispered, sniffing away her tears.

"Do you like surprises, baby? Because I have a great one for you."

I swirled the feather over each of her nipples, causing her back to arch while she whimpered.

"Oh my God! That's, that's torture!" Her unrestrained response at what I did to her sent tingles all over my body.

"That's right, baby. I'll make you love it and beg for more." I was a cocky son of a bitch, though she knew that from the start.

I continued down the middle of her body, making swirls as I went. She clearly enjoyed the way I worked down to the little triangle of hair she had left at the top, pointing the way to her pleasure.

"Should I keep going? I taunted her.

"Yes! Yes! Yes!" Yet I didn't. I blew on her wanton pussy with the intent of sending her as close to the edge as I wanted her to be.

"Do you trust me, Trudie? Do you promise not to run away from me again, to talk through your fears? Do you trust me only to have your best interests at heart?"

It wasn't fair of me to ask her this question when she was spread out so beautifully on her bed. She'd been right all along—I was an asshole. But I was *her* asshole, and I wanted a truthful answer.

"I do. Dr.—Alex, I do!"

Our future would be determined by what she did after I untied her, and it scared the shit out of me, wondering if she could distinguish me from my doctor persona. I set her free and took off the blindfold. Confused and scared, she sat up.

"What's going on? Why did you untie me? What's wrong?"

"Nothing is wrong. Everything is all right. I will always be your teacher for as long as you want me to be. However, it's your choice who you want to be with, the doctor or me. Who do you give your trust to? Who do you give your love to?"

She looked lost, almost devastated. The idea of the two men being separate from one another scrambled her mind. Her teacher, Dr. Pierce, stimulated her body and transported her from reality to fantasy. But that couldn't sustain us for the long haul. Alexander stimulated her mind, yet was bound in reality, a much more difficult proposition to accept.

Tears ran down her face and I fought the urge to embrace her. I couldn't make this easy for her. She had to make her choice. The buzzkill of going from an incredible high to a crashing low was earth-shattering—for both of us. Her mind and body craved release but neither would get it without her making a decision.

Trudie ran her fingers through her hair, pulling strands and tearing at the roots.

"What's happening, Alex? I'm so confused. I want you. I want everything you have to offer, including Dr. Pierce. You are Dr. Alexander Pierce. Aren't you?"

That's what I was afraid of. It was so Freudian. In her case it was a simple mental mix-up and if it wasn't settled, it would confuse and conflict her throughout our relationship. She didn't see this coming, and frankly, neither did I.

CHAPTER 7
TRUDIE

I struggled to get up the next day. We had our first mentor meeting with the kids and their teachers before lunch. I'd called off my first three periods, complaining of a severe headache that I couldn't shake. I wished I'd been lying, but I wasn't. I'd taken two rounds of Tylenol since my alarm went off. The hot shower did little to relax my neck and back, and I hoped that I could pull myself together before I had to leave.

Alex's revelation that I was in love with him as a doctor and not him as a man was jarring. Why would I want to separate the two personas? I had never done that before. Then again, there had never been a reason to. Hadn't I done the same thing regarding my father? Christ! What was wrong with me was that I couldn't distinguish between someone's professional and personal persona. It shouldn't be so difficult. I knew we all had a façade we presented to the world—some pieces of that façade were our true selves, and some pieces were an act.

When Alex and I had been in San Francisco for the convention where we met, I thought we had shucked off our outward appearances and grown to love each other for who we really were. I should have stayed with boring vanilla Sam and skipped over all this angst. Okay, no. That would have been a whole other kind of disaster with its own complications. Still, I couldn't piece together what I was missing in this whole situation.

I was a complete wreck. Alex had scooped me into his arms and held me for a long time. He whispered sweet nothings and words of encouragement until I fell asleep exhausted. When I woke up, I was tucked under my covers with a glass of water and two Tylenol on my night table and a note I will keep forever.

I love you, Trudie. Me—Alex and me—Dr. A. Pierce. Whatever persona you choose to love, I'll be there for you.

Oh. My. God! What was I supposed to do with that? I ran through our conversation and his explanations so many times I wanted to vomit. Could I have one without the other? Was he telling me he wouldn't teach me things anymore or that we couldn't role-play anymore? Or that he wasn't really an alpha-type guy in the bedroom, and that was the façade? I couldn't—wouldn't believe that. Alex knew who he was and what he wanted. Everything he did spoke to his self-imposed psychoanalysis. *Oh! My head was killing me.*

After my second nap, I found a comfy sweaterdress and tights to wear. It was the easiest outfit to put together, and my tights were already on the floor next to me. At the last minute, I pulled on a colorful scarf and my knee-high boots to improve my mood. While I shoved my feet into the boots, it occurred to me what assignment I would give a student who was in the same situation. I pulled out a piece of ruled paper from a notebook and sat down to write out the pros and cons of each Alex persona. If there was a shared attribute, I lined them up. Feeling inspired, I tore another sheet out to do the same for my father and an uncanny similarity became apparent. I shook my head, not believing what had occurred to me, and shoved both sheets away. I stood up abruptly and grabbed my purse and school bag, slung on my coat, and tore out of my apartment in desperate need of coffee and a call to Ruby.

I crept through the Starbucks drive-through and ordered those delicious egg bites and a warmed buttered croissant, along with my calorically pared-down vanilla latte with almond milk. Only full caffeination was going to work. What I really needed was a karmic cleanse, but I had to go to school. Twenty ounces of caffeine was the best I could do.

I pushed the speed dial to Ruby's phone and waited for her to pick up.

"Hey, Trudes! Aren't you at school today?" Her concern was well founded.

"I'm on m'way." Of course, she had picked up the line when I had half a pastry in my mouth.

"What? Half day today?"

I swallowed hard, giving myself heartburn. "I had a massive headache and begged off a few periods so I could release myself from its fiery hold." I can be so dramatic sometimes.

"Oh, baby. I'm sorry. Stress or period induced?" She knew me too well.

"Alex induced. It started last night and I couldn't shake it. I need you, Rubes. Hold me." I pulled over and the sobs crept up my chest, choking me. My eyes flooded with tears and I couldn't open them to drive.

"Jesus, Trudie. Where are you? Let me meet you after school. I'll leave work early and I'll squeeze you tightly."

I hiccupped several times, and Ruby waited for me to settle down.

"That–*hiccup*–that would be great." One more sob broke free and then my pulse slowed back down again. I wiped my eyes and checked my makeup, hoping it wasn't dripping down my face. Good thing I hadn't felt like wearing much today.

"Always, sweetheart. Hang in there. We'll get it worked out in no time." She sent a kiss through the phone and we said goodbye.

The high-risk kids were assembled, and we probed them about how they saw their future. It was a gamble to think these kids would be mature enough to play along, but our goal was to break down their barriers and rebuild them into more confident and resilient versions of themselves.

Eloise came by to ensure the kids understood that this group was to be taken seriously. Rules were put in place, and surprisingly, the group unanimously decided they could "fire" either a participant or mentor if they weren't living up to the expectations of the rest of the group. This was an amazing approach a sixth grader named Leo came up with. His bugaboo was equality. With five other siblings in his family, he felt invisible. Even when he asserted himself, someone else in his family always got the credit.

Robin closed our orientation session with a few final notes. "I'm sure you'll have questions as we go along—please don't hesitate to ask them. Good communication is the foundation of everything we will do the rest of the year."

Everyone stood except Leah. She was chosen to participate in the program to address her obstinance and defensiveness, and true to form, she was taking a stand.

"I don't want to be here. My teacher said I needed to go at least four times before he would let me join my friends on our field trip next month. Why am I here?"

Jody stepped in front of her and knelt down.

"Why do you think you're here?" she asked, saying nothing else.

Leah crossed her arms as her face turned red. Everyone in this group was expected to share openly and honesty with each other exclusively, therefore, she had to share openly like everyone else.

"I don't know," she whined.

Jack, a mouthy eighth grader, supplied her with an answer. "Could it be because you're bitchy to everyone? No one is smarter than you? Only you matter?" *Ouch, that hit the target.*

"Jack," Alex intervened, "packaging your comments so they aren't offensive will be part of our workshops. Whether you think someone is being bitchy or not, please refrain from being caustic and antagonizing your peers.

"What do you think about Jack's intentions with his comments? Are those the things you're here to work on?" Jody kept her voice low and her eyes warmed.

Leah pressed her lips together, keeping her arms crossed. "Maybe."

"Do you think you could improve on this attitude?" I loved how she could have made that comment personal yet chose to make it about Leah's attitude instead.

"If I have to," she replied, pouting.

"Well, that's a start." Jody pressed a hand onto her shoulder in a light squeeze. "I'd love to help you feel better about yourself, too."

The kids walked out, a jumble of energy, and the mentors simultaneously expelled a sigh of relief.

"Holy shit, that was intense," Bobby blurted out.

"Agreed." Jody fell into a chair and shook her hands out, swiveling her head from side to side.

Robin had the need to recap the session, saying, "Well, that went well for a first session. Honestly, I think the children who spoke up today will be the easiest of our kids. It's those quiet ones you have to look out for." We all nodded.

I sat down in my chair and folded myself over my desk in despair. How could I help these kids when I couldn't even help myself. Thank God this day was over. As soon as that thought entered my mind, Ruby burst into my classroom. When I lifted my head, the only other person left in the room was Alex.

"Oh, am I interrupting?" Ruby started to slink back to the door.

"No! I mean, I'm ready to go." I grabbed my things and crossed the room.

"Cool. Ah, hi," she turned to Alex and extended her hand, "I'm Ruby, her best friend."

He gave her one of his devilishly knowing smiles. "Hello. I finally get to meet the infamous voice-over actress." He took her hand and kissed the back of it.

She giggled at his formality, "You're everything Trudie said you were and..." she trailed off.

He quirked his brow. "And what?"

"Oh." she fluttered her hand in front of her chest. "Uh, that you are remarkable, uh, handsome. Maybe hot—very hot."

He let out a boisterous laugh, filling my room with his merriment. I smacked a hand to my forehead, praying for a bolt of lightning to hit me. This day would never end.

"Did she?" *Fine! Rub it in, asshole.*

Ruby's full smile at my expense was going to cost her dinner.

"What happened to solidarity among women?" I whined at her as I packed my bags.

He continued. "I like her, Trudie. Can I keep her, too?" He chuckled again, and so did my ex-BFF.

"You can have him. I'm done," I retorted and started walking down the hall in a huff.

Ruby called after me to wait up, and when they both caught up to me, Alex made a proclamation.

"The two of you will join me tomorrow night for drinks at Teddy's. My college buddy will be in town to do some recruiting, and I thought it would be more fun if you both joined us and your boyfriend, Daniel, of course.”

Geez Louise! He was inviting my friends out without even asking if I was okay with it. Ruby looked at me with glittery, expectant eyes. She had been wanting to meet him for weeks, and I had put it off longer than I should have. Now that she'd met him, she'd understand my predicament.

“You two are killing me. And you,” I pointed harshly at Alex, “don't play fair.”

“Noted,” he snarked out. “See you at nine tomorrow night.”

If I didn't know better, I swore he skipped down the hall. It's not like his ego needed any help. Ruby all but fell into his lap. *Bitch.*

“And, as for you, my pretty, you're buying dinner, and I'm officially now pissed off at you too.” I forced myself not to smile and slipped my arm through hers as we exited the building.

For the millionth time, I unpacked everything going on in my life with my dearest friend. She continued to stuff food in her mouth while downing margaritas. The girl was like Fort Knox. You made an emotional deposit, and she locked it down, never to be used against you. After my twenty-minute over-the-top emotional dump, she slurped down the rest of her water and sank back, prepared to deliver her prescription to my problems. Now it was my turn to eat and listen.

"Not to be flippant, but 'What we've got here is a failure to communicate.' You think you and Alexander are speaking the same language, but you're not," Ruby intoned.

With a mouth full of lettuce, I mumbled, "Why?"

"From where I'm sitting, it looks like he took a deep dive into your psyche and felt concerned you may have been confused about why you love him. Is he wrong to feel that way?"

"I've been racking my brain about that for the last day, trying to sort it out. I even made a pros and cons list for both Alex and my father. They started out so similar, except, as I continued, I think it's less that Alex and my father are similar and more like I respond to them in a similar way. It's almost like I can't separate the job from the person sometimes. For my dad, it was his insurance-induced job that produced his rage. For Alex, it was his parents and sisters. Sadly, every time both men came home to their families, it brought up so much guilt. My dad felt guilty for obvious reasons, and the way he wreaked havoc consistently on our family. And Alex felt guilty because he desperately wanted his parent's unconditional love. Unfortunately, his parents chose to put their needs ahead of his. Both men created two personas to cope with their forced situations."

Hmm. Ruby ruminated on my reasoning. "Alex was a kid when this all happened. He didn't consciously distance himself until he was an adult, whereas your dad did it *unconsciously* as an adult. Interesting. I'm not sure what to make of it, only that you are looking to be with Alex, not your dad," she observed.

"So where does that leave me now? If I can't trust my gut, then what can I trust?"

I had never felt so confused about anything in my life. I'd been thinking about the conversation I'd had with my dad. I certainly would be the one who got the better deal by forgiving him for his poor choices. And he would have to reconcile that he didn't do the best with his circumstances and suffered as a result.

We left dinner full yet simultaneously feeling empty. I resigned myself to let time be the healer of my problems. My only regret was that I couldn't have sex with Alex again until after I worked out my situation. Hopefully, he wouldn't be too dejected. His face had been so forlorn last night—it hurt me that I couldn't answer him concretely.

By the time I'd gone home and finished my bedtime ritual, there were two texts on my phone. One was from my dad asking when I'd be over to see him again. They had moved him to a nursing facility closer to my apartment, making it easier to help him if I wanted to. The other was from Alex.

Alex: Sorry for inviting your friends without asking you first.

Me: It's fine. She's been dying to meet you for weeks.

Alex: Did I pass her inspection?

Me: Please. You know you did. Your ego enters a room first, asshole.

Alex: Oh, so we're back to our love language, name-calling?

Me: Yes … asshole.

Alex: LOL. I'll be your asshole if you give yours to me.

Uh, oh. That was a trap! Damn it! I had walked right into that one.

Me: Let me rephrase. We are back to name-calling.

Alex: Darn. I was so looking forward to exploring your other assets.

Me: About that. I think it would be better if we take sex off the table for a while. I think it will help me sort through some of the feelings I have about you and your alter ego.

Alex: As much as I'll miss having my hands on you, I agree it's for the best. I still call holding hands as fair game though.

Me: Fine. Now go to bed. You exhaust me.

Alex: It's always a pleasure to do so. Goodnight, beautiful. <Heart eyes emoji>

Me: <Sleeping emoji>

CHAPTER 8

ALEXANDER

Our dinner at Peabody's was amazing. Jacob and I relived our glory days as we stuffed ourselves with lobster pasta. Jacob paid the bill and expensed it, per usual, and we hopped into my Audi rental, excited to meet Trudie and her friends.

"Tell me about your woman. Why are you so worked up about her? You haven't been interested in anyone for years." Jacob loved to ride me. It was time to lay my cards on the table.

"She's curvy with the most delicious set of tits I've ever seen. Her ass is, *mmm*, and she makes the most seductive sounds when we're together. It kills me."

"So, she's smoking," he deduced.

"Not in a traditional way. Her spicy Latina personality challenges me, pushed me. Pair that with her toned body and witchy eyes that change based on her mood, it's otherworldly. The frosting on the cake is that she always smells of vanilla and sometimes cinnamon. I literally want to eat her up."

"She sounds like a cinnamon roll with legs," he chortled.

"More like a caramel sundae," I laughed back.

"I'm happy for you, man. You deserve the best, and if she keeps you on your toes, then all the better. No one wants complacency in their relationship. Ellen and I struggle with that all the time. With two kids, a house, a dog, and then work, our love life has been diminished to a sliver of life's pie."

"The joys of settling down. I've counseled a lot of couples who, if they'd only made their relationship a priority, would have kept their marriages alive. I'm happy you are cognizant of your situation and are working together to keep things fresh."

"I fall in love with that woman every day. I don't know where she gets her kinky bedroom ideas, but I love them!" He rolled his eyes back in his head, overcome.

"Trudie says that her romance books have put a lot of ideas in her head, and I'm happy to oblige her with every one of them." I waggled my brows for effect.

I pulled off the road to parallel park and we entered Teddy's about a quarter to nine. Friday nights were banging at this place, and with a little patience we were able to grab a booth from a group getting up to leave.

I hadn't been to this bar since that night so many weeks ago, when Trudie lost a bet with me during Field Days at her school. I think she was pissed more about losing to me than just losing. That was the first time we connected body, mind, and spirit at her apartment, after grinding on each other on the dance floor. Our only other soul-ripping time together was in San Francisco after the conference and a very seductive sailing excursion on a tall ship.

That was the hottest fucking night of my life. She fell in love with Dr. Alexander Pierce, sex teacher extraordinaire.

The way she had let me handle her body and the trust she put in me was extraordinary. She was a gift and I intended on keeping it safe for. . .

"Alex!" Jacob yelled at me over the music. "Come back, dude." He snapped his fingers in front of my eyes.

I must have drifted off. The whole idea of Trudie made me light-headed. Speaking of which, I scanned the room and found her witchy eyes drinking me up from head to toe. The corners of my mouth pulled upward and I licked my lips, checking out the smoke show as she walked across the room. If I hadn't known she was walking over to me, I would have smacked aside the two guys who stood up to follow her.

"Do you need help picking your jaw up from the floor, Dr. Pierce?" she said, taunting me.

I bent forward and kissed her cheek, and whispered in her delicate ear, "I'd rather pick you up from the floor. I've been told I have to play nice with you, so I'll keep my thoughts to myself, for now." Squeezing her waist, I turned her around to press her back against my chest.

"Introduce me to your friends, sweetheart." My voice dropped an octave, eliciting a small arch from her back.

"You've met my best friend, Ruby, and this is her. . . " She paused, trying to find the right word.

Ruby interjected, "Boyfriend. This is Daniel, we work together at Miles & Stone Advertising in Birmingham. He's the managing director there."

I lifted my chin and extended my hand, "Good to meet you, Daniel. What are you drinking?"

Conveniently, a waitress came by just then and took our order. I gave her my Amex Black Card and opened a tab. I was planning on this being another epic night, even if I couldn't have my woman the way I'd like.

The girls chatted together and Jacob and I got to know Daniel while we sipped our drinks. I watched as Daniel casually slid his hand up and down Ruby's arm as she pressed herself into his side. They made a hot pair, with his athletic body and bulging arms and her gorgeous curves.

Speaking of gorgeous curves, I had to punch Jacob in the thigh under the table twice because he couldn't stop staring at Trudie's deep-V neckline. She purposely dressed to kill me. She wore a tan colored, long sleeved, skin-tight mini dress that the material gathered together at her waist accentuating her hips and tits. Jacob wasn't the only one having trouble finding her face. The dress only came halfway down her toned thighs—until she sat down, that is. Knees crossed, with one hand on her drink and the other above her crotch, was the only way she could sit without anyone getting a show.

Despite our agreement, I reached under the table and pulled her crossed legs closer to mine, "helping" her keep them tightly closed. Her incredulous look was worth it.

As soon as Trudie finished her second drink, she shoved Ruby and announced it was time to dance. Finally, I could get my hands on her without getting into trouble. Daniel licked his lips looking at Ruby's ass and seconded the motion.

"Don't mind me!" Jacob shouted behind us. "I'll just watch the table and look pathetic."

We all turned around and shouted back, "Okay!" We laughed the rest of the way to the dance floor, forgetting about Jacob.

Two fast songs later, I noticed Jacob wasn't alone anymore. Our eyes connected, and I lifted a brow, reminding him he was otherwise attached. His raised eyebrows of shock made my eyes roll. He was a big boy and traveled for a living. I knew he loved his wife and wouldn't cheat on her, though it wouldn't hurt to supervise his flirting for fun.

The tempo changed, and the bright lights turned purple and moody. The anticipation of putting my arms around my woman made my body tingle. She bit her lip seductively and dropped her head to the right, lifting her chin to summon me to her body, and I was all in.

"Hey, baby. Wanna dance?" I growled out.

"Only if you tell me your name," she purred, insinuating she wanted to play. Any other time would be great for it. Tonight, however, I wanted her with Alex. Only Alex.

"It's Alex, and you are?" Her pupils went wide and her hands clutched my shirt.

"I'm Trudie."

I pulled her hips to mine, letting her feel how excited she made me.

"It's a pleasure to meet you. You look fine in that dress. Is it new?" The way her cheeks turned pink was so sexy.

"As a matter of fact, it is. I was hoping to meet someone special who would appreciate the trouble I took to look my best." Trudie had missed her calling as an actress. Her dedication to this role was intoxicating.

"Every inch of you is exquisite and the color sets off your eyes." I cupped her face and placed a whisper of a kiss on both soft pink lips while running my hands down to her luscious ass.

"Careful now, Alex. We just met and I don't want you to think I'm easy." She smirked, placing a firm hand on my chest, cautioning me not to get too ambitious.

I nuzzled my lips behind her ear, pressing my hands up through her hair. "You, my dear, are anything but easy. I've never had to work so hard to be with a woman." I pulled back and looked directly into her eyes. "I have only the greatest respect and admiration for you. You're a force to be reckoned with, my dear." My lips needed more and if that was all she would give, then I was taking hers deeply and aggressively. Everything slipped away as I pulled her upper lip with my teeth then dove deeply into her mouth to explore her sweetness. Lime, rum, and sweet caramel. Delicious.

I felt an annoying tap on my shoulder. "Hey kids, do you need a room?" Ruby pushed her way between us. I was stunned back to reality and looked at Trudie's swollen lips and hooded eyes. *Shit!*

Something about a dance floor, great music, and this little vixen always got me into trouble.

"Oh, my God!" Trudie pressed her fingers to her lips. "We should never be allowed on a dance floor again, Alex." Again, our minds had followed the same train of thought. She grabbed my hand and dragged me back to our booth.

TRUDIE

Dancing at my favorite hangout with Alex's was evocative and his friend, Jacob, was gorgeous to look at. He was three inches taller than Alex, built with the same wide shoulders, a perfect bulge in both his arms, and a prominent bulge in his pants too. *Not that I was looking.* This became obvious when we went back to our booth, where he was sitting rather snuggly to a box blonde who suggested that they "work the dance floor." He had a little trouble standing and shifted his junk—it didn't look like he was ready to leave the table.

Alex stepped between Jacob and the blonde and recommended he go to the bathroom and wind down instead. Apparently, Jacob had been known to slug a few bourbons back and get overly flirty. I'm sure that was fine when he was single, but not so much now that he was married.

Jacob bobbed his head up and down, twirled his wedding band twice, and walked to the restroom quickly. His new friend stomped her foot and rolled her eyes upward, blurting, "Why are all the good ones taken!" Her hand shot out and she grabbed her purse, knocking over her drink as she retreated in a huff. I empathized with her plight.

When Jacob returned, he signaled that he would be at the bar. Poor guy. It must have sucked to not be with his family all the time. What choices did he have while traveling? Sit in his room reading or watching TV or going to a restaurant or club and watching other people being together. Talk about a lose-lose situation.

I took a long swallow of water and tried to make myself heard over the blistering thump of the bassline. Techno music just wasn't my thing. "Hey! Let's go somewhere quieter," I suggested.

Seriously, how could anyone have a conversation in a place like this? My head banging days were over, which was making me feel old. All heads nodded vigorously. Within minutes, we'd grabbed Jacob's coat and our things, hooked his arm at the bar, and emerged from the throng.

"Holy mackerel, was that place jumping!" Daniel blurted in a stilted cadence.

"No shit!" Alex echoed.

"I swear, I'm getting too old for places like that. Can't they play the music a few decibels lower so I won't need hearing aids at forty?" Ruby wrapped her arms around Daniel's waist for more warmth.

"Agreed, agreed, and agreed. What's up next?" I asked.

"Let's go back to my house. I'll make a fire and we can have some quiet conversation or play a game like the old people we've become," Daniel offered. Everyone laughed except Jacob.

"Listen, I resemble that remark, though you should know that my wife and I have held some pretty non-PG events at our home when the kids have gone to grandma's house. We give Chutes and Ladders a whole new meaning." He waggled his eyebrows and our mouths fell open.

Alex swung his arm around his buddy's shoulders and the other around my waist. "I love being old!" he yelled into the cold night air.

CHAPTER 9

TRUDIE

Before I knew it, Daniel had built a roaring fire, distributed beers, and turned the lights low. His home was beautiful, and the gourmet kitchen he'd renovated himself overlooked the entire family room. An island made of a giant geode-looking granite top set on a dark maple shaker-style base housed a bar sink, cooktop, wine fridge, and trash compactor. Six tan leather-backed bar stools lined up opposite the work area like soldiers awaiting their orders. The whole place looked like a modern Ethan Allen showroom, except the couch wasn't formal and the cushions felt like therapeutic foam—squishy and forming perfectly to whichever tush took up residence. Whatever he paid for it was well worth the money, and I considered staying the night since I was in no position to drive.

Ruby skipped across the room to the built-in bookshelves surrounding the fireplace and pulled out Jenga. I'm sure she thought it would be funny to have drunk people try to keep a steady hand. Jacob slid to the floor and announced that we were going to play *strip* Jenga. We all chuckled at how juvenile his idea was—if anyone else felt the tingle of anticipation like I did, they hid it well.

Daniel quirked his mouth and slowly drew out the word, "Sure."

Alex demanded everyone's phone and set them by the front door. "What happens at Daniel's, stays at Daniels," he ordered. The flush on his face was so sexy. I'd never seen him look this way before. I swear I could see teenage excitement spread across his features.

"Ruby, what's your rule?" Jacob asked.

"My rule ... is ... that ... after every turn, you have to drink." She struggled to find a fitting rule, just like in college when she chose the *Wizard of Oz* game where everyone picked a character, or thing, like "yellow brick road," and had to drink every time it was said. Very original. I rolled my eyes.

"Fine, Miss Fancy Pants. What's your rule?" Ruby asked.

Ugh! I had known this was coming, and Ruby had stolen my idea, leaving me struggling.

"How about—every time you take a turn, someone has to stand closely behind you but not touch you? You know, creating more pressure on you." Everyone looked dazed and confused.

"Come on! Let me show you. Alex, come here." Alex stood from the couch and pressed his chest into my back, placing his hands on my hips possessively and breathing heavily down my neck.

"That's right, big boy, but no hand action. Take a half step back." I waited for him to make those adjustments and smiled when he whined a little about not being able to touch me. "There. Do you get it now?"

Alex puffed out his chest and breathed rather loudly, trying to distract me from three inches away. I could feel every breath and all his pent-up energy. "Trust me, it's unnerving," I muttered, looking over my shoulder at a pair of smoldering eyes and a ticking jaw.

Daniel erected the game and Jacob insisted on going first. Anyone could choose to stand behind him, and I made sure it was me first. Jacob had been gawking at my chest all evening and I was sure he would like them as close to his person as possible. Alex, however, looked annoyed. *Poor baby.*

As prescribed, he drank after his turn, and we established a rotation that moved quickly for the next ten minutes. Girls stood behind boys and boys stood behind girls, though Jacob thought it would be fun to stand behind Alex, and Alex stood behind Daniel. My mind was racing with the possibilities of some kinky shit going down. All these beautiful people with their toned and muscled bodies. We could have made epic memories if we had been swingers.

"Trudie!" Ruby yelled as she put her bottle up to her mouth, announcing her turn was over.

"Yeah, okay." I rubbed my eyes carefully and walked up to the remaining twelve pieces, which seemed to sway. I studied the wobbly tower for a full two minutes until I heard a husky whisper behind my ass. Alex.

"I can't wait to see you naked again. You may not want to have sex but I would like to jack off on you spread out for me." *Damn him!*

"Sexual interference!" I cried. "He's goading me and I can't think straight."

Sadly, no one offered their sympathies, only their smirks and oh wells.

"I hate you all," I whimpered.

I shook my head again and extended my right hand to the only piece that could keep me in the game. My nerves were shot and I moved my left hand up to steady myself. Blocking out as much background noise as I could muster, I tapped my chosen piece through the tight space, moving it a nanometer at a time. Three more taps and I would be clear. *One. Two. Three.* I had done it! When I turned around cheering for myself, the whole thing collapsed. *I. Hated. My. Life!*

There were hoots and hollers, but they weren't mine. I closed my eyes, freaking out at my loss. The issue was my dress had only allowed for one tiny undergarment under the silky fabric. Once my dress came off, it was just me in my birthday suit, with the equivalent of a Band-Aid on my sex.

"I hope you're happy with yourselves. Do I now spend the rest of the night in a thong with two other men staring at me?" I shot daggers with my eyes and my sass as I pulled off my dress and threw it across the room. My full breasts jiggled at the motion and my nipples pebbled to tight points. I didn't need a fire to feel the heat of those stares. Even Ruby was in awe.

"Girl! Look at you go! Damn, you're hot. I told you, Daniel. My friend is one hot femme fatale," she whispered a little too loud.

She smiled so big and looked so proud of me I blushed for a totally different reason.

"Yup. She sure is," Daniel swallowed hard his agreement.

Jacob cleared his throat and started stacking the pieces again. "Ahem. Ready for round two?"

The crackling of the fire was the only sound in the room as I stood with my arms crossed over my tits, my hips shifted to one side, daring anyone to say one thing. Time stopped as we all calculated what to do next. No one else moved as Alex charged at me with his shoulder aimed at my waist, lifted me into a fireman's carry, and smacked my ass.

"Feeling powerful, baby? Let's see how strong you are in the bedroom. Daniel! A spare room, please?" Daniel pointed, and without stopping, Alex stalked past the kitchen and into a bedroom, slamming the door with his foot.

I could only imagine what my friends were thinking on the other side of that door. I knew what *I* was thinking. Alex yanked back the covers and threw me onto the middle of the bed. I was a little scared of what he would do. Would he use his persona as a teacher to teach me a lesson or would he admonish me as the possessive boyfriend I'd come to love? He said he would abstain from having sex with me, but I couldn't forget his twisted comments behind my back about jacking off while looking at me. Shit that had sounded hot. I hadn't been embarrassed to take off my dress as much as I would have thought. It was doing it in front of Alex with friends watching that made me more uncomfortable. But I did it anyway to get a rise out of him, and now I was biting my lip, wondering if that had been such a good decision.

"What the hell is wrong with you?" He jammed his hands onto his tapered waistline, accusing me of what—I wasn't sure. He looked yummy, all riled up, hair messy, and face reddened.

I covered my breasts and slid farther away from his wrath. His eyes widened and he yanked me back by my ankles, forcing a gasp from my mouth.

"No, no. You are not shrinking away from this, dear. I don't care what the "rules" were tonight, you knew you didn't have anything on under that dress and no other man gets to see this body!" He removed his large hands from his waist and used them to sketch out my shape in the air.

I came up on my knees, dropping my protective arms, and pointed at his face. "You don't get to tell me what I can and what I can't do. This is my body, and I decide with whom and when I strip."

His expression was priceless: high eyebrows and a gaping mouth. Did I really think I could confront this powerful man? *Apparently so.*

"You've got some nerve pushing me like this. I've only supported and encouraged your desires personally and professionally. I don't want to tell you what to do with your body, but I sure don't want to see you shocking our friends with your dramatics." He moved his hands from his hips and shoved them into his increasingly full pants.

"So, what's the problem then? Am I too dramatic for your highbrow taste? A poor Latina middle school teacher too base for you? Fuck you, Alex!"

I grabbed the duvet and sheet and pulled them over myself, turning my back to him in disgust.

"You are twisting everything I say. Why are you so mad at me? Is it so terrible I don't want to share your body with anyone else?"

I felt a dip in the bed and I peeked over my shoulder to see him sitting with his head in his hands. I wasn't backing down. Either he learned to love all my quirks or got the hell out. But the little voice in my gut was scolding me, telling me I was being overly dramatic, and to stop it immediately. I'll admit, I'd had my share of tantrums over the years when I didn't feel appreciated. I'd manipulated my mom and brothers to have pity on me when my dad missed my dance recitals and National Honors Society induction. I craved being my dad's special little girl and used whatever means necessary to get my way. Though now my antics felt more childish than they had in the past. *Ugh! I hate having to apologize!*

I rolled over and placed a hand in the middle of his back. He didn't move. I put more pressure on his spine and slid my hand down to his hip.

"I'm sorry." A timid apology was all I could muster. I slowly pulled my hand away when he didn't respond. I knew I had pushed him too far. Could this be the end of our relationship? If I threw him away over my insecurities, what would that say about me? Was I such a bitch that I couldn't have a simple conversation without pushing him away? I tried to roll away again when he captured my wrist in a vise grip.

"Trudie. I've never met a woman who tries my patience like you do. I've never given anyone, man or woman, as many chances to explain themselves as I do with you. Let me say this plainly. I want you. Not for a night or a weekend. I want more. I want everything from you—your mind, your body, your spirit, your heart, even the wild shit you pull. I don't want to own you. I want you to give me those things because you wholeheartedly want to give them to me freely."

Alex pulled off his shirt and socks and climbed into bed, straddling me and pinning my wrists above my head. His crop of thick brown hair, usually so stylish, fell over his brow, and his dark-green almond-shaped eyes bore into mine. His lush, dark-pink lips hovered inches from my own, sparking tingles down my spine to my sex. His breath was hot and spicy from his bourbon. He used his masculinity to soften me, making me pliant and vulnerable. It was unnerving.

"Tell me what I need to know to help us get past this mess. I need you to trust me. Help me to understand and I will do everything in my power not to provoke you again. Can you do that, sweetheart?" He kissed the end of my nose like a guardian and breathed into my mouth like God himself. My mind was scrambled and useless. I had to look to my heart for guidance and hoped it wouldn't fail me.

"Yes. I want to trust you, and I want to give you the opportunity to show that I can, but I feel like I'm standing on a ledge high above the ground, and I am terrified of falling and getting hurt again." His eyes stayed locked on mine, and he nodded, showing he had heard me. When his lips brushed over mine appreciatively, something clicked in my head: he was choosing to be with me, with all my daddy issues and my insecurities. My God! I had fallen—only it was for him, and not off a cliff, succumbing to my fears.

"I've got you, Trudie. I won't let you fall. However, I can't promise I'll never hurt you. I am human, and so are you. I can promise, though, that I will beg your forgiveness and make whatever stupid thing I did up to you as soon as I can. How about we agree to not intentionally hurt the other and we will own our mistakes and rectify them to the best of our ability?"

He let go of my wrists and threaded his fingers through mine, sending quakes of lust through my body. I swear this man had enough sexuality coursing through him to light up Manhattan. I strained to lift my head off the mattress and kiss him, but he pulled back, presumably waiting for my answer. I focused on his words and the intention behind them. If I didn't take a step forward at that moment, when would I? Courage. What a strange feeling it was. A surprising mix of fear, optimism, faith, and grit. I'd always known I could be courageous, that I could prove to myself I could achieve what I wanted. But taking this leap and trusting someone else to support me along the way? That was terrifying. What a turning point this would be in my life. Tears fell one by one, dampening the sheet on both sides of my head. My body trembled at the release these realizations caused, and I swallowed hard trying to stave off a full-on cry.

"I can do that." I pulled my hands from his and pressed them to his perfect face, while I prayed he wouldn't let me down. "I trust you will never intentionally hurt me. And I will talk with you, not run away or have a tantrum. I promise to share my feelings with you always." I hiccupped and more tears drained from my eyes.

His thumbs caught my tears and wiped them away lovingly. I was learning every day what he was capable of, and I needed to trust he only had my best interest at heart.

"Baby, I've got you. You don't need to cry. I'm sorry if I touched a nerve. More daddy bullshit?" The tilt in his head and the sweetness in his eyes were more fatherly than anything I'd ever gotten from my own stupid father.

I hiccupped again. "It appears so." I pulled his face to mine, pressing his lips open with my tongue and slipping it inside his sexy mouth.

I took a breath. "You've found all my hot buttons and diffused them." *Kiss.*

"It's exhausting." *Kiss.*

"And—liberating at the same time." *Kiss.*

I could feel his cock nudging my pussy, and the way he moved insinuated he wanted more. My determination to not have sex was waning as moisture dripped down my thighs.

Alex jumped off the bed and tore off his pants and boxers, returning seconds later to continue grinding against my mound.

He moaned as he rocked with more pressure, and his freed cock filled and pulsed. "Are we good, baby?" he choked out.

I nodded, mewling at the feeling of his gyrations. "Then I'm going to fulfill my promise to you and jack off watching your sinful body."

"Yes!" I hissed.

He pulled off my thong and spoke lovingly as he petted my pussy like a small kitten. "Get ready little pussy, I'm going to cover you in my cum and use my dick to paint every inch of you."

Jesus Christ! This man's mouth was filthier than I'd thought. Alex made Dr. Pierce look more like a teacher's assistant than a teacher.

"You are a freak talking to my pussy like that, Alex," I squealed.

"You don't even know the half of it, baby."

ALEXANDER

I delivered on my promise to dirty up my girl, and in the process, learned that she was almost as freaky as I was. Her openness to trying new things while not getting insulted when I wanted her submission, was liberating. But I also reveled in her freedom when she wanted to assert herself and ride me, taking control of our lovemaking and allowing me to please her the way she desired. The give and take we had in bed was soul inspiring and fulfilling in a way I had never experienced. Trudie made everything in my life better, and now that we had found a way to have meaningful communication, I couldn't wait to build on that foundation.

After I had collected a sleepy Jacob from the couch, I drove Trudie back to her apartment and my best friend collapsed back at mine. I couldn't have planned this evening any better: dirty dancing with her at Teddy's, getting her to trust me, and painting her body with my lust. Her eyes went wide when my hands moved my fluid up to her breasts, claiming every inch of her. She gasped and moaned and mewled like a kitten, giving me another erection. I came again when she held my cock like a vise and shared all her naughty thoughts of what she would like to do with it. *Fuck.* She wasn't a meek little kitten. She was a wildcat with a mind full of untried fantasies I would be happy to accommodate.

I had completely forgotten to invite her to the soccer match Jacob was scouting the next day. I shot her a text after I dropped into my bed asking if I could pick her up at eleven so we could grab a coffeehouse breakfast and watch the game together. Secure that we were in a better place, I deposited my phone on the nightstand, pulled the soft sheet up to my chest, and fell into the soundest sleep I'd had in weeks.

What felt like moments later, I heard my phone buzz, and I slapped my hand around trying to get a grip on it.

"Hey, good morning," a sultry female voice greeted me.

"Hey." I rubbed my eyes, crusted over from a night of drinking, and then noticed the time. *Shit! Didn't I set an alarm?*

"Are we still going to the game?" How could she be so perky after all that liquor we drank?

"Oh my God, I'm so sorry. I'll be there in twenty minutes. I forgot to set an alarm. Don't wait outside. I'll text you when I get there."

"Okay. I'll make us some egg sandwiches and coffee so we can head straight to the field."

"You're the best. See you soon." Wow! I found a woman who was forgiving. Unlike my mother who derived pleasure from inflicting disdain when her children and husband acted, "regular," as she put it. Who am I kidding? My mother wouldn't know how to be compassionate if her life depended on it.

I took the fastest shower known to humankind and was in my car twelve minutes later. I had no clue what time Jacob had gotten up and taken off, though I knew he'd made breakfast for himself because he had left a dozen dishes piled in the sink. *Asshole.*

My phone rang as I put my car in reverse. I didn't want to answer, but when I shifted my car into drive, my finger hit the answer button. *Crap!*

"Hello, dear." I hated that voice. All right, maybe hate was too cruel, perhaps disliked was better. Either way, it was my mother, and I didn't have time for her whining. I did what every bratty child did when they didn't want to speak with someone: I covered my mouth with my hand, muffling my words.

"Oh, hi, Mom. I can barely hear you." I was a shit and I knew it.

"Darling, I can't hear you. Please speak up. I need to talk with you about the holidays."

She sounded annoyed at having to discuss any plan that wasn't her own. In the past, she assumed all her children would be present for any and all public and private gatherings from Thanksgiving to New Year's Day. *Newsflash, Mom, I'm not a child anymore and I won't be present for any of it this year.*

I didn't answer her. She yelled into the receiver hoping I'd hear her. I let her carry on for a full minute and then she shouted, "I don't know why I even bother. Insufferable child." The line went dead, and so did my heart. Unbelievable. Am I the insufferable one? *No worries, you won't have to suffer any longer, Mom.*

I pulled up to Trudie's building, threw the gear shift into park, and pounded the steering wheel in frustration, wondering what other shit would rain down on my day. I took a page out of Trudie's meditation book and inhaled several deep breaths, slowing each one down until I was breathing normally. I needed to pull myself together and definitely didn't want to discuss this with my girl first thing in the morning. Maybe after dinner we could snuggle up on the couch with some wine, and she could console me as I dealt with my mommy issues.

I sent her a quick text alerting her that I had arrived, and three minutes later, I watched her sweet ass as she pulled the front door securely closed. Even in a Wings baseball cap, black leggings, an oversized sweatshirt, and a thick black scarf, she looked delicious enough to eat. She gripped two travel coffee mugs in one hand, and shook the paper bag she had in the other, making it clear that I would be eating food and not her hot pussy.

"Open the window," she shouted through the driver's side glass.

"Good morning, gorgeous."

She passed our drinks to me and ran around the car to jump in.

"It *is* a good morning, especially when you look at me like that."

I waggled my eyebrows and licked my lips. "Thank goodness you came packing food or I'd be dining on something else."

"I bet you say that to all the girls?" She giggled and handed me a sandwich.

"You give me too much credit. You are the only girl who matters to me." That would have sounded more romantic if I hadn't had a mouthful of egg sandwich.

She replied in kind, "Aww, thash show shweet." We both laughed as she buckled up.

Twenty minutes later we arrived at the field and climbed the small stands behind Oakland University's team. Jacob had a blanket spread out for us and we all hugged it out as we took our seats.

"Who are we scoping out today?" I probed Jacob.

"I've got two kids who have potential. The coach sent video introductions to me so I could get a feel for their personalities and dispositions. I don't have time for brats and assholes—I only have time for kids with a good work ethic. Jared Harris is a junior who has great handling skills, and his coach thinks he has the brains to be an integral part of a professional team. The other kid is Jaresh Singh. Wicked fast and doesn't hold back from bodychecking his opponents. His coach has him as a forward, but from what I can see, he'd be a better midfielder. He doesn't have the bulk needed for a strong attacker, especially playing with grown men who play for blood."

The stands were packed with shouting college kids covered in black and gold school colors, their faces painted with big Os on their cheeks. I remembered my days in college, where the only things that had mattered were good grades and having fun. My parents didn't visit me until graduation day, when they could be seen as doting parents whose son presumably made them proud. *Ha!* Rowing didn't attract a huge crowd and I didn't do it for adulation. I hated lifting weights and I got the same results pulling on long oars. Most of the time I popped in my earbuds, locked onto a boss playlist that simulated the same tempo we used for competition, and sculled for an hour.

"These guys are taking a beating," I said, sympathizing with the impact these guys were taking.

"Yeah, it's a rough sport. I played in high school and after several broken ribs and fingers, I decided that golf was a safer bet." Jacob nodded his head, remembering what a good decision that had been. He'd played golf for Columbia for four years, and I met him at a mutual professor's home for a sports psychology get-together. His attitude toward sports and how elite athletes lose life balance the closer they reached their goals had intrigued me. We got to talking, which had led to a friendship that had lasted over twenty years.

I patted him on the back, affirming his decision, and let him get back to doing his job. Trudie was sipping her coffee, and in between plays, reviewing her calendar app.

"Busy week coming up?" I asked, stroking the ponytail at the back of her hat.

"Yeah. I need to meet with our high-risk kids and then later in the week with our mentors. I want to be sure everyone is following our mission and resolve any student issues that may have arisen. They need to feel supported to do their best."

"I've got to get these kids to decide on a name for their group. Something catchy that says, 'It's cool to get your shit straight.'" She laughed at herself.

"You're cracking me up. It's a good thing you're already a card-carrying member of your own club."

She swatted at me, "You should talk. You're the president of the whack-a-doodle club."

"At your service, madam."

CHAPTER 10

TRUDIE

I'd never been to a soccer match before, and from what I was watching, I hoped I never would again. My body recoiled every time one of the players smacked heads with another player. I had a headache by the end of the match, and my teeth were chattering in the cold.

We stood and stretched, and I folded the blanket while the guys made plans to meet by the locker rooms, since Jacob needed to talk to the coaches down on the field first. By the time we met up, the players were exiting the locker room showered and goofing around, celebrating their win.

Alex held me by his hip as we leaned against the cinderblocks, and we were chatting about what we might want to have for dinner later when one of the players stopped in front of me.

"Trudie?"

Oh no! I remembered those dimples and sexy smile.

"Jared?" I was flabbergasted. I was so stupid—it hadn't occurred to me that the Jared we were watching was the Jared I had met on the plane last July. This was awkward.

"I've been thinking about you. Sorry I didn't call sooner. School and practice have been monopolizing my year so far. The season is winding down in a few weeks, so, maybe, we could get together and catch up?"

Alex's strong arm pulled me tightly against his side, and his tension was palpable. "Maybe not," he answered for me.

Annoyed at his possessiveness, I peeled myself out of his tight embrace and gave him a stern look to tell him to back down.

I took a step toward Jared, feeling that I owed him a private apology. Shifting my weight from foot to foot, I tried to find the right words that would let him down easily without sounding patronizing.

"We had fun on our plane ride, didn't we?" I smiled demurely and I got the feeling he thought he was about to get lucky with the date he suggested. "It was fun and exciting and I truly appreciated you holding my hand while I fought my uneasiness."

His smile really was beautiful and his dimple was so sexy. "It was hot as fuck," he whispered. He licked his lips as he stared at me.

"Yeah, it was. Unfortunately, you met me at a crossroads in my life, and after we parted I realized that you had so much on your plate with school, soccer, and figuring out your own life that it didn't mesh with where I was in my life. Does that make sense? It's not so much about the age difference as how the next few years out of college would work if we were together. I hope you understand that our attraction wouldn't be enough."

In response to my words, this handsome young man morphed into the equivalent of a five-year-old kicking the dirt. He pushed both hands through his hair, exposing bulging biceps and a snap-shot of what he would have looked like lying back on a bed of pillows with his hands behind his head. *Trudie! Get a grip.*

"I hear what you're saying but your eyes tell another story." His smile was devilish and he took another step forward, not intimidated by Alex just a few feet away.

I held up my hand, implying he should stop where he was. "That might be true in your eyes, but that guy over there, he's my boyfriend and he probably won't want you touching me the way it looks like you planned to. Finish school, Jared. Plan your career, and the right woman will be waiting for you—it just won't be me." I smiled again and gave a small wave. "All my best Jared. I can't wait to watch your professional soccer debut on television."

Alex stepped forward and pulled me again to his side with one hand while extending his other to Jared.

"Great game, Jared. Best of luck in the future."

Jared grimaced and walked toward the parking lot with his head hanging, and I watched, knowing I made him feel that way. All the logic in the world told me I did the right thing. However, being rejected never felt good. I wondered how Sam felt when I told him I wasn't going to Colorado with him. It appeared as though I was a two-time heartbreak offender. If it had been Alex walking away, it would have been the end of me. Jacob finally caught up to us and threw his arm around Alex's shoulders.

"What are you two love birds talking about?" He gripped his opposite wrist effectively putting Alex into a head lock. Alex shoved at him, determined to continue our conversation.

"How do you know that guy?" Alex turned me into an embrace, watching me closely.

"On the plane on my way to the conference. He ended up sitting next to me, and you know how much I hate flying, so he held my hand and then stayed like that for the rest of the flight. He's a sweet guy and wanted to stay in contact, except we never did. I met you, and he never called, so I didn't think about it again until today."

I suppose I could have told Alex about us making out and that Jared was all handsy, though that would only have made him jealous and he might have done something stupid. *Hmm.*

"Damn right you forgot about him. I'm your man and you'd be wise to put that guy out of your mind forever." He pulled me against his chest and planted a demanding kiss on my lips.

When he'd had enough, he pushed me back and took my hand to walk to his car.

Jacob followed us to the parking lot stopping at his Cadillac SUV he must have rented. "Sorry to interrupt your lovers quarrel, but I have to catch my plane. It's been great meeting you Trudie. I hope to see you again soon."

He smacked Alex in the head like a big brother might have. He then placed both hands on Alex's cheeks and whispered rather loudly, "Do not fuck this up, or I'll never speak with you again. Understand?"

Alex nodded his understanding and pulled Jacob into a tight hug.

"Love you, man."

"Back at ya, brother."

Jacob hopped into his vehicle and tore out of the parking lot leaving us standing there remembering what we were talking about earlier. I took his hand and started walking toward our car, swinging his arm when my thoughts came back to me.

"You're such a caveman. Get over yourself," I mocked him, and he immediately stooped down at my waist and drove his shoulder into my hips, flipping me over it. Apparently, this was his signature move.

He muttered, "I'll show you caveman. You my woman, arh, arh, arh." He slapped my ass for good measure. What a dork.

When we got back to my apartment, Alex received a text from Jacob saying he'd made it to the airport and thanked us for a great trip. He was a lot of fun, and I respected him for being faithful to his wife, in spite of the flirting. She must have trusted him completely, knowing his personality and the lifestyle of a recruiter. Being charming was part of the package and Jacob certainly played that role well.

I needed to visit my dad again. Although I didn't dread it as much as I had the first time, I wasn't ready to let go of our past. I'd spent fifteen years resenting my father and all his trespasses—missing birthdays, recitals, and other important occasions. I hated the way he'd treated my mom, making her his servant when he barreled back into the house. The fear and insecurities he instilled in me coursed through me every time my house wasn't cleaned before I left for the day. Whenever I found myself feeling unworthy, I recalled the person who created that emotion and all fingers pointed at my dad. I could have taken a first-class trip to Europe with all the money I spent on therapy and conferences trying to eliminate these feelings and improve my sense of worth. I had done the work. I had made something of myself. I was making a difference in my students' lives. I didn't want to deal with the past any longer.

Strong arms banded around my waist as I watched through the window the last of the leaves fall from the courtyard trees. I leaned back against Alex's chest and could hear the even thumping of his heart while he nuzzled into my hair.

"What are you thinking about? Not Jared, I hope." He made a soft caveman sound, making me smile.

"Not at all. I was thinking that I needed to go by my dad's nursing facility today and pay him a visit." He planted kisses along my neck, distracting me from my duty.

"I can go with you if you'd like?" His throaty offer was so tempting.

I rolled my head to the side, giving him more access, and hummed my approval.

"Are you sure that is how you want to spend your Saturday evening? He'll probably be a jerk to you too."

"Not especially, but if you're there, then yes. I wouldn't mind meeting the man that gave my girl her daddy issues. It wasn't good for you, though when we play, it's very good for me."

I spun around and punched him in the chest. "You're a sick person."

"Ow!" He looked so offended, mouth hanging open while he rubbed his chest with his open hand. "You knew I was sick the day

I met you and yet you still wanted more. So, who is the sickest of all now?" He stuck out his tongue like an overgrown child.

"I refuse to respond to your adolescent behavior. Get your coat and shoes. We're going to see Daddy dearest. Just remember, I warned you," I hissed over my shoulder as I whipped open the front door.

"Fine! I'm a big boy and can handle myself," he snarled, slamming the door shut behind him.

ALEXANDER

There were plenty of giggles and goofing around on our way to the nursing facility, but it stopped instantly as I pulled into the parking lot. Trudie's complexion had faded to a pasty pallor and she shivered with trepidation.

I slid my hand down her thigh, giving her a squeeze. "I've got you, sweetheart."

The tightness of her sad eyes pinched the sides of her gorgeous face as she attempted to take in my support.

"Just tell me what you want and it's yours. If you want me to rough him up a bit, I'll do that." I waggled my eyebrows, trying to get her to relax.

She slumped back into the seat, took a deep breath, and let it out slowly. There was no more pinching or pale coloring—on the contrary, her skin had pinkened up and she bit her rose-colored lips, which were set in determination. "Let's do this. If I tug on my left ear, he's all yours to do what you want with him."

"That's my girl!" I unbuckled my seat belt and met her at the front of my car. I was in awe of her resolve to get her issues worked out. I could only hope when the time came with my own parents, I would be the same.

After checking in we walked through the maze of hallways to her dad's room. From what I gathered, he didn't have any other family to rally around him—only Trudie and her mom. Her younger brother, Zander, refused to be involved, and Paulo, her older brother, had only agreed to see him once. These Gonzalez women were like many women who kept their families together, especially when their men didn't deserve it. My mother wasn't one of them.

We arrived at his room and I knocked on the open door. The mothball smell filled my nostrils and made it hard not to gag. I hated nursing homes. Death loomed everywhere. I looked into the room, and I couldn't picture the hard, difficult man who Trudie despised only a withered-looking, gray-haired man with a strained cough.

Trudie made to go into the room, but I grabbed her wrist. I wanted to know what I was walking into. She had mostly only given me her back story, not a whole lot about her last visit. I pulled her into a hug and whispered my question.

"What kind of cancer does he have? Do you know how long he has to live?"

I was a behavioral psychologist, not a medical doctor, but I'd treated hundreds of patients going through multiple types of cancer and their families seeking comfort while their loved ones passed or had already passed. I could be a great help to Trudie if I knew a few details about what her father was enduring.

"It's a kind of lung cancer from asbestos. I forgot the name. The last I heard he only had a few months to live." She hugged me tighter, not letting me go.

"Does the name mesothelioma sound familiar?"

"Yeah," she whispered. "Do you know what that is?"

I stroked her hair and whispered back that I did. Moments later she slid her hands down my chest and motioned for us to continue what we were there to do.

"Hi, Dad." It was evident that her pleasant tone was forced, but at least she was trying her best.

"*Cariño*. You came." He hacked up something awful into a cloth he held in his hand.

"Of course. I said I would and I don't make promises I can't keep." Regrettably, my passive aggressive behavior was more knee-jerk than I thought.

"You're an honorable woman. Tell me what you've been up to." He strained to speak—gurgling through a pained grimace.

TRUDIE

I took several steps forward to my father's bedside and then looked at Alex, not knowing what to do. He joined me then, pressing his hand to my lower back and pushing me closer to the bed.

"I'll get him some water," Alex suggested after looking across the room to his tray and seeing that it was empty.

Through a croaky hiss my father asked, "Who is that guy?" after Alex left.

I chuckled in response: "My boyfriend."

"I don't like him." His face became pinched.

"You don't have to like him. I'm not asking for your approval." I rolled my eyes at his audacity. I didn't want his opinion on anything at this stage of my life.

"Does he t-treat you w-well?" he stuttered out the words and then almost literally coughed up a lung. It didn't sound like he had much time, and I wasn't sure what his objective was in asking me to visit him.

"Very well. I don't want to upset you, but could you tell me why you need me to visit you? I understand part of it, though I'm not clear what's in it for me." I pulled up a chair as Alex returned with a fresh cup of ice water and a new straw.

"Here, babe."

I took the cup and straw and got it ready. When I slipped the straw into my dad's mouth, he took a sip and his face relaxed a bit at the cool water.

"Thanks, Alex. Grab that other chair while we catch up." I nodded toward the chair and swallowed hard, waiting for my dad's response. I wondered now if bringing Alex had been the best thing to do. I wanted my dad to open up and be totally honest with me, and I hoped having Alex here wouldn't interfere with that.

My dad pressed the automated bed controller and attempted to sit up, but to no avail. I jumped up to push him forward so I could fluff his pillows and help him get comfortable.

Of course, instead of a thank you, he became critical and blurted out his vitriol.

"Why are you dating my daughter? You look too uppity to be right for her."

Yikes! What the hell was that? The man had just gotten him some water and he didn't even thank him. He was still an ass.

"Hey! That wasn't nice or appropriate. Why we're dating isn't any of your business. Where are the manners you so deliberately beat into us?" Neither Alex nor I were going to be disrespected.

Alex stood up, throwing his shoulders back, spreading his legs, and crossing his arms, ready for battle. If he meant to intimidate my dad, he did all the right things. If he had done that in my living room, I would have been climbing him like a monkey.

"Mr. Gonzalez. With all due respect, your daughter came here at your request, giving up her time and energy to give you whatever it is you need to bring you comfort during this difficult time. I am here to support her and guide that conversation if she asks me to. As for your description of me, it is irrelevant. She chose me, and I chose her, and that's all you need to know."

Fuck, I loved this man! Alex was so smooth and calm delivering his speech. His tone was level and he didn't offer anything other than pure professionalism. I knew bringing him had been the right thing to do! If I could have skimmed off 10 percent of his impervious demeanor and infused it deep within me, I wouldn't have had my emotions running me ragged.

My father drank more of his water and stated, "I like him."

I smacked my hand to my forehead, dumbfounded. My dad just sat there smiling like the cat that ate the canary. "I just wanted to see if the guy had a backbone. All those rich snobs think they're better than everyone else. He'll do." I swear to God I was ready to suffocate him with the pillows I had just used to make him comfortable.

"Ha, ha, Dad. You're such a kidder. You know what, I'm ready to go. I don't need you to answer my question. You're still the ass I've come to know and hate. Goodbye."

I stood abruptly and motioned for Alex to follow me out. I was in the hall when I overheard Alex lying to him. My feet were frozen to the floor. I stood in the doorway, tears welling up, as I watched my man demonstrate he had my back just like he said he would. I listened quietly, praying for my father to hear his message.

"What the hell is wrong with you, Mr. Gonzalez? You've treated your daughter so poorly her whole life that she questions everything she does and can barely trust her own boyfriend. You've damaged her in ways I'm still learning about. Do you think you can behave this way and leave this earthly plane without hearing what a piece of shit you've been? Your daughter is the strongest, most resilient woman I've ever had the pleasure to meet. Her heart has an abundance of love to give when it isn't being taken advantage of. You have no right to treat her that way, and you haven't earned the right to ask her to come down here again. So help me God, if you say one more hurtful thing to that beautiful woman, I'll deck you. I don't care if you're dying!"

The look he gave my father was terrifying, and my father's face finally showed the contrition he should have had all along. Alex turned to face me and I burst into tears, rushing into his arms and wrapping mine around his waist. Tears turned to sobs and sobs turned to hiccups.

"I l-love you so m-much, baby." I cried wet hiccups into his chest.

"I love you too. Let's get you home." He wiped my tears with his thumbs and pinned me to his side as we exited the room.

CHAPTER 11
TRUDIE

I woke up the next morning in my bra and panties. A seasonal mug sat on a coaster on my night table reminding me of the hot tea Alex insisted I drink when we got back to my apartment. I was rolling over, flailing my arms wide, when I heard the crinkle of a piece of paper on top of the comforter. I was too tired to sit up and squinted, trying to focus with the paper held over my head.

Darling Trudie,

I stayed with you last night in case you had a bad dream but had to leave for an early morning conference call. Please take some time for yourself and regroup the best you can. I'll call you when my meeting is over.

Love, Alex

I held the note to my chest, marinating on how he ended his message. *Love.* Love? I'm still baffled as to how and when did we got to love. I pushed my hands through my hair several times trying to pinpoint when I had first felt that way. Last night he said it to me—or did I say it first?

I sat bolt upright smacking my hands to the sheets. *Jesus Christ, I really do love him!* Last night, he had said to trust him, that he had me, that he would support me. Man, oh man, he hadn't been kidding. I combed through the whole conversation—well more like tirade—with my father several times. Incredibly, Alex had summarized all my pain in a few sentences, and had managed to put my father in his place. Unbelievable!! He was my hero, my liberator, my lover—my true love.

I threw off the covers and grabbed my phone. I had to put this day in my calendar marking this historic change to my life. I shook my head in disbelief as I giggled through my shower and morning routine. I took extra care shaving all my bits for what I had planned for that night. We would celebrate with his favorite meal and then have each other for dessert. By midmorning I had our evening all planned out. I wasn't wasting any time thinking about my dad the asshole—only about Alex, my hero.

My phone buzzed, and I was thrilled when I saw Alex's face appear on the screen.

"Hey, there, gorgeous. Do you have time for lunch? Or maybe dinner, too?" I'm not great with sexy talk but I gave him my best seductress voice.

"I would have loved to eat you for lunch and dive into you for dinner, but unfortunately, I have to fly to Texas tonight to save a big client of mine from making some terrible mistakes. Can I take a rain check?"

If I was a balloon, his announcement would have been the pin. All the joy I was feeling whooshed out of me and I tried to keep the disappointment from my voice.

"Of course. You know where to find me when you get back." My sarcasm echoed in my head making me feel small. My insecurities had a terrible way of unnerving me when I needed to be strong and reasonable. I kept forgetting he didn't really live here. He only had a furnished apartment until the end of February, and November hadn't even begun.

"I'm sorry, sweetheart. I hated that I have to travel for my job before, but now, it's downright painful not being with you every night."

"Agreed. I've been thinking, what are your plans for Thanksgiving and then Christmas break? I'll be with my family for both and wondered if you'd like to meet them?" I bit my nails in anticipation.

"It's funny you're bringing this up, because later this week I need to fly home to settle some financial affairs and, sadly, I need to see my parents to accomplish these plans. I do not, I repeat, do not plan on being in New York over the holidays. I'm done with the façade, the hassle, and the anxiety my family produces. I'll have to figure something out with my sisters at some point, but definitely count me in for Thanksgiving."

My heart zinged at the opportunity for him to meet my family. My brothers were going to love him and my mom would melt at his handsomeness.

"Yay! I can't believe you're coming. Bring your stretchy pants because my mom goes all out, and I'll bring a book for my when my brothers steal you away to watch football." I laughed at myself.

"Or maybe you can show me your old bedroom and we can do shameless things in it." I could hear the dare in his voice.

"Ha! Not a chance. I've never lived in my mom's new house, so you'll just have to wait until later that night to do the things that shall not be said." I snorted into the phone and he belly-laughed his approval.

"Look in your email inbox. There is something you need to look at immediately. I have to go, but I'll call you before my flight leaves." The phone was silent, though he hadn't hung up.

"Alex? Are you still there?" The dead air had me nervous.

"Yeah. I told you last night, again, that I loved you, and those words still have me reeling. You said you loved me, and I never thought I'd hear those words again. In the short time we've known each other, our relationship has been a rollercoaster, yet I've always felt connected in a way I never had with anyone, including Sheila. I love you, Trudie. Never forget it."

His proclamation was so sincere and sweet, but it also felt foreboding to me. What might come between us? We had cleared the air about Sheila, so unless there was another woman lurking under a rock, what would keep us from growing our relationship? *You know what, I don't want to know.*

"Baby, I've got you and your love. That's all I need. Thanks for calling. I'll talk to you later."

Our call ended and I sprinted to my computer. There was a message from him with a gift certificate for a very high-end day spa a few miles from my apartment. I loved this man! He knew I could never afford a place like that. Heck, I barely had time or money to get a manicure twice a year. I grabbed my phone and sent him lots of heart emoji and a spa girl emoji, letting him know how much I loved this gift.

I printed the gift certificate and when I read all the details I panicked. *My appointments start in twenty minutes*. I grabbed my phone, purse, flip-flops, and a book.

I raced to my car and at the first stop light took a picture of the certificate and sent it to Ruby. She was going to flip out when she saw what I was doing. By the time I got to the spa, she had sent four messages calling me not-so-nice names, followed by a Bitmoji of her comic avatar image saying, "Yaaasss" and "You Go, Girl!" She knew how much I loved those things.

I indulged in an afternoon of a light lunch, facial, massage and mani-pedi. There was a fully stocked locker room with fluffy white robes and slippers and a sauna! Oh my God, I'd never been in one and because I wasn't raised to pamper myself this way, I had to watch everyone else so I didn't do something completely stupid. I knew I should have paid more attention to Queen Latifah in *the Last Holiday*. That girl got every treatment known to womankind.

"Ms. Gonzalez. I have a note for you. When you're ready, we'll do your eyebrows, makeup, and hair." I nodded like my students did when I gave them a pop quiz and they were thrown for a loop.

That wasn't on the certificate, and I couldn't afford to pay for all those additional treatments.

"Ah, miss, I don't think you have the right person. Those things weren't on my gift certificate." She smiled warmly and pointed to the note.

"You might want to read that now." She waited with her hands gently clasped in front of her. My eyes drifted to the note and the air in my lungs was sucked out of me.

Hey Baby,

Why not get dolled up and video chat with me when you're done? My flight isn't until later tonight and I'd love to see you all shiny and fabulous.

Love, Alex

That man!

I smiled at the attendant and slapped my thighs. "Well, let's do this!" I would be smiling like a fool for the rest of the day.

"Terrific!" she cheered and whisked me away for another couple of hours. I didn't see my phone until almost six thirty and was surprised by a message Alex had sent me.

"Change of plans. Can't video chat. Drive to Waterford and go to the Airport Inn Restaurant instead. Sorry for the short notice. Have dinner on me. Love you!"

What?! This day had been the longest and most relaxing of my entire life. But after that message I could feel my muscles tightening again and I got a sick feeling in the pit of my stomach. I knew I could go home, but the thought of wasting all this glamour on my couch eating toast sounded awful and wasteful. I grabbed my things and placed one foot in front of the other. I supposed I needed to be flexible with his work schedule. It's not like he had wanted to leave town.

Traffic was light, and I arrived thirty minutes later, my stomach still tied in knots. How had Alex found this place? I had never heard of it myself and this was my territory.

"Ms. Gonzalez?" The sexy hostess with bright red lips greeted me.

"Hello, that's me." I smiled brightly.

"Please follow me." Without hesitation, I followed her like a puppy looking for its master. I was mesmerized by this place. Airplanes coming and going, plush blue and gold booths that oozed of luxury, and a gorgeous woman in a red dress crooning jazz standards just loud enough that it didn't interfere with conversation. I was so caught up in looking around, I didn't realize she had brought me to a private booth that faced the landing field.

"Enjoy your evening." She smiled and extended her hand to the booth, giving me a wink. She was hot, but was she hitting on me? As I cocked my head to the side in contemplation, I noticed a large olive-skinned hand that looked very familiar, and I gasped in response.

"Alex!" I whisper-screamed and then looked around to be sure no one had heard me.

"It's Dr. Pierce, and you've kept me waiting. Please sit down, I've already ordered your wine."

My stomach dropped and I became instantly wet. I hadn't "seen" Dr. Alexander Pierce in over a week, and honestly, I missed him. He took control of both my mind and body in a way that left me speechless. His eyes were dark emeralds that looked obsidian in the evening light, and I remembered what that mouth could do to me if I allowed it. Alex and I hadn't had proper intercourse recently either. Jacking off on me, though exciting, wasn't reciprocal. I was so excited to give him the go-ahead and ravage me.

There weren't any chairs across from the bench seat—the only place to sit was in the small amount of space on the banquette that he didn't occupy. I had bolted out of my apartment that morning in only yoga pants and a slouch sweater and was terribly under-dressed for this place, especially since he was in a suit coat. It had always bothered me that as a Latina, I needed to dress sophisticat-edly to be taken seriously, so I was very impressed that the hostess didn't look down on me. More than likely, she knew who I was being escorted to and had been tipped handsomely. Again, another of my insecurities, though certainly not debilitating. I knew my value ... most of the time.

After sitting and giving him a small kiss on the cheek, I sipped my wine, waiting patiently for what was sure to be a great expla-nation for why he was here and not on his flight.

"You look incredible." His eyes stayed locked on mine as his hand slid down my slinky pants. "And you smell fucking fantastic." He nuzzled into my neck, inhaling my scent while sucking small nips along my neck.

"I know your taste is as sweet as honey. I can feel it on my hand." *Uhh.* He pressed his hand between my thighs pushing the thin fabric of my panties into my wet pussy.

I moaned his name into his shoulder, "Please, Dr. Pierce."

He pulled his head back and turned my face to cup both my cheeks. "Please what, baby girl." Shit, he was going to make me say it. That was the hardest part about being with Dr. Pierce. He made me ask for exactly what I wanted. He wanted to set my inhibitions free and pushed me when I hesitated.

"Please, take me."

He exhaled his warm breath on my face and the corners of his mouth turned upward—he was clearly thinking of all the things he could do to my body.

"I was hoping you would say that. First, we'll eat, and then—I'll see what I can achieve before my flight leaves. The good news for you is I booked a private flight and the captain will text me when he sends a car over to pick me up."

He brushed my cheeks with such reverence that my lips parted and my eyes rolled back into my head. The wet tip of his tongue glided along each pillow of my lips, taunting me, promising me what was to come, and my appetite for him skyrocketed.

"Do we have to eat dinner?" My voice turned husky and my hand pressed to his thick athletic thigh.

"Absolutely. You'll need your strength for what I have planned for you." The kiss he finally gave me was deep and wet and passionate. I didn't need words for Dr. Pierce to communicate with me, I only needed them from Alex.

"You're killing me," I whined. "Please tell me you already ordered."

His smile extended to his beautiful thick hairline. "Yes, baby girl, I did, and here it comes."

I turned in my seat to find the perfect dinner for me—a juicy burger with melting Swiss cheese and steak cut fries—times two.

"Oh my God, this burger is divine! So good," I mumbled my appreciation through not-so-ladylike bites. Rest and relaxation were hard work, and I needed sustenance immediately. "Great choice."

He laughed and then wiped a blob of ketchup from my cheek with his napkin. It wasn't just that he was being kind—he did it so lovingly and seductively that my mind fritzed again.

I stopped eating and stared at his face. All of his face. Generous lips, high sculpted cheekbones, and long, thick lashes framing sensitive, understanding eyes that had the power to lure me in. It was freaky how magnetic his energy was. It felt like I had to strain to pull away from him every time we parted. My soul cried out for him and I'd learned to listen to its voice. He made me feel that way with his love, his respect, and his patience.

"Thank you, Alex," I said quietly, "for today, for this, and for helping me become whole." I held his hands, hoping he'd understand that we could play with Dr. Pierce any time, but it was important to me that he knew where all this love came from.

"I love you, Trudie. You're everything to me. Thank you for loving me as I am, and not what I can buy you. I've never met anyone like you. People in my world only like you when they want something—it's disgusting. I would do anything for you, knowing that you loved me. Me, Alex Pierce, the psychology nerd."

"Psychology nerds have sexy minds. And it just so happens mine comes in the hottest body ever." My throat became parched as I said the words.

"I need to pay this bill so we can get out of here."

"Agreed!" I squealed. I slid out of the booth announcing, "I've gotta pee," and dashed off to the ladies' room before my bladder burst.

ALEXANDER

I wasn't kidding when I said this woman had changed me for the better. When had I ever hired a private jet just so I could spend a few more hours with someone? NEVER! Ending the call with her that morning, I could feel her disappointment about not seeing me that evening. The spa gift certificate was nice and she deserved it but giving it to her didn't feel nearly as good as being with her in person. One of the benefits of living an elite lifestyle was the connections to people and the resources most others don't have access to. My sister, Sarah, had a boss who owned a private plane and had offered on many occasions that I could use it to visit her. It was time to cash in on that offer, even if it wasn't to see Sarah, and I was happily surprised the pilot and the plane were available for a late-night flight to Houston. I'll never forget how sexy Trudie looked when the hostess brought her to me. It was a miracle I didn't slide under the table to have an appetizer of her pussy right then and there.

My little vixen always became submissive when Dr. Pierce was present. Most often I wanted my girl for myself, but sometimes

I liked to evoke my alter ego to entertain my alpha side. I've had my share of women to play with, however, most didn't like to be submissive. Now that I'd had the chance to meet Trudie's father, I understood why becoming submissive was an escape for her. She'd had to fight for control and recognition for years with her dad. And I may have been presuming this, but the horrible way Latina people are often treated may have kept her, from just being herself. The pressures put on her and that she freely accepted, appeared to shroud her natural state of balance. I've written and read hundreds of articles on the topic. Trudie was just starting to realize that something had to give, and I was more than happy to take charge in the bedroom when she allowed it.

After our rushed dinner we disappeared into a coat closet at the banquet side of the building. We cloistered ourselves deep in the back and I ripped off her yoga pants and made fast work of her soaking pussy. She begged me to fuck her—hard and fast—and I was happy to oblige. Her ass bounced and absorbed the impact as I drove my cock into her from behind. Holding her hands locked above her head, I described every filthy thing I wanted to do to her when I came back and told her that she better be ready to take me when I did. I was going to come too fast, but given that our time was short, I planned to enjoy the quick ride. I reached around her waist with one hand and found the plump nub of her clit hard and waiting for release.

"Come now, baby. Let me feel you pulsing around my cock." She moaned loudly and I released her hands to cover her mouth. The shriek she let out was explosive and my cock felt the same as I pumped into her every ounce of cum my balls housed. *Fuck.* Never had I ever been reduced to whimpering after coming so hard. I wished we had more time to come down from our high together but the buzz from my pocket informed me that I had to go.

We said our goodbyes, her hand in mine, as we walked to my awaiting car. I promised to text her when I arrived at the hotel and planted one last possessive kiss on her now reddened lips. "I'm not finished with you, Trudie. Not by a long shot. I love you."

Thinking back to the first time I met Trudie in San Francisco; I realized I should have known that we would be a couple. Anyone who could stand up to me was worth getting to know. I sent her my promised text once I arrived and fell asleep dreaming about how we would have looked to a stranger had they walked into that closet while I took her. So fucking hot. I wasn't sure I'd ever look at her the same again—the sexy, sensual, submissive, sassy, secondary school teacher. *Damn! I'm never going to sleep tonight.*

CHAPTER 12

TRUDIE

Monday morning felt like all the malaise memes I could remember. On the flip side, all the positive, perky ones seemed annoying too. Normally, I was a glass completely full person, but that was before I had Alex in my life. Not that he dampened my spirit or anything—it was that when I knew I wouldn't be seeing him that day, it took the air from my sails. I missed him. He added color to my life. Speaking of color...

"*Hola, chica!*" My good friend Jody blew into my room with nary a knock on the door.

"*Hola, chica,*" I responded less exuberantly.

"How was your weekend, and why aren't you all bubbly-like?"

I dropped my head into my hands propped on my desk and pouted. "It was great, and over too quickly."

Unaffected by my lack of enthusiasm, she continued, "I totally understand what you mean. I've been painting gourds and decorating my house with all-natural décor for the holidays. There isn't going to be one store-bought anything in my home this year." She placed a googly-eyed gourd on my desk to make her point.

"Aw! So adorable. I'm sure your family will appreciate all your efforts." I pasted on a big smile and wondered what my holidays would look like this year.

"You would hope, but highly unlikely. All they want is food. My kids finally launched and both are on shoestring budgets. Free washer and dryer and a meal keep them coming home, and I'm not embarrassed to say I like it this way. I might not see them otherwise, and that thought keeps me up at night." She twirled a dried maple leaf that had been sitting on the window ledge and stared out to a dreary, wet fall day. "Oh well." Placing the leaf back down she came to stand in front of my desk and mirrored my pose.

"Don't despair, darling. Whatever has you down will pass soon enough. In the meantime, I wanted you to know that Ella has been doing great with the art rotation. I've shown her several mediums she can use to express her anxiety. It's inspiring to see her mix colors and then assign emotions to them. Her emotional range is growing and I'm thrilled at how much growth she has made so quickly. I'd like to find a few contests where she could show her work beyond the district's regular Reflections program."

"Oh, my goodness, Jody! That's fantastic. I did see some subtle changes in her attitude this past week and noted them in her file to discuss later. I'm thrilled that our program is having an impact on these kids." I jumped up and ran around my desk to give her a big hug.

"We're making a difference. Ahhhh!" She screeched and hugged me and we jumped in a circle until Delano walked into the room.

"Uh, should I wait in the hall?" His deadpan question made us giggle and I motioned for him to come in.

As Jody walked out of the room, I shouted, "You're fabulous, girl!"

"I know!" She bellowed back. She knew how to change a mood, that's for sure.

I pulled myself back together by writing assignments on the board and lobbing questions at Delano about his weekend. I asked if he was feeling more confidence in his mastery of the vocabulary words.

"Ms. Gonzalez, I am a little confused about a few words I keep hearing, but when I spell them, they aren't right. They are *similar* and *frustrated*." He opened his vocabulary speller and showed me last week's words. "See, this is how they are spelled, except I keep hearing people saying *sim-u-lar*." He stretched the word out for clarity. "And the other is *flus-trated*."

I smiled at the seriousness of his comparison between the two. He was really applying himself and I could see how "frustrated" he truly was discerning the differences.

I asked him to join me in the Rest and Return area. I needed a minute to decide how I wanted to answer his question, and I thought he might like some time to ruminate on the answer.

"I can answer your question several different ways. I have a friend who has a speech impediment that makes it hard for her to say certain words. The only way she can say a word correctly is to slow it down and say each syllable. For others, it can be a cultural thing. Throughout history words have morphed due to lots of factors—regional and cultural—and without being mean, sometimes it's just lazy speech. I do love that you hear the difference and see the difference. Only you can decide how articulately you choose to speak, that is, so long as you don't have a medical issue affecting it. Do these explanations help you?" I sat bent over my knees with my hands clasped together awaiting his reply.

"Yeah. Just so long as I wasn't losing my hearing, I'm good." His wide-eyed look of relief and understanding told me he had picked up what I had put down."

"Wonderful. Please keep doing what you're doing and know that I'm here for you anytime." I patted his shoulder and stood up to take my place at the front of the room. A moment later he got up, too, and went back to his seat looking relieved.

"Okay class let's begin. It will come as no surprise that Thanksgiving is not far off and holidays can be challenging. Today's writing sprint will be describing one thing you are grateful for, and one challenge you might have to work through over the holidays. If you feel you would like some guidance on that challenge, please put a small star for your final period and I'll make sure to help you out. Any questions?" I looked for hands and then motioned for them to begin.

The rest of the day went smoothly until moments after the final bell. Bobby, the wrestling coach and a mentor for our group, dropped by my room.

"Hey, Trudie. Got a minute?" Bobby's swagger was on full display—he was wearing tight-fitted dark wash jeans and a black button-down shirt with cowboy boots. I'm not going to lie—he did look good, if not subtle.

I stopped packing my bag and sat behind my desk to keep some distance. Bobby was one of those people whose confidence was indisputable. He knew he had his act together and made sure everyone else knew it too. The kids loved the way he goofed around with them and pushed them physically and mentally to prove they were tough enough to handle anything life threw at them. Unfortunately, he intruded into my personal space and it made me feel uncomfortable. I didn't think he knew he was doing it and I didn't want him to think I was a bitch by pointing it out, but didn't he have a friend who told him not to do that to people? Sometimes it felt like he was hitting on me, except he was always going on about "his girlfriend this," and "his girlfriend that." I wasn't sure how to handle him, so I hid behind my desk instead.

"Ah, sure, Bobby. Have a seat." *Fuck my life!* He sat on the side of my desk! *Who does that anymore?*

"Bobby, I have to ask you to take a seat at any one of those desks. I'm not comfortable with you sitting on mine." His face fell, and he stood right next to where he was, crossing his bulging arms and posturing as if for a fight.

"I'm making *you* uncomfortable? Jeez, Trudie. I knew you were sensitive, but this is rude." His eyebrows pulled together, and his jaw ticked.

"I just don't think it's appropriate to park yourself on someone's desk."

I wasn't going to apologize for his presumed hurt feelings. He was wrong and I wasn't going to be a doormat to him being a dick.

"What was the reason you dropped by?" I changed the subject not wanting to prolong this exchange.

"I don't think it applies any longer—but I was going to ask if you wanted to join me for dinner. I have to be back here for a parent meeting, though now I think I'll skip the invitation and eat alone." Again, his jaw ticked and his eyes twitched—he couldn't understand why I wouldn't let him do what he wanted in my classroom.

"Thank you for thinking of me. I would have declined anyhow. I have a boyfriend and you have a girlfriend. I know we are colleagues, but I wouldn't want to have any tongues wagging if we were seen alone together." To my own ears, I sounded like an old-time schoolmarm, but the guy creeped me out.

"I don't get you. You're always so, 'Go, team. Work together.' So when I finally ask you out, you shoot me down. What did I ever do to you?"

I still couldn't figure out if this guy was being authentic or whether he had some weird agenda. There wasn't anything outwardly creepy, just a vibe I was getting, and after all the shit I'd been through, I had most definitely learned to listen to my inner voice.

"Bobby, please take what I'm going to say in the best light. You seem to be a great teacher and mentor, but your interpersonal game is off-putting to me, and I'm not comfortable having anything more than a professional relationship with you." You couldn't get more clinical than that. I was done with this conversation and stood to finish packing my bag. Robin walked by my room and I yelled to her to wait up, leaving Bobby to process what I had said. He was loud enough that I heard when he mumbled, "Bitch," as I passed him, walking out the door. *Saw that coming.*

CHAPTER 13

ALEXANDER

*H*ouston, we have a problem.

Not only did I not plan on staying in Houston for more than two days, but I also hadn't packed enough undies for any extra days. Now, I had two executives who thought what the CEO was trying to accomplish was bullshit, and, from his perspective, I should be the one to bring them in line with the program.

"Mr. Stanley, I am happy to assist you in helping your errant executives find their way back into the fold. However, it is not my responsibility to hold them in place." I stopped drinking my coffee, preferring water while I swallowed my rage pill.

I reset my expression to empathy mode. "You're in a tough spot, sir. Getting non-compliant people to do a one-eighty is nearly impossible. You will have to decide whether to keep your executives or let them go. Please schedule thirty-minute appointments with each of them before lunch. My flight leaves at four o'clock."

I stood and shook his hand, a little resentful that we hadn't had this conversation the day before. I gave him a reassuring smile and told him I would be back once I heard from his admin about appointment times and then took the elevator to the cafeteria to read my emails with some good coffee. Trudie had sent me an email about how the kids were progressing in our program, and Eloise updated me on the improvements made these past two weeks with her teaching staff. I loved making a difference, especially with kids. The only way we got functioning, community-oriented adults, was to nurture that in children.

A text came through directing me to the executive conference room, where I would try to persuade one of the executives to make a good decision. My recommendations would be recorded and submitted to the rest of the executive team and, from there, I would be on my way to the airport. I needed to get my hands on my spicy vixen tonight as we had unfinished business that couldn't wait any longer.

My phone pinged as I took my seat in the conference room. My parents, who contacted me at the worst times—such as during an intimate moment with my girlfriend or when I was with clients. They would pester me until I answered, like now, while I was between obstinate executives.

I chose an automatic response from my phone, *In a meeting*, followed by another text: *Can't talk. Will call later*. In response I got a message with four exclamation points and then a phone call. I wasn't going to give in to my mother's impatience. The time had come to stop that nonsense and use behavioral modification techniques to address her childlike stubbornness. I pushed her call to voice mail and shut my phone off. Whatever it was could wait until I was finished.

I shoved my phone in my pocket and turned back to the older woman on the other side of the conference table.

Dear Mrs. Reinhold went on and on about how preposterous that after all her years of service to this company, she had to change her ways. I unpacked all my behavioral psychological tricks to get her to understand that change was inevitable, and her choices were few in these circumstances.

"So, what you're saying, is that I will be fired over this? That my thirty loyal years of service will mean nothing?" Her fingers turned white as she strangled each digit in her clasp.

"I'm afraid so. Like every company out there, change is expected and inevitable." I said, stretching my hand toward the window as I stood and shoving my other hand in my pocket. It was time to pull a scene from my high school drama class final to illuminate her options. I hung my head and pushed out my bottom lip, walked across the room like I had just lost my dog, and then sighed the deepest sigh a frustrated consultant could politely get away with.

"Mrs. Reinhold, I can imagine how frustrated you are at this moment. Mr. Stanley and the rest of the team only want what is best for the whole of the company. Everyone is being asked to make sacrifices, and frankly, most will have to change more than your role requires. The question that only you can answer is are you ready to move on to new experiences outside this building or inside this building? I'm going to let you ponder that question while I pack up my things. Please let Mr. Stanley know of your decision by the end of the day Friday. Best of luck either way." Drop mic. Exit stage left. Cue the band. I was out of there.

By the time I remembered to turn on my phone, I was back in a cab, headed for the airport. Just as it came back online there was a call from my older sister, Tabitha. This surely wasn't a good sign. If past memory served me, after a series of texts and calls without me responding, a call from Tabitha meant that my mother had turned her histrionics in her direction. This was bad.

"Hey there, big sis. To what do I owe the pleasure?" I loved patronizing her whenever I got the opportunity.

"Don't you 'Hey there,' me, you dumbass. Why didn't you answer Mom's calls? She's been blowing up my phone for the past hour while I was interviewing Mariana Flowers, the biggest event planner in New York City." She made a choking sound in disgust.

"With all due respect, you're the dumbass. Did you actually answer her call? Why didn't you turn your phone off?" I would have thought my Mensa member sister would have figured out how to ignore her mother better.

"I was going to, but when Mariana asked who it was, I couldn't tell her it was my mother and then ignore her call. That would have been rude. I mean, the best thing I learned from Mom was how to keep up appearances."

I shook my head. "Yeah, appearances. Fine. Listen, what was so important that she couldn't wait an hour? A broken nail. Her cat is ignoring her again?" I let out a long, deflated sigh, feeling my own disgust regarding our mother.

I heard a pop and then a glug. "Thanksgiving," she belched without so much as a hesitation. "When would you arrive for the weekend?" Another belch. My sister was truly a sophisticated woman to everyone who didn't know her. For the rest of us, she was worse than a college coed bonging a beer.

I scrubbed my face, knowing it was time to tell her the bad news. I would then have to call my mother to inform her as well.

"Sorry, Sis, I won't be home for Thanksgiving this year. I'm hanging out with Trudie and her family. She's finally decided I'm worth the introduction." I chuckled.

"No shit! Alex! That's awesome, hashtag-not-so-awesome for the rest of us."

"I know. I'm really going to miss you and Sarah and your stupid boyfriend. Are you still in love with numbnuts?" My sole job as a younger brother was to aggravate my sister and she was due for some obnoxious behavior.

"When are you going to respect the men I date? Seriously, did I ever do that to you?"

Feeling bad, I conceded, "No, you didn't. Sorry."

"Thank you, but yeah, I dumped his ass last month. He was a good lay, but his grammar sucked, and my ears were bleeding listening to him yammer on about soil pH."

"Unbelievable. You're the worst! Have you ever considered dating someone who challenged you? Someone you may have interviewed who gave back to society something relevant or humanitarian. And I'm not talking about composting."

There was a loud "ugh" on her end. I guess I pushed one of her buttons.

"Sure, Alex. They are all lined up down the hall, waiting for me to pick one of them. God knows they would love to be in the family limelight or have our money to throw around. You know as well as I do that's all bullshit. Finding someone who loves you for who you are is a needle in a haystack." She went silent, and I gave her the moment she needed. "Do you love Trudie? Does she love you for you?" she whimpered.

She sniffed and honked her nose. Another sound only for her family. I felt her pain and frustration, which had plagued all of us siblings for many years. Had I not found Trudie by accident, I'm positive I wouldn't have found someone like her at all.

"I do, Tab. I really do. It took Trudie some time to trust me, and we've certainly had our struggles, but we have each other's backs and that alone is the link that binds us together. That and she does this thing with her tongue..."

"STOP! I don't need—blech!" She faked a gag into the receiver while I cracked up on my end. "You are the worst!"

"Yeah, I am, and you love it. If you decide to run away this Thanksgiving, come to Detroit, and I'll save you a seat." I knew it wasn't my place to invite my family to Trudie's mother's house when I was just meeting her for the first time, but hey, holidays were always more fun when unexpected guests arrived.

"Wow! Um, thanks, but what about Sarah? We can't leave her alone with our parents, can we?"

"Oh, hell no. Book your flights for Wednesday, and we'll call Mom and Dad when you arrive safely at my apartment. Then they won't be able to pull strings to put you both on the No-Fly List."

"You're evil."

"No, I'm not. I'm finally living my life on my terms, and so should you."

"I love you, Alex. I'll let you know what I decide."

"I love you too, Tab. You deserve the best—always."

Our call ended and so did my taxi ride. If this conversation had taught me anything, it was that I needed to stay close to my sisters and share my journey with them. They were the first women who always had my back. I often thought the phrase, "I'm truly blessed," was trite and self-effacing, though today, I finally understood the profound impact of having love and sincere support in my life.

CHAPTER 14

TRUDIE

The mentors were working with a new group of kids. Every two weeks each group rotated, and on this day, I was blessed with Tomás, RaeLynn, and Tina. They were grouped together due to their incredible shyness. One of these kids was a natural leader and I wanted them to have an opportunity to be heard over stronger personalities.

I took my group to the media center to sit in the cushy lounge chairs placed in a circle under a skylight. The natural lighting and the quiet were bliss after another chaotic day. I waved to Marsha as she walked out of her office for the day and motioned for the kids to pick a seat and get out their notebooks to write.

"Hello, my fabulous people!" I proclaimed. Then I took a seat and turned my decibel level way down, whispering conspiratorially, "Any ridiculous stuff go down today? You know, like anyone expel gas in gym while pinning another student to the mat?" The belly laugh they all gave was a terrific way to settle their nerves, and I wanted to help them remember that we're all human with human idiosyncrasies.

I was just getting ready to speak again when Tomás spoke up, "I don't know about wrestling, but I did hear Custodian Leonardo farting in his office when I went down there for a broom."

The kids most definitely laughed at that, though I should have thought through that joke a little more now that they were spying on the staff. Okay, not spying, just—poor timing.

"Thank you for that, Tomás. Like I said, we're all human. Moving on. Today's exercise will be twofold. First, a short writing sprint to open your mind to future possibilities and second, pranayama breathing." The inquisitive looks on their faces were priceless. These were the kids' teachers begged for. They were thirsty to learn and were the textbook definition of sponges.

"Your writing sprint topic is: If I possessed the ability to lead, how would I do it? You have fifteen minutes and then I'll collect them. I will not be sharing these with the group. Move wherever it's comfortable for you to write, so long as it's in the media center."

While they got settled and began their work, I stepped into the hall to catch up on my emails and texts. One was from my mom, who wanted to know if my "gentleman friend" would be joining us for Thanksgiving and what time I was coming over next week to cook. Another from Zander informing me that he was still dating Olivia, and she was coming to dinner so we should make enough food. And a very vague text from Alex saying he finally broke free from his client and that I would see him soon. Oh, and a second one asking if I could pick up some orange sherbet and some good champagne. *Hmm, wonder what he has planned.*

I caught myself up and walked through the media center door just as my phone timer played Donna Summer and Barbra Streisand's "Enough is Enough." It was decades old, but I loved the message and the beat.

"All right, my pretties, please put those over by my bag and let's stretch out by the windows to empty our minds and fill our souls." I grabbed a tufted pillow, set it to the side, and laid myself perpendicular to their position so they could see me better.

"It's important to empty your mind every day, much like brushing your teeth. Please tell me you're brushing your teeth?" They all giggled and followed my lead, lying in corpse pose, Shavasana. "Breathe in and out through your nose, doing your best impersonation of Darth Vader." I demonstrated and let them play with that for a while.

"Sometimes, when I'm stressed, or need to get focused on something that means a lot to me, I use my yoga breathing, called pranayama, and settle myself down with just a few repetitions. Obviously, we won't always have a place to lie down, so you can find a chair or stand by yourself somewhere, and I can assure you after practicing daily for a few minutes you'll become masters and move from minutes to seconds to gain your control. It's very effective. Let's do ten as a group."

Breathing as a unit was immensely powerful. It was like we were one organism connecting on a cellular level. You might be skeptical until you experience it yourself. Even though we reached ten together, I let them breathe for two more minutes on their own. Incredibly, they continued feeling each other's energy and rhythm, growing stronger because of it.

I sat up cross-legged and held up the pillow, asking if anyone needed it to help them sit straighter. Tina grabbed it and got comfortable next to me. She was so sweet. I closed my eyes and placed my hands on my knees—not everyone believes in placing their hands at heart center, and it wasn't my intention to offend anyone. And my incantation wasn't typical of a yoga class—nevertheless, it was just as powerful.

"I would like you to repeat after me a closing mantra I use when I need to feel brave." The kids nodded and mirrored my pose.

"I am warrior! I am strong enough, smart enough, and brave enough to conquer all my fears. I might need help sometimes to do it, but I will be successful. I will prevail!" My whimsy and theatrics were more for their age group than my usual practice.

I knew about these kids' parents—sometimes I had more than a glimpse of their family life. Tina was half of a set of twins whose brother passed shortly after birth. You could see the gaping hole in her heart, and I had no way of knowing how to fix that. Rae-Lynn, well, she was in sixth grade and since her parents were in the military, this was her fourth school since kindergarten. How does a kid make friends when they can barely finish a school year in one place? And then, there was Tomás. He came from a loving family that barely spoke English. He was incredibly resourceful and had created his own company, working as a Spanish tutor for parents who wanted their children to learn the language at a young age. Since he was eight years old, he'd been making money for his family and now at the ripe old age of thirteen, he was tutoring no less than ten kids a week, making over a thousand dollars a month. Unfortunately, that didn't give him much time to make friends and find other interests that kids should explore.

I praised my kids and we all walked to the front of the school. After they were picked up, I pondered more about what some of these kids had to endure at too young an age. Shit, when I was that age, I was dancing three nights a week, and had my head in a book all the time, or I was writing the next teenage super novel. I had sleepovers, and played miniature golf, and so much more, without thoughts of making money for my family or having to move for my parents' work the next day. It was no wonder we all had childhood trauma, even with seemingly ordinary lives.

I stopped at my mom's favorite bakery and brought her favorite cookies and the book I had finished while Alex was away. Oh, was it steamy. I helped myself to a few cookies myself, trying to satisfy my craving for something sweet. I hoped Alex planned to come over that night. Those few lines from the book had made me horny.

My mom and I planned out our menu for Thanksgiving and split up the grocery shopping. It was a big deal for our family to have each of our favorite dishes. There was something symbolic about marshmallow-covered sweet potatoes, spicy corn relish, and cornbread. Beef filled tamales and empanadas filled with chicken were also crucial for our Hispanic family. The only other American dish served was cranberry sauce. Mom always added orange zest to hers, though Ruby's family insisted it be from a can and cut into slices. To each her own.

It was almost seven o'clock by the time I got back from the market and unpacked my groceries. I was pooped! I ate my Lean Pocket and mandarin orange as I undressed and laid out my clothes for the next day. It was Friday, and Eloise had promised to meet with me and Alex to read through the initial reports he planned to submit to the school board.

After a long, hot shower, I decided to skip watching TV and crawled into bed, opening a new book I had picked up at the grocery store. Of course, it was a romance, but my tastes had changed after meeting Dr. Alexander Pierce. He had turned my mind inside out, and when his eyes bore down on me, I thought I'd given my soul to one hot devil. One of my favorite authors had just started writing taboo romances with innocent illustrated covers—I don't think the grocery store knew what they were carrying. Not that I was complaining.

A knock on my door startled me just as I read those exact words in my book. Freaky! I tiptoed my way down the hall, hoping it was Alex so I could fling the door open and dive into his bulging arms. I looked through the peephole and smacked a hand over my mouth, screaming internally. It was Jared! What the hell was he doing here? I couldn't open the door to him looking like this—I was half naked. But it turned out I didn't have to answer the door—I heard a deep rumble of a threatening voice barking at Jared to get lost.

There was only one voice that put fear in my heart like that and it wasn't Jared's.

"Hey, man. I-I was just checking in on Trudie. She, uh, looked nervous when I saw her last week." I wished I could have seen his face because his words reeked of wishy-washy nonsense.

"Nervous about seeing you again or nervous having her boyfriend meet a four-hour fling from a plane ride four months ago?" *Oh, snap!*

"What's your problem, man? You don't own her. She can see who she wants." I could almost picture the maniacal grimace on Alex's face when he heard that.

"She can do whatever she wants with whomever she wants but don't assume that includes you. She made her choice, and it wasn't you. Nothing personal, man, but she's mine. I think it's time for you to go."

There was silence for a full minute before the heavy steps of a pissed-off Jared faded down the hall. I was so happy with myself for not opening the door. That was a no-win situation, and the fact that my indecision about what to do saved me from having to deal with both men was a huge relief.

There was another knock—actually, one hard bang, followed by, "I know you're in there." My heart raced, and my juices began to flow. I could have opened the door immediately, but instead, I hopped from foot to foot in a playful mood. "Who's there?"

I pressed my cheek to the door and heard his husky chuckle. It made me smile. I traced circles with my finger on the door, first in one direction, then the other, waiting for his next move.

"I'd like to say I'm the Big Bad Wolf, except you told me Daniel said that to Ruby when they first got involved, and I'm no copycat. So, I'll say it's Santa Claus bringing my little girl a very special gift."

He was very good. I clapped my hands like the little girl he'd just described and sang with glee, "What did you bring me, Santa?"

"Open the door, sweetheart, and I'll show you."

Not wasting a minute, I unlocked the door and slid the chain off. There he stood, his pecs stretching across a straining cotton t-shirt under his long wool coat. His hair fell over his forehead, and he was wet and wild, looking like an animal ready to pounce on his prey. *Come and get me, baby.*

Alex stepped in, slammed the door, and pinned me against it. His head pressed against mine as he breathed in my scent and gently combed my hair through his very talented fingers. I'd thought he would already be inside me, but he'd downshifted his adrenaline from full throttle to coasting, which I loved even better.

"I love this time of year, Santa."

He pressed his palm into my breast while he blew in my ear, "I missed your smell. Your shampoo turns me on." More wet little kisses pressed down my jawline, sending tingles to my toes and my womanly places.

Strong hands pulled my hips tightly to his own and we both moaned our pleasure, knowing how good we were when we were together like this. He moved his mouth over mine, hovering and breathing in small gasps, absorbing my aura and connecting us even closer. *Mmm.* I pushed his coat off his broad shoulders, letting it puddle on the floor while his hands moved to my ass cheeks.

Somehow, his massive hands covered more than each cheek, making me feel small beneath him. I was small in stature but not in curves. It took a sizable man to handle all of them, and Alex was my perfect partner. He peppered kisses across my shoulders, pushed my pajama spaghetti straps down, and then surprised me by licking me from my clavicle to my ear. *Fuck did that feel good.* He had said he'd brought a surprise, and so far, he hadn't disappointed me.

"Baby, your skin smells like vanilla and cinnamon. I can't figure out how you do it, but I could eat you like a caramel sundae. My caramel sundae." The trail of his tongue was replaced with his index finger tracing down between my breasts while the other hand still kneaded my ass. My mind was reeling with these powerful sensations, not knowing where to focus first.

"Alex," I purred.

"Tell me what you want, baby." I cupped his cock through his trousers and he hissed his appreciation. "You want my cock, huh?" I nodded. "How do you want it, sweetheart? Clean or dirty?"

Oh my God! A low moan started in my belly and traveled up my throat until I could only respond with a croaky "Yes."

He gave me a devilish smile. He had to know by now when he spoke to me that way, my brain turned to mush. I wasn't even sure what the question was, only that I wanted what he had offered.

"Dirty it is, then." His tone deepened and a sound I'd never heard him make rumbled through his chest and came out as a guttural growl. "Go to your room while I lock up."

He didn't have to ask me twice. Once I found my land legs again, I hobbled down the hallway, pulling my top off and dropping it somewhere along the way. I waited on the edge of the bed, thinking how amazing tonight was going to be. We had only been apart for four nights, yet it felt like a year. When had this relationship grown into dependency? My cells craved to be next to him. Feeling the energy and strength and comfort from him was something I'd never experienced with anyone, not even Sam, and we had dated for six years.

I almost went looking for him because he was taking so long, but he finally entered the room carrying the uncorked champagne bottle and the container of orange sherbet. So that's what this was all about. He walked past me and entered the ensuite bathroom, placing each item on the edge of the tub, only pausing to look over his shoulder into the counter mirror and then back to the framed mirror hanging on the wall above the tub. He rubbed his jaw, assessing something as he peered into the reflective glass. Moments later, he strutted up to the bed and used his knees to spread my thighs, and a rush of wetness pooled at their apex. He placed his hands on my shoulders and looked down at my face, licking his lips while his forehead crinkled. I wrestled internally, wondering if I should ask him what was on his mind or just let him lead me down the filthy path I knew he was dying to tread.

My courage spiked, and I asked a question that ended up sounding like a child's: "Why is dessert in the bathroom?" I could have added the word, 'Daddy' after that question, but that was a fantasy we hadn't explored yet, and tonight was already a treat with a visit from Santa.

He ignored my question and rubbed my shoulders more firmly instead.

"Unzip my pants and take me out." *Gulp.* The confidence and directness of his statement ignited me into action immediately. The ratcheting sound of the zipper's teeth being pulled apart was an aphrodisiac to my ears. When I reached the bottom, I saw that his crown was peaking up past his boxers, ready to greet me. Moist beads of precum glazed his smooth, velvety head, making my mouth water. I leaned forward, flattening my tongue, and licked it off slowly like eating salted ice cream from a spoon. So good.

"Yes, baby, yes. You're such a good girl."

"Mmm," I moaned as I sucked his head, finishing with a pop. He lifted me under my arms and yanked off my pants before removing his just as quickly.

"We need to celebrate this holiday in decadent style, Trudie. Walk." He took my hand and pulled me after him into the bathroom, placing me against the empty countertop. In a flash, he was on his knees, pressing his nose into my wet pussy. He used only the tip of his tongue to dig into the flesh above my clit, challenging me to keep it together.

I gasped and my head fell back in ecstasy. I may have mentioned how talented his fingers and dick were, but did I mention the unspeakable things he could do with his tongue? He could lick his lips, and my imagination would do the rest. I've almost come just from that alone.

I ran my hands from the short hairs at the base of his neck to the long tufts on top and gently pulled at them—he rewarded me with an appreciative moan. If hairpulling got my man excited, then he would be in perpetual bliss. I loved his thick hair. I pulled it again and he stood, grabbing my face and forcing his tongue into my mouth. He entwined his tongue with mine, branding my mouth with my essence and his own distinct taste.

"My God, woman. I can't get enough of you. You keep finding ways to make me go wild."

"Then we are a perfect pair because I don't see an end to the possibilities you keep presenting to me. I love you, Alex. I think I did from the first time I met you—asshole and all."

"I should have known you were the one for me. No one has ever made me work so hard to please them. You make me better."

CHAPTER 15

ALEXANDER

I felt like an animal every time I was within fifty feet of Trudie. The roughness with which I commanded her and pushed her to explore the filthiest of things blew my mind. She may not have trusted me as a person, but it had nothing to do with whether she trusted me in bed.

I lifted her up on the counter and reached for the champagne bottle. I poured a small sip between her bruised red lips and devoured her mouth in a sparkling sweet kiss. "Yum," she replied. Yum, indeed. I tore myself from her mouth, leaned her back, and poured a river of sweetness down to her stomach that pooled in the sexy swirl of her belly button. I lapped up every inch of its trail and poured another round as she squirmed and moaned my name over and over again. The orange sherbet sitting next to the bathtub was just an arm's reach away, and by the way she screamed when I dropped a dollop on top of the pooled belly-button drink, I knew I was on the right track to make this night one for the ages. The combination of treats created an elixir of delight in my mouth. Her skin, the wine, and the orange was the most extraordinary taste I'd ever eaten.

"Fuck, baby, you taste incredible. I want to eat every bit of you with this stuff."

I kept returning to her mouth, letting her enjoy every bite, and when her eyes rolled back into her head, I knew she was long gone.

"More, Alex, more!" She cried. "I want your cock in me, please, Alex. I want to come." Her hips bucked twice, encouraging me to stop her torture, except I wasn't done. Not by a long shot. The ice cream was melting, and I could only think of one place the cold would cause her to go mad. She stared at me wanton and drunk on all the erotic sensations I'd placed on her. Going back on my knees again, I scooped an extra-large spoonful of orange goodness and placed it just above the small patch of hair prominently displayed on her mound, watching as she came undone while it slowly melted into the seam of her pussy, over her clit, and into her tight hole. I was out of my mind seeing it happen. If I were a real pervert, I would have videotaped the whole thing to watch a million times while getting off.

"I wish you could see this, baby. Your pussy is the perfect Creamsicle. I hope you don't mind me eating it because it would be a waste to let it fall off." My taunting was cruel, though Trudie had learned it was part of our playtime—I played hard and I played to win.

"God damn it, Alex. Eat me now! I can't take it anymore." *Yes, ma'am.*

I commenced enjoying the best meal I'd eaten in a week. I dove deeply into her folds, flicking her clit in short bursts and then flattening my tongue to envelop her whole organ. Her hands returned to my hair and I felt like a king pleasing my queen. She panted each time I passed over her swollen bud, and when I inserted two large fingers into her hole, I had to clamp down on her thighs so she wouldn't fall off the counter. When I looked up, all I could see were glazed-over eyes and submission written all over her face. She was in bliss and I would make sure she came all over my face before I set her free.

I repositioned her farther onto her back as I found her G-spot and vowed to suck and finger fuck her hard until the end. I didn't have to wait long—she squirted liquid all over my face, screaming so loud I'm sure the neighbors all around her could hear.

"My God, Alex. I can't breathe. Please sit me up." I gripped her hand and pulled her upright. I was so deep into getting her off I didn't realize she was bent unnaturally against the mirror and the counter.

"I'm so sorry, baby. Are you hurt?" I hugged her tightly, pressing her wet brow against my shoulder. Her euphoria left her unstable and a little disoriented, and I was concerned that maybe I pushed her too hard.

"No. The angle was weird on my neck and I needed a full breath after . . . after those wizard-like moves you just did. I'm okay now."

"I think you're the magical wizard. I'm just Santa Claus, and I've never read a story starring Santa Claus as a sex star." We both cracked up, still absorbing the shockwaves of our sexcapades. I bent down and opened the lower drawer to get a washcloth. The food I had poured over her was starting to get tacky and I didn't want her to get any kind of infection that would keep me from having her again.

I was still hard, not having given into my desires yet, but as I wiped her pussy clean, I kissed my little vixen softly, licking her sweet lips each time I finished a kiss. My cock needed release and I knew from my reconnaissance earlier just how I would take her.

"Come here, gorgeous, I have one more special gift for you." She focused quickly and directed her laser eyes at my throbbing purple head.

"Please, Santa, I've been a very good girl." She licked her lips in anticipation, though those lips wouldn't touch my dick again tonight.

"So I see. Put your hands on the side of the tub and don't move them."

I stepped back looking at her toned full ass. She needed to have her legs farther apart so I could press deeply into her crack when I was ready. I used my feet to kick her legs wider, enjoying the goose bumps that popped up in her excitement. I looked again pleased with her posture. I opened the top drawer of her vanity to pull out a hair tie. Stepping back and positioning myself where I was before, I collected her hair into a single ponytail and threaded my fingers through her mane until it was smooth and tightly wound into place. I gave a quick pull to get her attention.

"It's time to take this body for a ride, sweetheart. Use your safe word if it becomes too much. Your pussy has already come three times, but I know you have it in you to bring me home."

"Anything." She was back in her euphoric zone, and when I pressed my hand to her back, a visible shudder rippled up her body.

I hummed into her spine as I placed kisses down to the top of her ass cheeks. She had the cutest little beauty mark that looked something like a bumble bee, and I loved to focus on it whenever I took her from behind. I looked in the mirror at her heavy tits hanging down in full globes, her nipples pinched into tight nubs. I grabbed hold of my cock and pulled from the root several times, getting my blood to pump harder.

I watched as my girl waited for my first full push into her pucker. Her eyes closed, concentrating, and preparing herself. As I entered her slowly, I tingled all over as her ass muscles clenched around my cock. I would remember this moment for the rest of my life. Her face strained taking my length and girth. The way her mouth hung open trying to breathe stole my senses. As I became fully seated inside her, my throat let out a strangled sound that was foreign to me. It was wild and throaty, and fully expressed how deeply connected both physically and emotionally I was to her. Nothing had ever felt so good.

"Yesss!" Trudie hissed out. "So good, Alex. Thank you. Thank you," she repeated in between whooshes of air. I couldn't take my eyes off the picture we created together in the mirror.

"I'm so proud of you, baby. You take my cock so well." I growled.

I smacked her ass until it was pink and she whimpered with pleasure. I was reaching the brink of my orgasm and collected her ponytail in my hand, pulling it back tightly and forcing her neck to bend backward.

"I'm going to fill your ass to overflowing, baby. You'll come again when I do. Do you understand?" She didn't answer and I wasn't sure her mind was even in the room, so I asked again. "Trudie, do you understand me?"

It only took a few seconds, but I got the most perfect answer I could ask for: "Yes, sir." *Fuuuck, yes!* I didn't want her to be submissive all the time, just when we played. I wanted her to completely let go of every thought in her head and float off to a place of pure bliss. She was there and I was going to rocket her even higher.

"Now, baby. Give me what I want." I reached underneath her and gently pinched her clit and she exploded immediately. I pulled her hair one last time and held myself tightly against her ass as I came like I had never come before. My legs were wobbly from the exertion and perspiration beaded my brow. The only thing that really mattered was that my woman was sated beyond comprehension.

"You—that..." I couldn't finish my sentence, so I pulled her up from her waist and sat down on the floor, pulling her into my lap exhausted and complete.

She rested her head on my chest, her eyelashes brushing against the few hairs I had there. I rubbed her arm and cooed into her ear everything I was feeling. When the sensation of her eyelashes turned from butterfly kisses to wetness, I stopped in concern.

"Trudie. Are you crying?" I pushed her away from me so I could scan her dreamy face. Big droplets of salty tears dripped down as she tried a couple of times to speak through her hiccups.

"I don't know where my mind went, Alex. I'd never felt that feeling of weightlessness. It—was incredible. Scary. Full of freedom. What happened to me?" Her confusion and naivete about what pure bliss felt like were refreshing. Most people would never know how freeing it was to allow someone to own their body. It couldn't be accomplished unless there was 100 percent trust, and that alone spoke volumes to me about how far we had come as a couple. We'd finally found safety with each other and that feeling was priceless.

CHAPTER 16
TRUDIE

We should never be separated again. There was a seismic shift in the earth's tectonic plates when we'd been apart too long and then reunited. I wasn't sure if I'd ever walk straight again. What I could tell you was that for the first time in my life, I was at peace. A perfect stillness with tiny figurative sparkles of confetti coated my body, and in that peace, I felt an energy source I didn't know I'd possessed. It was heavenly.

I sat at my desk Friday morning unable to teach my rowdy class. It was the week before Thanksgiving and I'd already had three kids drop notes on my desk saying that they were leaving for an extended vacation and requested next week's homework to complete so that they could email it back before their break began. Was there ever a time that a teacher could do that crap? Never!

The bell had sounded for class to begin, and I was still looking out at the dusting of snow that swirled through the parking lot. If this kept up, I was going to have to dig my car out, and I haven't broken out my snow boots, or my winter coat, for that matter. There was a knock at my classroom door, and in fear of looking negligent, I pushed my chair back and announced to the kids to look at the board for their writing sprint prompt. I promised to be back shortly and headed for the door. It was Eloise. Busted.

"Good morning, Ms. Gonzalez. Feeling a little despondent this morning?" She pulled her glasses down her nose, eyeballing me.

I stifled a yawn and said, "Not so much despondent as exhausted. I barely slept last night, and the two cups of coffee this morning don't seem to be doing their job well enough."

She pushed her glasses back up and assessed me from head to toe.

"I'd say you even forgot to look in a mirror before you left this morning, because your shirt isn't buttoned correctly and your eyeliner is pretty uneven." *Yikes.*

"Jeezus," I hissed looking down at my cockeyed buttoning job. I turned to the lockers while reorganizing them one at a time so I wasn't exposing myself. Eloise didn't waste any time and began her questioning.

"Trudie, do you think Dr. Pierce is on top of the school board's project? I know he was supposed to be out of town for several days, but I haven't heard from him all week. Has he shared with you the status of his findings?"

Had he? My brain felt tased by her questions, and I wasn't sure which project was which anymore.

"I-I'm not sure really. We are having amazing results with our mentoring kids, and all the teachers I've spoken with over the past month seem to like Dr. Pierce. They have been implementing his suggestions, though there are several teachers I usually never see. I wish I was a 100 percent clear about what the school board's target is supposed to look like."

Her exasperated sigh confirmed my suspicions. "You don't know either, do you?" I asked.

Eloise pursed her lips and rested her hands on her ample hips. She looked conspiratorially left and right, making sure no one was listening. "From the get-go, this project seemed like a set up. Our school has the highest state testing records, more masters certifications, and better after-school programs than any school in our district, and not just middle schools."

I nodded, impressed, and took a step closer. "I knew we were the best. They spent a shit ton of money on Dr. Pierce, so what do you think they are really looking for?"

Eloise closed the distance and whispered in my ear. "Do not quote me on this, but I think they are trying to scare some teachers into early retirement. Budget cuts are coming, and this little charade might screw us all with huge class counts." She took two steps back and turned in a circle, scoping out the hallways around us.

"What?!" I whisper-screamed. "They laid off five teachers from our school last year. How the hell are we supposed to provide a quality education with thirty kids in a classroom? If they do this again, we'll be up to thirty-six. Even the best of us can't keep up with all the extra work." My arms were flailing all around my head like a sprinkler out of control.

"I understand, and don't think for a minute it's any easier on administrators. We get to deal with all the fallout: ranting parents, kids riddled with anxiety, and teachers losing their shit in ways that put their jobs in jeopardy. Trudie, I need you to get Dr. Pierce to include something about this in his reports, and not just once—like a lot!"

I'd never seen Eloise fall apart like this. She was the queen of cool, and the way she leaned on me for support meant she was at her wits end. Alex needed to sit down with us and help us figure some of this out. Did he know this was the board's hidden agenda? I wanted to believe he didn't know anything about this, but then again, he neglected to tell me about his ex's antics, and that caused a huge problem for us. He was leaving this evening to go back to New York to handle a few things and would return on Monday. I hoped he would have time today to come in.

I returned to my classroom later than planned and, of course, they were all either on their phones or sitting on their desks goofing around. *Kids.*

"Sorry about that, kiddos, let's take our seats and get back to work." The end of the day couldn't come fast enough. I sent a message to Marsha in the media center, hoping she would let some of my classes come down today to do some research, lightening my teaching time. God bless her, she moved her plans around to accommodate me.

By the end of the school day, I still hadn't seen a text from Alex. Every time I thought of his name, my uterus clapped her hands. The previous night had been off the charts, but he'd had to leave when my alarm went off. No morning sex or shower. Not even a cup of coffee.

I pouted and blew a raspberry on his belly. "You're no fun. How am I supposed to start my day off right when you have to leave so quickly?"

He ran his fingers through my hair like he was petting a cat.

"There, there, little one, I'll be back soon enough and we both know that your pussy is more like a kitten this morning. Better give her a rest." He did, however, give me a panty-melting kiss before he rolled off the bed and slid into his wrinkled trousers.

"Would you mind standing there, maybe turn just a little, yes! Right there. Don't move. You look delicious. Hmm. Okay, you can go." I breathed out a deep sigh, relishing his coy smile, cut abs, and the intentional flexing of his biceps.

"I'm glad you got your fill, baby. Now go get in the shower before I pin you back to that bed and then you'd have to explain to Eloise why you couldn't sit down all day." He chuckled and I was appalled that he would even think of doing that. *Wait for it. . . .* Okay, I had wanted that, and I was deliberately being a brat.

"Fine! Have it your way, but you'd better text me later." I rolled out my lower lip just for effect and flipped the covers back dramatically. "Have a wonderful day without me!" I called over my shoulder as I headed for the bathroom.

He had shouted back, "I won't have a wonderful day. I refuse to feel good when you're not with me. You are my queen!" I loved it when he picked up on my flights of fancy.

ALEXANDER

She was my queen and after last night, I was her minion. It crushed me to have to take off so quickly, but I had woken up moments before she did and looked at my phone. There were two emails from my parents, one each, the same topic. And a third from Dr. Williams, the micro-managing school board president demanding an updated report by the end of the day. It appeared that my morning habit of getting a jump on things had bitten me in the butt.

When I reached my car, I called my father, knowing he wouldn't pick up his phone that early and waited until I got home to do the same with my mother. Sadly, she kept her phone by her bed and always answered it like there was a five-alarm fire.

"What's wrong? Are you all right? Where are you?" Someday she'd learn to just let the call roll to voice mail.

"It's me, Mom, Alex. Nothing is wrong. I'm fine, and I'm still in Detroit." I tried to keep the disdain from my voice but failed miserably.

"Don't give me that tone. It's barely seven in the morning and already you're irritated with me?" Her shrill reprimand sounded like fingernails on a chalkboard.

I shook my head and resigned myself to being a "good boy."

"Sorry. Perhaps I should call later after breakfast."

"No, no. Just tell me why you had to call so damn early."

Telling her I wasn't coming home right after I irritated her wasn't going to go well. Nonetheless, it had to be done.

"I'm sorry to tell you I won't be home for Thanksgiving this year. I've made other plans and wanted you to know who to expect." The key to winning a negotiation was to stop talking after you've made your offer. *Zip it!*

"What do you mean, not coming? People are expecting you. How will that look to our guests?" See, that was the real problem with my family. It was always about optics, and that day I was drawing a permanent line in the sand about not giving two fucks how it made my parents look. That's a "them" problem. Not a "me" problem.

"I'm coming in later tonight to handle some business and personal things and leaving again Sunday afternoon. I'd love to see you and Dad for brunch on Saturday morning. Say eleven, at your club? Terrific. Love you, Mom. Have a great day." I hung up on her mid-dramatic breath and didn't answer the three calls she placed immediately afterward. I've taught countless parents and business magnates how to apply tough love. Of course, my family was a different breed altogether. I knew I should have practiced what I preached decades ago, but like most of us, I was waiting for a miracle to intercede so I didn't have to. Plain and simple, I was a hypocrite, but not any longer. I pulled up my big boy pants, laid out my plan, and so long as I didn't answer my phone all day, I could deal with the fallout the next morning.

With that behind me, I turned my focus to work, Texas work that is. Mr. Stanley had apparently grown a backbone in the previous twenty-four hours and accepted Mrs. Reinhold's resignation, effective January 1. *Hallelujah!* It seemed she liked the idea of mentoring and wished to share her wealth of knowledge at a center for underprivileged teens. *My best to you, madam.* The other guy decided he wasn't ready to retire and found it in his heart to learn some new business tricks to keep him relevant in the world of millennials. *Way to go, buddy.* See, tough love. It does business and family good, although kind packaging goes a long way to helping those people get over the hump of change.

My mind was mush, and coffee wasn't doing what it was designed to do, so I finally took a break for a shower and a short nap. My girl knew how to get the best out of me and I couldn't fault her for my lack of energy. I pulled up the messaging app on my phone, sending her a text to tell her how amazing she was, and then threw my phone on the bed.

I awoke to my phone alarm going off. *Shit!* I overslept and needed to get it together to catch my plane. Shuffling through the sheets, I found my phone, ordered a car to take me to the airport, and shoved it in my pocket. I hadn't unpacked since I had come home from Texas and thankfully, I was going to my apartment where I had everything I needed, so I slung my computer bag over my shoulder and whipped open the door.

By the time I looked at my phone again, I realized I had indeed typed out a message to Trudie three hours ago but never hit Send. She was going to kill me. I completed the process of touching the damn button, and sure enough, moments later those exact words showed up on my screen.

I sent ten bawling emoji followed by, "I'm sorry. Can you forgive me? I mean, it was kind of your fault."

Trudie: My fault? Qué?

Me: Yeah, you sucked all the life out of me, and I barely had enough energy to call my parents and answer my most important emails today.

Trudie: Like the one Eloise sent you? Or the one I sent you?

Me: Uhh, no. Just the one from Dr. Dinglehopper. He is so annoying.

Trudie: Dr. who?

Me: LOL. Dr. Williams from the school board.

Trudie: <laughing smiley face> What did he want?

Me: He wanted a report on where I was with the project.

Trudie: Did you send one to him?

Me: Not yet. I was able to make a draft but was too tired to finish. I'll work on it this weekend so he'll have it Monday morning.

Trudie: NOOOOOO! DO. NOT. SEND!

Me: Why? What's going on?

Trudie: Eloise thinks there is some sort of hidden agenda. Please don't send it until we talk. OK?

Me: A hidden agenda? Sure, I'll wait. Just arrived at the airport and I'm late to check in. I'll call you tonight once I get settled.

Trudie: Thanks, baby. Have a safe flight. I love you.

Me: I love you too. <heart>

Hmm. The plot thickens.

I was sliding my phone over the scanning device just as the gate person signaled to the counter person, she was shutting the door after me. *Phew!* I didn't normally cut it that close to boarding a plane but I stand by my earlier comment to Trudie that she threw off my game. My strict schedules and pristine work timelines had never been so sloppy. Another thing my parents would be appalled to hear. "To be early is to be on time, to be on time is to be late," had been deeply ingrained in my hypothalamus since my first swim meet as an eight-year-old. It made sense then and it made sense now, only the self-flagellation wasn't as deep as it had been in the past. Sometimes shit just happened and I was tired of turning myself inside out with their modus operandi.

The first thing I did when I landed was text Trudie asking her to call me after ten. The next was a conference call with my sisters to discuss the Turkey Troubles, as I had so cleverly named it. We needed a comprehensive plan that sealed any loopholes and another plan that included the upcoming Christmas holiday season. I was done with that too.

Given that I had already briefed Tabitha on my intention to miss Thanksgiving, I called her first.

"Hello, my darling sister."

"Ha! Right. Currently, I'm the only sister who knows how incredibly devious you are. Connect Sarah, and we can both blame you for leading us away from the family fold.

"I would like to amend my salutation to 'Hello, Miss Smart-as s.'"

"Exactly," she snarked.

I pushed the conference button and dialed Sarah. I wasn't sure which continent she was on at the moment—she was the luckiest of the siblings, always somewhere other than New York.

While we waited for her to pick up, Tabitha informed me she had pulled up the airlines' websites hoping we could book our flights immediately. I couldn't remember if I had mentioned this to Trudie yet. My days and conversations were a little messed up that week.

"Well, hello, little brother! To what do I owe the honor of your call?" I always loved the brightness of her voice. It changed my mood and always gave me hope when I felt down.

"I'm on the call too!" Tabitha yelled.

"Jeez Louise, Tabs. Relax. We can hear you," I scolded.

"I'm just so excited. We haven't had a three-way in a long time. I love them!" Did she even hear herself?

"Not a three-way, sis. That's taboo for me and my sisters. Hard no on that."

"Yeah, Tabs. Take it down a notch." Sarah jumped on my bandwagon.

"Fine. Alex, tell her why we're calling." That was my cue.

"Right. I'm not coming home for Thanksgiving this year. I'll be spending it with Trudie and her family." I plowed right through so we could move this along. "I am inviting you to bail on the traditional family get-together and join me in Detroit, Wednesday through the weekend."

"Uh, isn't that going to be the next *CSI* episode— 'Suicidal Son Sabotages Seasonal Ceremonial Dinner?' Huh. It has a nice ring to it." You could always count on Sarah to create an interesting TV show title.

"Ha! I love it!" Tabitha shouted. Again, with the shouting.

"Very funny. Tell me again why you wasted hundreds of thousands of Mom and Dad's dollars to get a business degree when you could have been sitting in a writers' room ripping off one-liners," I said, yawning through my own one-liner.

"Are you kidding? I'm too beautiful to waste behind closed doors." Sarah cracked herself up noting the obvious truth. She was gorgeous—not that I was one to check out my sisters. Sarah had an ass of steel from all the lunges she did, and Tabitha could choke any guy with his head between her thighs. *Not a bad way to go.*

"Noted. Anyway, are you in or out? Tabs was on the fence, with you being her deciding vote, I presume," I said, baiting them. "I suggested to Tabs that you both fly in and then call our parents to break the news. What's done will already be done and, well, we can always set the phone down and walk away while Mom wails about the injustice of it all. So what do you think?"

Again, I used my negotiating technique on my sisters and shut my mouth, letting them do what they'd like. While they carried on, I sent a note to Trudie inquiring about having a few extra guests for Thanksgiving. That's the kind of guy I was: ask for forgiveness, not permission. The girls laid out all the pros for us, and the cons of the fallout. Given the way their voices rose, I made the assumption they were excited for the change-up this holiday season.

"So, where are we ladies? In or out?" I had already made my choice so staying on the line for them was more of a courtesy.

They yelled their agreement unanimously, and I felt like a king on a throne. All my people were following me and we'd just won the war. Except, we hadn't. All I had was an army, not a victory.

Tabitha interjected, "I'm booking the flights now and we'll ar-rive about two o'clock. I'm hoping this party starts at a bar and ends, say, at a bar with me dry humping a hottie on the dance floor."

"TMI!" Sarah shouted. I laughed just picturing it.

"What do you mean too much information? How am I supposed to manifest my happy ending when I don't put it out to the universe?" More laughing from me.

"You sound like Trudie and her manifestations. I can't wait for you two to have some quality time with my girl. She's going to love you even more."

"Wait! She said she loved us?" Tabitha inquired carefully.

"Her words. She loved your banter and style. Too bad Sheila fucked up that night or you would have learned that yourselves. I missed so many opportunities to…"

"Enough! I don't need to visualize that any more than my sister's dry humping," Sarah cried.

"Good point." I cleared my throat and decided we needed to clarify one specific item that would make this scheme viable. "One last thing: when will you tell our parents you aren't coming? I already did this morning and I'm prepared to suffer through tomorrow's brunch hearing about it. I'm not mentioning your plans, if you thought I could soften the blow for you. We are all adults here and you'll have to take your tongue-lashings yourselves. I'm going to run back home to Detroit and hide under the proverbial covers." For this reason, I'd been known to my friends as a fast talker, who escaped the effects of his mouth while exiting stage left.

"I vote to wait until we get to Detroit. That way they can't get the FAA to keep us from flying," Sarah suggested.

I guffawed. "I said the same thing earlier."

"I'm with you on that, but won't that mean not telling her in advance? She puts on such a show with her guest list and catering and all. Her heart will be broken. And I bet Dad would want to join us." Tabitha said, and we all laughed.

"I'm not trying to be mean, guys. I've tried any number of strategies to get out of their events, but they always manage to wiggle enough guilt my way about not making them look like bad parents. I'm forty-two and if I don't make this change when I have solid reasons to do so, when will I ever break free?"

My car pulled up to my building and it was time to say goodbye to my sisters. We had sorted out enough of our escapade, and I had to call my lawyer.

"I've got to get going. Send me your flight information and I'll make sure you have a ride to my place in Detroit if I can't get you myself. Mum's the word on Mom, okay?" Ha, now I was cracking myself up.

"Good night, troublemaker," Tabitha quipped.

"It feels like we've established an underground movement to thwart parents all over the world. Okay, maybe that's too much high drama. I love you guys." Sarah's enthusiasm was moving, and it did feel like we were on a quest of sorts.

I smiled at my doorman and asked about his family—going through the necessary pleasantries that went with living in a high-end building. Unlike most though, I did care about his family and sponsored his kid's soccer team every year. Housekeeping had freshened my condo since I had alerted them of my arrival yesterday, and as always, a seasonal bouquet—this one with sunflowers, roses, and sprays of wheatgrass—adorned my counter.

I peeled off my jacket and kicked my shoes to the mat stationed by the door. I grabbed the remote that ensured I barely had to lift a finger around my home and pushed a series of buttons that closed my blinds, turned on some mood lighting, and started playing smooth jazz. My impending conversation would require me to be as calm as possible.

I ordered dinner through the building's catering app and then called my lawyer to discuss my financial future. While the phone rang, I walked over to the fireplace to study a family picture taken during my teenage years on a ski slope in Breckenridge, Colorado. If I recalled correctly, it was the last time we had taken a family vacation together with my dad's side of the family. My cousins and I had been close and spent most vacations together—however, that ended when my philandering Dad thought it was funny to grab my aunt's ass that same night after dinner. He claimed it was the alcohol. She, on the other hand, felt assaulted and chastised him for not knowing when to stop drinking. The worst part was that we all saw him do it, and we knew it was meant to be sexual, given the way he had draped himself over her shoulder. #NotGoodTimes.

Finally, Phil picked up the line.

"Hey, buddy, I almost forgot we had an appointment." Phil's breathiness could only mean two things, since he didn't exercise: he was having sex with his wife, or he'd just run up the stairs to have sex with his wife. Ever since college this man had had it bad for one woman, and let's just say, she had to be ready to go on a dime's notice.

"Uh, if this isn't convenient, we can reschedule."

"Nope. Just give me one sec." The sounds over the next few minutes were muffled but even a novice could figure out he was two yanks from getting off, and his wife, Amy—a very vocal woman—was close too. More shuffling and a noticeable kiss on the cheek, and he was back.

"So, you're finally cutting all your ties with your parents, huh?"

"Mostly. I'm sure after they learn I've cashed in the whole of my trust and sold off my shares in their businesses, they'll disown me anyway." My need for reassurance was high, thus my self-deprecating dismissal of the severity of my actions.

"Alex, I wouldn't be doing my job if I didn't tell you these abrupt changes will cause some repercussions, not only with your family but your community. People will see you pulling out and think something is going down, and then they will pull out too, causing a domino affect your parents will not survive."

Phil had only given me one serious speech in my life and it was a warning not to marry Sheila. I should have listened then, so this time, I agreed, I would take a pause and slow my roll on this request.

"Any suggestions to do all this another way that will save some face for my parents?"

"Wow, Alex. You've never listened to me so easily. First, why do you need to make all these changes, and, second, why are you hearing me for the first time?"

Yeah, I'd been an asshole to Phil on more than a few occasions. He took my shit because I paid him well and he was loyal to me to the end.

"I know, right? It's a girl—a woman—who has opened my eyes to a variety of things I've let go in my life. Things like being a better listener and getting what I want without being a dick. Learning how to breathe and relax and focus on what really matters and letting go of the shit that doesn't."

"She sounds amazing. What's her name?"

"Trudie. She's an English teacher at a middle school in Michigan, and I'm pretty sure she's the one."

"Whoa! The real one? Not the one your parents want you to have? Or the one who will make them look good?"

I laughed. "Yeah, the real one. She made me see how not dealing with my past was fucking up my life. It meant that I needed to take a deep dive at the way I've been living, and I'm done with it. No more standing in solidarity for pretense. No more putting up with my parents' guilt trips and whining to get what they want. And don't get me started on the foundation. They can keep it. No more worrying about optics."

"Damn. You're going all in."

"Yes. Help me put a plan together—now," I demanded.

He turned away from the phone and yelled, "Honey, I need a rain check. Alex needs me for a few hours." Phil putting a pin in sex—that's what real friendship looked like.

"Let's get to it."

CHAPTER 17

TRUDIE

I'm not going to lie, when Alex texted he wouldn't be able to chat the previous night my heart sank. His explanation was authentic, and so was his apology. Nonetheless, the ache I felt when he wasn't around was becoming problematic. I'd never been a clingy girl, especially after being raised by a man who had pushed me away all the time. My mom had taught me to be resilient, independent, and practical. All very important things a woman should learn—except it was exhausting not having someone else to ease the load at times. That's where Alex had weaseled his way into my mental fortress. I had trained my brain to be Fort Knox. Impenetrable. I wish I could have figured out what he did to alter my reality, allowing softness to percolate to the top. I could have rationalized it as the result of mind-blowing sex or all the delicious dinners, and parties, and flowers. All those things alone could have broken down my walls—though that wasn't what did it. It was the way he looked at me, held me, comforted me, and most importantly, protected me from my father's manipulation. He didn't have to do any of those things, but he did. Willingly, sincerely, and lovingly. I loved him for all of it. I wanted to give him my heart completely and without hesitation—so why, when he had to cancel a call or text or meet up, did I get all squirrely?

Ruby and I had plans to catch up later that afternoon for coffee and holiday shopping. In the meantime, it was self-care Saturday, starting with a full hour of yoga and meditation. The biggest feature of my tiny apartment was that it had a bath. I could sit and soak in a kelp mineral bath and forget all my troubles. I turned the water temperature as high as I could stand it and slipped in. I rested my head on a tiny inflatable pillow and languished in the rejuvenating liquid. I ruminated on the past months like I was watching a movie. I watched the transformation of both Alex and myself as we traversed our life experiences, growing stronger together. I rewound the movie again from the beginning and watched from a different perspective, one that sparked my soul and my sex. This version was much more intense, if not as fulfilling. Giving myself to a veritable stranger, letting him do things to me that words couldn't describe, was incredibly freeing. Never in my life had I felt as light as I did that first time we were together in that old moldy motel room. How could vulnerability equal safety? The two didn't seem to equate—yet for me, they did. My mind still couldn't figure that one out.

When the water had cooled to tepid, I pulled the plug. As I watched the greenish-gray liquid swirl around the drain, I felt my trepidation about being with Alex go down as well. I believed in him. I believed in us. We just needed a little more time to let things gel. To know if what we had would last forever. Unfortunately for both of us, his involvement at my school was coming to an end and that would be the true test of where this relationship would go.

Another hour later I was shaved, masked, and pleasured by Big Ben. *You can always count on that guy to deliver.* My phone buzzed and I was thrilled to see Alex's picture pop up. Truth be told, it wasn't just his picture. It was us at Belvedere Castle with me between his thick, athletic thighs and one of his hands on my boob while the other took the selfie. Yeah, butterflies danced in my lower abdomen when I thought of all the wonderful memories I'd had between those thighs.

"Well, hello there handsome," I purred just to rile him up.

"Well, hello to you too, gorgeous. I love the sound of your voice this morning."

"Too bad you don't get all the perks of being here in person," I taunted him.

"You're killing me, Trudie. Not fair." Poor baby.

"How is your trip going? Making mommy and daddy proud?" Why was I being so bitchy to him?

"Listen, smart-ass, that's one of the things I'm here to correct. I've already told my mom that I won't be at her Thanksgiving table and now I'm on my way to brunch to listen to her wail about how unfair and rude I'm being. The good news is that this will be the last time I'm ever going to have to deal with this. I'm drawing a permanent line in the sand with my parents. Of course, I'll be spending the rest of my life defending it. Nonetheless, it must be done."

"Wow! I'm impressed, Alex. You haven't talked about this since the gala. Are you sure you're ready to go to war over this?" I was biting my lip, genuinely nervous for him.

"Oh, this won't be the worst of it, sweetheart. The main reason for this trip, and why I couldn't speak with you last night, is that I'm divorcing my involvement in all their foundations, trusts, and businesses." He said that with much bravado, but I couldn't imagine him not freaking out internally about doing this.

"Alex! Seriously? Why do you have to go through all that? Can't you just say you're not going to be involved anymore?"

"That's what I have been doing for the past ten years and look where it has gotten me? Nowhere. It's time to sever these business relationships, and maybe sometime in the future, they will want to spend time with me, just because..."

"Oh, baby. I knew your relationship was complicated. I thought they appreciated you for the kind of man you are, not something they could use as a pawn. I'm truly sorry."

There was silence on both ends of the call. I don't know why I thought his troubles were merely superficial. The way he described his parents, and having met them, I knew they were ridiculous people, though I never thought they didn't love him for himself. Pretenses sucked.

"Thank you, baby. Don't worry about me. I'm emotionally dead inside in regard to my parents. My lawyer has drawn up papers relinquishing any hold on their assets beginning today. I've already been to the bank to withdraw any trusts and monies at my disposal now and opened a new entity to house those funds for future nonprofit ventures. I make a good living and don't need their money for myself. I would like to use what they have given me for other good causes though, like the mentoring program at Hart Middle School.

"My God, Alex. Who are you? You're like a modern-day Robin Hood. It's no wonder I love you."

"I wish I had my arms around you." His voice was husky and oozed sexiness.

"Me too. When will you be done with your parents?" I wanted to be available for him the moment he finished the war he was charging into.

"Probably by one o'clock. I'm going to the gym to burn off my anger and resentment immediately afterward and then visiting a colleague of mine from Columbia, Marco. We're considering expanding his business into new states and I thought that since I'm in Michigan so much, that maybe, if we—"

I cut him off, "You mean move here? Permanently? Because of me?" I gasped, trying to understand what he was getting at.

He gave a full belly laugh at my disbelief. "Yes, Trudie, mostly. Detroit has some resources we can tap into for a faster return on our investment than in other cities, specifically the car and medical industries."

"Never mind them—for me?" I knew I was being selfish, but hey, I had started this whole thing.

"Yes, sweetheart, because of you," he said, sounding like a devil. I wished he could fuck me with his voice because I felt impaled every time he spoke to me with his porn persona.

My heart was thumping and full of love and possibilities. I crossed everything in hopes that the meetings he had planned for today went well. He deserved to feel at peace about his family even if they couldn't see what an amazing man he was.

"When will you be back to your apartment?" I was fishing. I needed to see him as soon as he came home. *Home? Ha, would I be his new home?*

"Late, I'm afraid. My flight won't take off until six, and there appears to be a cold front with some snow behind it. Wish me luck getting out on time."

"Good luck, Alex. I miss you." There may have been a whine in my tone. Sometimes I can't hear well.

"I miss you too. Uh, Trudie?" There was trepidation in his voice. He was holding back something, and that never worked out well.

"Should I be nervous?"

"Maybe? I may have invited my sisters for Thanksgiving. Do you think it would be okay for them to join us at your mom's house?"

"You 'maybe' invited your sisters? Are they or are they not coming for dinner?" Ooh, schoolteacher tone. I should have been delighted they were coming.

"Yes. They are coming. Just themselves, no boyfriends. I'll call your mom and pay for the additional food, it's just, I needed to provide them an escape route out of dinner with my family this year. They always get the brunt of the blowback from my parents when I'm not present, and I couldn't do that to them again after bailing on Memorial Day. I've been meaning to ask you for a couple of days now. The three of us had a conference call only yesterday, so, yeah, sorry for the short notice."

"Alex, I'm thrilled they're coming. I'm sure my mom would love to meet them. I'll give her a heads-up and you can call her directly when you have a minute. Bring some booze. Everyone will love it. Let's do something fun on Friday. I'll start putting something together. Maybe ice skating, or skiing, or, I know, curling!" I switched gears so fast that I gave myself whiplash.

"Slow down, woman. One thing at a time. I've got to get inside and take my beating. I love you and will call later."

"Bye, baby. Fight like hell!"

I would be his champion just like he was mine. Who knew what a pair we'd be, taking down our parents at the same time? Speaking of which, as much as I didn't want to think about my dad and his imminent passing, I wondered how he was faring.

I left my apartment, sporting a knit headband, scarf, and mittens, and drove the handful of miles to Royal Oak. I pulled up the nursing facility's number at the first stop light and asked for the charge nurse. After several minutes of waiting, she came on the line to inform me he had lost his ability to speak and was being fed through a tube. *Shit!* I guessed he wouldn't be smarting off at me anymore. Mom said when his time was up he would fail fast. Last week he was being an ass to me, and this week I was being the ass with the smart remarks.

"Take the high road," my mom had said. How fucking high did I have to go here? I'd said what I needed to say, and I suppose he had as well. My gut instinct was that no one should die alone, especially when you had family literally five miles away. Why then was visiting him so difficult?

I closed my eyes at the next stoplight to settle my brain and allow what was in my best interest to come forward. What was the right move? When should I make it? I figured I'd just have to sit with it until I had an idea. It was time to catch up with Ruby.

I was meeting her at our favorite coffee shop, the Proving Grounds, and shuffled through the masses to find a small booth in the back. It had been a few weeks since we had been able to physically be in the same room and I missed her warm hugs. She arrived and I pointed to the pickup area to wait for our order while I manned the table. She didn't have to tell me what she wanted, it was the same every time, so I watched the animated conversations all over the shop until she made it over. One couple held hands under a table, while another chastised their kids to sit still and finish their cocoa. A rather hot man stood facing the window, and my curiosity about why he stood there looking concerned was satisfied when two teenage girls with high ponytails and checked tights walked in nonchalantly. His grimace said it all: *Where have you two been? You kept me waiting? I thought you were lost or taken.* At some time or another, that was every parent's nightmare—when their kids didn't show up or call. *Yeesh! Glad I wasn't a parent yet.*

Ruby made her way to the booth with our goodies, plopped down next to me, and burst into tears.

"He's going to fire me!" she sobbed.

"Who? Why? Hey, it's going to be okay." I patted her shoulder and pulled her head to my voluptuous chest.

"Daniel. He thinks I took advantage of him and now he doesn't trust me. How could he know it wasn't my fault. Patrick told him I had nothing to do with that bitch." She wasn't making sense, but I wasn't going to stop her ranting until she was out of steam.

"I just put a deposit on an apartment and I'm moving out of my parents' house today. I can't take their pity anymore. Will you help me with some boxes instead of shopping?"

There was a lot to unpack in this conversation, so I just said yes to everything she asked. I was about to pick it all apart for clarity, when a big, beautiful man with chestnut hair and a chiseled jaw came barreling across the room. Daniel. I couldn't tell if he was pissed or concerned, only that he was looking for Ruby and relieved he had found her. He peeled off his snow-soaked coat and looked like he was ready to tear the top off this booth to get to her. He pushed his hair out of his eyes and addressed me in a controlled and quiet voice.

"Hi, Trudie. Would you mind helping a guy out and let me have a few words with Ruby—alone?"

Daniel waited while I looked at her and then back to him. With all the howling she had done about how he was going to fire her, I was leery about letting him get too close. However, everything she had told me about this guy did not indicate that he would be aggressive, so I stood and took my coat with me.

"Ruby, I'll be over by the windows, watching. Give me the signal and I'll come to your rescue. And you—you better make this right. She would never knowingly do anything to hurt you. Got it?" I pointed my finger for extra emphasis and gave him my ugliest stink eye.

He must have been a little intimidated because he took a step back and let me through. Men. So easily thrown off-kilter when a strong woman stands up to them.

This afternoon was not looking good for shopping, so I opened my notes app and began a holiday shopping list of things I thought my family would like. Alex's gift would take some creativity and Ruby's, I'm sure, would be bawdy and memorable. Now that Alex's sisters were coming, did I need gifts for them too? I wasn't sure how long they were staying or if I would even see them at Christmas, so I decided to put a pin in that one. I'm one of those girls who had a basket full of cute last-minute gifts that would be perfect for a number of occasions, so I knew I could dip into that for Tabitha and Sarah.

I looked back at my desperate friend and saw dread in her eyes. Unfortunately, for both of them, there was dread in Daniel's eyes too. Two puppies who had lost their owners would look happier than the two of them, and my heart broke. A minute later, he was placing a chaste kiss on her cheek and getting up from the booth. He slung his wet coat over his back, stuffing his arms into the long sleeves, and left the building. I ran over to my girl and slid back into the booth, ready to make plans to take him down, but she dropped her head to my shoulder.

"I made a big mistake." Her broken words caught in her throat making her sound like a record playing at the wrong speed.

"What do you mean, you made a mistake?" I must have missed something.

"It wasn't my fault we recorded the tampered script that Elena, the senior copywriter, demanded we tape—but I should have contacted Daniel *immediately* when I realized what she had asked us to do. I knew she was trouble and so did Angelo, the sound engineer. We figured Daniel would need to approve it anyway, so ultimately it wouldn't matter. It seemed insignificant, but it went against what he specifically asked me to do—to come to him with any unusual demands from Elena. Trudie, I broke his trust and now he has to find proof that Elena was trying to sabotage his account."

My hand flew to my mouth. "Oh shit, Rubes. That doesn't sound good. So, what else did he say. From across the room, it looked horrible." I rubbed her back trying to soothe her distress.

"I'm not allowed back in the building until after the investigation, and we can't speak to each other until this is resolved. I could lose my job. More importantly, Daniel may never trust me again. I was sure our relationship would go the distance, but now, I don't know." She began weeping again, making the snowflakes on my sweater feel like real ones.

"I'm sorry sweetheart. I know it seems unfixable, but you can't give up hope. He is just doing his job and you'll be exonerated in no time. Why don't we pack our stuff up and get those boxes to your new place? You can come over for a sleepover just like in the old days so you don't have to explain any of this to your parents. Okay?"

"I don't know," she moaned.

"We can get some wine, and I have a fresh pack of Double Stuf Oreos we can demolish." I nudged her shoulder and wiggled my boobs side to side with her nose right between. She gagged and giggled at that.

"Good girl. Let's go."

And that's how you become someone's best friend. Not the wine and cookies and unending support—it's by motorboating their face between your boobs.

CHAPTER 18

ALEXANDER

Forty-eight, forty-nine, fifty.

I hated squats, but my girl loved my thick thighs and I couldn't let her down even if all I wanted to do was become so inebriated, I'd forget my name. I pushed myself farther than I ever had in the gym that afternoon and quite frankly, I still had energy to burn after that hideous scene at brunch with my parents. To think, they wouldn't accept my resignation and discounted every feeling I had. They were despicable. The icing on the cake was my mother's moan of despair that stopped eighteen tables from eating their gourmet lunches and caused a waiter to drop his full tray of dishes when he looked to see where the call of the humpback whale had come from.

"Who do you think you are, dropping this bomb on us at our own club?" my father spat.

"Are you kidding? I've been telling you this for over a decade and you haven't even given me the courtesy of sitting down for an adult conversation. Who do *you* think you are?"

He huffed out his indignity, "I am your father and you will treat me with respect."

I laughed. Was he serious? "Respect is earned, Father. When you give it, you will get it. I'm done with this. My lawyer will be in touch with you. Have a lovely Thanksgiving with all your paid guests."

I threw my napkin onto my uneaten meal and stormed out of the dining room without a backward glance. So much for being dead emotionally. I was volcanic!

Getting stupid drunk still sounded enticing, so I called my sister Tabitha to see if she was free. Catching up with friends was out of the question. I was a hot mess and all I wanted was a blackout bender. Even calling Trudie wasn't an option while I was in this state. She'd want to help, but the only thing she would be able to do was say, "poor baby." I wasn't poor and I certainly wasn't a baby, even if I was acting out of control. I deserved to have a tantrum given what I'd been through. I deserved to be my own man and not be treated like a corporate pawn.

"You're being irrational, Son. Why do you think we built this conglomerate? For us? No! For you and your sisters," my father said.

SHUT. THE. FUCK. UP.

"What are you talking about? You totally built all this for yourselves. Have you ever once heard us begging to be out front for photo ops? Or pleading with you to miss our school events? I can count on one hand the number of times you or Mom showed up to support our passions," I hissed loud enough that the surrounding tables heard the venom in my voice.

More bullshit. More denial. More demeaning platitudes Fuck that!

I wished I could have stopped this loop of shame and despair and anger that had been riding on my back all my life. I truly understood firsthand what Trudie had experienced with her father. The reasons may have been different, but the manifestation was the same—low self-worth. I'd worked hard at improving how I felt about myself. As a psychologist, it's required to work your shit out in psychoanalysis, but even the masters had trouble maintaining their equilibrium with asshole parents. I hated regressing when I was around them, and it was high time to shut that tap off.

My call went to voice mail, so instead I walked down a block to a local bodega and bought a fifth of bourbon, a family-sized bag of Cool Ranch Doritos, and a hero sub. Dinner was served. Keeping to my plan, I went home, stripped out of my sweats, turned on my emotional support video game, *Hell Let Lose*, and shot the fuck out of everything on the screen. I know, real mature. Rationalizing this was better than taking my rage out on my parents, I set my liquor intake on *constant* and proceeded to obliterate myself and the game.

I couldn't tell you what time it was when my phone buzzed, though I can tell you that half my bottle of bourbon was gone, along with my sandwich and most of the bag of chips. I felt like a loser and certainly looked like one too. *Seven o'clock. Shit!*

"Heeeeyyy, baaaby," I slurred out of my numb mouth. I felt the remnants of drool on my chin and rubbed at it, not knowing if my skin was coming off with it.

"Alex? Is that you?"

Trudie's concern was sweet. She was the best. She had big tits and an ass that could take my dick. Where was she? For that matter, where was I?

I hiccupped and laughed, "I'mma heeer. Can you shee me?"

"Oh, brother, you are shitfaced. I take it your meeting with your parents didn't go so well, huh?" Her pity was palpable.

"Noooo. It dinnit. I hate dem. Where are you?" Wetness formed on my lashes and I thought for sure I was broken.

"Baby, I'm in Detroit, but I wish I was there with you." She always said nice things to me. She made me smile. I just wished I could make my lips cooperate with my thoughts. My head was hurting. I think I swallowed a cat. "Listen, baby. I want you to get yourself a big glass of water and drink the whole glass down. Can you do that?"

"Yeah." I rolled off the couch, smacked my elbow on the glass table, and howled, "Ouch. Motherfucker!"

"What happened?" she yelled, "Are you all right?"

Whining loudly, I said, "God damned table attacked my elbow." I rubbed it again and staggered to the kitchen to complete my assignment. "I got it!" I yelled to her. "I got the water!"

"Good, boy. Now drink it all up and then get into your bed. It's time to sleep off whatever you've had and we'll talk in the morning."

She sounded just like a good mom. I wanted her to be my mom. She loved me. She had said so. I loved her, too. I wonder if she would be a mom to my sisters. They needed a good mom, too. Fuck, I was messed up.

"Are you in bed yet?" she whispered sweetly.

I snuggled into my pillow, imagining they were her tits. "Yes, Mommy." Oops, did I say that out loud?

TRUDIE

Did he just call me, "Mommy?"

I knew he was in bad shape, but referring to me as his mother was on a whole other level. How could this forty-two-year-old man, who was built like a professional baseball player and commanded respect, spiral down to a drunken little boy looking for a mother? It seemed we all had a façade that we used to make ourselves feel better in front of others. How awful we didn't allow ourselves, in all our forms, to be just that—ourselves.

My big burly man was broken and I had no way of making it easier for him. I hoped his sisters would step in and offer some support. Goodness knows they had traveled the same path Alex had, although he was the sole male of the siblings. The pressure he must have faced had to be crushing, and to have the courage to walk away and not look back was admirable. I was so freaking proud of him, and when he became conscious again, I would tell him so.

I had finished my call with Alex while driving home and figured I'd do some laundry to pass the rest of the night. Dirty underwear waited for no one, and I wasn't a flip-them-inside-out kind of girl. I sat staring at the dryer window, letting my mind numb out as my delicates flipped and flopped. It was mesmerizing. For a brief moment, I even considered climbing on top of it and taking a short nap. It worked for babies, so why not me? Yes. I sounded ridiculous. No. I wasn't losing my mind. Maybe, however, I wanted to go back in time to when life was simple and unfettered with complex emotions. I had never realized how boring my life was before I met Alex. I usually looked forward to laundry night coupled with a quart of ho fun Chinese food, and some *Friends* reruns. Not so much now, though.

Twenty minutes later, I was on my way back to my apartment with my laundry basket, wishing I had someone to curl up to when my phone pinged with a message from Sam. Ex-Sam. Boring, vanilla Sam. What did he want?

I dropped my stuff, bolted the door, and filled my water bottle. This disaster of a day was over, and for me, it was lights out. Ignoring Sam's message, I got ready for bed and had just turned off my bedside lamp when my phone pinged again.

Sam: Hi Trudie. It's probably a little late there, but I just got off work and wanted to check in to say hello.

See? There was absolutely nothing wrong with him. Polite, conscientious, and caring.

Me: Hey, Sam. I'm already in bed. Can we talk tomorrow?
Sam: In bed? So early? What are you wearing?
Eww! What the hell?
Me: Not discussing that with you. Why are you really calling?

Sam: I-I wanted to see if you might have changed your mind about moving out here with me. I miss you.

Sure. Missing your home care provider.

Me: Sorry, Sam. I haven't. I hope you make new friends and love your job. Best of everything to you. Good night.

Sam: Wait! Are you sure? We were great together, weren't we?

Me: We had fun and were good company for each other, but I didn't love you like a forever love. Do you understand?

Sam: What's the difference?

Me: Exactly. All my best, Sam. Bye.

I flipped my phone onto vibrate mode and then turned my body away from my nightstand. Seriously? He was so obtuse and childlike. It gave me the creeps now that I'd grown up and seen what a real man looked and felt like. I would never have gone back to him.

It was time to close out this night with a kiss to my lover, so I flipped back over again and pulled my phone close to my chin, sending Alex a good night message.

Me: I'll be your mommy only for the right reasons. But you'll be my daddy forever. Good night, sweetheart.

Sunday couldn't come fast enough. With the impending visit of his sisters, I put myself into overdrive and cleaned my apartment so well that even my mother would have been proud. Then I tried to imagine them in my apartment, and it made me laugh. Where would I put them? I literally had seats for four people, two at the kitchen counter and two on the loveseat. I suppose the ottoman could be called a seat, but then where would my guests put their drinks? I had a really cool lacquered wood tray with daisies all over it, and it made the perfect sturdy surface for appetizers and drinks when I put it on the ottoman.

Who was I kidding? Alex was going to wine and dine them all weekend and they'd never step foot in my apartment. But I could hear my mother clearly: "Always be ready for company." *Sure, Mom.* So I cleaned, grocery shopped, and bought a holiday poinsettia and garland to make the room more festive. Clearly, I didn't make a show of decorating for Thanksgiving, unlike Ruby and her family. Mrs. Michaelson started her accessorizing the minute the leaves began to fall. Pumpkins, gourds, leaf chains, and don't forget seasonal linens, pillows, and front doormats. I used to envy Ruby every year until I started shopping for all those things myself and realized seasonal decorating required a second job. That was a hard no for me. An occasional tchotchke would have to suffice.

My hair hung in sprays around my face, and the coat of grime that glossed over my skin felt like dried potato starch—sticky and gross. I needed to get out of my filthy clothes and into the shower. If it had been up to me, there would have been a new Olympic sport added to the list of highly competitive events called bra wrestling. Even Houdini would have had a tough time with this. I turned on the shower to scalding and stepped in front of the sink to assess the damage of my overly ambitious day. My messy bun was, indeed, messy, and my complexion was ruddy and in desperate need of a mask.

With my Dead Sea mud mask in place, I carefully squeezed out a dollop of argan oil to moisturize my hair. I loved the smell and feel of freshly oiled hair. So smooth and silky. Alex had commented on how silky my hair was for someone of my ethnicity. During several of our conversations, I had educated him on my multinational Hispanic background, including some of our mannerisms, so he wouldn't be left out at dinner this week. One Hispanic woman was one thing, a house full, with the men and their machismo, well, that was another. I hoped my brothers wouldn't razz him too much. Alex was a good sport about most things, but I wasn't sure how he would take being ganged up on.

He must have known I was thinking about him, because just then, a video chat rang on my phone.

"Hey, baby, don't you look pretty." He snickered.

"Thanks, sweetie." I blushed.

"How long before you turn to stone?" His laugh exploded into hysterics.

"What? Oh shit. Ugh, I can't believe I forgot I was covered in beauty products. Well, now you know all my secrets. If you tell anyone, I'll have to kill you." My mafia voice wasn't really forceful enough to drive the point home, though the added pointing of my finger settled him down.

"Yes, ma'am," he murmured behind a dazzling smile.

"Moving on, when will you be home?" I took our call down the hall to the kitchen, where I put a kettle on for tea.

"Soon. I think you should look out your front door. I sent a package over and want to be sure you got it before your neighbor steals it." His remark and pulled-in brows implied I had a nefarious neighbor. While I agreed that stealing my Sunday paper occasionally would indicate Gary was a bad neighbor, he only borrowed it because he knew I didn't pick it up until after ten o'clock and thought he could return it before then. Regardless, it didn't make him a criminal.

"I think you misunderstand Gary. He wouldn't take a sealed package. It is sealed, right?" Now I was concerned. I held my phone toward the door and opened it slowly, hoping whatever Alex sent was still there, proving him wrong.

I looked down and didn't see anything directly outside my door until a giant person jumped out.

"Gotcha!" he yelled.

Before I knew it, my hand shot out, and I palmed his neck, pressing on the carotid artery. The gurgle he made didn't sound so good.

"Jesus Christ, Trudie! Are you trying to kill me?" Alex coughed and rubbed his throat.

I jumped up and down, waving my hands, not knowing what to do. "Oh my God, I'm so sorry. What the hell, Alex? Jumping out at me isn't funny."

"I thought it would be funny and surprising," he whined.

"Yeah, are you as surprised as I am?" I whined back.

"Completely. Surprise! I'm home." He coughed one more time and spun me around, then smacked my ass as he pushed me back into my apartment.

"Hey! That smarts." I turned to pout in his direction.

"Prepare yourself, that was just a sample of what's to come. I have a lot of pent-up aggression, and your ass is going to bear the brunt of it."

I gulped. I had been the recipient of his moods before, though none of those times was fueled by anger caused by his parents. It was possible I'd need to use my safe word.

"Uh, Alex. Please remember I will need to use said ass for sitting tomorrow," I implored him.

"Noted, now let's get you back in the bathroom to finish your regimen."

"Yes, sir," I mocked him as he smacked my ass again, forcing me to high-step it back down the hallway.

I'm not a prude or self-conscious, so it didn't bother me when Alex stepped behind me while I was removing my mask and massaged my full ass. My muscles deeply appreciated him relieving the tension the day had brought on. His strong hands kneaded and tugged, and when he neared my most private hole, he ran his fingertip around the rim, sending a million volts of electricity throughout my entire body. My brain went offline, and all I could do was hold onto the counter for dear life.

His breath at my earlobe startled me back to consciousness. Warm and sultry vibrations made the hair on my neck tingle, and when he spoke, I felt weightless.

"Do you like that, naughty girl? Are you ready to let me have you completely?"

Fuck! Every time he spoke dirty to me, an imaginary switch in my head flipped from In-Control Trudie to I'll-Follow-You-Anywhere Trudie. At first, it felt shameful to have him poking, literally, back there, but Dr. Alexander Pierce had knocked that notion out of my head the first time we were together in California. Never had I once felt threatened by him, and the idea of letting him through my backdoor was heady, though a little unnerving. Alex was a big man, and the idea of his cock impaling me felt a little threatening at the moment.

"You're doing that thing again—going all Dr. Pierce—and it's killing me." I moaned as he traced another circle around my hole.

He chuckled. "But you like when I do that thing," he murmured and then sucked hard on my neck, making me wince.

"I do. It makes me wild and drains all the resistance out of me."

"So, I should keep Dr. Pierce on the roster? Let him out of the dugout every once in a while?"

"Oh, yes, please," I cried.

"Good. Give me some of that oil you put on your hair and spread your legs. Dr. Pierce has another lesson for his dirty girl."

Ugh! I'm a goner.

He nudged my legs farther apart, took the bottle of argan oil, and squirted a generous amount on my ass. The good doctor resumed his ministrations, taking the liberty to insert one of his thick, long fingers inside.

"Ahhh, Christ, that feels good." I barely comprehended how this could be pleasurable, and yet it was.

"I knew you'd like that. Follow my instructions precisely and you'll be begging me for a repeat performance. This is one test you do not want to fail." He smacked my thick haunch hard; the oil on his hand made it smart even more. "You must stay relaxed and control your breathing. You'll feel a lot of pressure and you'll want to tense up—don't."

"Yes, sir." Remembering our rules had become more natural to me. Our communication flowed and my trust soared. He made me his queen and I adored him for his lessons. I could let go of everything in my head and just be in the moment. It was an amazing gift he gave me every time we were intimate.

I felt the velvet crown of his cock run up and down my seam. My legs quivered and a deep moan escaped my mouth as jumbled words rolled from my throat. He pressed one finger, then two, into my tightly puckered hole and coaxed the thick membrane to relax. Scissoring his fingers back and forth, he massaged the muscle wider, creating space for his hefty cock.

"Jesus, Trudie. You're so fucking tight. I need you to relax more."

Slowly I felt his fingers retreat, wondering if he'd changed his mind. I felt hollow back there and wanted him to continue exploring. His hands pulled my torso up, palming each of my breasts as he stared lovingly at them over my shoulder.

"Change of venue, baby." He bent and lifted me into his arms, cradling me as he walked me to my bed, and then laid me down carefully. It felt like the calm before a storm, and, for some reason, I didn't hear the warning bells.

In a flash, he jumped on me, straddling my legs, then flipped me to my belly and yanked my hips up until I was on my hands and knees. *Wow! That was hot.* Not stopping his onslaught, he reached around my waist with one hand and slid those perfect fingers over my hot aching pussy, bringing me to a blissful orgasm. My juices covered Alex's hand, and the look I saw on his face when I peeked over my shoulder was full of carnal desire.

"Yes, baby. The way you arch your back when you come is so fucking sexy." All I could do was hum at his approval. He scooped the juices from my pussy and rubbed them onto his swollen dick, muttering dirty words that worked me up again.

"Once I have your gorgeous ass, I'm going to do so many dirty, delightful things that will have you begging for more every day. The doctor may even have to give you a note to take a week from work to recover.

"Shit, Alex, I'm not even sure I'll survive your giant cock in my ass the first time. Calling a medical doctor might be required."

He laughed at my comment, but I was serious. I did my best to relax as he put two thick fingers in me, but then he announced he was adding a third.

"This finger will tell the tale if you're ready for me, and I sure hope you are because my patience is fading."

I knew my yoga breathing settled me down, so I inhaled as steadily as I could and exhaled the same way as I concentrated on relaxing my lower half. Five cleansing breaths later, Alex's third finger slid in along with the rest. He twisted and flexed his fingers, massaging every inch of my asshole, and I was pleasantly surprised at how it made me feel.

"I'm doing it!" I exclaimed. "Fuck, Alex, I had no idea how amazing this would feel. I feel so full, and the stretch is incredibly erotic."

He patted my ass and gave me a good whack. "It's Dr. Pierce, and that was for not trusting me. I thought we were past that, but I see I still have some work to do." He smacked me harder.

"Yes, sir. I will trust you. I will." My whining was pathetic, but I should have trusted him. I told him I did, so why was I still questioning him?

"You're mine, Trudie. After I take this sweet sexy ass, you'll be mine forever."

Forever?

I looked over my shoulder and was immediately transfixed by his face. Tension pulled his eyebrows together, and sweat beaded along his lip. The control he was using to get me ready was taking a toll. I watched as his fingers pulled on one side of my ass cheek while he tugged on his engorged cock. His eyes laser-focused on pressing his cock right into its target, and my God, the pressure was enormous.

"Fuck. Fuck. Fuck. This is so intense. You feel—I feel—God, it's so—good." I hummed and wiggled my ass, trying to get him to fit better.

"Stop! Do not do that. I'm holding on by a thread and you wiggling your ass isn't helping." I had no idea.

"More, Dr. Pierce. Please, more," I cried.

ALEXANDER

This woman and her wiggly ass were killing me. I have tracked every freckle, vein, stretch mark, and beauty mark there, and when she waved them in front of me, I began to shake. The control it took not to drive my raging cock into her ass in one agonizing stroke had my thighs burning, my body sweating, and my nerves fractured. I had one goal in all this—bring Trudie pleasure. But also, if I was successful, not only would her level of trust go sky-high, but we'd be able to reenact this erotic scene over and over again. I was still a selfish asshole. So sue me.

My dick swept over her hole, and each time, her body shivered in delight. I did the same after coating my cock with her juices after the body-racking orgasm I had pulled from her pussy not two minutes earlier. She needed every trick I could think of to relax her and bring her the ultimate pleasure she deserved. When I felt her taking deep, measured breaths, I knew she had gone to her tried and true mechanism of relaxation—breathing. I was impressed with how therapeutic it really was in every situation.

With my crown inside her mucus membrane, I pressed in slowly another inch. Her muscles tugged at my dick, creating the most incredible sensations—I had no words for them. For us men, this was what heaven felt like—nothing in this world could match it.

"Baby, you're so fucking tight. I can barely push any further." I grunted as I thrust my hips forward.

"You better fucking push harder!" She scolded me, and I smiled a wicked smile.

"Push your ass back toward me. Seat that perfect ass all the way to my crotch. Take control, baby, and fill that sweet ass up with my cock." My encouraging words made a difference and a feral growl erupted from her throat. My girl wanted more cock, and she took it without shame.

"Fuck! Yes, that's it. Take me, baby. Take my cock and make it your own." I felt like a cheerleader at a championship game the way I hollered and smacked her ass one more time.

"You're too fucking big. I can't take any more." I couldn't have her lose confidence; I wouldn't allow it.

"You will take all of my cock. Relax. Breathe. You're almost there. When you do, I will twist your nipples until you beg me to stop."

She rocked forward and back, forward and back, and her efforts found purchase because her cheeks rubbed against my balls. I'd arrived at the Holy Land. Fuck me, she was perfect.

"I did it! I feel your balls on my ass, and it's incredible." She looked over her shoulder and smiled so brightly through her tears.

"You did, baby girl, you did, and now you can have your reward." I held her hips in place with one hand and pulled her torso up to my chest with the other, rolling a hardened bud between my fingertips as promised. My lips pressed to her shoulder, and I traced a line to her neck, leaving puckered kisses along the way. She consumed me in every way, and I needed her to come again so I could feel her ass clenching around my dick.

My hand on her hip slid back to her sweet spot between her thighs and rolled it back and forth until she came again.

The way she leaned into me, pushing her ass deeper onto my dick, had my voice thick with lust. "Yes, baby. You're perfect."

It was time for me to finish what I had set out to do, and I gently released her back to all fours, settling my hands tightly on her hips for leverage. "It's time to fill this ass with my cum."

I pulled out almost to the head and drove into her ass again, eliciting an anguished moan from both of us. I did it again, and her moan grew louder and less pained—I hoped she was allowing herself to get emotionally lost in the moment. I pulled out completely, waiting for her response. I knew it would be indignation, but because I'm an asshole, I wanted her to beg for it.

"SIR! Where did you go? Please PUT THAT BACK IN! Dr. Pierce, please!"

My girl was hooked. I knew she would be. Anyone who is flexible internally and externally would love the challenge of that kind of stretch. I understood some of what she was feeling. The way her ass milked my cock rode the border between pain and pleasure. Conquering an ass for the first time was mind-blowing.

I rocked my hips like a pile driver blasting through her ass. Every stroke was pure heaven. A few more thrusts and my eyes rolled back in my head with the most incredible release I'd ever felt. Never—and I mean never—had I come so hard in my life. I shook from the exertion, and the electricity that pulsed through my veins felt like continuous static.

"Sir—sir. Are you okay?"

I may have whimpered in gratitude. The sexual Holy Land we'd just entered was a deeply spiritual place, and I needed time to reflect before departing.

"I'm floating. Give me a minute." I didn't recognize the hoarse sound coming from my throat. It was a mixture of pain being released and gratitude and humility at how much she gave me.

Trudie held her position while I gathered myself back together. Very slowly, I pulled out from her ass as we both expelled a deep sigh. I fell to her side, tugging her gently into my chest, me the big spoon and her the small one. If I never moved from this position, I would die a very happy man.

We didn't speak for quite a while as we fell in and out of sleep. What words needed to be said that we didn't already feel? I let my fingertips slide up and down her arms, laughing to myself at the things that pop into my mind when it's relaxed and happy. Trudie rolled over and curled tighter into my chest, and I twirled her silky hair around my fingers, imagining what the future held for us. Travel, marriage, kids? Did she want kids of her own? She had thirty a day at school already.

"I can hear you thinking," she mumbled.

"Yeah, it's pretty loud in my head. All good things, though." I pressed a kiss to her head, inhaling her intoxicating scent.

"Tell me." Her lips nipped at my nipple, sending shockwaves through my body. *Dirty girl.*

"If I tell you, it will sound all mushy and over the top, and you'll stop seeing me as an alpha asshole."

"You'll always be my alpha asshole. Tell me anyway."

"To steal a line from a movie, 'You complete me.'"

"Aww. That's so sweet. I feel the same way." Featherlight kisses trailed across my chest, making my dick wake up.

"I'm serious, Trudie." I sat up quickly and looked directly into her eyes. "I'm in love with you. I've told you that. After what we just did—what I just did to you—things became crystal clear to me. You actually complete me. Your touch, your voice, your kindness—they all fill gaping holes in my psyche. I haven't felt complete since my grandmother held me. I'm not sure if I'm re-born or freaked out."

I scrubbed my face with my hands, reeling from the absurdity. Then I took her hands in mine and kissed her knuckles. "Do you know what this means?"

She let me pull her up to her knees. "You're going to tell me I'm the best thing since sliced bread, right?"

I burst out laughing and planted a deep, wet kiss on her plump pink lips.

"Yes! Exactly. That, and I want to plant my salami-sized dick between those slices of multigrain ass cheeks." I tickled her mercilessly until she cried out for me to stop.

Her tiny hand held my face while her thumb traced the corner of my mouth. "You are magnificent, Alex. You fill all my holes physically and emotionally, too. How did we get to this place? We are so different and from such different worlds. Are we really that lucky?" Her whispered musings penetrated my soul. She was right. We were lucky—so very lucky.

"It was my grandmother's doing that we found each other," I suggested.

"Really? You said she passed over thirty years ago." Her confused face was adorable.

"Yes. As a scientist of the human species, I know that we wrestle with the physical manifestations of our mental health." Yeah, I went all clinical with her. "But you know very well we need to remember that faith and spirituality manifest just as much healing as hard-core medicine, probably more so. I believe my grandmother found a way to bring me to you, and because of that, I can't discount how important and necessary you are to my life now."

Her mouth hung open, and her eyes went as wide as saucers at my declaration. I had never made a clinical analysis sound so romantic if I must say so myself.

"That was deep, Alex. Profound and incredibly romantic. So where do we go from here?"

I kissed her again more softly, more reverently. "To the shower." I waggled my brows and tickled her one more time before rolling out of bed and dragging her behind me.

CHAPTER 19

TRUDIE

The Wednesday before Thanksgiving always presented a classroom management challenge. A third of the class had already taken off for the long weekend. Another third couldn't leave and wouldn't pay attention. The last third wanted to do something fun. Poor babies. I was stuck here, too.

This year was going to be different—we were going to try a new exercise in progressive storytelling.

"Listen up, today all your classmates who bailed on us will wish they hadn't. We will spend the entire day doing a progressive storytelling exercise in three parts: first, writing it, then rewriting it into a play, and then acting it out. Ms. Robin and Ms. Jody will be assisting us in the acting out portion, so you'll be able to hang out with more of your friends this afternoon. Keep in mind, they can't help until we have a story to give them, so let's get going."

Mumbles, sighs, expletives. All signs of tweens hiding their excitement. I loved it.

"Everyone, take out a sheet of paper and a pencil, please. Write the first line of a story you would like to tell. This is a one-minute exercise. Go!"

I sent Robin and Jody a text letting them know we had begun and that I'd share the story at lunchtime. A moment later a weird text came through from my father. The spelling was atrocious, leaving me to decipher the actual message.

"Gimmel a fall betta ton suner."

What the hell? The closest I could come to deciphering it was *give me a call better soon*. More than a week had gone by since I last saw him, so I suppose he was reminding me to call again. After the holiday.

"Okay. Pass your paper to the person in front of you—the head of the row, please run yours to the rear. Great. Now, looking at the prompt you have in front of you, write what happens next. You have five minutes. Go!"

I scanned the room, and to my delight, everyone was diving into the project. Last week, I'd woken up from a weird dream and this idea came into my head. I wasn't sure if it was unique, but I loved it and thought how cool it would be to infuse the ideas of all these beautiful minds into one cohesive manuscript.

"Wow! Is time flying for you too?" Their heads nodded excitedly. "Awesome. Let's do it again. Pass your papers forward, and I'll set the timer for five more minutes."

As I walked around the room my thoughts kept shifting back to Sunday night. Something had changed in Alex. His bravado had been strong during the wildest sex I'd ever experienced, and then it mellowed into what I can only describe as reverence when we were finished. His aura had shifted and his speech pattern softened. He spoke of his deceased grandmother like she had exhumed herself from the grave and rejoined her grandson. It had been magical the way his eyes shone and crinkled in the corners as he described his childhood with her. It warmed my heart that he had a woman in his life that focused solely on feeding his heart and soul. Goodness knows that his mother wasn't capable of it.

Moving my concentration back to my kids, especially my high-risk kids, I realized that we should plan to discuss that topic at our next workshop. I was very curious to hear what they would have to say about who completes whom. *Hmm.*

We continued the page shifting three more times and took a break. Afterward, I collected the four stories and read them to the class, who then got to vote on which story we should turn into a play. Before I knew it my stomach was growling and lunchtime had arrived.

After dismissing the kids, I collected the stories and met my lunch buddies in Robin's classroom to review them.

"You won't believe these stories. You'll never guess which one they chose!" I was so excited to get started on writing the script that I tripped over the music stand right in front of me.

"Hey! Are you okay?" Robin whirled around to see what had crashed.

"Yep, just excited."

"I guess so," she quipped, pulling her mouth to the side.

Jody came in and slammed the door behind her. "Hey, bitches."

"Wassup?" Robin drawled out.

"Girls, we have work to do."

We dove into our lunches as we read and rotated stories until we each had reviewed all of them. I loved the comments they chirped out as we read.

"So, what do you think? Which one would you choose?" It was killing me to know so I could let them know what the kids chose.

Jody pulled off her readers. "You didn't prompt them?"

"Nope," I said, popping the *p*.

"And the first person never saw anything other than what they wrote?"

"Yep." Again, with the *p*.

"Unbelievable. You need to document this exercise." Robin stopped eating altogether. Not me. I was still stuffing my face with tuna and cottage cheese. She continued, "My father was a psychiatrist, and he would refer to this as zeitgeist, although it's actually an old French game."

"How do you know this?" Jody retorted.

"I may have read some of his doctoral students' thesis papers lying around his office. He taught at Wayne State, and, well, dozens of these documents were strewn around, and I was bored."

"Seriously? How bored do you have to be to read doctoral theses as a teenager?" My chastising tone was painful to my own ears. "Sorry," I said.

"Pretty bored. My dad hired me to answer phones, make appointments, and file a couple of times a week. Don't look at me that way. I made fifty bucks a week. How much did you make in high school?" Robin said as she chewed on her nail bed.

"Settle down. I just thought it was weird. Would you mind breaking that down for us laypeople?" Jody said with disgust. *Ooh! Girl has lots of tone today.*

"Sure. It literally means "spirit of the time" in German. In this case, all your front-row students didn't want to spend time with their families over the holiday, and each kid behind them echoed their opinions of why they didn't." Robin continued chewing on the other hand.

"Geez. Why, then, did they all end well?" My question was met with blank stares.

"Maybe they are nervous about sharing anything really honest about themselves or being called out for stuff," Jody suggested, and we all nodded.

"Maybe talking and entertaining all weekend seems overwhelming to them," Robin concluded. We all nodded again.

"Or maybe they are just kids who want to blend into the wallpaper. Listening, but not talking. Or the opposite—they want attention and are afraid they won't get it. Oh! What about not being heard when they speak?" Robin suggested.

"I love you guys but read the concluding paragraphs of each one. They are almost identical. All your thoughts are valid. Look carefully at what this class of kids wanted from this weekend." We all reread them and stared again at one another.

"Love. They all just want to feel loved." My statement was like an arrow hitting a target with a resounding *boing*.

"I think I'm going to cry." Jody sniffed.

"God damn it. This is why I went into education. The fucking kids are teaching us more than we are teaching them." Robin sniffled, then pushed back her chair and started walking around the room, throwing out ideas for staging and choreography.

"Don't you want to know which one the kids picked?" I interjected.

Four eyes locked on to mine. "The story where only the nuclear family is at Thanksgiving. Lots of gameplay, movie watching, and loving each other. Nothing fancy."

"Wow. Those little buggers got it right. Okay, just a little movement and lots of dramatic expressions and arms flailing." Robin suggested. Jody went to the board and sketched out a table scene and a couch scene to connect with the story, and ten minutes later, when the bell sounded, we had a plan.

"You gals are the best. See you at one for the first rehearsal. I gathered all my bits and headed back to the classroom. This was going to be a blast.

I set the kids up to organize the short story into a play and sat behind my desk. I needed to shoot off a few texts; they couldn't wait.

Me: Are you free to come down to the choir room at a quarter after two? Jody, Robin, and I and our students would like to share the project we've been working on today. Bring whoever you'd like.

Eloise: Oh! What have the three of you hatched today? I'm sure I can. How many classes can we cram into the choir room?

Me: Uh, better not bring other classes this time around. Things got a little heavy and I don't want the kids feeling awkward around their peers.

Eloise: You've piqued my interest. I'll bring Ricky along. He loves a good play.

Me: Terrific. See you then.

So far, so good.

I'd been noticing a confrontation behind me, though I couldn't stop my conversation with Eloise to address it. Now that we were finished, I jumped in to break up a potential incident.

"Jack! Come on, man. Give Ella a break for once," I barked at him. I think he liked her because he was always trying to get a rise out of her.

"Ms. Gonzalez, she started it," he complained. Really? Ella was standing up for herself? You go, girl!

"Ella, is that true?" I pointed my pencil at her questioningly.

"Uh, I guess I did. Jack wanted to change a line we had already agreed on and we don't have time to waste with minutia."

Minutia? "Did you just use a vocabulary word from last week?" I sat forward, intrigued.

"I did." Her smile was bright and proud. Something I hadn't seen from her all semester.

"Amazing! Well done, and you get five extra credit points. Jack—let it go."

I went back to my texting while the two of them shot daggers at each other. That looked like an exchange I had myself this past summer with Alex. *Ah, young love.*

Me: Hello, gorgeous. What time do you pick up your sisters?

Alex: I just picked them up.

Me: That's terrific. Any chance they would like to see some kids do a play?

The dots bounced in a wave while he typed.

Alex: What time and where?

Me: Yay! Two-fifteen in the choir room. It's going to be really good.

Alex: If you created it, I know it will be.

Me: Charmer. Except the kids created it. I was the conduit.

Alex: I can't help it. You bring out the best—and worst—in me.

Me: So true. Love you. Gotta go. XOXO

The rest of the day was a blur. I taught the kids about the key components of playwriting, rewriting, staging, and, of course, the performance. It helped that there were only six roles in the play, and the rest of the kids played directors.

Showtime arrived with my invited guests, both Jody and Robin's classes and a surprise visit from Dr. Dinglehopper from the school board. How the hell had he heard about this?

The kids settled into chairs arranged in a semicircle with the adults flanking them. Robin dimmed the room lights and aimed a spotlight at the stage area. Jody and her team stood off to stage left and stage right, holding props. And me, well, I was the ringmaster. If this was going to be an epic fail, it would fall on me. Fingers crossed.

I walked across the room and stopped by Alex to ask if he could step outside for a minute. I didn't want to make a scene, but I needed to know who invited the board member. He'd never come to any other event at the school, and it was weirding me out.

Fighting to keep my hands off his pristine suit coat, I spoke quietly with my hands behind my back, trying to look nonchalant.

"Hey, baby." He purred.

"Later, Alex. Did you invite Dr. Williams from the school board?" I hissed.

"It wasn't me. Eloise?" His confusion was palpable.

"Then who? It's so strange. Anyway, let's talk afterward."

"Break a leg, beautiful." He looked up and down the hallway and leaned in to kiss me on the cheek. *Rogue.*

With everyone seated, I stepped up front to welcome our guests, praised the kids on a job well done, and thanked my friends for hopping on my kooky plan to make this show happen. The kids took their places at the Thanksgiving table, looking slightly petrified, and Robin dimmed the rest of the "house" lights.

I sat at the corner of the stage to offer direction if needed, but these kids erupted with laughter and hysterical banter over passing the rolls or if one of the family members wasn't sitting up straight enough—just like at home. Even Ella made a show of demanding that her request for game time be heard. It was so cool to see each kid bring a little of their home life to the stage. As I thought that, I noticed that one family member on stage sat quietly, saying nothing—waiting to be seen. Delano played that role and my heart broke. He'd never said he was neglected in that way, though now that he was "pretending," I could see it right in front of me. Tomás played his older brother and, during all the cross-talk, yelled for everyone to stop what they were doing. Then he quietly asked Delano's character what movie he would like to watch after game time. I'm not sure if Delano was acting or if he had something in his eyes, but a single tear fell from his face in appreciation for this simple kindness. He wanted a voice at home. He wanted to be loved too.

It wasn't scripted, yet Tomás must have sensed his distress and got up and stood behind Delano's chair. He put his hand on his shoulder and made it clear to the audience what was really happening on stage. "Hey, little brother. Your voice matters."

The crowd jumped to their feet in appreciation. Both boys laughed together, bonding, and hopefully made a new friend for life.

Fifteen minutes later, the whole thing was over. What a memorable time it was.

"Oh. My. God! Did you see how authentic Delano's tears were?" Jody said, bursting into tears herself.

"I didn't know Tomás had a flair for acting. His improvisation was spectacular!" Robin clapped her hands, knowing she'd snag him for the spring play.

Alex and his sisters approached me from behind.

"Trudie, sweetheart, I had no idea the depth of your teaching. I found myself living several of those kids' lives. So heartwarming," Tabitha gushed and gave me a hug.

"You do this every day? So many emotional moments in a twenty-minute production. You have a real calling." Sarah threw her arms around me in a sisterly hug as well.

I stepped back, holding her hands, and looked at both sisters lovingly.

"Thank you so much for coming and sharing your time with my kids today. Alex and I, and the rest of our mentors, have been working with a few of these kids in our workshops, and I can really see a difference after the few sessions we've had."

"Excuse me, Ms. Gonzalez." A crackly voice interrupted our conversation. I turned around and was met with a pair of pale brown skeptical eyes and a rumpled gray suit.

"Dr. Williams. What a surprise. How did you know about our little play?"

He shuffled his feet, looking annoyed. "Your front office admin informed me that the principal wasn't available until after school and I wanted to know why she couldn't take my meeting." *Oh, poor Ricky.*

"I see. And, did you like the production?" I was fishing and hoped he wouldn't surprise me with a slap on the wrist for not following a prepared lesson plan.

"It was interesting. I couldn't relate to either the table or couch scenes, as my family always traveled over the Thanksgiving holiday. It was always a cruise to the Bahamas or something. I suppose these kids wouldn't do that since they are still in school the day before the holiday. Your methods are unique, Ms. Gonzalez, and I'm happy that your students are benefiting from your cleverness. Happy Thanksgiving." He retreated with a grimace on his face. I felt bad he'd never had a traditional holiday experience—no wonder he was so grumpy.

CHAPTER 20

TRUDIE

"Whew!"

I loved new experiences even if they exhausted me. I wished we'd have time for a proper celebration, except Alex got us a table at the Fox & Hounds for dinner and I wanted to hug him properly. Public displays of affection at school the way I liked it were frowned upon at school.

The restaurant bar was packed with beautiful-looking, well-dressed people. The area between where I worked and lived was extremely affluent and certainly wouldn't fit my budget any day of the week. The décor resembled Tavern on the Green in New York City, where Alex had taken me for lunch in Central Park. The banquettes were ornate, upholstered with lush, heavy leather and brass tacks. The lighting was so dim you couldn't even see twenty feet in front of you.

I had been walking around for a few minutes trying to locate my peeps when a thick arm caught me around the waste and pinned my back to a broad chest. I assumed it was Alex and wriggled my ass against his stomach, encouraging his advance. Warm air swirled around my earlobe, and I melted against him. I was turning my face up to kiss his jaw when I saw a blond shaggy-haired man that looked a lot like Bobby.

I tried to pull away, but the arm that banded around me tightened even more while the other one grabbed my ass and pinched it ruthlessly.

"Ow! What the hell, Bobby?" I turned around to set him straight. "Leave me the hell alone," I screamed loudly. I looked at the people around me for assistance, but they didn't get that I didn't want this asshole's attention.

"You're such a sweet fucking tease, Trudie. Did you think I would give up on you so soon? You have no idea what you're missing. My big cock will be in your tight ass soon enough and you'll be begging me for more." He spat the words, leaving moisture all over my face. He was revolting.

I screamed as loud as I could, "Get your filthy hands off me!"

By the time I said the last word, blood was spewing out of Bobby's nose and another strong arm pulled me away.

"If you ever touch this woman again, I swear I'll kill you."

My legs felt like Jell-O and my head swam in disbelief. Everything had happened so fast; I didn't see it coming. I assumed Alex had been looking for me, heard me, and came to my rescue.

A bleating cry came from behind us. "I knew you were fucking her!" Bobby screamed.

Both Alex and I ignored him while adrenaline chased our peace.

When we got back to the table, he spun me around giving me a blistering kiss.

"That's for an incredible production today." He raked his fingers through my hair and planted another intoxicating kiss on my lips, which now felt like a dozen bees had bitten them. "And that's for scaring the shit out of me over there. What the fuck was that all about?" He paused. "I'm sorry. I should be asking if you're okay first." He looked carefully at my face trying to to ascertain any lasting trauma.

See, this was why I got into trouble. Little incidents, like the thing with Bobby, would happen throughout the week, and I'd either minimize them or let them go. But then sometimes these problems would double back and bite me, or in this case, pinch me, on the ass. I needed to learn to shut this shit down when it happened.

I adopted a calm tone and said, "Bobby came on to me in my classroom a week or so ago and I told him we would only be friends. He was insistent that, with time, we could make a go of it. I told him unequivocally that I had a boyfriend and wasn't interested. He then called me a bitch and that was the end of it. He's only in school a few hours a week, and it was pretty easy to stay away from him. Given the size of the beer he was drinking, I suppose he was drunk enough to think he could take whatever he wanted when I got close to him.

"I don't give a shit how close you were, that display of aggression will not go unanswered. As of now, he is off the mentoring team and by Monday he will no longer be an employee of Hart Middle School or anywhere in the district. Who the fuck does he think he is pushing himself on someone like that?" Alex scrubbed his face and was breathing like a dragon after the chase. If I wasn't so distraught I would have jumped into his arm and wrapped my legs around him. He was hot in all the right ways.

"Alex, you saved your woman's honor! Gallant never looked so good," Tabitha swooned.

Sarah pulled me into the booth and held me tightly, "Are you okay? Here, drink mine. I'll get another."

I wasn't going to argue with her and downed the rest of her drink. "Two more!" I called to the closest waiter.

My butt buzzed as I entered my apartment later that night. I dug around my purse, looking for my phone. The illumination faded, and so did my interest when I saw that it was a call from the nursing home. It was the holiday. The season of generosity, kindness, and love, except I wasn't feeling any of those things toward the man I called my father. I suppose I could have texted him. Unfortunately, now that he was back in my life, he became an afterthought, which I wasn't going to acknowledge today.

I needed to make a pie. Sadly, I had been in no shape to drive my car and called an Uber. Alex and his sisters stayed for another round, but after three cosmos, I would be lucky to find my keys in my purse when I got home. He made me promise to call him when I got there, and I licked the side of his face because I'm weird like that.

"Even your face tastes salty," I slurred out, feeling proud of my sexy sense of humor. The look on his face was priceless, though his sisters screamed, "TMI!" Tomorrow would be fun, if not outrageous, especially since I had a few surprises to spring on Alex throughout the day. With my family's loudness and his sister's sharp sense of humor it would be a dinner for the ages.

I did not manage to get a pie together after all. I did, however, find all of the ingredients and got up an hour earlier so I could bake it before I left. My phone buzzed and I happily answered Ruby's video chat while I put on some makeup.

"Happy Thanksgiving, pretty girl. Are you so excited for today?" I asked. Daniel was coming to her parents' house along with her brother and new wife from Colorado.

"You too, *chica*. Me? Excited? More like nauseated. What if he hates my family? My parents can be a bit condescending sometimes, and my brother is usually cool but sometimes he can be intimidating to my men friends."

"Don't you remember what happened to Arnold during freshman year of college?" Hmm, Arnold? *Oh, shit, yeah.*

"I see what you mean. The wedgie your brother gave him at your Halloween party gave him a hemorrhoid. Best of times." I chuckled as I was putting on mascara.

"Not for Arnold. Regardless, they have to like him, even love him, because you know I love him, and I can't lose that gorgeous hunk of man. No one, and I mean no one, can lick a clit like he can."

I laughed so hard I peed a little in my pants.

"Girl, you really know how to express yourself. I would not lead with that comment anywhere but behind closed doors. And anyway, Alex holds that record, and before you say it, no, we will not be boyfriend-swapping to prove your point."

"You're no fun," she giggled. "Send me a text later and let me know how things are going on your end. I can't believe you have the NYC elite dining at your mother's humble abode. You're moving up, princess." I really was.

ALEXANDER

Gift for her mom. *Check.*

Sisters warned not to be the snobs they'd been known to be. *Check.*

Comfortable clothes for overeating—and easy access. *Check.*

I yelled across the apartment that we needed to leave and was met with, "For the love of God, Alex," in unison. A phrase they had picked up from my mother. I stood in my foyer, flowers in hand for both my girl and her mom, a case of craft beer for her brothers, and slippers in a bag. I hated cold feet.

My darling sisters emerged with their hair in single ponytails pulled tightly above their heads and wearing simple black leggings and slouchy sweaters. Who were these girls and where did they take my sisters?

"Who are you people?" My bugged-out eyes and slack jaw must have concerned Sarah because she ran over and pushed my jaw back into place.

"Are you having a stroke? You can't have a stroke on Thanksgiving! None of the good doctors are at the hospital today." She felt my forehead and then tickled my sides, making me almost drop the flowers.

"Ha. Ha. Seriously, what happened to you two?" I deadpanned, then flicked off the lights.

Sarah put her coat on first and I handed the flowers off to her.

"Darling brother, we don't always dress to the nines. We have simple, comfortable clothes like the regular folks. I rather enjoy looking sloppy."

"The regular folks, as you refer to them, are the majority of people in our country. You really are snobs. For the record, even when you choose to dress down, you still look impeccably put together." Not that I was checking out my sisters but they are hot women no matter what they wore.

Tabitha stood on her toes and kissed my cheeks. "Aren't you the sweetest baby brother?"

Yes. Yes, I am. "It's about time you noticed. Let me lock the door and we can get going."

It had been a really long time since the three of us walked arm in arm. Today was the best Thanksgiving already.

In a million years, I would never have concocted a Thanksgiving table like the Gonzalez family did. Nina, Trudie's mother, decorated the table in the living room with fuchsia-colored flowers in cobalt blue pots and emerald green and yellow turkeys. Each colorful place setting had a folded card with quotes of gratitude, and there was a Christmas ornament on each seat. *Interesting.*

Like every Thanksgiving I'd ever been to, we ate all the traditional American favorites but with a twist. At this table, we had cranberry sauce with jalapeños, roasted turkey tamales, mashed yucca and potatoes, sweet fried plantains, assorted vegetables, and other Latin treats. A stunning ring bread with bright bands of colored sugar buried in light white frosting adorned the middle of the table, and Trudie later told us it was a *Rosca de Reyes.* My mouth watered while Trudie explained its origins.

My family always began dinner at seven sharp, followed by drinks and politics for the men, and I don't know what for the women since we were in different rooms like the cast of Downton Abbey. Everyone sat straight, knees together. There were no confrontations and definitely no slang. Not here. All those rules were broken, especially the confrontation policy. Nothing was sacred, and therefore, Trudie and I were ruthlessly grilled by her brothers, with my sisters bandwagoning along with them.

"Alex was a crier when he was young. We never figured out why, so we ignored him." Story of my life.

"Zander, too!" Paolo shouted, outing his brother.

After dinner, we sat on the furniture, off the furniture, and on each other in Nina's living room. She pulled a chair from the table and sipped her tea, taking in all the drama and laughing to herself occasionally.

"To be fair, I had horrible parents who ignored me and sisters who dressed me up like a freak show. I rest my case." Alex was indignant, jutting his chin out.

Zander, not to be outdone, retorted, "My father abandoned me, and my brother took out his anger on my kidneys. Where was my sister in all this? Punching my other kidney." We all laughed at our pitiful circumstances. But we had all survived to tell the tale with less vehemence than in the past. We were healing, and for that alone, I was grateful.

"*Todas las niñas y niños*, please get your ornaments and sit back down, we have a tree to decorate." Nina was as sophisticated as any of my mother's snobby friends but without the air of entitlement. Once we were all assembled again, Trudie stood and looked over to her mother, who gave her a small nod.

"When I was five, my amazing mother and I started a family tradition of making new Christmas ornaments. We agreed that each year we would make ornaments designed for each person in our family so that our collection would grow and reflect our journeys." Her voice trembled and her hands fingered her ornament as she did her best to keep it together. She was adorable as she shifted her weight from foot to foot, doing a little dance.

"This year, we continued our tradition and expanded it to the other loved ones in our cherished circle. The twist will be that next year, you will make one of your own ornaments to hang on our tree by decorating it with what is in your heart. Mine is sappy and looks more like a Valentine's ornament. Olivia has a similar one since her romance with Zander is almost the same as mine with Alex.

I hope you like your designs. And I love you all, but you'll have to participate in this tradition moving forward—I'm done making all of them. Mwah!" she finished, blowing us a kiss. This woman was a freakin' rockstar. Always giving and never asking for much in return.

I would be remiss if I didn't mention that shortly after we arrived and introduced my sisters to her family, Trudie pulled me upstairs for a personal tour of her mother's home.

"In here is where I..." She pulled me into a walk-in closet and closed the door quickly. Her hand slid down the front of my pants before I could kiss her, shocking me into silence.

She unbuckled my belt and unzipped my pants like a woman possessed. In her haste to yank down my boxer briefs, she tore the waistband almost in half.

"Guess you'll have to go commando the rest of the night," she sniggered and licked my shaft from root to tip.

"Jesus Christ, Trudie. Uh! That feels amazing." She sucked my crown and finished with a pop. The confidence she exuded was hot as fuck, and I was sincerely impressed at how well she played the seductress.

"Yep. That's the plan. Surprise." Her grin was borderline maniacal, and I wasn't sure what to expect next.

I guess I should have taken responsibility for creating this sexual monster, but I wasn't at all unhappy about it. This seductress was waiting for the right person, and thank God for all that is holy that I got her.

She grabbed my ass to pull my cock fully into her mouth and down her throat. I gasped at how deeply she took me—my legs strained to keep me upright. Her eyes were closed as she concentrated on her task, and saliva dripped from the corners of her mouth each time she came up for air. I held her hair back, watching how dedicated she was to my pleasure. Later I would thank her profusely for being such a good student.

"Fuck, fuck—fuck. I'm going to come. Trudie, baby . . . " Her surprise attack had gotten me rock hard in seconds and she sucked me off in record time. I felt like a teenage boy with how quickly I came. Though, in all fairness, it had been three days since we were together, and in "man" days, it felt like a year.

Like a good girl, she cleaned me up with her tongue, looking quite proud of herself. My eyes were glued to her face, and incredibly I was hard again, ready for more.

"Now, now, Alex. Don't be greedy, we have guests to entertain." She tugged my underwear back into place as she stood. "Sorry—not sorry—about your underwear." She bit her lip and fluffed her hair before cracking the door to the closet.

"You're going to get it, Ms. Gonzalez," I warned her.

"I hope so, Dr. Pierce," she retorted and left the room with a swish of her ass and a devilish grin.

She left me standing there like a cliché, with my pants down literally and figuratively. I grabbed my khakis and put myself together, having rather enjoyed her brazen moves. I walked toward the door and caught a glimpse of myself in the bedroom mirror. I did look like a cliché.

After the ornament ceremony, I went to the refrigerator with feelings I couldn't describe. My heart had constricted in grief over never having had a holiday like this one. It left me bereft. Is this what a real family feels like? I'd earned a PhD in human emotional health and I'd never experienced these feelings myself. It was as though they actually held me in esteem without backhanded swipes at my profession and without making me feel insignificant in any way. On the contrary, I made Trudie's brothers look like slackers, and they were well respected in their fields, too. We bonded as equals over Jenga and poker, and gratefully, no one brought up politics or other trigger topics. Yep! This was the kind of life I had aspired to, not one that systematically tore me apart from the inside out.

Listening to my sisters call my parents the previous night to inform them they wouldn't be home for Thanksgiving had been priceless.

"Yes, Mother. You heard correctly. Sarah and I are in Detroit with Alex this year. Yes, he knew we were coming. No, we didn't make that decision until this past weekend..."

Tabitha fielded questions for five minutes before Sarah grabbed the phone from her ear.

"Listen—oh, hi, Dad. I know this isn't what you planned. Okay. I'm sure you're very embarrassed your own children aren't coming. That's not fair, we always do what you ask. It's only been one time..."

Tabitha got her second wind and went in for round two.

"Listen, Dad—hi again, Mom. Here's the bottom line, you barely talk to us during your dinners—we are just props in your world and we are done. Yes, all three of us are done. If you feel that way, then okay. See you whenever. Happy..." They had hung up.

Sarah stepped up to her big sister to give her a hug. "Ouch. That hurt, didn't it?"

Tabitha grabbed the back of her neck with both hands, massaging herself.

"Hurt? I'm long past hurt. The whole thing is pathetic. Don't you find it ironic, no, narcissistic, that neither one of them asked if we were all right? If there was anything they could do to ease the pain—fix the problems our family suffers from? Nope! It's all about them and will always be about them. Fuck it! I'm just happy we are here and that we were well-lubricated from all the tequila before having that conversation."

We had all huddled on my bed and took strength from each other as we broke free from our parental manacles. This was by far the best Thanksgiving ever.

Zander followed me into the kitchen and plopped down on a barstool as I passed him a bottle of beer. He lifted his chin in appreciation, and the two of us stared into our bottles, enjoying the quiet. A few minutes passed, and I felt like we'd had enough time together. I was just getting up to return to my woman when he cleared his throat.

"You okay?" He asked.

I pulled my lips to one side, "I'm good."

"Are you planning on marrying my sister?"

I almost spit my beer all over the counter. "Jesus, man. Way to cut to the chase. Uh, we haven't discussed that yet, but I can keep you in the loop."

"That's not an answer." Zander's look was serious, his eyes not leaving mine. They were eyes that resembled those of a fiery vixen I knew very well. Only a straight answer would suffice.

"True, true." I pursed my lips together and tried to buy time to come up with an appropriate response.

I put my beer on the counter, flattened both hands on the marble, and leaned in.

"We love each other. I adore her. Do I see a future together with your sister? Hell yes. Is marriage imminent? Probably not. We are still figuring out our own shit, and until this project at her school is over, I can't imagine how we could talk about getting married."

He sat back on his stool, taking an assessment of my words, weighing my sincerity.

Moments later, he shifted out of his seat and stood up tall, mirroring my stance. "Fine. Trudie has been through too much to get fucked again. Here's the deal. You make her happy, and I'll keep you in one piece. Sound good?" His eyebrows lifted, and he tilted his head to the side.

Had I just been threatened? "I have a better idea. I'll make her happy, and you keep your fucking threats to yourself. Sound good?" I was no one's punching bag.

He smiled brightly, apparently happy with my response, and walked over to clap me on the shoulder. "I knew you loved her and would stand up for her. I like you, Alex." Zander walked away as if we'd just discussed a football game. I had a lot to learn about having brothers, and I planned a lifetime with these two formidable opponents.

When I returned to the living room, Trudie wasn't in her chair. I casually looked around, not wanting to attract attention to myself and wandered down the hall toward the bedroom on the other side of the kitchen. I admired the family pictures and graduation photos arranged on the walls so I wouldn't look conspicuous. The open door at the end had to have been Nina's room. Would Trudie lure me back there? Maybe. After all, the blow job she gave me earlier came out of nowhere.

I peeked into Nina's room, but there were no sounds indicating anyone was in there. When I turned, I caught sight of a finger in the basement doorway beckoning me in a "come hither" way. Clever girl.

"Is this my second surprise?" I inquired. My husky voice sounded unusual to my ears.

She grasped my wrist and led me down the stairs with only a flashlight to guide us. Once in the basement, I saw two candles lit on the far side of the room, giving off enough light to take in the simple yet comfortable TV area. Adult-sized bean bag chairs, a deep couch, and a coffee table were arranged in a semicircle in front of a giant television.

"What's with the huge TV?" I asked, momentarily distracted from Trudie's seduction.

"Football, basketball, hockey, baseball, and soccer. It's our family game room," she explained while pulling me away from my fantasy weekend hangout. "Do you know what other ball-type games I like?" Her purr had me snapping back to attention. I gulped in anticipation of her answer.

"Tell me," I demanded.

"Your balls, baby, and a little game."

Gulp. Clearing my throat, I asked, "What kind of game?" I put my hands on her hips and pulled her small body to my growing dick.

"Let's call it baseball. You sink your bat into me, and when your balls slap my ass, it's a home run. What do you think?"

I growled my reply, "You've seen me compete, sweetheart. I never lose a game," and twisted her body around, bending her over the side of the family couch. Time to start making my own memories in this house. "Put your hands over your mouth and don't make a sound."

I unbuckled my belt and slid my pants to my thighs. We'd need to be prepared to make a quick exit if anyone opened the basement door.

I knelt down and ran my tongue over her wet pussy from behind. That's when the first strangled moan rumbled from her beautiful throat. I loved that sound more than life itself. Encouraged me to do it again, I finished with a nip to her clit. The squeal she made was too loud, and she had to be punished.

"Quiet!" I hissed, smacking her ass and licking my lips as I stood up. Too bad I couldn't feast on her longer.

Another beautiful moan. My cock bounced in anticipation, and I couldn't wait another moment. I tugged my wet-tipped dick a few times, then dragged it down her crack. She wiggled her ass at me, but if she thought I'd take her there with a room full of people upstairs, she was far more of a risk-taker than I was. Then again, I took her to a gallery of a hotel with hundreds of people milling around at a party. We made the perfect pair.

I slid, "my bat," as she referred to my thick cock, into her juicy hole and drove it to the hilt in one swing. A low throaty *mmm* filled the room, and I echoed her response.

I ran my hand under her loose sweater, feeling her stomach pulling in and her tits hanging heavy. Every curve of this woman was full and fucking fantastic.

"Is this what you wanted, baby?" I granted her request by pumping into her so hard that the only noise besides our grunting was my balls slapping against her bottom. "I think I hit a homerun sliding in and out of you over this couch. I don't think you'll ever watch a game again without hearing us slapping together, will you?"

She removed her hands from her mouth, breathing heavily.

"Fuck, Alex. I love it when you win. You should never lose a game—ever." She threw her hands back to her mouth when I changed her position to hit the spot that always sent her over the edge. "Uh, yes, yes," she sighed into her palms.

"I'm coming, baby. Are you there, too?" My legs were quaking as my fingers dug into her hips, most likely leaving marks.

"Now, Alex. Please!" She hissed.

I heard footsteps above us and pounded her pussy as hard as I could. I exploded so intensely that I crumpled over her back, hearing her heart thumping as she came with me.

"Trudie, you leave me speechless."

The people stopped moving above us and I held my breath.

"Alex, we've got to move." She pushed me back and we both grabbed our pants just as the door handle turned.

She shoved me toward the back bar in a panic. "You and your monster dick get behind the bar. Grab something out of the fridge to drink and give me one too."

I obeyed, not wanting to explain why we were leaving our DNA all over the family couch.

"Trudie, are you down there?" Paolo called as several footsteps followed behind him.

She pulled her tiny self onto a bar stool and ran her fingers through her tousled silky locks. Yeah, she looked well and truly fucked. Anyone with half a brain could see that.

"Over here by the bar. Alex was telling me about his trip to Texas." *Not.*

CHAPTER 21
TRUDIE

I'm a fucking animal. Literally!

I had assaulted Alex twice in my mother's home, and I wasn't even ashamed. Who had I become? A modern-day Jezebel or just a woman who knows what she wants, how she wants it, and who she wants it from? The latter, of course. I deserved to let my she-beast out after years of muting her with my last boyfriend. The line about "men having needs" was bullshit. Women's needs were just as strong. I'd seen a movie a few years back that revealed that women of the early 1900s were called "hysterical" because they complained about needing affection. They couldn't even articulate that their "gardens" needed to be watered and cared for by their neglectful husbands. Those poor Victorian women who couldn't admit they were desperate for an orgasm went to see their "female" doctors for "medical stimulation" to relieve their distress. Interestingly, according to the movie, that's why the vibrator was invented. By a man. A man too busy or uninterested in his wife's pleasure. Argh!

Alex, on the other hand, had been more than pleased with my forward approach. His balls were completely empty by the end of the day, and my vagina was very proud of herself for taking what she wanted. The newly sexualized Trudie would never again be caged.

"Yoohoo. Trudie. Where are you?" Sarah called.

It was Friday morning. I had gone to Alex's apartment for brunch, and began making coffee as soon as I arrived. I must have zoned out while looking at the huge piles of snow forming outside. Soon after, I poured myself a cup of coffee and sat with crisscrossed legs on Alex's ridiculously soft microsuede couch. Once you sat down, you never wanted to get up. I know this because twice now, we had fallen deeply asleep after a romp, only to be wakened for work by my trusty phone alarm. *Fucking phone alarm.* I returned my gaze outward toward the blizzard, balancing my cup between my palms, when I realized Sarah was speaking to me.

I shook my head, "Sorry. I totally zoned out and didn't see you walk in." I took a sip of my coffee, slipping back to the present.

"Where did you go?" Sarah teased. Her eyebrows were raised cartoonishly high.

Hmm. Where had I gone? What did I want to share with her?

"Is it that obvious?" I grimaced.

"Well, it could be, though you do seem to have quite a bit on your mind these days."

"Yep, but I don't think that was what you were thinking about." Damn, she was intuitive.

I reached over and put my coffee cup onto the side table and twisted myself to face her directly.

"Are you sure you're a pharmaceutical representative and not a psychologist?" I chuckled a nervous laugh. I didn't know her well enough to unload all the deep stuff in my life. She'd find out about my dad and all his bullshit at some point. It was probably best just to give her some highlights.

"I'm sure. But I used to read all of Alex's papers and edited his first thesis, so I've picked up a few bits and signs here and there." She sipped her coffee to fill the gap as I let her comments settle. This woman was stealthy. Not only had she walked into the room without me knowing it, she had walked in, poured herself a coffee, and sat down on the couch.

"Sarah." My chin dipped. "Like you, I've been sorting through a lot of baggage from my childhood. Alex has been a superstar in helping me see those experiences through an adult lens instead of the child's lens—one I had been stuck with for years. One result of that lens shift has been letting go of stuff my father inflicted on our family."

I continued with a one-minute summary of the current situation with my dad, though only revealing what was necessary.

"I'm perplexed about how I can ease his suffering without losing myself emotionally. Any thoughts on how to make that happen?" I lifted my chin and looked into eyes that were very familiar, although her eyebrows were finer than Alex's and mysteriously without his crinkle lines.

Sarah didn't have to get involved in my troubles. She had her own family issues to deal with. Nonetheless, an outsider's perspective couldn't hurt, and I was running out of time. I needed to see my father that weekend. The texts he kept sending were barely coherent. His time may have been coming sooner than I expected.

She put her cup on the coffee table and moved forward to grasp both my hands. "I don't know your father, and honestly, I don't know you well enough to give you any specific answers. My gut, though, says to do the things that will leave you with as little guilt, or residue, or remorse as possible once he passes. You can't fix him at this point. Your only responsibility is to protect your heart—to accept that you gave what you could. That will be a gift you give yourself. A well-deserved gift—given what you said he did to you and your family."

I hadn't planned to cry. I'm not a crier. But Sarah's surprisingly uplifting, soulful words wrapped around my heart in a way no one else had. She understood me just like her brother did. This weekend kept filling me up in ways I hadn't expected. Something more to be grateful for.

She wiped my tears and took my face in her hands like a caring mother. "You're going to get through this. We're here to help. You have captivated our brother—which is no minor accomplishment—and you have also endeared yourself to me and Tabitha as well. We've got you."

I was sniffling, feeling like a blubbering idiot, when Alex walked into the room.

"Jesus, Sarah. What did you say to my girl?" His annoyance at her was endearing, especially because he flipped himself over the back of the couch to get to me more quickly.

"What did my evil sister say to you?" He said in a baby voice. He pushed his ass in Sarah's face, crawled to my spot, then flipped me on top of his body. "Do you want me to send her home?" he hissed.

His boyish responses to a conversation he knew nothing about was adorable and sweet. I had never seen a childlike playfulness in Alex. The more I was around him, the more I saw him let his guard down to be the man he wanted to be. Someone without pretense or façade. Just Alex.

"Don't be a dick, Alex, I was comforting her. Ask her yourself," she shot back, not so playfully.

He gently lifted my chin to look into my damp eyes. "Is this true?" Those dark emerald eyes melted me every time.

I nodded. He brushed away the last remnants of my tears and placed a gentle kiss on my lips. He was such a good kisser that I forgot Sarah was sitting in front of us.

"Ahem," she interrupted. "I'd say get a room, but I don't want to hear you fucking like bunnies. I'm going to take a shower. Then I'll be ready to walk through your town's version of a Dickens novel." She bent over and kissed each of us on the cheek while her reassuring hand squeezed my shoulder. I had made a friend that morning, and I was grateful it was one of Alex's sisters.

An hour later we were walking through Shain Park in Birmingham eating roasted cinnamon almonds and drinking hot cider with rum—the rum generously donated by Tabitha and her flask.

Every girl needed a concealed flask just for this reason. Birmingham was one of those quiet towns that valued a big show of holiday decorations, sparing no expense to invigorate their citizens' shopping. Window displays were a form of art in these parts—from dancing children in bright holiday outfits to ones with animatronic dogs jumping over each other. Another one looked like a live snow globe with tiny bits of paper floating over a Victorian dollhouse.

We shopped among the throngs vying for the perfect gifts for the people in their lives, laughing as they dipped and dove around stores, grabbing at things like they'd won the lottery. By lunchtime, we called it quits and found a quaint spot to eat a mile down the road. The snow was falling again in earnest, causing us to reconsider going out for the night.

With a new drink in hand, Tabitha slid into the wooden booth, raising her glass.

"To Alex and to us. Freed from the bondage of parental dinners. Freed from the lecherous stares from their bulbous-nosed politician friends who dared to think they could help themselves to an unappreciated hug." The alcohol had loosened her lips and I was pretty sure she had just revealed another piece of her family's secrets.

Sarah concurred and drank deeply herself. Alex, on the other hand, went stiff.

"What do you mean when you say unappreciated hug?" His hands were flat on the table, his drink forgotten. I laid my hand on his thigh in hopes of settling him down, but to no avail.

The sisters looked at each other conspiratorially. I couldn't believe the level of table talk these two could accomplish with their eyes only. This was not good. Not good at all.

"Tell me!" Alex slammed the table, making our drinks spill.

Sarah started, her face somber: "There were several times when we were young that a few of dad's friends thought they could pat our asses, or rub their arms over our breasts, or hug us closely to feel them while kissing our necks."

"Fucking-A," Alex bellowed. "Why didn't you say something to me? Or better yet, our fa—? Never mind. I know the answer to that question. Did you ever try, though?"

Tabitha put her arm around Sarah's shoulder, giving her the support she appeared to need. "We did try, Alex. We tried lots of times. Neither Mommy dearest nor our ignorant father gave our complaints any merit. 'You must have misunderstood their intentions.' Blah, blah. Or, my favorite, 'You're such a pretty girl, you should be flattered.' I swear to God, Alex, if I hadn't stomped on the mayor's foot or retaliated every time after trying to be heard, I would have killed someone."

I sat dumbfounded, hearing what they had to endure. For me, I was just neglected. For them, there was physical abuse on top of emotional abuse. I was still not processing that rich and entitled people experienced these horrors the same as poor people. I felt so naïve. Weren't they supposed to be more evolved? Beyond us simple folk? Maybe I was the ignorant one. Sadly, this shit was pandemic, and no one was beyond its reach.

Alex scrubbed his forehead. His lips were pressed together so tightly that a white line appeared. I could hear his molars grinding in his head and I needed to do something before he went ballistic.

As quietly as I could, knowing this was none of my business, I interjected, "You were right to fight back. Having each other to lean on must have been your saving grace. I'm sorry you were subjected to this behavior from all parties involved."

Now that I'd said that, I was concerned that maybe I should have kept my mouth shut. Sometimes in my desire to help, I'd unconsciously add to the problem. Alex looked at my mouth and then my eyes, looking at what, I didn't know. *Yep. I should have kept my mouth shut.* Slowly, he turned his head back to his sisters, who looked guilty and shocked.

"She's right. If I'd known that was going on, I'd, I—fuck! I don't know what I would have done. Our parents suck. I'm sickened by how callous they were in the face of your revelations. I'd ask who did this to children, but for fuck's sake, it happens everywhere!" He buried his face in his hands. Watching this big, strong man shutter with emotion was killing me.

I wrapped my arms around his shoulders, offering what strength I could. He turned and returned the hug as if I was a raft he was hanging on for dear life. There had been so many blows to these beautiful people, it was a wonder they had become so successful and strong. But there's the rub: strong on the outside, deeply wounded on the inside.

The waiter who came over to take our order stopped short when he saw our faces.

"I'll come back in a few minutes to take your order," he suggested.

"Bring another round of drinks when you do. We're calling a cab tonight," Tabitha quipped. Leave it to her to bring levity to a devastating moment.

Sarah wiped her eyes and pushed herself upright, proclaiming, "I'm done with this conversation. What's done is done, and it can't be changed. I know who my parents are and are not, and I'm not spending the rest of my vacation playing the 'What if' game. Alex, thank you for wanting to step in and save the day. You've done it plenty of times, including this weekend. We're moving forward, setting new boundaries and forming new traditions thanks to Trudie and her delightful family. Thank you." She polished off the rest of her bourbon, clasping her hands on the table when she was through.

"What she said," Tabitha mumbled, pointing a finger at her sister.

"For the record, I'm not fine with this nor will I ever be. As far as I'm concerned, I have no reason to spend a moment more with them for the rest of my life. If things go as planned, I'll be opening a new office in the Detroit area soon, and visits back to New York will be few and far between." He, too, polished off his drink and then placed his hand on my thigh, caressing me softly.

I shook my head, wildly choking on my spit in the process. "Hang on. You're moving here? Soon?" I looked to his sisters hoping for some clarity. "What the hell is he saying?"

"I think it's true. Alex told us last week when he invited us for the weekend that one of his partners wanted a Midwest presence. He can travel from here just as well as from Manhattan." Tabitha looked at Alex to be sure she was telling the right story.

Alex shifted in his seat and placed his big hands on my shoulders. His face softened and his dimple popped out when he smiled at me. If I had ever questioned whether he loved me, it was the face he made when he looked into my eyes that obliterated the last molecule of doubt in my body.

"I can't be away from you anymore. I want to be close to you. When you're happy, I'm happy, and when you're sad, I need to hold you. Trudie, I love you. I hadn't planned to ask this now, but what the hell—will you move in with me?"

Gasps of joy rang from his sister's mouth while mine gaped in surprise. My head swam with what this might mean. The room seemed to spin around, with the two of us stopped still as if in the eye of a hurricane, as Alex waited for my answer. What did I want? What about the projects we were working on? I needed to speak to Ruby, my mom, and my friends. My heart wanted this so badly, but words were not forming on my lips. What was my hesitation?

I wrapped my hands around his neck and pulled him into a long deep kiss instead. I needed time to marinate on his proposal. It wasn't marriage. It wasn't forever. But it was a bridge to our future, if only I'd cross it. He'd proven to me over and over again that he would protect me both physically and emotionally. He'd changed in ways I couldn't have imagined the first time I met him. He was honorable and respected. Imaginative, dominant, playful, and possessive. When I thought of the perfect physical manifestation of a man, he ticked off every box, notwithstanding his penchant for cleanliness. I finally trusted him. I finally believed we could have a future together. So what the hell was holding me back?

Our kiss ended, and I smiled.

"Trudie—baby. That was some kiss, but I need your words. Would you move in with me?"

I searched his eyes, and finally, I saw what had held me back.

I put my hands on his chest and played with the button of his shirt. The chambray material was soft and soothing, exactly what I needed right now. We were making the biggest decision in our relationship to date in front of his sisters, and I felt very exposed and vulnerable. I didn't want to pressure him or make him feel something he wasn't ready for, but I needed to let him know exactly how I felt about moving in together without creating a wedge between us. I guess this was what was meant by putting your big girl panties on. I sighed, and his eyes widened. It was good to know he was as tightly wound as I had been. *Here we go.*

"I would love to move in with you. Unfortunately, the timing is poor. We work together. You are a hired contractor, and I'm not sure how Eloise or Dr. Dinglehopper would warm to the idea that we've been distracted by each other."

His eyebrows came together in disbelief. "Really? That's the only reason you're not moving in?"

I'm not sure I liked his tone when he said that. Of course, it was one of my reasons—though there was another that took precedence.

Fine. Pulling up my proverbial panties again, I took another stab at making my feelings known. "Okay, you're right. It's not the only reason." I looked to his sisters for support. They opened their hands, palms up on the table.

"I'm laying down all my cards, Alex. Please know that I love you so much when you hear this." My lower lip pushed out slightly and I slouched against his chest.

"Just be honest with me. That's all I ask." He placed his thumb on my chin and cupped my jaw, sending shutters of lust down to my belly.

"I'm afraid if we move in before we are committed to each other our relationship will fail. I'm not a prude. Not in the least. I've never met anyone I would even say this to because I've never loved anyone like I love you. I want us to go the distance. I want forever."

ALEXANDER

Forever?

Is that what I was asking by proposing she move in with me? Was Trudie my forever person? Wouldn't we figure that out by living together? So many questions I hadn't even thought of. When I had been engaged to Sheila, we lived together long before we were engaged. Was that what Trudie was afraid of? Why hadn't I put that together?

Trudie came from a very traditional family, like I did, yet hers seemed so different from mine. I couldn't deny the statistics of people who married after living with each other had an high divorce rates. Even though being engaged and cohabitating had better results, both were big risks but I wanted to try–for her. She was younger, much younger than I was. She wanted the fairy tale, the kids, the whole nine yards. Her hesitation was becoming crystal clear to me. I was living for today and she wanted to live for the future.

"The student has just schooled the professor. I mean—wow! I guess we need to figure some more of this out." I was crestfallen. I wanted all the benefits of living together without the pressure. What a jackass. I placed my hand on her heart and kissed her lips gently. "This is exactly what I mean. You make me a better man. We'll figure something out—soon." I pulled her in for a hug and saw hearts in my sisters' eyes.

"You two are so fucking cute," Sarah said, choking on her words.

"I think I'm going to be sick," Tabitha mocked, putting her finger down her throat.

I signaled the waiter scurrying across the room. I was starving and this dinner needed to be over as soon as possible. My sisters could have the apartment tonight, I was sleeping at Trudie's.

CHAPTER 22
TRUDIE

Alex took his sisters back to the airport Sunday morning while I caught up with my mom at my house. She had started visiting the university library more often and I was fairly sure it wasn't for the new releases. After some prodding, she admitted to flirting with one of the librarians, and he had suggested she get a part-time job there so they could spend more time together. I had always wondered if my mom still desired another relationship after my dad. Not having sex or intimacy for fifteen years seemed horrifying.

"So, are you going to do it? The job part, not the man part." For an English teacher I'm embarrassed to say my words weren't always packaged well.

I could hear dishes clanging in the background. "Maybe," she replied, sounding unsure. "I hoped to cut back on my hours at my current job on campus, and if I did get the library position, I could still make enough, keep my benefits, and get to know Clark better."

My mother couldn't move forward until she had all the answers straight in her head. Not me. If I had half a story, it would be enough to go for it.

"I'm proud of you, Mom. You deserve to slow down and enjoy life more. If this guy, Clark, is a good man, then I think you should definitely take the leap. You love books and you're there all the time anyway. Why not get paid to do what you love?"

"That makes perfect sense, Trudie. Once I meet with human resources about the move, I'll apply. Thank you for your support and encouragement. You're the best daughter in the world." I could hear the smile in her voice. She deserved to have someone who adored her.

"I know!" We both laughed like little girls.

I hesitated to bring up the past, but I needed to know how my mom decided to divorce my dad. Her opinion mattered the most when it came to helping me decide if moving in with Alex was a good idea.

"Mom. I need help with something. It's a tricky situation that involves Alex." I sat down at the kitchen table with my coffee to describe my dilemma. "He asked me to move in with him,"—I could hear her gasp on her end— "and I told him that I didn't want to take that step unless he was committed to me—like with a ring committed. Did I do the right thing? I do love him and we're great together. Most of the time, that is." I left my seat and began a circuitous path around my living room.

"*Mija!* That's amazing! You're right to pause for a moment and think this through. My experience with your father was vastly different. We were married before we lived together. There was no back door to escape through. I don't think that kind of commitment has gone out of style, though so many young couples your age feel living together is a way to see if they are compatible enough to get married. But to me it just sounds like one or the other doesn't want to fully commit and therefore won't give everything they have to make things work. Trudie, marriage is arduous work. The hardest, most fulfilling work you'll ever do, until you have children. That's when the true test of your relationship happens."

I was beginning to wear a path in my carpet as I circled my tiny living room listening to my mom's words of wisdom. They were exactly what I was feeling. I hadn't even considered adding kids into the equation. Alex was so good with them at school. I'm sure he'd be a great father and me a great mom. But she was right, we had to go all in to make this work.

"My thoughts exactly. Mom, please tell me how your marriage ended. I was too young and self-absorbed to understand." She had evaded my original question for a reason, but I needed an answer, now.

"Leaving your father was the hardest decision of my life. I weighed the pros and cons dozens of times over the first three years after he took that god-awful job. But each time, I remembered my vows and how good we were together when he wasn't away. I felt I could keep the family together until you all graduated from high school. Unfortunately, toward the end of those three years, he started coming home angrier and angrier. The way he took it out on you kids broke my heart. I could handle his jabs at me as long as he wasn't doing the same to my children. When he came back from those forest fires in California, I decided I was done. He raised his hand to Zander. He threatened Paolo. His words shredded you into mute, shuddering in a corner and fearing for your safety. That had to stop. I had to make it stop." There was a tremor in her voice I hadn't heard before. It sounded like there was more to say, but she was choosing to hold it in. My own breathing became shallow and my pulse quickened.

"Mom, did he … ah … ever hit you?" I was pushing her. I needed to know the whole truth so I could finally reconcile my feelings toward my father.

"*Mija, por favor.* I don't think it's necessary to divulge every detail to you. My relationship with your father was mine to deal with, not yours."

I pushed again. "He did hit you then?"

"Trudie, don't."

"I'm not letting this go, Mom. Did. He. Hit. You?" Pity turned to anger, with volatile coming up right behind it.

The long pause was all the answer I needed.

"Okay then. I'll respect your privacy, but I have my answer. I hope one day you'll say the words out loud and set them free. It's been fifteen years, Mom. You're entitled to let them go. It won't change how I feel about you. You'll always be the best mother in the world. You saved us. Words cannot describe how grateful I am that you were strong enough to do what you did. It's remarkable."

"*Te quiera, cariño.*" She cried—hopefully happy tears.

"I love you too, Mom."

My head was filled with emotions, none of which were happy. I needed to see my father one last time. I needed to be able to shut that door permanently and move forward from the lessons learned from that part of my history. I sent him a text letting him know that I would be coming to the nursing home later, and that it would be my last visit. Closure. It's what I craved and would get before this year was over.

Blinking lights and squiggly lines covered the monitor attached above the hospital-style bed. The facility the social worker had found was designed for hospice care. Thankfully for him, there was an aide who watched him diligently, allowing me to feel less guilty that he lay there alone. It was late in the afternoon and the streetlights had already come on. The end of Daylight Savings Time put us in darkness way too early. I could feel the reaper in the room.

His eyes were closed, and his arms sat limply at his sides. An IV port in his bruised hand pumped life-sustaining fluid to his veins. I was pulling up a chair alongside his bed when a young male nurse aide with a chopped haircut came in to check on him.

"Why is he attached to all this if he is dying?" I pointed to all the things connected to his body as if it was a waste of time. Implying that *he* was a waste of time.

The aide and I sighed. "He hasn't allowed us to remove them yet. Sometimes our patients wait for their loved ones to show up or leave before invoking their DNR. Others want to have some control at life's end. Either way, our facility specializes in patient dignity, so until he can't communicate, we'll let him make his own decisions."

Waiting for loved ones. Interesting. Did he mean me?

My experience with death had been minimal. A guinea pig, a neighbor's cat, and a professor I once knew in college. So far, nothing as monumental as losing a parent.

"Has he been declining recently?"

"A few things have. His sight is mostly gone and we are feeding him through a tube. That white one there." He pointed to my dad's nose. "He's a funny guy, especially when we have to change his catheter." I'm sure he was.

"We can't make out much of what he is saying so we gave him a pad and pen to help him communicate. This morning he wrote out a message that I needed a haircut." *Huh. He's not wrong.*

I patted my dad's hand like he was a dog, "He's a real charmer." My disdain was evident, but I didn't care.

The aide left after taking his vitals and I removed my hand from his. So many thoughts stomped around my brain that it was hard to think straight. Alex warned me that today's visit might be difficult and to prepare myself for the worst.

"Babe," Alex had said. "It's time to tie up any loose ends in case you don't see him again."

He had held me tightly to his chest outside the hospital doors. He wanted to come up but I wouldn't let him. As much as I loved him protecting me, this was my fight to fight and my problem to solve.

"I know," I said, fiddling with the shirt buttons under his coat.

"I'll be here in the waiting room until you're done. Take your time."

This was why I loved him. Always ready to give me my space, then stepping in when I needed him the most.

I sat there looking at my old, broken father, wondering if we had said all there was to be said. Beeps and whooshing of machines made me drowsy. It didn't help that Alex had kept me awake the previous night as he explored my body in new and exciting ways. His repertoire of sensual moves was expansive, to say the least. Now, however, I was paying the price. My eyelids were drifting closed when I heard a big snore. It was so big that it triggered my dad, who woke up in a panic.

"Whass goin' on?" His slurred speech resembled that of a stroke victim.

I jumped up to let him see me better.

"Hey, Dad, it's me, Trudie. I came to visit." I pasted on a smile for his benefit even if he couldn't see it.

Gathering his pen and paper he wrote out a scribbled message and turned the pad for me to see. "You came." He reached out a hand and I held it gently.

"Yeah, I came. Do you need anything?"

He swallowed a few times and worked the saliva around in his mouth.

He took back the pad and wrote, "Your forgiveness."

"Why? Nothing can be changed and you won't be affecting me in the future. Our problems are history, Dad." I stared at the bruises on his hands, feeling like one myself.

He reached over and clasped his hands over mine. His droopy eyelids kept me from seeing his eyes completely. It was the one part of him I saw every day, because he had given me the same eyes. I loved the shape and color. My long thick lashes made me look like I had mascara on all the time. It was the best part about them. But looking at myself in the mirror and seeing his eyes always aggravated me.

He cleared his throat and croaked out, "Our legacy. Clear the air."

Crap! One second he sounded like he'd had a stroke and the next he sounded like a God damned poet. I was conflicted.

"Why would I say it if I didn't mean it? That would make me a hypocrite," I argued back.

He took up his pen again. "Doesn't matter. You'll grow to mean it someday." *Not possible.*

He pushed the button on his bed to raise himself higher and wrote his longest message yet.

"I'll go first and then when you say it, I'll ring for the nurse to pull all this shit off me and I'll die a happy man. Does that work for you?"

Disgusting! Then I'd have to carry the burden of his death. No fucking way. This man was a narcissist to the end.

"Do what you want, Dad, but I'm not saying it until I mean it. How dare you bargain with your life, leaving me to deal with the guilt. Fuck you."

I pushed back from the bed and grabbed my purse. "You can live and die by your decisions. I have nothing to forgive myself for. You're projecting your guilt onto me and I'm not buying into it anymore." I began to walk to the door and spun around vehemently, "Good luck on your passing. You're going to need it."

I stormed out of his room again. I couldn't seem to leave a room he was in without stomping out angry.

"Wait!!" he cried out with what little voice he had left, but I kept walking. "Trudie!!" he wailed. I made it to the lobby when someone called after me. Alex jumped up from his seat and ran over to hear what the commotion was about.

"Ms. Gonzalez. Your dad is coding. He can't speak and I need a family member to make a decision about his life." My insides turned upside down, and we ran back through the maze of hallways to his room.

Every freaking buzzer was going off and my dad looked stricken. Another aide entered the room with a defibrillator, asking if a decision had been made. I wouldn't make it. I couldn't. I had just told him he had to make it. Then why did I feel compelled to have him brought back to life?

"Revive him," I grunted, and stepped back by the wall while they worked.

They zapped him twice with no conversion. Then again, two more times, with no luck. I stepped forward to the end of his bed as they called the time of death.

I knew theoretically I hadn't caused this. Not forgiving him wasn't likely the reason either. I refused to believe any of this was my doing. Didn't I come more than once to try to have a happy ending with this stubborn man? Didn't I put my best foot forward and listen while he unburdened himself to me like I was a fucking priest. He wanted absolution. Fine. "I forgive you, Dad." Did that change anything, no! It changed nothing!

The aides gave me their sympathies and told me I could have as long as I wanted to sit with him. I poured my heart out, beating his bed and saying horrible things. I hadn't wanted to be here when he passed. It wasn't fair that I needed to deal with his shit again. I can't be sure how long I cried at the idea of losing him or the dashed hope that he would have changed back to the man who read me stories, protected me from spiders, and bought me a new ice cream cone when mine fell in the park. Hope was gone for that part of my life. It left a chasm so wide I wasn't sure how I was ever going to fill it.

Alex knocked on the door at some point, reminding me he was near. He pulled me into his arms and whispered reassuring things, but I can't seem to remember what they were. Then the chasm shrank. Not much, but some. I didn't want Alex as a father or protector. I wanted him for this—knowing how and when to make me feel whole.

We left the nursing home without speaking a word. The hospice director slid a packet of information into my hands and said she would take care of all the cremation details and that a clergyperson would contact me tomorrow to arrange the funeral. None of it mattered any longer. He was gone. Never coming back. Never.

The rest of the evening was a blur. Alex took charge and called my mom, who then called my brothers. We met at her house and had dinner, sharing only the good stories we could remember about our father. My brothers had accepted that my dad didn't have the capacity to become a better man. I was the only one who had clung to that hope. When we got older, my brothers also saw the way all the drinking and anger had corroded his mind. We had never spoken about that. They had protected me from additional pain, and I appreciated them so much for their efforts.

Alex sat quietly on the couch while we sat around the kitchen table. I watched him twirl his phone around in his hands, then watched him walk around picking up pictures and knickknacks around the room. He was infinitely patient and it helped the chasm close some more.

I nuzzled up behind him near the fireplace as he inspected a photo on the mantel of all of us on a beach when we were young. I wrapped my arms around his slim waist and leaned against his muscled back, inhaling his smoky scent.

"Thank you," I spoke into his back.

"You're welcome."

We stayed like that for a while just enjoying the closeness and sharing each other's energy.

"This would be a great picture for your dad's funeral. I'm assuming it's one of your last happy family pictures?"

I unlocked my hands from around his body and stepped around him to look more closely at the picture he was holding. "It was. You're right. It's time we focus on what was good about our father and let go of the rest. It's too heavy a cross to bear."

He took the picture from me, placed it back on the mantel, and took me in his arms. He rocked me gently and placed kisses into my hair. It felt so good, and the chasm closed even more. This day had been a whirlwind of emotions. I was so tired.

"Come on, baby. Let's get you home," Alex said, stepping back from me with his hands on my shoulders. All I could do was nod.

One week later, during a colossal snowstorm, we cremated my father and held a small memorial service with a couple of his work friends, a set of old neighbors, Alex, and even Sarah and Tabitha, who had flown back for it. A snowstorm was very apropos since he'd spent the last twenty years assessing damage from terrible storms. But the only damage assessed that day was the estrangement of a once loving couple and their children. And you couldn't put a dollar amount on that kind of loss.

Once the funeral proceedings were over and the last guest had left my mom's house, we went to the basement to watch a Wings game on the big screen. Alex sat in the seat where he had fucked the life out of me on Thanksgiving, and I sat in his lap, wiggling occasionally, reminding him of how naughty we were. The rest of the gang screamed at the screen, completely forgetting why all of us were together. It seemed that he had been out of our lives for so long that there wasn't much need to mourn him. Life went on after death, and my family flowed smoothly into our next chapter.

ALEXANDER

The semester was winding down at Hart Middle School, and my assessments were also coming to an end. After I gave my recommendations to Eloise and the school board, I wouldn't be required to be at the school until early February and then again during the first week of April. Follow-up was paramount to change, and I planned on taking advantage of every day available for the kids' sake as well as my own. After all the activities the teachers had executed and all the unexpected issues with the kids, I had grown to love this place. Also, there was a dirty part of my brain that was banging to let me run free in this school—places and surfaces I wanted to fuck Trudie on. Her desk, for one. In the locker rooms, behind the stage, and so many others. I remember being a kid and fooling around after school behind the drama stage or under the bleachers. Apparently, I wanted more of those experiences, but this time with a certain fiery Latina. Speaking of Trudie, watching her walk down the hall at that moment in a pencil skirt that was hugging her ass while she swished back to her classroom popped a tent in my pants.

Thank goodness my satchel had a cross-body strap because I needed to keep the front over my dick until it got itself under control. I trailed Trudie to her room but was stopped abruptly by Eloise just before making the turn.

"Dr. Pierce, what a lovely surprise to see you here so early today. How was your holiday?" Why did I get the feeling she was fishing for something?

I pulled a hand from my pocket and threaded my fingers through my hair, lifting off my brow.

"Good to see you too, Eloise. It was ... memorable." Sharing the news of Mr. Gonzalez's death wasn't my story to tell. I had no idea if Trudie had shared her backstory with anyone at school, and I sure as hell wasn't going down that rabbit hole.

"Mine was the usual. My kids came home from college with their arms filled with laundry and their pockets empty. They made a huge mess of my house and we played board games, which elicited some much-missed smack talk. Then poof! They took off on Sunday, leaving me with a week's worth of cleaning. In short, it was the best." She smiled, reflecting on her memories before pulling herself back to me.

"Sounds delightful. Well, I have a few things to discuss with Ms. Gonzalez before class starts. if you'll..."

"Uh, before you go, I have a few things to discuss when you're finished talking to Trudie. The first being Bobby." Her stern expression frightened me. That woman could turn you to stone if you looked at her too long.

I cleared my throat and stood straighter. "Sure. See you soon."

Crap! I knew this conversation was coming, though I didn't think it would happen before nine in the morning. I wanted to take that prick down and would do anything it took to make it happen. No one touches my woman, especially that creeper.

Trudie's classroom was filling up with kids dropping homework onto her desk while she wrote out some lesson elements on the whiteboard. I saw Ella speaking quietly to Delano, *interesting*, and Tomás sharing his cell phone screen with Tina. They were laughing, and for the first time, I saw each of them sincerely engaged with their classmates. The positive effects our mentor program was having on these kids were more meaningful, and my response was more visceral than I would have imagined. I couldn't have been more pleased.

I stood next to the board and blew a stream of warm air toward Trudie's face to get her attention. Her response was priceless—she dropped her head back ever so slightly as she exhaled. Nothing noticeable to the children, yet ridiculously hot to me.

I whispered softly across the two feet between us.

"Good morning, Ms. Gonzalez. You look edible." I smiled, making the dimple in my cheek pop out. She loved that dimple, and I loved using it to my advantage.

Looking hot as hell, she shivered and then peeked over her shoulder to her class, taking inventory to determine whether anyone was close enough to hear my comments.

"You as well, Doctor. How was your Thanksgiving?" She taunted me.

"Now that you ask, it was eventful and illuminating. Did you know that I asked my girlfriend to move in with me and she declined my invitation?" I waggled my brows and hoped she would spend a minute bantering with me.

She stopped writing and threw the pen onto the ledge, turning quickly toward me.

"She what?" Trudie's eyes went wide realizing how loud she was. Whispering now, she tried again. "She what? That ungrateful bitch." She covered her smile with her hair.

"I know! I'm absolutely crushed. Would you be able to help me get over this affront after school today?"

She threw her head back, laughing, and grabbed at her belly. "Dr. Pierce, you are a piece of work." When her laughing ended, I took a step back, held up four fingers, and whispered, "Here. Four sharp. Your desk." I pointed two fingers at my eyes and then back at hers as I backed out of her room.

I chuckled to myself as I walked down the hall to the office and then peered through the glass wall that housed the administrative staff. I would miss these people. Mona and her mothering and Ricky and his infectious flamboyant mannerisms. It was rare that I found such a cohesive group of people all working equally for the greater good of their organization.

I felt very melancholy that morning and it was starting to bug me. More often than not, I did my job and left. Typically, no one called or wrote to stay connected, and it felt more professional to keep some distance from those who I was working with. Trudie had been the only exception. And in order for her to succeed here, I needed to be sure her programs were solid and protected. Eloise was key to this process, so I knocked on her door, ready to defend myself for defending the woman I loved.

Knock, knock.

"Whose there?" she called and then chuckled a deep belly laugh. "Never mind, I know who you are."

This meeting was starting off well. I was very interested to see how it finished.

I smiled and took my regular seat. In an unusual move, Eloise turned the seat beside me and sat down.

"It seems there was an altercation over the holiday weekend. Would you care to tell me your side of the story?" From the look on her face, this was less like a question and more like an inquisition.

"I would love to. What story have you been given so far?" I wasn't laying down any cards until I knew what I was dealing with here.

"Bobby sent me an email last Wednesday. Since Trudie's father had passed the Sunday before, I made the assumption you and she would be working through her feelings and busy with more pressing matters. His complaint was that you punched him in the face unprovoked with a hundred people looking on at a local eatery. His statement had a million holes in it and I was hoping you could fill them in for me." She stopped talking, grabbed the mug of coffee she'd left on the end of her desk, and sat back in her chair.

I shook my head in disbelief. Of course, he'd omitted why I'd decked him. Did he think he could get away with that kind of behavior?

"You are absolutely right about missing information—more like the whole story." I scrubbed my face with my hands and sat back, laying out all the details that Trudie gave me about what happened before I saw her and everything that happened afterward. Eloise gasped and slammed her hand down on the arm of her chair.

"Damn it, Alexander. I knew something was up with this dude. I've been trying to find any reason to fire him. Now that I have your story and Trudie's, we'll have enough to do it. Did Trudie press charges against him?"

I hadn't thought about that. But pressing charges would also have called attention to me throwing the first punch, and we all know how that would have gone down.

I hung my head, feeling guilty about my own actions. "She did not. I protected her and promised this guy would get his due. But she wasn't physically hurt, and moreover, by the end of dinner, she seemed fine emotionally. Eloise, I've treated traumatized patients who had been raped, and Trudie didn't exhibit those responses. Since the incident, she hasn't mentioned any difficult feelings or shame. I feel like an ass for not suggesting it to her." I sat forward with my hands clasped between my knees, running that evening through my mind over and over. "She was fine."

Eloise had an exceptional intuition about her staff, and Trudie was a favorite of hers.

"Dr. Pierce. Alexander. Your interest in Trudie hasn't gone unnoticed by me. I see how fond you are of her and the sparks that fly between the two of you. While I appreciate that you are, let's say, exploring your relationship, I do need you to maintain your professionalism in the building." Her eagle eyes seemed to be staring deep into my psyche, making my spine tingle. *Did she know what I planned for later?*

"Furthermore, the way you protected her outside the building was exceptional and heartwarming. Trudie is more than just a teacher here. Her instincts are invaluable and if she doesn't feel that Bobby is a safe person to be around, I trust her."

I nodded my head. "I couldn't agree more."

Eloise stood and returned to the opposite side of her desk, taking her coffee with her.

"I have already filled out the termination paperwork for Bobby, and after I speak with Trudie to corroborate your stories, I'll submit it to the superintendent of schools. The fact that he already has a black mark on his record for harassment a few years back certainly will help settle this quickly. Do I have your word you won't speak with Trudie until after school today? I don't want you coaching her or skewing her story in any way."

"No, ma'am." I pinched my fingers together and pretended to zip my lips and throw away the key. Her sly smile was encouraging. She was definitely onto me and Trudie and because I respected her greatly, I would follow her instructions.

"Good. Regarding your assessments of our teaching staff, test scores, and the overall climate at Hart Middle School, do you have a quarterly report you are prepared to turn in?"

I reached into my satchel for the half-inch thick document and handed it to her. She took her seat and picked up her reading glasses to review it.

"This is just a draft," I explained. "Trudie begged me not to turn it in without your review first. Something about hidden agendas. What were you thinking?"

Before she said anything there was a knock at her door.

"Come!" Eloise said, raising her voice.

Ricky turned the handle and poked his head in. Not his body, just his head. It was so Ricky.

"Sorry to intrude. Ms. Gonzalez is here to see you." He gave me a wink. It appeared Eloise wasn't the only one on to us.

"Send her in. Please hold my calls." Eloise waved her hand dismissively.

"Got it." He turned his head dramatically. "You can come in now," he said, directing a fidgety Trudie to enter. She sat down, crossing her toned legs and giving me a direct line to the split between her ample thighs. They framed her sex so prettily.

"Welcome. I was just starting to respond to Dr. Pierce's assessment." She went back to reading the first page and then looked at both of us.

"Our discussion a few weeks back revolved around possible hidden agendas from the school board. The scuttlebutt is that they are looking to fabricate loose reasons to let go of some of our staff and to reduce their bottom line. I'll be straight with you, Dr. Pierce. Is there anything in this document that indicates we are being wasteful in our resources or that any of our teachers or staff aren't necessary?"

I shook my head, puzzled. Normally, an organization makes it clear to me why they want an assessment. This board didn't mention firing or fiscal reductions in any of our conversations.

"Really? They've said nothing of the sort to me. What have you heard?"

Trudie took the opportunity to voice her thoughts.

"Not in our school, but in two others in the district, the board made severe cuts in their teaching staff, implying it was due to lower enrollment figures trending over the next five years. However, in our part of the district, enrollment's growing. I can only surmise that they want equity throughout the entire district and may penalize us using that metric."

Her fidgeting continued as she recrossed her legs the other way.

"Exactly, Trudie. In addition, our school has fifteen tenured teachers, with five more reaching that bar in the next eight months. If they could fire those teachers, they wouldn't have to provide the pay bump, saving them tens of thousands of dollars," Eloise explained.

I scrubbed my face, thinking about what they'd said and what my initial recommendations were in the document in front of her. Was there anything in there that would get a teacher fired for any reason other than money?

Seconds went by and I watched these fine women hold their breath, waiting for my answer.

"First, I don't think there is any incriminating information in that document." I pointed over to her desk. "Second, I would like to beef up some verbiage regarding how necessary it is to keep all personnel in place given the growth trends in your part of the district. I'll have to do my own research to be sure your assumptions are correct. Not that I'm questioning them, just covering our asses."

"Agreed," Eloise concurred.

"And, last, I would encourage you to collect letters from both parents and students about their teachers to fortify their positions. Any shred of documentation could make the difference." I wished

I had something more formidable than letters, but that was the only thing I could think of at the moment.

"No problem. I'll have my class write essays tomorrow and have them bound together by the end of the day. I'll encourage my friends to do the same. Eloise, would you send out an email to all the other teachers when we're finished? We could say it's for a time capsule so no one freaks out."

I jumped up, "That's brilliant! A time capsule. If we weren't in school, I'd kiss you."

Her face blanched at my words. Eloise pressed her lips together, fighting back a smile.

I looked into Trudie's eyes very intently, causing her to squirm in her seat. I'd love to be that seat. "She knows." I jutted my chin toward her principal. "I think Ricky does, too. Heck, I don't really care who knows, only that we keep our hands off each other during school hours."

TRUDIE

She knew! How was that possible?

"It's true. I do. When you two were in the conference room last month throwing daggers with your eyes and making a fuss about God knows what, that's when I knew something was happening." She smiled like a detective who had solved a crime. "Just keep your hands to yourselves—and stop smiling at each other so much. I don't want the kids catching on." Eloise motioned for me to sit down. We both laughed, finally relieved not to have to hide our feelings so much.

Alex held his hand out to Eloise. "Let me have that back and I'll confirm my remarks aren't going to give them any ideas about firing anyone. I'll inform the board that I'll have their report before the holiday break next week. Also, I would like to sit down on Friday so we can go through this together. There are a few minor changes I'd like to see resolved. Nothing to be concerned about. It's not my normal mode of operation to confer with my subjects in this manner, except I'm thrilled with what I'm seeing. Even Chip has dropped the tough-guy routine with his students, and their test scores have gone up 10 percent across all his classes. That's a great success rate."

"That's fantastic," I exclaimed.

Eloise looked impressed, too. "What did you say to him?"

Alex was clearly trying not to look cocky when he said, "I told him to stop acting like a tough guy to his students. I promised him they'd like and respect him even more if he built them up instead of threatening them with his large size and smart-assed mouth." He laughed then.

"And he didn't blink an eye at that?" I said in shock.

"Truthfully, he looked relieved. He said the teacher he learned most from in high school was an asshole who used the same technique to get his students to learn. He'd thought nothing of it until it became exhausting this past year. Who'd a thunk it?"

"Huh. I suppose we do what's been modeled for us. I'm making a note to put that on our discussion list with our high-risk kids," I said. "Additionally, I wish they would come up with a name for their group already."

Eloise stood up and pushed her chair back. "I think we are done for today. We will reconvene after school on Friday, and Trudie, I'd like you to give me an update on our kids' groups then as well. Have a great day." Eloise walked ahead of us out of her office and over to Ricky.

Alex shoved his papers into his satchel, and as we both stood, he placed a light kiss on my lips, making me tingle all over.

"You are one gorgeous, deliciously smart lady," He growled seductively.

"Yeah. You're right." And I left him watching my ass as I strutted out of the office.

CHAPTER 23
ALEXANDER

"Somebody better tell me what's going on over there."

My business partner had made plans to come to town today and neglected to tell me where and when I was supposed to meet him.

"I'm sorry, sir," Rita, Marco's admin squeaked. "Mr. Demascus said he would contact you himself when he landed. The last thing I heard was he was meeting you in Birmingham at the Lexus Hotel at one o'clock. Did you check with the front desk to see if he left a message?"

"Yes, Rita. Twice. He's not in the lounge, the restaurant, or booked into a room. I've canceled two other meetings this afternoon to accommodate him and now I'm wishing I'd canceled this meeting instead. Sorry, Rita. It's not your fault. I'll wait a while longer, and then I'll be back at my apartment for the rest of the afternoon. Thanks for your help," I said.

"You're welcome, sir. Have a better day." Her voice wavered in her distress at the situation.

Marco Demascus was a lifelong friend who drove me up the wall with his harebrained ideas that remarkably always worked out—which was why I was still sitting there twiddling my thumbs. Over cigars and cards two years ago we'd bounced some business venture ideas around. After a ridiculously long research process we had founded PsychMasters, Inc., a practice offering virtual and in-person psychological consulting and treatment options for all types of mental illness and general emotional well-being.

Each center focused on one or two core issues: the one in Detroit focused on educational and business psychology. When we mapped out the country into zones, we felt having one of each specialty—educational, business, sports psych, and diagnoses management—in each zone would be enough to create a microcosm of what our business was about: overall good mental health. Utilizing the magic of the internet, we could connect each zone's support groups and collaborate across the country for clients who exhibited unique traits. It was like a sudoku puzzle, whereby when you had the same values vertically and horizontally, they equaled out. I was still out of my mind excited about this venture and the infinite impact we could have.

Trudie turned me on when she spoke of the mentoring program for her school and her plan to help these kids improve their self-worth and start believing they deserved the best in life. When I wasn't thinking about her, I was dreaming of a nonprofit piece to integrate into PsychMasters. In order to truly make an impact on those who needed it most, we had to give back with outreach programs that families were desperate to access. This was precisely the conversation I was supposed to be having at that moment with my dipshit friend instead of scrolling memes on social media. Yes, even highbrow people like me laugh at dogs riding on goats' backs.

"Hey! My man, Alex. How are you buddy?" Marco walked across the lobby like he owned the place. *He just might.*

I stood to greet my friend, giving him a bro hug with clasped hands and one arm across the shoulder.

"I'd be better if my dumbfuck friend showed up on time. Water under the bridge. Let's talk."

Two hours later we had mapped out the nuances of our new Detroit location. With any luck, if this paradigm worked, we could duplicate it across the country. Having it operate as a franchise allowed us to maximize our advertising budget and encourage local mental health specialists to own a piece of the pie.

"I wish I had more time to hang, Alex, but I'm meeting with some potential franchise owners over dinner and I need to check in and pull everything together."

Marco never stopped. He was the only person I knew who literally closed deals in his sleep. He was just that good at schmoozing and negotiating. My focus was on programming and building results from them. That's probably why we worked so well together—we stayed in our own lanes and collaborated when necessary.

"Next time. I have a few ideas for locations I'd like to toss into your freaky head. Our offices should reflect the high-quality services we offer, but I don't want to intimidate those who don't live in this area. We need to be advertising our brand as servicing all individuals, not just the elite."

He nodded his agreement and we shook hands, taking our leave. I had to work through my Hart Middle School assessment with a fine-toothed comb for the rest of the evening. No one would lose their job on my watch ... except Bobby, that is.

December had always been a tricky month for me to balance work and family. Many organizations earmarked money for projects beginning the following year and needed to empty their bank accounts before the end of the current year for tax purposes. I had twelve meetings to trudge through before New Year's Day. Also, at the top of my list was getting our high-risk students shored up for the holidays. I didn't want them to lose traction with their newfound skills. Throw in my problematic family and my lovely vixen and I'd maxed out the rest of my year. Something had to give, though, and I knew exactly what it would be: traveling to see my parents. I didn't have four days to kill dealing with their guilt trips and annoying pretenses. For once, I wanted to choose for myself how I'd spend the week between Christmas and New Year's. Like those students, I did not want to lose traction in my efforts to set boundaries with my parents, even if it was difficult to do so.

As I left my meeting, I saw Roots, the Canadian outfitters store Trudie and I had walked through Thanksgiving weekend as we strolled around town and stopped in to buy us matching sweatshirts, sweatpants, and slippers for Christmas. I also stopped at the corner jewelry store we had browsed. My sisters had insisted that we look through the sparkly cases, and I watched my girl get excited over a few brilliant pieces. I wouldn't be surprised if they had been setting me up to know what style of jewelry Trudie liked for future purchases. *Those sisters of mine. Always with an ulterior motive.* I asked the clerk to show me a one-carat single-stone necklace with tiny round diamonds dotted along the chain. It was spectacular. I imagined her lovely neck adorned with this gorgeous piece and knew she'd still outshine every diamond on it. She deserved everything in this store and more. I knew what her salary looked like and was shocked at how cleverly she could make ends meet and still save something for a rainy day. Being thrifty wasn't a word in my family's vocabulary. Nothing in our home was secondhand, handed down, or on loan from someone who didn't need that item for a while. I would venture to say everything in Trudie's apartment was secondhand or borrowed and it was still decorated with spectacular style. It was another reason I loved her. My money didn't impress her—though the cashmere winter coat I was wearing was a favorite of hers. I caught her last week covering herself with it on the couch while she watched TV.

"Were you missing me?" I had asked, rubbing the coat draped over the side of her body.

"Umm. Yes. How do they get those little cashmeres so soft anyhow?"

"You do know they aren't from bunnies, right?"

"I don't care if cashmeres are goats or giraffes. I love them." She was so damn cute when she was neither sleeping nor awake.

"For the record, cashmere is from goats," I expounded.

"Then I want a goat for Christmas and a pen to keep it in. What the hell, buy me a farm!" That had both of us laughing for a full five minutes.

"Something tells me you're more of a city girl. Besides, I don't think you'd like the sheering process those goats go through. Traumatizing, to say the least."

"...and this is why I steal your coat when you're not wearing it." Her sassy remark broke my resolve to keep from bugging her. That's when I tickled her until she cried.

I was entering my building after my shopping excursion when my phone rang. It had to be my lucky day—it was my mom. I considered smashing the phone onto the brushed concrete in the foyer but decided it would be too much of a hassle to get a new one, so I answered begrudgingly.

"Good afternoon, Mother," I deadpanned.

"Don't you 'Mother' me! I'm still trying to recover from you and your sisters deserting us for Thanksgiving. Have you any idea how embarrassing it was to make excuses for all your children? Our cook even asked us to take your meals to a shelter. A *shelter*, Alex!"

"I'm sorry you were traumatized by these circumstances, even though several hungry people benefited from our desertion. You have to understand that we aren't young children. You don't get to decide where and when we are to appear. We aren't intentionally"—although we really were—"trying to make you and Dad look bad. We have lives, responsibilities, and relationships of our own. Please try to make an effort to respect us and what *we* are trying to build."

That was my last plea to my parents. I'm still not sure if they were truly obtuse or if they were narcissistic. I hoped it was the former because I did love to be around them when they were relaxed and without an agenda, which wasn't often.

The silence on the line went on far too long. "Mother?"

"I'm here," she said sullenly.

"What are you feeling right now?" My psychoanalyst mode had engaged.

"Do you really believe your father and I are ruining your lives?" she said with dramatic melancholy.

I breathed in and out slowly and decided that platitudes and my efforts to soften the blow weren't going to get the job done.

"I never said ruining. I said in not so many words that we aren't pawns. Sarah is achieving status and financial success on her own as a pharmaceutical representative. Tabitha has her hands in a variety of organizations I still don't know anything about. And, as for myself, I'm running three businesses, including your foundation, which I don't have time for. I'm building a life in Detroit, Mother. I have friends, and work, and a woman who makes me feel alive and special. Why wouldn't I want to stay here over the holidays? I'm not saying I'll never come home for them, but not this year. It's less about you and Dad and more about me and my needs. Can you understand that?"

More silence.

"I love you, Mom. Please let us grow up and have our own lives."

And more silence.

"Why don't you think about what I've said and we can talk later. Okay?"

"I love you too," she whimpered. This was the moment I'd dreamed of, and now that she truly heard me, it made me afraid for her mental well-being.

I knew her so well that I could set a clock by her neediness. My father neglected her, her friends tolerated her, and now her children were creating lives that didn't include her. I was sure she felt a stab of pain hearing everything I said, but I knew she'd learn to live without. I'd make sure of it. In my heart of hearts, I knew we were doing the right thing. I just wished it didn't hurt her so much.

CHAPTER 24
TRUDIE

Alex and I had planned to do some holiday shopping for his sisters and parents that evening. He may have drawn the line with his parents, but I knew he was upset at having to do it. I had my own boundaries to set, though not with my family. The decision to move forward with holding Bobby accountable for his actions at the restaurant had been made that afternoon. During my prep period, Eloise had pulled me aside to review his and Alex's stories of what happened that night. I'd clarified a few things for her and filled out a disciplinary form to be filed along with her completed letter of termination, which would be presented at the school board's next meeting. The three of us would need to attend, and I hated the thought of another confrontation with Bobby. "Big Girl Panties" moments terrified me. Did I mention my favorite things to do are non-confrontational? Like yoga, and meditation? Alex assured me I was doing the right thing, and I truly wanted to believe him.

"Have you thought about what you'd like to get for your sisters?" I shifted my mood to enjoy our evening together. Nobody liked a Debbie Downer.

"I'm clueless. Can you think of anything?"

"Well, they can afford anything they want, right?" I asked.

He nodded.

"I have two ideas: Pretty nightgowns, although that might be weird coming from their brother. Or a subscription to an audiobook club. It travels well, will get used often, and it fits anyone. What do you think?"

"Both sound great. What if you give them nightgowns, and I give them a year of free audiobooks? I'm paying for both, though."

"Fine. Now for your parents." I would find something personal from me. I may have been a poor teacher, but I was a clever shopper, if nothing else. "This one is going to take some planning. Let's eat first."

This guy followed me around like a puppy sometimes, making me feel like I was running our relationship. I had more than enough wit, talent, and smarts to nurture it, but I also knew that it was honesty, trust, and the belief in your partner's abilities that made the difference. Patience, when you didn't have any more to give. Friendship, to know when to let your partner shine. And compassion when they were hurting. The more I meditated on what love truly was, the more I understood that it involved sacrifice and trust and lots and lots of humor. Sadly, I had learned much from my parents about why they weren't able to go the distance in their relationship. I needed to do better in my own with Alex. His parents, ironically, stayed together even though they weren't happy with each other in order to keep up pretenses. That was a life I never wanted to live. We found a corner booth in a local bar and shared a plate of Mediterranean nachos while throwing out ideas for parental gifts, my mom included.

I unconsciously slid my hand up his thick thigh while eating my dinner. When my hand dipped to the inside of his leg I heard his chest rumble in appreciation. I loved the way his lips parted when I turned him on. Not an O or a pout. More like he was trying to remember how to breathe."?

So sexy. I had to be careful when I touched him in public. We'd gotten stares when he made that face, probably because I was usually licking my lips when it happened.

"You know Trudie, if you keep doing that, our shopping trip will be postponed to another day." He licked his lips now and flicked his tongue over the rim of his beer bottle, sending electricity straight to my clit.

I batted my eyelashes, placed a hand on my chest, and in my coyest voice asked, "Whatever do you mean?" Scarlett O'Hara had nothing on me.

He didn't speak, but his hand grabbed my wandering fingers and placed them on the rather large bulge beneath his napkin.

"Oh, my!" With my other hand, I stroked down my throat to my heaving chest.

"Oh, yes!" His voice lowered as his eyes locked on mine.

I took this opportunity to meet his challenge. Alex almost always took the lead in our foreplay, but not that evening. I wanted him panting for me. I wanted to experience a fantasy I'd had for years and tonight was the night.

I pressed my hand harder to the ever-growing bulge in his jeans.

"It must be painful to have such a large cock in such constricting pants."

He pushed my hair aside, kissed me behind my ear, and sucked on the spot that drove me wild. *Mmm.*

"Very." His breath hissed loudly.

"I have an early Christmas gift for you if you're feeling daring." I turned my face to see his red lips barely an inch from mine. I could feel his pulse beating out of control and it pushed me to continue my plans.

He outlined my lips with his tongue and then drove it through the seam, making me light-headed and wet.

"The most daring man you'll ever meet. Give me my gift—now." He was so hot when he demanded sex.

I turned so I could see where my coat was and pulled it up over my head before sinking lower on the seat. The table linen came halfway down, which hopefully would be enough to hide the rest of my body.

"What the fuck, Trudie!" he whisper-screamed.

"Shhh. Try not to look affected." I laughed.

"Christ! Are you kidding? This place is packed," he hissed.

Not my problem. I got to work unzipping his pants and working his boxer briefs over his purple-tipped cock. It didn't take much, since it was already peaking over the briefs. My man was hung and I had plans to attack all of it.

I pushed his velvet-soft crown into my hot waiting mouth, eliciting a rough inhale. I licked around the head and then sucked deeply before ending with a *pop*. Muffled expletives drifted over my head as I wrapped my hand around his member, turned it upward, and then formed a line with my tongue from his base to his tip. I chuckled when his hand smacked the table above me, reflecting my clever work.

"Jesus Christ, Trudie. I can't take much more." His hand hit the table two more times when I swallowed most of his length.

I was so lost in my fantasy I barely heard Alex beg me to hurry. He would have to wait until I was good and ready. I loved the way he pulsed in my throat and the salty taste of his precum. The fact that I could hear the waiter talking to Alex didn't slow my tongue down. Instead, I pushed down again even deeper.

"No! I mean, no, she'll be back shortly." He spoke to the waiter like he was having a heart attack.

A few moments later he scolded me. "You are so fucking going to get it later. The waiter wanted to know if you were finished. Uhh! I told him you were still eating and to come back later."

"Yeah." I hissed out. "Still eating." Sadly, he couldn't see my Cheshire cat smile.

"Please, baby. Get me off. Get me off now," he hissed back. Thank goodness the music in the restaurant was loud.

He had to be losing his shit trying to keep a straight face, but I didn't care. He had made me wait, panting hysterically for release on more than one occasion, so fair was fair. I used my other hand to cup his balls while I took him all the way again. That was all he needed. He went stiff and choked his climax back so as not to scream it to the whole bar. His hot cum squirted down my throat in thick ropes of salty goodness. I hummed while I drank him down and felt my own desire nearly reaching its climax. I was so close I didn't want to stop sucking him down. I continued my task and reached between my legs to apply enough pressure to bring my own release making me hum louder. Now both of us were happy.

The sweet sounds of him repeatedly saying, "Fuck, fuck, fuck," was music to my ears. I was so happy with myself and my brazenness that I giggled as I tucked him back into his pants. I used the napkin conveniently placed on his lap to wipe the rest of his orgasm from my face and slowly pulled myself back up to look into his blown pupils.

We stared at each other for a long time. For me, it was disbelief that I'd actually sucked him off under a table at a packed restaurant, and for him, I couldn't say. He'd never looked at me this way before—it was awe inspiring. He trembled as he lifted his hand to cup my jaw, brushing his thumb over my swollen lips. No words were said, only the softening of his eyes was a clue to what he was feeling. He kissed me, sweetly. Once, and then again. His hand moved to tuck a loose curl behind my ear and he let it trail down to the top of my V-neck sweater. That look created a burn in my belly I'd never experienced before.

The waiter came back with our bill and slid it across the table, no wiser about what I'd just performed underneath. Alex pulled out his billfold and slapped a hundred-dollar bill on the little black tray, sending the waiter into shock. He grabbed my hand and our jackets and wished the guy "Merry Christmas" as he dragged me out the front door by the hand and into an alley one storefront down.

He pulled my hips to his, inadvertently leaning us both against the freezing-cold brick wall behind me and I wrapped my legs around him. I grabbed his face, kissing him hard, and he returned the kiss with the same intensity. Any passersby would have seen two people devouring each other's faces, but we didn't care. We were in another world. A world without words—only hands and tongues. He pulled back when our lips were raw and pulsing, gently setting me back to the ground and staring at me like he had before, except now he was smiling all the way to his eyes.

"Well done, Ms. Gonzalez. You have exceeded my expectations and set a new bar for our relationship. Seems to me I need to up my game."

He pulled me to his side as we began walking down the sidewalk. I threw my head back, giddy with his praise and loving how excited we both were to play out in public. "I suppose you do."

With great timing, we walked inside a home décor store that specialized in candle making when a demonstration was just beginning. I knew his mother wouldn't appreciate such a simple gift, even if it should have been the thought that counted. Regardless, the choices we made regarding the container, the scents, and the colors made this gift really special.

"If they hate it, I'm stealing it back next time I'm at their house," I said snarkily.

"I'll do you one better; I'll light it up every time we come over just to piss her off." He preened at his clever idea.

I stood behind his chair and rubbed his heavily corded shoulders while he mixed the vanilla and cinnamon oils in the vial they'd provided.

"Hmm. I love these smells together." I nuzzled his neck from behind. "It's so cozy."

He turned and kissed my cheek. "You mean sexy as fuck. You smell like this all the time and now I can't drink a latte without thinking about you." I kissed his lips, drawing stares from an older woman sitting next to us, making a God-knows-what smell at her station.

"You might become a milkaholic having so many then." I mocked and giggled.

"Guilty." He chuckled back.

We made it back to his apartment soon after and he pinned me to the front door, resuming our make-out session from the alley.

"Why is it that every time you open your mouth now, I want to put something in it?"

"These lips, or these lips?" I asked, pointing to my mouth and then moving my finger to the apex of my thighs.

"Jesus, woman. You are insatiable."

He dropped to his knees and unbuttoned my jeans, speaking to my pussy like it was a bad child.

"You know you're going to have to pay for your mommy's bad restaurant manners?" He looked up at me through a lock of hair. His face was ruddy from the cold and when he put his nose to the top of my seam I squeaked with pleasure.

"I know it wasn't fair for your mommy to neglect you while I came so hard down her throat. She's a bad mommy," he mumbled while parting my nether lips and gently touching my swollen clit.

I moaned.

"Yeah, it's time to punish mommy," he said as he stood and threw me over his shoulder. He smacked my ass as he walked down the hallway to his bedroom, laughing maniacally. He didn't bother turning on the light or pulling the shades. He was going to punish me by moonlight, and I couldn't think of a better way to enjoy this lesson.

The hot bath we sat in after he graciously pulled three orgasms from me was heaven on my battered body. Alex had a sexy playlist on his phone that started before we got in the tub that added to the sensual mood he created earlier. He twirled my hair and circled my nipples as I lazed back against him. He had tortured me earlier as he sucked my pussy and teased my asshole with his enormous fingers. He lingered so long, nipping and flicking my bud, that I gasped, begging for release. He just shook his head, reminding me of my earlier indiscretion. After twenty minutes of exquisite torture, he edged me closer and closer to climax as I screamed like an animal. When Alex wanted to get even, his conscience went on hiatus.

"Fuck, fuck, Alex! I–I–can't breathe. Stop. Please stop. I'm so sensitive now," I had begged. He kept at his task until the last tremor left my body, delivering another aftershock orgasm. I'd never experienced that before. I was spent, although my bad little pussy clenched, demanding Alex's battering ram of a cock back deep inside me.

He looked like the devil incarnate in the way he crawled up my body and sucked hard at my hipbones. The way he gathered my abundance of bosoms in his large hands made them look small, which was no easy feat. When he pulled my nipple between his lips and teeth until they were long and flat, it rode the fence between pleasure and pain. At last, I could feel his hot breath panting on my collarbone, and I exhaled at the anticipation of his lips finding my mouth until. . .

"Do not leave a hickey on my neck! I can't explain it to my students, though they probably already know what one is ... just not on their teacher!" I cried.

"A tragedy, to be sure." He laughed and waggled his brows.

The bathwater turned tepid as Alex scooped up handfuls of water and dripped them down my breasts while I hummed an old standard. My fingers trailed along the outside of his muscular thighs, pondering our journey up to this moment.

"Baby," I purred. "I know that my decision about moving in together was rather quick. I still stand by that decision, though I have considered some alternative options I'd like to run by you."

I used his knees to pull myself to a seated position and turned to face him.

"What would you think about me—us, living together on the weekends? We could both stay more focused on our work during the week and have the benefits to enjoy on the weekends." The idea had come to me yesterday on the drive home from school, but I decided to wait until the time was right to bring it up. I didn't let my hopes get too high, knowing he wanted us to live together now fully—but thought that maybe he'd be flexible on this point.

He offered a tentative smile, tipping his head to the side. "You're comfortable with that? It's not too much of a compromise? The last thing I want, baby, is for you to freak out because it's too fast or too much commitment."

My smile grew slowly as I made an effort not to jump into his arms. Instead, I moved forward between his legs and pressed my belly against his hardening shaft. I ran a finger over his lower lip and then replaced it with a soft kiss, finishing with a slight pull that made his dick jerk against me. I wanted this to work so badly, even if we had much to work out. I was ready and excited to leave my panties in one of his drawers. I wanted to brush our teeth together every morning and night. I wouldn't even mind nagging him about picking up his undies off the floor if I could wake up in his arms and tell him I loved him.

"I want this—I want you, Alex. Let's do this," I spoke in a breath. "I don't want to try and make this work; I want to do this for real. No running away—either of us. I want to depend on you, and you on me. I want us to be a team that never gets defeated." My decibel level grew increasingly as I spoke until I was a cheerleader rooting for Team Trulex! *It just popped into my head. Don't judge me.*

He threw his head back, bellowing a huge belly laugh.

"Team Trulex, huh? We should get T-shirts and bumper stickers." Fine. He could mock me. I could take it.

"I was thinking more of a banner to hang outside our window, but shirts and stickers would do." He tickled me until I shrieked.

"Out!" He barked and lifted me so I could step out of the tub. I found my towel on the floor and threw him the other as he stood up. "You have ten seconds to get in my bed, or I'll tie you to it for the rest of the night."

Uh-oh. "On my way!" I said, running out of the room. Don't get me wrong. Getting tied to the bed was exciting for me. However, all night—I think not.

CHAPTER 25

TRUDIE

"What do you mean you're engaged?" I cried loudly into my phone at Ruby. "Why the hell did you wait so long to tell me?"

Friends don't let friends get engaged alone. They need a wing-woman. Someone to plot with. Someone who doesn't hold back things like, "He has too much nose hair" or "He drives a Corolla."

"I'm the worst! I'm so sorry," she faked cried into the phone. I knew her real cry and it was heartbreaking. This? These were crocodile tears that a toddler made when cookies were withheld.

"You are! I swear, one day when Alex pops the question you won't know until the wedding invitation arrives." *Ha!*

"I really am sorry, Trudes. Daniel popped the question, surprising me on Thanksgiving, of all days. The sneaky bastard had spoken with my dad and brother about it the week before, and they all had the inside dope while I looked like a deer in the headlights. Besides, sweetheart, your dad just passed, and, well you know…"

I chuckled. "Yeah, you were right to wait to tell me. Overwhelming joy and sadness cancel themselves out. But I could totally see your family laughing their asses off at your expense. I guess you showed them who got the last laugh when you said yes." My best friend was engaged to a stud of a guy who adored her. What more could you ask for?

"I wanted to text you right away. It's just that Daniel took our phones and locked them in a drawer for the weekend while we consummated our engagement—like twenty different ways." Since we were Face Timing, I could see that she was biting her lip and had a familiar dreamy look plastered all over her face. "I'm still in wonderment that my life went from disaster to dreamland in a few months. This must be what Cinderella felt when she met her Prince."

That's when I hung up and drove to her apartment.

I banged on her door so loud the hall light fixture threatened to fall. She flung open the door yelling, "What!"

First, I gave her a bear hug because I loved her so much and was genuinely happy for her.

Second, I smacked her tits for the stupid Cinderella comment because, seriously, we aren't cartoons, we are real women.

And, last, I hugged her again like the sister she was to me, and we cried for a really long time. We spent the rest of the afternoon drinking wine and sharing the best about our men, especially the fantastic sex we were finally having and the ways they made us feel empowered and appreciated.

"Enough about me," Ruby flipped the conversation, obviously tired of me teasing her. "Where did you land on moving in with the good doctor?" She nudged my side as we snuggled on the couch.

"We, or I, rather, landed on a part-time arrangement with the complete understanding I was in this for the long haul." I slurped down the last of the wine she had so generously supplied. "I need my weeknights for grading papers, errands, and laundry. As much as I'd like to laze around like a concubine in his bed, I'm a busy woman."

"Agreed! Just because we have men now doesn't mean we have to give up our hard-earned lives when they snap their fingers." Ruby snapped her fingers on both hands for emphasis.

"My mom said she'd support whatever decision I made, as long as I am true to myself."

"Your mom is the best—next to mine of course. Yours definitely gives the most practical advice, though."

"Practical and wise." I nodded my head and tried to recall if she had ever given me bad advice. Nope! "Did you pick a wedding date yet? I always pictured you with a spring wedding."

"Close—fall—like in nine months. And congratulations—you're my maid of honor and thus, you are responsible for traipsing through the Metro Detroit area with me, looking for the perfect venue, tasting cakes, and picking out dresses. And that's just for starters. You'll be great."

I didn't share her confidence in me. I'm a big idea person, not a planner. That's Ruby's forte. Did she have any idea how many people she wanted to invite? Or the style of her big event? There were no less than a million details to attend to—no exaggeration.

"Sweetheart, while I appreciate your confidence in my ability to help, you should look into an event planner. At least someone for the day of the wedding so you can relax and enjoy it. In the meantime, swing by a bookstore and get a wedding planning book to start. We need to create a timeline before we do anything."

I stood up and rearranged my shirt, which had slid up too high, and carried my glass to the kitchen. Ruby rambled on about who she wanted to invite, and I was cool to let her go on until she mentioned my ex-boyfriend, Sam. I spun around quickly and held my hand up with the universal gesture of stop.

"That's a hard no for me." I stared her down, wondering why she thought that was such a great idea.

She frowned and bit her bottom lip. "But he's been a friend since middle school. He would be offended. Come on, Trudie, I'll seat him on the other side of the room. You'll be standing up for me so you wouldn't have to sit near him anyway. Then there's Alex, who would break his arms if he so much as touched you. Pleeaasse," she whined, chasing me around her apartment. Her hands were in prayer position as she followed me to her door and knelt down while I put on my shoes.

How could I deny her? She was my best friend and I had only said no because I didn't want to make Alex feel uncomfortable.

"Rubes. Go ahead and invite him. Hopefully, he'll bring someone with him, so be sure to put "and guest" on the envelope." She beamed and threw her arms around me, placing kisses all over my face.

"Thanks, Trudes. You're the best." She did a little dance, though I didn't know why having Sam there was so important to her.

"Yeah, I've been hearing that a lot lately." I gave her one last hug and left her apartment to grade papers at home.

Holiday break was the following week, and Alex and I hadn't spoken about where we would be celebrating and with whom. Being away from my family wasn't something I could imagine. As with Thanksgiving, the casual nature of our gatherings was what made me love the holidays.

Before I committed to reading thirty-two papers on classical authors of our time, I was inspired to dig out my plastic tub of holiday decorations to decorate the windowsill with my snowman collection. Some lit up, while others wound up or had to be shaken so the whimsical flakes of snow floating through the water would land on the snowman's hat.

I loved winter. I loved everything about it except brown snow, clearing off my car, and those deep frigid days in February. Each year I pulled out all my funny mugs and lined them up on the counter, and every day I pulled one from the queue to enjoy a mug of green tea, hot chocolate, or a chai latte. No matter which, I enjoyed sitting in my overstuffed chair, warming my hands on the mug, and appreciating all that I had in my life.

This year had new blessings and sorrows. Alex, for one, had changed my life for the better. My father on the other hand, had helped to bring closure to my troubled childhood, but also agitated those old wounds. I was proud of myself for not being bullied into his stupid forgiveness deal. I was also proud that I did forgive when I truly felt it, even if it was a few minutes too late for him to hear it. Consequences. Every decision had one. I prayed that most had little cost associated with them.

After forcing myself to the kitchen table to grade papers for three hours, I allowed myself to call Alex to see if I could see him that night. But I barely had a chance to touch his contact on the screen when it lit up with him calling me.

"Hey you. That was some good timing—I was just about to call you." I put the phone on speaker while I packed up my papers.

"I've been working on it." His laugh was so freaking sexy. "What were you calling me about?"

"Whether I should order Chinese for one or for two?" I bent myself over the table to stretch my hamstrings and imagined him behind me.

"That sounds like a good plan. Call it in and I'll pick it up. See you soon, gorgeous."

"Bye, baby." I hung up and placed our order. I danced my way down the hall to freshen up, enjoying the anticipation of his arrival. Every time I saw him my love seemed to grow. I felt comfortable and safe like I'd never been before and it was intoxicating. I was pushing the sponge applicator back into my lip gloss tube when my phone rang again. Hoping it was Alex, I answered with a bright hello.

"Is this Ms. Gonzalez? The haughty tones of the man at the other end of the line made my hair stand on end.

"Who may I ask is calling?" I wasn't about to hand over information to a strange person from a strange number.

"This is Maxim Pierce, Alexander's father." His tone was riddled with disdain, having to explain who he was. People of his world would never require this of him.

"Yes, Mr. Pierce. This is Trudie. How can I help you?" I answered politely, not wanting to sound rude.

"I understand that you and Alex are still dating and wanted to be sure he was coming home for Christmas. His mother had been deeply distressed about him missing Thanksgiving. It's his duty to be home by Christmas Eve, and I'm holding you responsible for making that happen."

"Me? You're holding me responsible? While I may be dating your son, I am not his keeper. As a matter of fact, we are discussing our plans this evening. I'll urge him to call you when we're finished."

"So long as they include him coming to New York for the holidays, there won't be any problems." His rudeness and innuendo of a threat were very off-putting.

"With all due respect, Alex is a grown man who makes his own decisions. Why do you feel that pressuring me will help change that?"

"Because if you don't insist that he come home, I would hate to hear you'd lost your job."

What the fuck?!

"You can't do that. Who do you think you are, trying to extort me like this? I wouldn't spend one fucking minute around you—especially at Christmas."

"I'm Maxim Fucking Pierce!" he growled. "I own half the Eastern Seaboard and sit on more boards, that have more pull, than anyone in this whole damn country. Get my fucking son home for Christmas or you're through!"

The line went dead and I collapsed to the floor. I was shaking so hard I almost peed myself. In my whole life, with all the bullshit my father had thrown at me, I'd never felt so assaulted. His scathing tone eviscerated me like paper through a shredder. Could he really steal my job from me? Would Eloise allow that? I couldn't think straight.

I had to get off the floor before Alex arrived. I had to find a way to get him home, even for a day. His father wouldn't—couldn't erase everything I'd achieved. I hated that fucker! How dare he threaten me? Alex would see right through me pushing him home, and then what would I say? I didn't have to wait long when a knock sounded at my door.

I stood behind my door and let him in, and then sat down on the couch, covering myself with a fleece blanket and staring out the window.

"Hi, honey! I'm home!" His cute entrance fell on deaf ears. The food aroma that should have smelled good battled with my nauseated stomach. I only hoped I wouldn't heave up my lunch.

"Where's my hug for bringing the food? Trudie?"

He walked around to stand in front of me. His coat dripped snow on my rug, but I didn't care. Gently, he knelt in front of me and placed his hands on my legs, scanning my stricken face.

"Baby. What happened?" I didn't move. "Honey, you're scaring me. What's going on?"

I opened my mouth to speak, but nothing came out. My muscles were frozen as well as my vocal cords. All I could do was point to my phone, but that was enough of a clue. Alex opened the call log to see an unnamed number that triggered an unearthly response.

He jumped up and roared with such force it frightened me. "When? Who was it? My family?" My nod was all he needed to launch into a tirade that could have been heard from outer space.

"Did that motherfucker call you? What did he say? I swear I'm done with him and the whole fucking Pierce empire."

I couldn't answer him. He was out of his mind, and his being upset compounded my emotional state. His fit of rage could only be described as that of the Beast from *Beauty and The Beast* when the villagers stormed his castle. I knew from my training that trying to rationalize with an irrational-minded person was a lost cause. I needed to wait for him to burn himself out. I only hoped it would be soon because my nerves were shot.

He pulled at his hair and stomped around the apartment, cursing his father, then his mother, finishing with his life. When he slowed his diatribe, he fell to the floor in front of me. "I can't do this anymore. Trudie, please tell me what he said to you."

My fingers rose to his head, threading themselves through the long strands on top and over the shorter ones at his neck. I pressed harder as I came over the top again to settle his nerves and help him relax while I told him what had happened. Every time he tried to stand, I cupped his jaw and kissed his twisted mouth.

"I couldn't keep this from you, though my first instinct wasn't to tell you at all. But then I realized we couldn't let him have that kind of power over us. You've been working so hard to break from your parents without causing them pain. Unfortunately, I don't see any other way to go about it."

A single tear fell from his eye and my heart broke. I pushed a box of tissues closer, not sure if it was more for him or for myself. My man was broken, and all I could offer was my shoulder to cry on, a box of tissue, and my belief that better days were on the horizon for both of us.

I leaned forward to place a soft kiss to his nape and kneaded his shoulders as he rested his head in my lap.

"I can't tell you what to do from here, but you can definitely trust that I have your back every step of the way. Let me hold you and lift you up while we find a way out of this hellish situation he has put us in."

He sat back on his heels, looking at his hands, forlorn and lost in his thoughts.

"Please promise me you'll visit me in jail because I'm going to kill both my parents before the end of the year." His face became set like stone, and I blanched at the thought of what he might do.

"You'll do no such thing!" I shook his shoulders. "I mean, yes, I'll visit you, but no, you can't kill your parents. I forbid it!" While I was freaking out, his stone face turned into a grimace. "You're pulling my chain, right?"

"I can't promise anything, though I love the way you fight for me. You are one hell of a woman, sweetheart."

I smacked his chest hard. "Don't ever scare me that way again! I thought you'd lost your ever-loving mind. You don't own a gun, do you?"

I stalked away toward the kitchen, doing my best to shake off the feelings of the rollercoaster I had been forced to ride. "I thought my dad was the worst. Well, congratulations, Alex, yours wins all the prizes for crazy rich Americans."

He finally pulled off his wet coat and hung it by the door. Even when we were at our lowest, simple gestures like his hand through his hair, turned me on. Maybe it was the look on my face that settled him, or the way I was staring at his mouth—either way that storm had passed and a new one was rolling in.

"Good thing that movie has already been made. Maybe they'll get cast for the sequel."

ALEXANDER

As much as I wanted to kill my parents, I was hungrier for dinner—first Chinese, then Trudie. Her strength and passion for me was incredible. She trusted me to make this right, and I would. As for the threats against her job, I had friends in high places too and I wasn't afraid to use them.

Calling her out of the blue and threatening her into railroading me to come home for the holidays was the worst thing he had ever done to me. This would never happen again. After dinner Trudie excused herself to take a shower, and I called my lawyer, Phil.

"Come on Phil, pick up." My annoyance with my family needed to settle down. Phil hated when I was annoyed. It meant more work for him.

"Hey, Alex. These evening calls are starting to interfere with my love life." I heard a thwack in the distance.

"Jesus, Phil. Tell your wife to unchain you for a minute so we can talk. I promise to make it brief."

Muffled shouts went on until he came back on the line. "Okay. Be quick about it. Amy hates when the ice cream melts on her sheets." *Why was this guy my lawyer?*

I explained what went down with my dad. Phil agreed that legally, Trudie had a case of verbal abuse along with threatening behavior. I had no intention of actually filing that case, I just needed confirmation of how the law read. I could threaten people too.

"Last, are all the separation papers signed regarding the foundation, my trust, and all the other organizations affiliated with my family?" Given what had happened today, I was thrilled I'd had the foresight to start this process last month.

I heard some papers shuffling and then his wife calling "Yoo-hoo." "Everything is zipped up tight except your share of the summer home in the Hamptons. What do you want to do about that? It's the only one among these transactions that will get your parents attention."

Good question. I scrubbed my face thinking of how to settle this matter, when another call came through from Sarah. *Yes!*

"Phil. Split my portions evenly between Tabitha and Sarah. I've gotta go and I don't want to hold you up any longer. Please get it done first thing Monday. Bye, friend. Enjoy your ice cream!"

Just then, Trudie walked down the hall in a silky number that gave me tingles. I unseeingly answered Sarah's call as I took in every sexy curve my woman swished in front of me.

"Yeah?" My tongue slid across my lips, excited for my second dinner.

"Alex? You sound funny. Are you okay?" Sarah's concern was cute. If only she had known.

"I'm good. Can we talk tomorrow, I'm waiting to be tied up right now." *Uh, I don't think that came out correctly.*

"Oh shit! Sorry to interrupt. Say hi to Trudie. Talk to you tomorrow. Love you!" The line went dead and I left my phone on the table.

There would be no more interruptions tonight. I turned off my phone to be sure of it. The lavender sheath sliding over Trudie's toned body didn't leave much to the imagination. All I could think about was whether she was wearing panties. The lacy cups that held her voluptuous tits didn't hide her ruby-red nipples. I hadn't thought I could want her even more at this point, but I did. She finally trusted me and even stood up for me. She should have run the other way, given the kind of family that I had, but she didn't. Her steadfast, unselfish heartbeat for me when I could barely do it for myself. I had to be inside her now. I needed to fill her with my cock like she filled the void I'd carried for decades. I thought I had been in love before—now love had taken on a whole new meaning.

She stopped where the wall ended, leaned her back on it, and bent her knee like a pinup model. *Damn*! She sure looked like one.

I cleared my throat, which suddenly felt glued shut. "I do. Not only do I like everything I see, I love it."

I unfastened each button of my shirt as I slowly walked up to her soft, sexy form and then took her hands. "Do you want to play, baby girl?" She bit her lip and slipped into a pouty grin.

Her hands were soft and unadorned as they threaded through mine. The energy between our palms rocketed through my body and my breathing became stilted. I raised her arms above her head, pinning her to the wall. Her hair hung in silky strands that I pushed away with my nose as I kissed her behind her ear.

"You are my hero and will be rewarded as such," I whispered seductively. Sweet scents of cinnamon covered her skin, and her hair smelled of vanilla. My two favorite aromas mixed together on her exquisite body.

"How am I your hero?" She inquired innocently.

"You stood by me when I was at my lowest. You didn't have to. It wasn't your problem to fix. You stayed and supported me and I'll never forget that."

Trudie turned her mouth to meet mine. Time stood still as she hovered over my lips, breathing in my breath moment by moment. I could feel her heart pounding. She astounded me, and I gave her the time to express herself in whatever way she desired.

"Dearest Alex, standing by your side will never be a chore or obligation. My love for you has grown so deeply that I can't even find words to express how much I care for you." She pressed her lips to mine in a blindingly euphoric kiss far different from anything we'd shared before. It was a promise and with it, my mind shut off. *My God! What has this woman done to me?*

"Make love to me, Alex. Let me show you instead of trying to find the right words."

I didn't have another moment to think about her beautiful words because when she finished her next kiss, she slid her hands from mine, turned us so my back was now against the wall, and licked me from my neck to my left nipple. My legs wobbled when she pushed her sexy ass out and bent at the waist to continue her onslaught of kisses and nips down to the top of my pants.

She deftly unbuckled my belt and yanked it off in one motion, then kneeled on the floor, pressing her nose to my throbbing cock. I could hear the ratcheting of each tooth of my zipper like a hall clock. It made my dick bounce beneath her hands. She pushed my pants down to my ankles and then looked up at me with desire, licking her lips while she palmed my balls.

"I love when your cock peeks over the top of your boxer briefs. He's so large and eager."

"Jesus Christ, woman. You're killing me here." I banged my head against the wall and forced myself to keep upright while my vixen did unspeakable things to me.

I didn't have to wait long. She licked her lips again, then flattened her tongue to lick the precum off my purple head. Her eyes came up and locked on mine as she did it again, sucking at my slit each time.

"How is my sad man doing now?" she asked. If I were a real man, I would have told her I was terrific. But because I was a bruised little boy, I replied, "A little better, but I think I need more sucking from your perfect mouth." She smiled and kissed my head one more time before taking me in her mouth.

I tried to keep a straight face but failed miserably. Inadvertently, I shoved my dick farther down her throat and made her gag. "Uhhh. Yes—oh my God, are you okay?"

She never gave me an answer. Instead, she grabbed the back of my thighs aggressively and took me deeper into her throat. I couldn't breathe. I clawed at the wall to stay upright and prayed I would always be this deserving of her talents. Saliva dripped from her mouth when she pulled out, and she eyed my veiny cock, seemingly to inform it telepathically that it was no match for her. It was as if she challenged herself to take me deeper in her throat and hold me there longer and longer, and if I wasn't as in awe as I was, I might have been concerned she would asphyxiate herself.

She stopped suddenly and locked her eyes back on mine. "Promise you'll always have my back?" Was this a standoff? Of course, I had her fucking back. She had to finish me off, or I'd die.

"Forever and then some!" I wailed. "Please, Trudie, fucking finish me off." Yeah, I heard it that time. I did whine. Holy fuck, she reduced me to a blathering idiot.

Her hands gripped every inch of my cock and she fed it back into her throat greedily. And that, my friends, was all she wrote.

"Good boy," she muttered to herself as she stood to kiss me. I tasted myself on her lips and fuck, if that wasn't hot.

I swept her off her feet and with her cradled in my arms, I walked her back down the hallway to her bedroom, kicking the door closed behind me. After yanking the covers back, I gently set her in the middle of the bed and arranged her hair around her head to make her look like the queen she had become to me.

"Open your legs, sweetheart." And she did. I could see the tiny lace thong she hid under her silk nightgown. "Umm. This is so pretty." I pressed my tongue to the delicate fabric, pushing it from side to side. She moaned her appreciation, and I sat back to study her magnificent body. My woman wasn't one of those fashion model types. Her curves gave me something to hold on to and her tits hung just heavy enough that I couldn't milk them with just my mouth. She was fit and healthy and absolutely made for me and my thick cock. I pushed my hands through my hair as I tried to decide how best to please my woman tonight, but no sex trick in the world could substitute for what I wanted to give her.

I stared deeply into her brown eyes, admiring the thick, long lashes that made it look like she wore mascara all the time.

"Do you trust me now?" I feathered my index finger down her midline from her throat to her almost bare mound. Her eyes rolled back in her head as she arched her back in response to the delicious sensations I was giving her.

"Yes. Always," she moaned.

I carefully pulled that thread of material from her thighs and flung it somewhere over my head before bending again to pull her lower lips apart. Her clit was engorged and red and desperate for attention. I flattened my tongue and bathed her pussy from ass to hood as she writhed above me.

"You're mine," I whispered. Whether it was to Trudie or her sweet pussy, I couldn't tell. They were both mine and I couldn't wait another minute to enter her.

I crawled up her body like a panther to its prey, ready to devour her completely. Her hungry mouth was my destination, and when I reached it, I plunged my tongue and found my treasure. Our teeth clashed and her nails drew blood along my back as we grappled for control. We were animals that couldn't be tamed and I'd never felt so alive.

"Now," I grunted into her mouth like a fucking caveman. I rocked back and grabbed hold of my cock and lined it up with her soaked pussy. Without thought, I drove hard into her in one thrust.

"Trudie!"

"Alex!"

I found her hands and threaded them above her head, using only my knees for balance as I tried to get some control of myself. I kissed her cheeks, then her nose, and slowed my pace to focus on her face. Those witchy hazel eyes that turned amber when she was mad or euphoric. I pushed in, and her mouth twisted as she adjusted her body for a more comfortable fit. When I pulled out to the head, she bit her lip, exposing a small dimple in her right cheek.

Moving at this slow tempo, the sensations were so good, so perfect. I didn't want it to end. I was making love, to my love, for the first time. We'd fucked plenty of times in the past, but this—this was next level.

My brow was damp and our bodies were drenched with perspiration from our leisurely exertions. I never knew how wildly sexy it was to have two bodies wet and slapping against each other for one purpose alone—love. If Trudie hadn't been on the pill, this night would have produced a baby just from the looks we gave each other.

Her irises were blown and her body began tightening. Her pussy walls clamped down hard, squeezing my dick mercilessly. She bucked her hips hard against mine and screamed, "Baby, please! I can't hold on any longer. Make me come, Alex, please." Her head swiveled on the pillow, maddened with desire. I moved her hands, placing one beside her head and using the other to push her knee toward her shoulder for a new position. I sent a prayer to God Himself to give me strength to be patient a little longer.

"Fuck, you feel so good. I don't want this to end, but I have to come," Trudie moaned.

I doubled my efforts, and in exchange, Trudie touched her clit once and went off like a rocket. One more thrust and I followed her to the moon. Exquisite sounds of moaning and humming filled the room, along with prayers of thanks, until our bodies fell back to earth, whole and satisfied.

I rolled to her side, fitting our bodies like spoons, and whispered the only thing that mattered into her delicate ear, "I love you so much."

CHAPTER 26

TRUDIE

Chinese food for breakfast was the bomb. Not as good as cold pizza, but almost as good as that boxed macaroni and cheese shit. That should be the number one cure for hangovers. Alex showered after we pounded one more out that morning. The man was a machine and I loved him for it. However, my lady bits needed a break, so I let him have his shower alone while I pulled out last night's food. I wasn't sure how it got into the fridge. Unfortunately, being alone gave me more time to think about how we were going to thwart his father's evil plan.

"Look at you, all college-like with your cold leftovers. I hope, at least, you made some coffee. We're going to need it today." He walked past me as I sat in my college sweatshirt and undies—placing a tender kiss to my forehead before he entered my tiny kitchen.

"Coffee is almost ready. I put a plate and silverware out for you." I chuckled into my chicken fried rice. "I guess we need to add 'thwart an evil villain' to our holiday plans," I groaned, sharing my disdain for the burden.

He poured two steaming mugs of heaven's elixir and walked the short distance to place them on the table. Returning to the refrigerator, he grabbed the almond milk creamer and an apple.

"That item was definitely not on my to-do list, unfortunately. Sorry, sweetheart." He set the creamer and apple on the table and leaned over for a proper kiss that ended with his teeth trapping my lower lip. God, I loved when he did that.

"Can we first figure out how we want to spend the holidays? I don't think I can be without my family this year, especially since my dad died. I know it sounds silly, but I think my mom never stopped loving him despite all his flaws." I reached a hand across the table and Alex took it, nodding.

"I wouldn't have it any other way. How do you feel about conferencing with my sisters in our planning? I need them more than ever. Obviously, our family dynamic has changed—kind of like Brexit. What's more is that they really like you and your family and would love to experience how real people celebrate the holidays." His smile was contagious.

"You mean how poor people celebrate the holidays." I tipped my head to the side.

"Not poor, that is very different. If I use 'average,' will I get slapped?"

"Are you calling me average?" I leaned over and slapped him.

"You? Totally not average. How does 'average American' sound? Better?" He put his hands out in supplication.

"You still sound like an elitist pig, but I'll forgive you. Your sincerity outweighs your pompousness."

"Oh, thank you, miss. Your kindness knows no bounds." He bowed his head reverently.

I set my cup down and sat up straight. "Seriously, though. Do you think our class difference is the reason your parents hate me? I can't control who I am or who I was born to. We are all God's creatures, and I never want to be treated again the way your father treated me yesterday. It's too much."

We looked at each other with frustrated faces. He laid his other arm on the table, silently asking me for my other hand. This would be the first big problem we would have to solve together. We had to get it right. Do or die.

"No one, especially my father will ever treat you that way again. Not while I'm at your side. I've been thinking and I may have a solution to my daddy problem. We'll save my mother's issues for another day. Let's decide how we want to spend that week between holidays and I'll call my sisters."

"Okay, but what's your daddy solution?"

"I'm still working on that," he said thoughtfully.

We spent the next hour talking about what we could do for the holidays, and who we would like to include in our fun. Ruby and Daniel were at the top of the list, then my mom and brothers. Alex didn't know many other people in the Detroit area. However, he did say he met some guys at the gym who were movers and shakers in the city. Besides building a work circle of friends, there was one he thought he could build a real friendship with."

I shifted to the other side of the couch and we intertwined our legs, looking at each other while we listed some fun activities.

"I've always wanted to try axe throwing," I offered, flipping my pen over and over.

"I heard fowling was fun, though I haven't a clue about what it is." His raised shoulders were an exact replica of mine. I grabbed my phone—the encyclopedia of the world and everything in it—and found a YouTube video of the sport. We leaned in to watch together and cracked up.

"Bowling with a football. That's a real thing?" Alex asked, incredulously. "Why am I feeling like I live under a rock? I'll try it, if you will. I suppose a few beers beforehand wouldn't hurt. I know, let's call Jacob and see if he's tried it. That fool has tried everything."

"Sounds great, but let's call your sisters first."

Shortly afterward, we firmed up our plans for the holidays, none of which included his parents.

"As most of you know, there will be fewer and fewer of us by the end of the week. But this holiday vacation will only be a vacation for you if you complete this essay, typed double-spaced and grammatically correct. And include the outline you've been taught to create before you begin writing. The grade you'll all start with is an A—it's up to you to keep it."

The best part of the last week before vacation was that I could leverage each day with mild threats against minimum effort. I walked back and forth in front of the class, stopping occasionally to stare down at an aloof student who didn't think rules pertained to them. I had one kid a few years back who thought it was okay to put his feet up on the desk and eat ice cream. In response, I asked, "Did you bring enough to share for the whole class? If not, you can finish that with Vice Principal, Schultz. I'm sure he'd love an ice cream sandwich." That got his attention. I didn't like being a hard ass to my students, nevertheless, I wouldn't be a doormat either.

"Your topic will be clever ways to get out of a hard spot. For instance, you're being made to do something that is distasteful to you. Or you're feeling pressured to make a decision when you don't have all the facts. Use your past experience to guide yourself and then step out of your comfort zone to find new ways to tackle that situation. I'm looking forward to reading two hundred and fifty words of your best ideas. If you have forgotten how to write a five-paragraph essay, look on the board."

I knew it was cheating, but I was hoping one of these rug rats would open my eyes to a clever way to get around Maxim's ultimatum. I wasn't going to lose my job to that asshole, no way. If I could find some common ground, perhaps I could finagle my way out of the situation.

By the end of the day, only two kids had finished their essay and they informed me of their early departure for a cruise they were being "forced" to go on. Apparently, a fully paid vacation to the Bahamas was a hardship. *Please. Sign. Me. Up.*

I had a three o'clock meeting with Alex and Eloise so we could put the final changes in our first report. The next report wasn't due until the end of February, and the final one in April. I was getting ready to go when I heard Jody shout, "Hey, girl," down the hall.

"*Hola, chica. Como esta?*"

"*Muy Bueno!*" That was about all the Spanish Jody knew. I gave her an A for effort.

"Excellent, my friend!" Her eyebrows pressed together and her mouth scrunched up. Maybe I needed to expand her vocabulary. "*Excellente, mi amiga.* Four more days and counting."

"Oh my gosh, right? I'm already missing four kids today, but I'm not complaining. I'd be the happiest teacher ever if I could sit in my classroom reading a rom com all day Friday." Jody finger combed her hair into a ponytail and grabbed the elastic she always kept on her wrist.

"I'm right there with you. Do you have plans for break?"

"Absolutely. My new beau, Mike, and I rented a cute place up north. Four days of glorious sex, warm fires, no Wi-Fi, and lots of good food. I'm even leaving my dog home." I loved the animated antics she performed when she spoke, complete with a "stuck the landing," pose with her hands in the air and a winning smile.

"Wow! That does sound good. Need a third wheel?" She looked so stricken, I laughed. "I'm kidding. I have out-of-town guests coming in, although I don't know exactly when. I'm hoping Alex and I can find some alone time for a few days." I bit my lip, looking off into the distance, thinking about alone time with Alex, and then remembered our meeting. "Whoa, I've got to go. Talk to you later, 'gator."

"Bye, baby. Have fun." She gave me a quick hug and we went in different directions.

I wasn't nervous about my meeting with Alex and Eloise. It would be perfunctory at most. Nonetheless, I wanted to report on our secondary agenda: "The Victors," which was the name the kids finally chose for their mentoring program. I liked it—it conveyed the value of being a participant.

The front office staff stayed until three-fifteen, so I was able to catch Ricky.

"Hey there. I haven't seen you in a while. Is everything okay?" When Ricky wasn't smiling, there had to be a serious reason.

His face was solemn, save for the slight lift at the corners of his mouth. "Thanks for noticing. There are a few things troubling me, namely impending staff cuts."

WTF? "What do you mean, cuts? I haven't heard anything, or at least not in the near future. Were you sent something?" I crossed my arms over my body, suddenly feeling chilled.

"Nothing has been sent yet, but my friend at the district office said there was a short list of support staff getting pink-slipped on Friday." He looked around the office and stepped closer, keeping his voice low. "Can you believe this bullshit? And right before the holidays, too."

This *was* bullshit. Here I was going into a meeting to make sure no cuts were made at our school and the district was already plotting to destroy good people's lives. *Argh!*

I put my hand on Ricky's, hoping what I had to say would be helpful.

"I'm not supposed to say anything, but given what you've just told me, I think you should know that Dr. Pierce's report advocates keeping all Hart Middle School personnel in place to uphold the exemplary school status. Maybe you won't be chosen, or your friend is wrong."

He sighed, showing the stress of the situation. "Maybe. Either way, I've started looking for other employment opportunities. I've canceled my trip to Europe this summer, and I'm purging and selling a bunch of knickknacks that are collecting dust." He scrubbed his face with his hands and then slapped them against his thighs. "Well, it's been nice knowing ya!" he squawked dramatically.

"Stop that!" I swatted his shoulder. "You aren't going anywhere. Have faith. It's not over till it's over," I said and patted where I'd just whacked him. "Now, go home and sell your junk. I bet you're a hoarder anyway."

That got a smile out of him. "If you only knew." He threw his arms around me, giving me a bear hug, just as Alex made his presence known.

"Ahem," he said, faked-clearing his throat. "Are you two lovebirds done fluffing each other's feathers?"

Ricky chimed in first, "Well, if you must know, we were just getting started. Bug removal was next." We all laughed at that, but Ricky still looked so sad. It hurt to see my friend so upset.

I cupped his face with one hand and whispered, "It's going to be okay. I've got you," and gave him a sad smile. He mouthed a thank you and then collected his things.

Alex waited outside Eloise's office for me. His sincere look of concern was touching.

"Is everything okay with Ricky?"

"No. It isn't. He has some insider information that some support staff will be let go by the end of the week, and it's breaking both our hearts." I continued into Eloise's office, shifting my attitude to something more positive so as not to divulge the information I'd just received.

Eloise sat poised behind her desk. A small pink poinsettia adorned the corner, with a snowman bowl of puffy peppermint candies next to it. *Don't mind if I do.* Reading glasses decorated with candy canes were perched on the end of her nose while she read through what I presumed to be Alex's updates. I sat sucking on a candy and twiddling my thumbs, hoping the work we'd accomplished so far this semester would make a difference, not just for our students but also for our staff.

"Everything looks to be in order here." Eloise dropped the papers on her desk and sat back. "Is there anything else to discuss before it's sent?"

Alex and I shook our heads and Eloise clapped her hands once. "Well, let's hope we did our jobs well enough that we meet the school board's expectations. I know we still have two more assessments, but I'm feeling good about receiving our exemplary status from the state very soon. Good job to you both."

In any other circumstances, we'd be celebrating, but it appeared Eloise sensed something was up.

"What's wrong? Why aren't you two ecstatic?"

Alex and I looked at each other again, and he raised his hand to stop me from saying anything. "We *are* ecstatic, unfortunately, we just received some news that despite our efforts to keep all our personnel here at Hart, some might be losing their jobs before the end of the week. Can you corroborate that information, Eloise?"

She became ashen and her jaw dropped. "Who told you this? I only heard a rumor this afternoon."

Alex stayed the course, handling her questions. "I don't have a name. Is it true?"

To see my principal and friend so upset was disheartening to say the least. She put her elbows onto her desk and let her head fall into her hands. "What's happening? I can't get straight answers from the district anymore. I feel like a puppet the way they keep pulling and pushing me and my people around." She wiped her eyes and leaned back into her seat.

"I'm sorry for my lack of professionalism, but I am mad!" She slammed a hand down on her desk, making both of us cringe. "Trudie, you're too young to remember how things used to be in our school district. Administrators cared about their teachers. They gave them space and creative freedom to build programs that developed whole children, not anxious, obsessive ones. We didn't teach to a standardized test. We taught our kids to be lifelong learners. They learned to try and fail and pick themselves up on their own. They learned what it was to have grit—to persevere even when things were difficult. Now..." She shook her head. "Now, we can't hug a kid, pat their shoulder, or speak to them sternly so they can understand how important their actions are, that compassion is interactive, and life isn't a video game you can restart when you mess up."

"Eloise. You are making a difference to our kids, and you're so supportive of your teachers. I know how much teaching has changed. Some of those changes are good, and, well, as you stated, some are not so good. Your work here is relevant, and I speak for all of us when I say that you matter more than you know." My words sounded like platitudes, but that was all I could offer. Times had changed, and we had to change with them. Change being the only constant.

"All I can tell you is that these budget cuts were a plan B if we didn't get enough enrollment this year. Funding from the state has been reduced 15 percent, and there is nothing we can do shy of robbing a bank to keep all our people employed. Twenty people will be let go now and another twenty in the spring. I'm not going to sugarcoat this, Trudie. You don't have tenure, and therefore, you're subject to dismissal as well."

Whoa! What just happened here? "Are you kidding? All the things I did for this school won't matter to anyone?" I was dumbfounded and sickened by what I'd just heard.

"Sadly, no," she whispered. "I'm sorry to have to make you aware of these realities."

"Uh, you and me both."

Alex sat there watching two grown women fade into despondency. I couldn't tell what he was thinking, but I didn't have to wait long. He jumped to his feet and jammed his hands on his hips.

"Listen, you two. We don't have anything concrete in front of us, so let's try to stay positive." He knelt beside me and took my hands. "Trudie, be patient. Everything will work out how it's supposed to. You're an amazing teacher. They'll see that. I know you want to stay at this school, but if it doesn't work out, another lucky school will hire you."

Alex was trying his best to be supportive, but his words only angered me more.

"You're right. I want to stay here, where I built a system that works and relationships that support me. It hasn't even happened, and I'm already feeling despair, if not for me, then for some of my beloved friends."

Well, this meeting had turned out to be a buzzkill. Discussing our new program would be a waste of time if the teachers supporting it were going to be fired. This would have to wait. Plus, I needed to get out of here and smash something.

ALEXANDER

Well, fuck me!

I felt like a rotting sack of shit watching highly qualified people lose their jobs while a dumbass school board wasted good money to get a status that won't mean shit when the people who earned it get dismissed.

I brought Trudie back to my apartment. The roads were terrible and there was very little visibility, so I was genuinely concerned she wasn't fit to drive. Thankfully, she followed me through some back roads and we made it safely before the really heavy snow began to fall. Despite the crappy end of our day, tonight would be a perfect night to snuggle by the fire and just be with each other.

We didn't talk while we rode the elevator or entered the apartment. I uncorked her favorite pinot grigio, poured a hefty glass, and set it in front of her. Taking a chance, I placed a gentle kiss on her head, hoping to relax her from her recent trauma. *Could this girl catch a break?*

I warmed up sourdough bread and soup and then turned on the gas fireplace. I'd let her soak up all the energy she needed to heal her heart and stoke her internal fire, so she could go back to school the next day with the positive attitude she always managed to muster.

After dinner, I carried her to the couch, then went back for our wine. Once she was settled into the cushions, I asked her to put her head in my lap, reaching for a small pillow to support her. We watched the weather report—it didn't look like the snow would let up. I was banking on a snow day so my girl could have more time to wrap her mind around everything that had happened.

I reached for the fleece blanket Trudie had so thoughtfully let me borrow while I was in town, tucking one side under her bottom and letting the other drape over her body and up to her neck. Who knew we would be using it as often as we did? I played with her hair, twirling strands around my fingers as if I had done it my whole life.

Trudie's breath softened, and the hand she had on my thigh slid off onto the cushion. My beat-up beauty was sound asleep. I couldn't think of a better way to spend an evening. I reviewed my emails while watching the rest of the news, deleting junk and sorting the rest into folders. Tabitha texted confirmation of her plans for the following week, and Nina sent suggestions for gifts for Zander and Paolo. My relationship with those guys had been growing, with a "hey, buddy" here and threats that I'd better take care of their sister there. I still wasn't sure if the threats were real or not, so I was watching my back. Not having had brothers growing up was something I missed, and I'd grown attached to the idea of building a brotherhood with these guys. Now, if Sarah could survive giving her excuses for not attending Christmas with our parents this year, it would be the best holiday ever.

I woke up to six inches of snow on my windowsill and a weather ticker tape indicating school closings. My heart sighed, looking forward to a cozy day in my home office with stunning views of Trudie practicing yoga and meditating on a cushion in the corner. I chuckled thinking of what our breaks would look and feel like. Her mouth was on my cock under my desk, eating her pussy for lunch, and then an afternoon break of mind-bending anal. Glorious orgasms all day long. What more could we ask for?

"What are you laughing at?" she mumbled, pushing her hair from her drool-dried face.

"School is closed tomorrow. What do you think about having a sexathon?" I waggled my eyebrows, hoping she would agree.

"Of course. Isn't that what everyone does on a snow day?" Her mumbles morphed into sarcasm with a bite.

"It is when we're together." I smacked her fleeced ass, giving her some attitude right back.

"Hey! Watch it!"

Ooh. Cranky, huh?

"What time is it?" she asked.

"Time for you to get a watch." I loved laughing at her expense. *Sometimes.*

She sat upright and glared at me. Okay, I deserved that.

"It's twelve thirty?"

"I'm going to get ready for bed," she grunted.

"No, you're not," I said belligerently.

"Why the hell not?"

Maybe handcuffs tonight. I really don't want to get punched in the nuts. "Because it's tomorrow, therefore, to wit, the sexathon has begun."

I didn't wait for a negotiation. Instead, I yanked her up from the couch in a reverse bear hug and carried her down the hall. I probably should have set her down gently; however, playing defense seemed like a more prudent decision. I stopped, dropped, and she rolled over, irate.

"God damn it, Alex. I'm barely awake, and you want to fuck me when I'm still pissed off?"

I'm sorry, was that a question? "Yes. Yes, I do." I smiled coyly and bolted for the toy chest. Not really a chest, and certainly not toys for children. I loved the name anyway. She jumped off the bed and made a play for my hand as it opened the drawer stuffed full of sex toys she'd insisted we try.

"No!"

Her rant was adorable.

"Yes. Trust me. You'll feel so much better afterward. I promise you'll sleep like a baby," I said in earnest and offered my lips to kiss as an incentive. Sadly, she rebuffed my love and tried again to close the drawer. I thought about locking her in a half nelson, but considering the potential repercussions during our sexathon, I stuffed her head into my armpit instead.

Her protestations were aggressive, but her tone implied she knew we were playing, so I kept going.

Found them! I managed to wrap one cuff around a hand and dragged her over to my bed, locking her wrist onto the headboard where I had previously installed a clip. *One down.*

"I swear I'm going to cut your nuts off while you're sleeping!"

As a psychologist, I was able to observe the various levels of grief, and since Trudie's job was being threatened, I ascertained that she was in the anger phase and needed to burn off some steam. Enter me.

"I have it on good authority that you will not do that as it will prevent us from making beautiful babies in the future." *Babies? WTF!*

"I hate you!" she ranted.

I located the second cuff and returned to the bed, tackling her legs and fastening it on. After jackknifing off to the side, I clipped that arm into place and caught my breath.

"You look stunning, and I couldn't love you more if I tried." I stood there with my hands on my hips, catching my breath while I drank in her disheveled hair and smudged makeup. Her chest heaved as she struggled against the bindings, swearing at me at the top of her lungs.

"Why are you treating me this way? Haven't I been punished enough? I'm at my lowest, Alex. Take pity on me and let me out of these things," she cried.

I pulled my shirt over my head and let it drop to the floor, followed by my pants and underwear. Socks were staying on—it was winter for God's sake. I sat on the side of the bed and pushed her hair from her watery eyes. A new tear formed and fell as I studied every freckle on her face. She was broken, and as her teacher, her mentor, her coworker, friend, and lover, it was going to be my honor to help her repair herself. I loved her and couldn't let her stay in this mindset. She needed me in a very different way.

"Sweetheart," I whispered. My throat closed and my voice cracked. "This is not a punishment. This is your rebirth. I will pull from you every orgasm it takes to rid you of your pain. Let your mind empty. There is nothing more to fix right now. Give yourself permission to let go of your pain and anger so that you see things for what they really are. Give yourself twenty-four hours of reprieve to get a new perspective. Give yourself to me and I will care for you and your heart until you can do it for yourself. Please, Trudie. Let me care for you." I pressed a tender kiss to her swollen lips, tasting the saltiness of her pain and vowing to fix what was in my power to do so.

She looked like she was watching a tennis match, with her eyes shifting from side to side. You could almost see the gears turning in her head as she weighed what I was offering. A minute later, she relented.

"You have fifteen minutes, and if you don't remove these fuckers, we are over. Do you hear me?" she hissed.

"I will." Trust me when I tell you no seconds were wasted in bringing my vixen to orgasm. There were three minutes of sucking and pinching her nipples until she cried out, "Alex! Fuck that feels so good."

Three minutes dragging my tongue to each hip and her belly button, pressing wet kisses that left marks that would certainly turn purple tomorrow.

Four minutes teasing her drenched pussy with a thumb in her ass. "Yes. Yes. Yes!"

And five minutes later, entering her so slowly that I was about to scream from the excruciating pleasure of popping my head in and out of her pussy.

"Jesus Fucking Christ, Alex! I'm coming. You have ten seconds to get me there, or, or..."

She didn't get a chance to finish that sentence—I reached between us and pinched her clit.

"Oh—my—God!" she screamed, and that was all I needed to hear to blow my load deep inside her. Time seemed to stop whenever we had sex, except tonight, it didn't start again. I fell to my back, out of breath, sweating, and spent. I heard the snowplows scraping pavement down the street and the eerie calm of no other sounds in the air. It felt like we were in a cocoon, wrapped tightly in bed, wrapped in snow, wrapped in silence. Blissful.

A minute later, I reached up to uncuff Trudie and looking down at her, chuckled to myself. She was out cold. *Way to go, Alex. You fucked the life out of her.*

CHAPTER 27

TRUDIE

I woke up with a start, not sure where I was. I looked next to me and took my first breath, seeing my beautiful, incredible man. He had some wicked ways of getting me to calm down and it excited me to know there was so much more to learn from and about him.

As I went to the bathroom to relieve myself, I noted the red numbers illuminated on his bedside clock. 5:00. Who needed an alarm when your inner clock woke you up on time daily? Alex had said something about school being canceled, so I walked to the kitchen to locate my phone and turned it on. That stinker had shut out the world so he could get me sane again. We had a lot to figure out, and I thanked heaven for the snow day.

Sure enough, school was canceled. I opened my class distribution lists and sent out reminders about turning in their essays on time and a few minor things they could do if they wanted extra credit. I pressed send and left my phone on the table. Orange juice screamed my name from the fridge, and I ripped open the door to save it. I'm not a calorie counter, but I'm sure last night's sexcapades burned thousands of calories I had to replenish.

I crept back to bed and faced Alex, staring at his handsome face. I could see him as a teenager when his face relaxed. And when he scrunched up his eyes, he looked like a little boy.

"Are you staring at me?" he croaked out in his husky morning voice without opening his eyes.

"Yes," I whispered, tracing my index finger along the large vein running down his arm.

"Do you like what you see?" He fought a smile and cleared his throat.

"Very much." I stroked the inside of his palm, seeing the pleased reaction on his face.

"Did you need something?" *Did I need something?*

"So many things, but for now, just a kiss." I leaned closer, pausing above his mouth feeling the energy spark between us, then closed the distance to brush a sensual kiss on his pillowy lips.

"You're the best kisser." He rolled to his back and pulled me over his body, pressing me onto his impressive bulge.

"I have my charms. But, you sir, have so many of your own." I kissed him again, harder.

He opened his eyes and stared into mine. I expected a sweet, sexy reply from him, but instead, he did a one-eighty and landed one of his raunchy lines on me.

"I'd like to insert my finest charm deep into your pussy." I rolled my eyes, amused and horrified at the same time. He thought he was a riot.

"Charming," I deadpanned.

I tried to pull away but without any luck. He rolled me to my back to insert his charm without hesitation. The sexathon was back on, and honestly, I had no wish to fight it.

Despite two rounds of sex before noon, we managed to come up with a plan to shut Maxim down and still have a great holiday. Let me rephrase that, we had one plan and one punt. The punt being that we'd buy cruise tickets for his parents and send them out of the country for the holidays, leaving us free and clear to do what we wanted without guilt.

"I don't know, Sarah. Don't you think the cruise plan is pretty transparent? Us, all of us, getting COVID would be more of a realistic strategy."

Alex had his sisters back on a conference call to plot their excuses.

"Now that's the best damn excuse we've come up with all week!" Tabitha cheered.

"No loopholes there unless he asks to see test results," I offered. The collective sigh was deflating.

"Listen, I don't care about finding an excuse not to come. My only concern is that he doesn't retaliate against Trudie. Her school needs her. I have no idea who he knows who could interfere with that, but it's not worth taking a chance." Alex. Always my protector.

While the three exhausted their options, I opened my weather app on a whim, wondering if we'd have school tomorrow. To my delight, I saw blue—lots of dark blue starting Friday and ending Tuesday, two days after Christmas. A severe freeze was forecast, and every traveler who didn't get out of Dodge before Friday would have to plan to stay home for the holidays.

"Uh, guys. Pull up your weather apps and check out the forecast for this weekend." I turned my phone screen so Alex could see it and his eyes bugged out. He jumped up and swept me into a hug, twirling me around in a circle.

"You're a genius!" he shouted.

"Would you look at that." Sarah sounded impressed.

"And here I was preparing to lie my ass off." Tabitha sounded bummed.

"No lies, no deception, no threats to my livelihood. Christmas miracles *do* happen," I sighed.

"I'll buy a ticket for Christmas Eve, and then I'll be grounded," Alex proposed with glee. What a tragedy. Even *I* can't control the weather."

We all agreed this was a great plan. Alex booked his flight and texted his parents to say he would be arriving on the evening of Christmas Eve. The girls would do the same in their respective cities, with Tabitha being "called out of town" to go tomorrow. I invited her to come early and stay in Detroit as long as she'd like if it got her here before the bad weather.

"Thank you, ladies, for your cooperation in planning The Great Escape." Everyone said their goodbyes, and for the first time in forty-eight hours, I was able to stop worrying about the damage if Alex didn't go home.

I got up from the kitchen table and pulled my spare yoga mat out of the front closet. I laid it out in front of the fireplace to soak up the intense heat to warm my body for a slow flow of poses designed to relax and rejuvenate. If I had my way, I'd push all the desks in my classroom to the walls and lay out mats every day for the kids to use to unwind and clear their minds. It would be a mainstay in my lesson plan that would work miracles for anyone with anxiety, stress, or frustration. Yeah, one day, when standardized testing wasn't in my way, I would transform the world with yoga.

Alex granted me thirty minutes of practice before he requested a certain pose, dropped his pants, and said, and I quote, "Suck my cock into relaxation." Obviously, I complied.

ALEXANDER

Nina's home was a winter wonderland, with fake snow blanketing the mantel and no less than fifty snowmen and snowwomen in every available space in every room. Besides the main tree we had begun to decorate at Thanksgiving, she had added three more: one in each bedroom and another in the basement. I'd never seen so many gifts in my life. I deposited ours and hoped they wouldn't create an avalanche.

The kitchen counter was laden with dips, cheeses, fruit, veggies, and some unidentified soups Nina kept bugging me to try. Zander brought enough beer to stock Oktoberfest, and Paolo supplied three kinds of tequila. We all grabbed a plate and headed to the basement bar.

"Give me a shot of 1921," Trudie called from across the room.

"One girlie creamed tequila for my sister!" Paolo yelled from behind the bar.

"I love this stuff." She waggled her eyebrows and drank half the shot. "Tastes better than Baileys." She drank the rest, then dropped her head in feigned ecstasy. "It's the nutmeg." I smiled and nodded, watching her.

My sisters had their own charms and weren't holding back with Trudie's brothers, even though one had a girlfriend. Sarah swung her arm over Zander's shoulders. "You better lock down that girlfriend of yours or I'm going to have to step in. You're hot." If I wasn't mistaken, there was a small slur in her statement. Perhaps it was time for me to step in.

"Sarah, sweetheart. Don't threaten the man. He already knows how difficult our family is. Why would he voluntarily go anywhere near us? Poor Trudie is a prime example." I nodded dramatically, encouraging Zander to agree with me.

"Yeah, he's got a point. By the way, how did you get out of going to New York for the holidays?" Zander asked, staring at me not so friendly like.

"The weather did it for me. I bought a refundable ticket for when I knew the winter storm would be its worst—knowing the flight would be canceled. I took a picture of the ticket to assuage my dad, then forwarded him the email of the cancellation notice. How could he be mad at me?"

"I'm sure from the description you gave us, he was very mad," Zander said.

Tabitha appeared and leaned over my shoulder, inserting herself into the conversation. "He was pissed as shit! He blew up our phones and made idle threats, but in the end, Mother Nature took the blame. I love that gal."

The call to come upstairs ended our conversation. As I sidled up to my girl at the bar, she threw back another milky shot. "You sure like milky drinks, baby," I snickered in her ear.

She snorted. "I suppose I do." She winked as she walked past me up the stairs and I started pushing her ass with my head. "Behave, Dr. Pierce or you'll be put in a time-out."

"I have been a naughty boy these past few days."

"I wonder if Santa changed your presents then. Let's go find out."

Thus began two hours of round-robin-style gift-giving, with each person handing out one gift to everyone and then watching as each was opened. I looked at my sisters, who were as stunned as I was at how this family shared in the act of giving and receiving. It was exceptional how patient everyone was while the paper was torn and the bows reapplied to someone's head. There were jokes and jabs and chasing around the room like they were young children. Beautiful, dignified Nina watched her kids play as if this behavior was common for adults. She took pictures and clapped her hands when a joke gift hit the mark and placed her hand on her chest when she was touched. When I stole a look at her just before giving Trudie my presents, her hand was there, too. She had as much anticipation as her daughter.

"I was going to give you yoga clothes, but face it, you already own all of them." That got a good laugh and a grimace from Trudie. I handed her a green apparel box with the sweats and slippers.

"Roots! Oh my God, they are the best!! How did you know I love these?" Trudie clutched them to her heart.

"I didn't, though I did see you look wistfully in the window as we walked by a few weeks ago. I bought the same ones for myself. I've always wanted matching pajamas, but since I don't..." Oops! Too much information. "Well, you know what I mean, right?" The room nodded, and Paolo tossed out a wiseacre remark—"What a bonehead"—which I took as a bonding comment. At least I had the decency to look sheepish.

I had to wait another forty-five minutes before I could hand Trudie my final gift—the one in a small red box.

She eyed me over the wrapping, inspecting the embossed logo on the bow. She cocked her head to the side, wordlessly asking if this was what she thought it was. It broke my heart to shake my head no, but she had been so emphatic about not rushing into an engagement.

Her delicate fingers pulled off the white satin bow, which she looped around her neck. She looked at me again for more assurance, but I still shook my head. She cracked the box open, and her eyes blew wide.

"Alex! Oh my God!" God was a big part of my girl's vocabulary. "It's too much! It's, it's so beautiful!" Tears formed at the corners of her eyes and that made mine begin to fill, too.

"Here. Let me put it on you." I moved around her on the floor and affixed the diamond necklace around her delicate neck. The whole room exploded with appreciation for the gift, but all I could see was the love in her eyes. She was mine. One day soon, the small red box would have an engagement ring, and I would forever claim her as my own.

The rest of the evening was a blur. Tabitha and Sarah downloaded their audiobook apps and loaded up their queues with dozens of books. Trudie didn't know I had upgraded their subscriptions to unlimited plans since Tabitha was a voracious reader and Sarah adored biographies, so everyone got what they liked. They were both genuinely pleased with the lingerie Trudie had picked out and promised to wear them often. The guys liked their Beer of the Month Club subscriptions as well. Then it was time for Nina's gift. I suggested that we all pitch in and get her a cruise. She hadn't been able to afford a trip in decades, and we were sure that the all-inclusive cruise package would be the safest, most enjoyable vacation of her life. By the time the booking was complete, we were able to upgrade her to first class and add an extra week to her trip.

Trudie crossed the room and laid a thick blue envelope in her lap, smiling profusely as she did.

"What's this?" Nina looked around the room, and we were all antsy, waiting for her to open her gift. "What did all of you do?" she chastised playfully.

Very carefully, she snapped open the seal and read the letter explaining her gift in detail. I got nervous for a minute as she swayed in her chair, presumably from the shock of our thoughtfulness and generosity.

"T-two weeks! A cruise? All-inclusive?" It seemed our gift had hit the mark. She was speechless. She dropped the letter in her lap, unable to continue. "My children. I don't deserve you. This is more than I could have ever hoped for. I just don't know what to say . . . thank you."

This was followed by a mass hug huddle around her chair that included my sisters and me. I was living in another plane, sharing this much joy and love with my new family. *Please, God. I need this family.* It hurt to compare it to my own, which resembled an Arctic tundra. The most joy exhibited at my home growing up was when our parents sent us to ski camp while they left for two weeks in the Swiss Alps.

By the time we had dinner and cleaned up the house, the snow had eased up enough that we could go back to my apartment and celebrate quietly under the sheets. We said our goodbyes and expressed our gratitude, and I left carrying the most meaningful gifts I had ever received.

After a perfunctory video call to my parents on Christmas Day, I announced to my sisters that Trudie and I would be going up north through the New Year and told them not to call unless someone died. My sisters stayed in Michigan a few days longer to hang out shopping the sales with Nina and checking out the nightlife downtown with Zander and Paolo. The only thing hanging over our heads was whether Trudie would be able to keep her job in the spring. There hadn't been an email with a pink slip this week, but there had been one for Ricky that ruined the rest of that day. I assured her I had a plan for him and would present it when we went back to school for the last three weeks of the semester.

Knowing I wasn't going to New York, I had placed a call to Daniel, Ruby's fiancé, to find out where they were staying up north and was happy to find a cancellation at their resort so we could all hang out together when we felt like it.

"Being with you is like Christmas every day. It's one surprise after another," Trudie remarked as we drove up I-75 to Traverse City.

"The same to you, sweetheart, since you are the gift that keeps on giving." I smiled back adoringly.

The rest of the week was timeless. Snow, skiing, sex, food, fireplaces, more sex, fun with friends, and, well, sex. Lots and lots of funky sex.

CHAPTER 28

TRUDIE

I have to keep remembering that the universe provides us with what we need more than what we want. Case in point: Ricky. He looked like a starved tree sloth moving through the office at a glacial pace, gaunt and humorless. It was a horror show. Pain emanated from his body and I found myself slogging along like he did as I walked to and from the main office. I left him little love notes and his favorite chocolate squares, wishing they would perk him up. Alas, it was not to be—until Alex came in on Wednesday.

I was in the copy room before lunch when Alex walked through the front door beaming. His dashing smile and perfectly styled outfit made my mouth water. They clearly made Ricky's mouth water too—he was sporting the first semi-grin he'd had all week.

"Good morning, everyone. I trust you all had a delightful holiday break and are restored to your vibrant selves." He looked at Ricky, who made a noise like a balloon that had been untied and the nozzle pulled to make a gassy, gurgled exhale.

Alex stopped at the side of Ricky's desk and put his satchel down on it, extending his arms and inviting him into a hug. "I'm so sorry for your loss," he said while squeezing him unreservedly. The look on Ricky's face was priceless.

Alex let go, and Ricky blurted out, "I'm not dead, you know." I knew his snappishness was merely a sign of his despair.

"If you have a moment, I'd like to share something with you in private." Alex tilted his head toward the conference room.

"Alex, it's too late for you to share your privates with me. Trudie would kill me." He looked at me sporting his first full smile of the day, so I lifted my chin, indicating my consent. Alex looked over his shoulder and smiled brightly—I gave him a knowing smile right back.

Ricky followed Alex down the hall, and when the door was shut, I knew what would happen in 3 ... 2 ... 1. I heard a giant *whoop* and chuckled to myself as I walked back to my classroom.

By the end of the day, I had met with The Victors and their teacher mentors to rehash the holiday break. We shared what had gone well and options for the future when they didn't. We also planned our next semester, including an outing to a college campus to help them visualize themselves reaching their goals at a school that fit their needs. I gathered my things, stowing them in my schoolbag, and was about to walk to my car when a holler from behind halted my exit.

A wild-eyed Ricky had run out of the office and across the expansive lobby flailing his arms dramatically. *Because everything Ricky did was dramatic.*

"Trudie, wait!" He stopped abruptly, placing his hands on his knees and puffing out air. After another dramatic pause, he stood, placed his hands on my shoulders, and tilted his head adoringly.

"You knew, didn't you? Don't deny it. You suck at secrets."

I hummed, fully aware of my part in this deceit. "I did, but it was Alex's story to tell. The miraculous timing was the hard thing to get my head around. He made an off-the-cuff comment to me a few weeks ago about how Ricky's talents weren't being utilized very well. Apparently, Alex did a little web surfing and found out about Ricky's education and true skillset. It was just incredible that their paths crossed at the right time. I know you'll be a terrific office manager at PsychMasters. Of that, I have no doubt."

Ricky hugged me like I'd just saved his life. "But, why me? I'm a lowly secretary." *More drama.*

"Hardly. You know, I did a little digging, and this "lowly secretary" has a business degree in administration. Are you aware of that, or did you forget while wasting your talents in this school?" He blushed.

"That's what I thought. Alex needs people he can trust, who have the natural talents and compassion you exhibit every day with all these kids, and especially with us whacky teachers. Congratulations, darling. You have risen." I bowed deeply to his magnificence. I laughed on my way back to standing and my air was hugged out of me again.

"Besides being the sidekick of this story, I'll get to keep seeing you, and your sexy man." He winked.

Again, more people knew about our romance than I was aware of. *Big deal.* Alex's job performance hadn't been affected and his role at this school was almost complete. My bigger concern? I needed to figure out what would happen at the end of January when he left.

ALEXANDER

Having Ricky on board made organizing my new offices so much simpler. He started February first, a few weeks before I handed in my semifinal report to the school board. I was thrilled things were starting to take shape for PsychMasters. I would be lying if I said I didn't want Trudie to lose her job at the school, because I wanted her as my new program director. She was an exceptional human being: organized and incredibly creative. It was exactly what I would have had to advertise for. But sharing these thoughts with her now wouldn't be good timing. I didn't want to sabotage the rest of the year for her. However, I would be having many think-tank conversations with her to build our program, while I secretly prayed she'd be able to hit the ground running if she lost her teaching position.

Several weeks had come and gone without issue, if you don't count back-to-back tirades from my parents and then Marcus Demascus yelling at me for hiring staff before we'd settled in a building. *Too bad.* Ricky handled all the minutia in my world and that made me a very happy man. At least I thought so, until dinner one night.

Trudie and I went to a quaint Italian place downtown. The room was dimly lit and the furniture appeared to be at least a half-century old. Our waiter was a small frail man who spoke beautiful Italian and could carry a tray of dishes half his weight. It was the perfect place for us to talk without interruption or loud music. It would have been my preference to sit in a booth so I could run my hand up her thigh and kiss her while we chatted, but we barely got a table at the last minute. Finding an open table in Detroit was like finding playoff tickets for the Stanley Cup. Impossible.

After our wine arrived and the antipasto plate was laid down, I extended my hands on the table for Trudie to take hold of. When she did, she also licked her lips, which put me in a very awkward situation since I had to lean over the table to kiss them.

"You're so romantic, baby," Trudie said as she beamed at me.

"Be happy this table is between us or I'd have already given you your first orgasm of the night." *Damn. I needed to slow my roll.*

She let her head fall forward and her silky locks covered her face. Her lips were pursed and I sensed she was holding back her thoughts. That wouldn't do.

"Something on your mind, beautiful?" I coaxed.

She pressed her lips together and took a deep breath. "What happens next for us? What if I lose my job and have to move somewhere else to get a new one? What if they let me keep my job and fire Eloise? They'll probably bring in some hack who will run the place like a gulag. Then I'll be miserable and will want to quit. Look what . . ."

She was nearly hyperventilating. "Hey, hey. Slow down, baby. Take a breath." She took a long deep inhale and exhaled trying to get control of herself. She followed that with a long pull from her wine glass, leaving it empty. "Better?" She nodded.

I held one of her hands and rubbed the back of it with my thumb. "Good girl. I didn't want to have this conversation with you now, but given your state of mind I think it's appropriate to share some ideas I've been kicking around." I poured more wine into her glass and let go of her hand to sit back in my chair.

"Ever since I met you back in July, you have exuded an astounding amount of confidence, intellect, and knowledge about child maturation, mental health, and compassion. All excellent traits for a teacher. They are also great traits for a trainer, a program director, or counselor. I love that you're organized without being obsessive, patient without being a pushover, and that you use your voice to champion your causes."

"My goodness," she exclaimed. "You make me sound fabulous." She blushed and waved a hand in front of her face.

"Because you *are* fabulous, sweetheart. That, and formidable. You are exactly what my new venture needs to provide a desperately needed niche of mental health care opportunities for people who can and cannot pay for those services. I haven't had much of a chance to discuss my latest project with all the interference we've had to deflect, but I have time now." I stared at her face, assessing her body language. Interest. Confusion. Openness. There it was—openness. That was all I needed to continue.

"What exactly are you getting at, Alex?" She put her elbows on the table as she held her glass by her ear.

"What I'm saying … is … that … if you decide, or the school board decides, that your teaching career at Hart is finished, you might consider joining me at PsychMasters in one of many capacities." *There! My idea was out in the open, finally.*

"Work with you? At PsychMasters? Am I even qualified?" she asked, putting her wineglass down with a *thunk*. She'd clearly missed what I had said earlier, so I took her hands in mine again and said it slowly in simple terms.

"Yes. Work with me at PsychMasters. Yes. You are qualified, and if you'd like, the organization will pay for your master's if that would help you feel more relevant. I'd like you to be my program director for the nonprofit division. You'd be working with children much like the ones you're working with now. You would still be making a difference in your community and in the lives of children who need you most. The only difference would be that you'd be paid your full worth. Are you following me?"

She was frozen in her seat, her eyes unblinking. If I hadn't seen her bosom rise and fall, I'd swear she was dead.

"Baby? Trudie? Talk to me." I pinched the top of her hand and she jumped.

She picked up her wine and polished it off before replying.

"I–I don't know what to say. I think I might cry." She waved her hand, gulping in mouthfuls of air. "I'm so torn right now. I wouldn't want to leave my kids hanging like this. They were making such great strides. And, my friends, I'd miss them so much. But I'd have Ricky, right?"

I nodded. "You don't have to make any decisions right now. If you want to be a part of building this business from the ground up, let's work in the evenings a couple times a week. I'll pay you well, and maybe you'll trade in that piece-of-crap car of yours for a big-girl one that has heated seats and a stereo from this century." That put a big smile on her gorgeous face, which allowed me to focus on her adorable dimple.

"Me and that piece of shit car, as you put it, have history together. She has a name. A family she belongs to."

"We'll have a wake for what's-her-name," I mocked gently.

"It's Zelda! Her name is Zelda. She is a caring, gracious, and self-sacrificing vehicle, just like the video game character. She watches over me, Alex. She isn't garbage. The stories I could tell you about how she's saved me would make you cry."

"Well, then, Zelda will get a superhero's send-off complete with cake and fireworks," I said with as much seriousness as I could muster.

She dipped her head to her chest and looked back up at me. "All right then. I'll let her go—begrudgingly."

"Noted," I quipped.

Is it possible to fall in love anew every day?

During the following weeks, we met in the evenings for dinner and discussions about the various positions and departments and our hopes for PsychMasters. For obvious reasons, we couldn't give all our services away for free, but we could offer them on a sliding scale for low-income families. And we could partner with any number of agencies to bring in highly trained counselors and build a meaningful program. Opportunities abounded for any of Trudie's friends who might find themselves out of work one day. To quote my favorite not-quite-a-dog animated creature, Stitch, "No one gets left behind or forgotten."

I went to Trudie's apartment most weeknights to snuggle, talk, and plan and we unleashed our inner passions on the weekend. There was no end to the things Trudie would try, though there were a few she said she'd rather not try again. Honestly, I agreed. I may have been athletic, but I wasn't a gymnast, and quite frankly, I just wanted to worship my woman in a deeply meaningful way. Which was how I came to the conclusion I was ready to take our relationship to the next level.

"Ricky!" I yelled across the office space currently under renovation. "Did you find it?"

I was juggling a ridiculous number of responsibilities. If Ricky hadn't started when he had, I would be rocking in a corner somewhere sucking my thumb.

"Hey, boss. Not only did I find it, it will be available for you to review and acquire tomorrow after two. Also, your lunch will be here in twenty minutes—please don't forget to eat it this time. I'm not driving you to the urgent care again when your blood sugar crashes." He whirled on his heel and marched back down to the only quiet place on this floor, a closet.

Marcus had been masterful in acquiring this building. He kept two of the existing five businesses on the third and fourth floors while encouraging the others to relocate to another building he was trying to fill a mile away. This was why I kept that bastard around. Certainly not for his bedside manner. The first and second floors would be more than sufficient for PsychMasters for the next couple of years, and then we'll move out the other renters and renovate those floors, too. Currently, we have a small conference room to hold six people, a classroom for twelve and a multipurpose suite where kids can work in small groups with their counselors or mentors.

Trudie had the brilliant idea of installing a sensory room for kids who had trouble with loud noises, bright light, or similar characteristics of autism. She was made for this business, and I couldn't wait until she came on board full-time—if she came on a full-time, that is.

CHAPTER 29
TRUDIE

I needed my mommy.

I walked into my mom's condo to find piles of clothes on the couch, enough toiletries for a small country, and her sitting in the middle of it, catatonic.

I ran and fell to my knees in front of her. Shaking her shoulders, I cried, "Momma, what's going on? Why are you on the floor? Are you okay?"

Slowly, her eyes found mine and I saw that her pupils were blown wide.

"I'm calling an ambulance. Did you take anything? Are you feeling weird?"

"*Mija,* please. Sit down. I'm fine." I helped her up off the floor and pushed some things off the love seat so we could sit together.

"What the hell, mom. You scared me." I cupped both sides of her face, turning it side to side to get a good look at her.

"It's this trip!" she shrieked. "I'm so excited to go that I'm overwhelmed with—everything." She bowed her head to her hands.

I pulled her into a tight hug, "Oh, Momma. I've got you. I'll help. Why didn't you just ask me?"

She pulled back. "I didn't want to look helpless. I'm not a child. I should be able to pack a bag without help."

"Of course you're not, but this isn't a weekend getaway, it's a major trip, and you've got to plan outfits for all the adventures you're going to have. Let's have some fun with it, *si*?"

The tissue box sat on a small round table nearby and I pulled out a few for her to freshen herself up. "Come on. This will be fun."

Together we chose several blouses and capris. I laid them out in a group and showed her how to mix and match them to form several outfits and then add a few accessories to stretch them into a few more. By the time we were done, she had more ensembles than days to wear them.

"Holy Mother of God. How did you know how to do this? You're a wonder!" We danced around the now empty floor.

"I'm a poor teacher, Momma. Mixing and matching is the only way for us. Now, let's see what we can do with all these creams and stuff." We sorted through everything on the kitchen table and managed to fit it all into a hanging toiletry bag and a pouch for her makeup. She kept shaking her head in amazement and I felt pleased to be able to relieve her worry.

Alex texted during our packing to say he wouldn't be available that night and that we'd talk later, so I threw some dinner together and spent some more time with my mom. It wasn't often that we could hang out like that. It was good to sit and talk when we were both in a good place. I was in love with a remarkable man, and she had finally been able to put her past to rest.

"Do you miss him?" I asked quietly.

"Your father? Not really. Only the good times. I hoped that he would eventually have some remorse for his actions. We both know how that turned out," she said with a sad laugh.

"Yeah. I do. Ultimately, you can't fix anything when the other person is dead, right? I'm good with everything, and I'm very happy to have the extra energy I don't expend energy thinking about what-ifs."

I collected our plates and put them in the dishwasher.

"*Ver dad*, Trudie."

I sat back down. "It's definitely the truth, Momma."

"You are wise beyond your years and stronger than I could ever have been. I'm so proud of the woman you've become. You blow me away with all your talents, and love of life, and that sassy mouth of yours that only speaks the truth. I love you so much, *cariño*. I wish you could come with me on this trip." She was tearing up again and I choked up myself.

I held her hands and let my tears fall. "Me too. You're going to meet some incredible people, and who knows, maybe you'll meet a hot older man who will treat you like a queen." She harrumphed. "It's possible. Please tell me that you'll keep your heart open to new love. Or lie to me to keep me happy. Worst case, you'll date the librarian." I pressed my lips into a one-sided smile.

"Fine. I will keep my heart open. Now go home. You have to teach tomorrow."

She was leaving in two days, and I had some trepidation about whether she would be well taken care of. Alex assured me he had made arrangements to assist her and not to worry. *Easy for him to say.* I kissed and hugged her tightly, making promises to be good, and walked to my snow-covered car.

My phone pinged with a message from Alex to call when I got home safely. I sent a kiss emoji and made my way home.

ALEXANDER

I'd been a wreck all day. First, my contractors didn't show up until noon. Then Ricky informed me that the bakery Trudie loved was closed until noon as well. And the coup de grâce was my parents calling to say they were coming into town that night for a "discussion," whatever the hell that meant. Their timing was stupendously off. I planned to surprise Trudie at school and couldn't be distracted with whatever they were up to. I also intended to have her clipped to my headboard soon after, and a "discussion" with my parents was not going to happen.

"Ricky!" I'm sure I sounded like Lucy Ricardo.

He ran over and knelt by my makeshift desk (also known as a door laid over two file cabinets). "Yes, my liege," he intoned.

Since he had started the job, Ricky had come up with no less than twenty ways to address me. If I didn't like the guy so much, I would have shown him the door.

"You may get up." I paced back and forth reading back the list of things that had to happen in order for this afternoon to go smoothly. "No lunch today. I'm too wound up to eat. You will leave at noon to pick up the cookies. Next, you'll drive to Astonia's to pick up the flowers I ordered yesterday. Be sure they have them in a vase so she doesn't have to arrange them. She hates that. In the meantime, I will go to the jewelers and get the ring and meet you in the school conference room at two-thirty. Eloise promised she would have a lookout and Jody and Robin have everything else planned for the proposal." And then I froze.

I was getting engaged again. Again! What if she said no? I'd be embarrassed in front of everyone I was working with and everyone she was working with. I had thought I was ready before I put all these plans into action. It was Valentine's Day, for God's sake. How cliché!

"*Señor. Como esta?*" Ricky was snapping his fingers in my face. Maybe *he* was Ricky Ricardo.

"Knock it off, Ricky. I–I was just having a moment. I'm fine. Go! Do my bidding and I'll see you at the school."

I sat down to marinate in my feelings. I took comfort in knowing Trudie loved me—deeply. That she trusted me to protect her, guide her, and give her the space she needed to work through things herself. I could provide a good life for her, and she could save me from myself, my parents, and my loneliness. I'd never met two people so right for each other, but I realized love alone wasn't enough to go the distance. It needed time and understanding like a plant needed air and water. It couldn't be rushed if you wanted it to last forever. She'd taught me that. She'd taught me to love myself without judgment or limitations. She had to say yes. That's all there was to it.

I arrived at the jeweler with the owner opening the door himself. He knew I was spending a lot of money, and wanted to make a good impression but I'm pretty sure I wasn't the only one who had dropped a ton of money in the past. Trudie wasn't impressed by over-the-top things but when I had found this ring by a designer highlighted in an in-flight magazine, I made some inquiries. It was exquisite and the designer herself agreed to sell it through a local dealer for a reasonable price. I prayed Trudie would love it too.

"Dr. Pierce, please, have a seat while I get your ring." His exuberance was impressive.

"Thank you, Mr. Frank." The shop was small, decorated in blues and ivory. "Simple sophistication" I believe it's called. My armchair was tufted velvet with gold filigree through the arms and legs, and the mirror on the small desk matched perfectly.

"So sorry for the wait," he called as he glided to the chair opposite mine. "You have exquisite taste, sir. How did you find this piece? I've ordered several more of the designer's creations for my fall collection." He continued gushing even after I told him how I found it.

"She's going to adore this," I said as he put the ring down in front of me. "I love the emerald cut sapphire center surrounded by round diamonds. But do you think it's too gaudy?" I asked, just to mess with him.

His face blanched. "Too gaudy? Never, sir. Do you see the filigree between the diamonds? This piece is timeless. Given the shape of her hand and her skin color, it's perfect." I almost felt like fucking with him some more, but I had to go. This ring was exactly what I wanted and my queen was going to be more than pleased.

"Thank you, Mr. Frank. You're absolutely right. No need to wrap it. Just a box please. A red box. I'm proposing shortly."

Five minutes later I was back in my car heading for the school when my phone rang. *Damn it!*

"Hey, Mom. I'm busy at the moment. Can I call you later?" My head started to pound with the amount of adrenaline coursing through it.

"Of course, dear. We are landing now. Talk to you soon." Was that a pleasant tone I heard? No pressure to drop what I was doing to attend to her every need? *Hmm.*

I pressed my head against the front door window of the school to see if Trudie was in the main hallway, and to my relief, she wasn't there. *Step one accomplished.* It felt like *Mission Impossible* as I swept through the main office door swiveling my head for any signs she might be there. Mona, the head secretary shook her head. Obviously, she was in the know. *Step two, done.*

Ricky was inside the conference room with my flowers and the Mexican wedding cookies Trudie loved. Or was it her mother who loved them? Regardless, she was getting them.

"Are you ready, big kahuna?" Ricky's smile was contagious, and I softened and hugged my goofball office manager, showing some love for all that he did to make this big day happen for me.

"Yes, I am young Padawan." He snorted with glee. "Let's do this."

School was going to let out in fifteen minutes, and as planned, when I arrived at Trudie's classroom, Ricky plastered himself against the wall outside the room, along with Eloise, Jody, Robin, and Marsha, the media consultant. Trudie was lecturing to her students on the virtues of truth in writing. A beautiful sentiment on any day. I knocked on her closed door and she turned with a confused look on her face. I was waiting like a wet-behind-the-ears teenager holding flowers and a box of cookies.

When she opened the door, I stepped forward, shouting, "Happy Valentine's Day!" and shoved the flowers and cookies into her hands. Clearly thinking I was a lunatic, she walked back into her classroom as the kids whooped and hollered their joy for her.

"Wow, Alex! This is amazing, but couldn't you wait until tonight?" Her eyebrows pulled together in confusion.

I pushed a hand through my hair and wondered if I was doing this all wrong. But when Jody came in throwing flower petals on the floor, and Robin started singing "This Night," by Billy Joel, I knew this was right.

There was a hush in the room as I bent down on one knee, and no one moved as I reached into my coat pocket and pulled out the small red box. Trudie set the flowers and bakery box on her desk and trembled as she looked into my eyes.

"Alex?"

"Trudie. You are a comet that burst into my life, and ignited fires within me I don't think I'd ever felt. You fought with me—about everything. You pushed me out of my comfort zone right from the start and haven't stopped since."

The kids giggled, and I could sense more people slipping into the classroom, but I continued.

"You said I was obnoxious, and I was. You said I did things to you no one else had. And for the sake of the children, I'll leave it at that. You said we would be nothing without trust, and you were right—again. I found every way I could think of to prove my devotion and respect to you. I showed you just how far I would go to win your love and keep it. I've been your teacher of many things," I said with a wink. "I've been your friend and confidante while you worked through your issues. I have given up every shred of dignity I possess so that I can be open and honest with you. There isn't anything or anyone who could get in the way of my love and respect for you. You promised me you'd always be by my side, and now I'm holding you to it. My beautiful, brilliant queen, will you marry me?"

She wobbled on her heels as she looked at the ring and back to me. My heart stuttered as I waited for her answer. She opened her mouth to speak, and I leaned in even closer.

"What the hell took you so long? YES! I will marry you!"

She launched herself into my arms, landing me on my can with her on top of me. We made quite a scene as I pulled the ring from the box and slid it onto her finger, lying on her classroom floor. The kids rushed over to see us, and by the time we were both standing, Robin had her phone out, snapping pictures of Trudie's hand, and Jody snapped a million more pictures of us rejoicing.

I finally kissed her properly but kept it chaste, given all the horny young minds watching us. To her credit, Trudie even made our proposal a learning experience.

"Listen up, kidlets. Let this be a lesson to you of what true love is. Don't forget, you have a homework assignment due by Friday. Please write yourself a love letter describing how much love you deserve, and I'll be sure to send it to you on your graduation day."

The bell sounded and the kids skipped and ran from the room, shouting their congratulations. The teachers cleared out quickly, too, until only two people remained beside us: Delano and Ella.

"Ms. Gonzalez, I just wanted to tell you that … that I'm so happy for you. You deserve so much love to replace all the love you have given me this year. You're the best." Ella threw her arms around both our waists in a giant hug.

"Thank you, sweet girl. Be sure to write your letter and include some examples of how you love yourself. That's how you get the big love payoff in the end." We all smiled at each other, and Trudie walked her to the door.

"Miss G.," Delano spread his feet apart and crossed his arms like a great protector. "You make sure he takes good care of you, or you call me." His bravado was priceless.

"I will. But it's good to know she has you to watch over her." I winked at him and he nodded his approval.

Delano walked to the door and turned back around. "Don't tell nobody, cuz I'll get my ass kicked if anybody finds out, but … I love you." Trudie's hand smacked her chest and her mouth dropped open, and she just stood there blinking. She didn't even have a chance to respond to his declaration before he ran down the hall.

"Holy shit, Alex. Did you hear that? I don't even know what to do with that." I was as stunned as she was.

"Well, you better not be loving him more than you love me. That ring cost a small fortune!"

She walked to the door to close it, flicking the lights off as she came back to her desk. The way she swayed her curvy ass made my dick swell, and I wasn't going to wait to let him out.

"Sit that pretty ass down right here." My voice morphed into one I knew she would obey. I pointed to a messy desk that took one swipe to clear off, and I leaned over her hot body, not giving her any room to move.

"Did you like your proposal, little girl?"

She nodded demurely.

"Good. Unbutton your blouse." The hazel in her eyes turned amber as she unfastened each button provocatively.

"I like the lace." My voice turned raspy when I saw that her buds looked like raspberries as they pushed at the flimsy material of her bra.

"I've been respectful of your position as an educator in this building, but since our relationship has taken a turn, I'm going to push this pretty skirt up to your waist, yank down the delicate fabric that has been hugging your sweet pussy all day and fuck the life out of you on this desk."

Her mouth turned into a perfect O as I laid her back. I knew we didn't have much time, but I was pretty sure I didn't need it.

I threw off my coat, unbuckled my pants, and shoved her skirt up as promised. My hands pulled her thighs apart, revealing a lace thong that matched her bra. It didn't stand a chance of weathering this storm, so I got rid of it. I pulled my pants and underwear down to mid-thigh and jerked my rock-hard cock up and down. After leaning forward to sniff her essence, I licked open her labia to uncover her treasure trove of pleasure.

"Alex," she moaned. "Someone could walk in." True, though anyone with half a brain knew not to enter after that proposal.

I didn't waste a moment and plunged my cock deep inside until my shaft was completely sheathed. The feel of her wet pussy was incredible. I slowly pulled back to my crown several times until I couldn't hold back any longer.

"Fuck, baby. You're so tight. You feel so good."

"Jesus, Alex, you're so fucking big. I can't get enough of you—ever. Please, baby, make me come."

No other convincing was necessary. I hadn't planned to fuck her on her desk, but damn if it didn't check off one of my favorite fantasies about her. Less than a minute later, her moans began getting louder and I pressed my hand to her mouth. It was one thing to fuck her privately, but I didn't need her getting in trouble for announcing it to the whole school.

Her muffled yeses met with my final slam into her pulsing pussy. She clenched and unclenched as I came until there wasn't a drop left. My fiery vixen really knew how to play now, and I would forever enjoy the fruits of being her teacher.

We stayed attached for several minutes before I pulled out and straightened her skirt. I helped her sit up and then tucked myself back in my briefs and fastened the rest while she buttoned her blouse. *Damn! I hadn't even made time to play with them.*

"I feel like I did back in high school when Tony Hill wanted to see my boobs in my locker block." She giggled adorably, slipping the last of her buttons into place.

"For the record, if you ever introduce me to Tony, I'm going to fucking punch him in the face. These," I twirled my finger in a circle in front of her tits, "are mine."

"A little possessive, are we?" she taunted.

I kissed her deeply once and then again with a hand on her breast. "I am my beloved's..." I whispered and kissed her gently.

"...and my beloved is mine," she answered correctly.

CHAPTER 30

ALEXANDER

If I thought my happily ever after started on Trudie's desk, I was sorely mistaken. Not long after we both made it back to her apartment, I got a text to meet my parents at the Fox & Hounds, the same place Bobby had assaulted my woman. I better not be getting fucked by my parent's tonight because if they started anything, they would be out of my life forever.

"Do I have to go?" Trudie whined. So, I whined back.

"Yeeessss you have to go. We're a package deal, and when I suffer, you get to suffer too. That's how a marriage works." I was beyond ornery, but I liked to be sassy when I was like this.

"How would you know? You've never been married," she sassed back.

"Have you met my parents? They are the most insufferable people I know. We don't have to stay long, just until my mother unburdens herself. We'll have champagne and celebrate our upcoming nuptials." I walked around her tiny apartment for what I hoped was the last time. I wasn't taking no for an answer about her moving in with me permanently.

"Excellent. Let's get Dom Pérignon since they will be paying." She waggled her brows and shook her tailfeathers provocatively in my direction.

"Stop doing that or we're not leaving. In fact, meet me at my car when you've changed. I can't keep my hands off you, and I'm not walking into dinner with a boner."

"Fine—I only need a few minutes," she called as she walked to her room.

After I got in my car, I turned on the engine to stay warm and dialed Jacob. I had an important question for him.

"Hey, dick knob, where are you?" I asked, specifically to get a rise out of him.

"Hey, weasel dick, I'm at home. What's happening with you?" He crunched down on something and chewed in my ear, being the ass he really was.

"I need a favor only you can provide." I took on a haughty tone for effect.

"I'm intrigued. What pray tell arest thou needing?" He sucked at this.

"I need a best man. Since I took a bullet for you already being your best man, you owe me one."

"What the fuck, man? You got engaged? It better be Trudie or I'll punch you in the nutsack," he threatened.

"Of course, it's Trudie, dickweed," I scoffed at his incredulous tone.

"Then, yeah, man. I would love to be your number two. I'm sincerely happy for you, Alex. Well done."

"Thank you. Now don't make me cry, you motherfucker," I choked out, speaking our love language. "I'll call you back later."

"Love you, man," he said and hung up. I looked at my phone, knowing that not only did I have a truly awesome best man, but I was also getting a truly awesome best woman.

I chuckled to myself as Trudie opened the passenger door.

"You look happy."

"Yeah, I called Jacob and he agreed to be my best man." I felt my eyes welling up but kept it together.

"Aw, sweetie. I'll eventually get around to calling Ruby. Can you believe she shut me out for almost two weeks before telling me?"

I drove the short distance to the restaurant while Trudie put on her lipstick and called her mom. Nina was leaving the next day and needed to hear the good news. Lucky for me, I didn't have an uphill climb to get in her good graces like Trudie would have with my parents. I planned on very little contact with them in the future so she wouldn't be subjected to their bullshit very often.

We entered the restaurant and the hostess directed us to their table. My stomach flipped when I saw them both smiling. *What's happening?* We were clearly in the Twilight Zone. My parents never smiled at the same time unless they were entertaining donors. I was very afraid.

"Darling! So good to see you. I haven't been to Detroit in years. Look at you Trudie, you look absolutely radiant. Alexander must be treating you well."

My mother's over-the-top gushing was freaking me out. Trudie and I looked at each other. I telepathically asked if we should make a run for it. She messaged back, *please hold*.

"Son." Oh shit, he sounded just like she did. What did they want to discuss? His and hers frontal lobotomies? "Please, sit down. You both look terrific," he said lovingly. *WTF?*

"Yeah, hello. Good to see you both, too. Don't mind me asking, but why are you in town?" I asked with trepidation. I had to tread lightly, not knowing who these people were in front of me. When had they ever commented on how good we looked?

My mother poured us some red wine and thankfully got to the point of our discussion. "Alexander, your father and I had a rather profound realization this Christmas, and with your approval, perhaps, we could..."

My father jumped in. "What your mother was about to say is, we wanted to apologize for taking advantage of you and your sisters all these years." His face looked ashen and repentant.

"You see, when you were younger, we had all these responsibilities, and because you were children, you came with us and did as you were told," my mother added. "Our mistake was not realizing you were adults decades ago and asking if you wanted to be a part of our organizations." She, too, looked apologetic.

Wow! This really was a revelation. Though much of what they said was true, it still didn't account for their attitude toward us, and how they treated Trudie. But I supposed this was a monumental start and shunning them wouldn't help, so I accepted their apologies.

"That's, incredible. Thank you for stepping back and reflecting on that. I'm curious, though, did you have any other realizations you'd like to share?" I probed, anxious to see if that was the end of their trip down memory lane.

"Not entirely," my dad offered. "We were perplexed that our children preferred to be out of town on Christmas and not together as a family. A dear friend, a psychologist with the foundation, suggested we stop by to discuss why this could be. I would be negligent if I didn't share our findings with you, and therefore, planned this trip."

I, we, were stupefied that they would even see a therapist, let alone someone they knew. It was preposterous, really.

"Please, I'd love to hear what they had to say. You do know I'm a therapist as well?"

"Of course we do. We just didn't understand why you became one..." Her comment trailed off.

"Please, continue," I suggested.

"It appears that we are consumed with pretenses. We pushed everything aside—including our children's feelings—in order to be seen as proud, upstanding citizens only working for the greater good," my mother explained. We know you aren't proud to call us your parents. We've paraded you all around like ponies at the fair, and I'm disgusted with myself that not only didn't I see it, but it took a veritable stranger to point it out to us. No wonder you hate us." That's when the waterworks started.

My father detailed their additional failings, even adding bullying to the mix. I looked at Trudie, exhausted. This heart-wrenching hurricane of feelings and purging of souls shocked my system, leaving me numb and speechless. It was my generous, courageous fiancée who rescued the evening for us.

"Mr. and Mrs. Pierce, your words today are worthy of praise. Your transgressions against your children have been noted, released to the universe, and we will all begin to heal because of your bravery. It takes courage and fortitude to not only dig deep within yourselves for the truth, but to share your truth with those you love. I, personally, had to become a warrior to persevere when things got excruciatingly hard. Alex couldn't fix me, and I couldn't fix him either. We could, however, lean on each other until we could stand on our own again. We believed in each other like you are starting to believe in your children. You can offer them your love and support, but they are still responsible for making themselves whole.

"I also wanted you to know that I forgive you for treating me poorly, and I hope in the future, I'll give you reasons to like me, if not love me. Forgiveness, for others and for ourselves, is the greatest lesson we can learn."

She took my hand and stretched her other one over the table to my father, who took hers and picked up my mom's hand to connect our circle. Trudie then recited a prayer for healing that will stay with me for the rest of my life.

"Self-love allows us to love others completely and sincerely. Tonight, my wish for us all is to continue our own work so that we can bring new lives into this family in peace and love."

The looks on my parents' faces were astounding. Years fell off, and the crinkles at the corners of their eyes went up instead of down for once. My beloved had built a bubble of love in less than a minute and my whole world changed forever.

THE END

ACKNOWLEDGEMENTS

While I like to think I'm getting a better handle on being a published author, I can assure you that every book brings with it new challenges and a deeper understanding of how important it is to have a strong support system of friends, family and a small army of generous readers, editors, cover designers, and marketing warriors. To all who had a hand in this book and the whole Perfect Series, thank you, and God bless you all!

To Evan, who works tirelessly (okay, more like very tired, but it helps anyway) to keep my website, IT, and social awareness skills up to date. You really do "complete me." Thank you so much for everything.

To Daryl–who reads my books with gusto, love, and a neverending supply of cheers and encouragement. You complete me, too!

To Ma Mère–We sit, we talk ... and talk, and talk, and we still have more to discuss. You are my sounding board, my best and loving critic, but most of all, my mother and friend. Every book has your DNA in it. Thank you for always wanting the best for me.

To Nora–My trusty steed. You're always, literally, at my back, waiting for a snack to fall or the ball you deposited on my seat. You remind me to get up and move, if not to go outside. Your presence soothes me and writing with you at my side is truly a blessing.

To Robin & Jody–Yes. They are real people, and yes, the dialogue nuances are exactly who they are. FYI-I do have their permission to use their names in the book. LOL. Thank you for always checking in daily to be sure I'm still alive, writing, and offering me food and fun to balance my work. I love you chicas!

To Megan & Jennifer–Super editors and educators of the written word. A million thank you's for saving my biscuits and keeping me on the rails editing, formatting, guiding, and generally, keeping me from losing my marbles during the publishing process and beyond. Muah!

The Perfect Series may be over, but I'd love to hear what you think about it.

Please consider leaving a review on any or all of the below links. They really make a difference!

REVIEW LINKS:

To leave a review, Click here for Bookbub Review
Still hungry for another Beth Gelman book?
Read this sexy, fun, social media fantasy, *Socially Satisfied.*
On my website: or Amazon: Click Here

Sparks fly when Ella and Viktor meet on a second-rate social media platform. Ella, a midwestern ER nurse, is cautiously optimistic after ogling her on-screen hottie, while Viktor, a Ukrainian-born actor, risks his career to text a beautiful face and soulful eyes. When they find themselves unexpectedly entwined in a whirlwind of romance and adventure, they embark on a journey that tests the limits of trust and explores the depths of compassion. In Socially Satisfied, readers will be taken on a roller-coaster of emotions as the characters grapple with their desires and fate. If you enjoyed the tumultuous love story of 'The Fault in Our Stars', you'll be captivated by the passionate romance of Ella and Viktor. Buy now before the price changes!

Thank you so much for being an Insatiable Reader!
Join my newsletter to get all my new release dates and offers at"

www.BethGelman.com

9 798989 994 6747